Praise for

Hunting Teddy Roosevelt

"*Hunting Teddy Roosevelt* by Jim Ross is that most valued of historical fiction —a well-written novel with great characters and a great story, and we also learn about an important period. Imagine a fascinating nonfiction book that the reader doesn't even know is nonfiction. It's the trick of good novelist."

– Tim Sandlin, author of the *GroVont Quartet*

"Having enjoyed Edmund Morris's Pulitzer Prize winning biographies of Theodore Roosevelt, I was delighted to encounter *Hunting Teddy Roosevelt*, Jim Ross's fine novel, based on TR's African journey after keeping his promise not to run for a third term in the 1908 election. This is engrossingly plausible fiction, drawn from historical fact. Was someone trying to kill the still-electable and hugely popular Roosevelt while he hunted big game for New York's American Museum of Natural History? Very possibly. Was there a chaste love interest? Who knows? Wonderful, too, was the subplot about Kermit, Roosevelt's son, who accompanied him. Ross's captivating, suspenseful story may not have actually happened, but it certainly could have and that's the point."

– J R Lankford, author *The Jesus Thief* thrillers

"A thrilling blend of historical fact and fictional adventure, *Hunting Teddy Roosevelt* takes the reader on safari with ex-president Theodore Roosevelt as he pursues big game while contemplating an unprecedented third term. But his African exploits may well doom his political career. He encounters predators more ferocious than lions and rhinoceroses, including an assassin with a personal grudge hired by determined political foes. And when an old flame turned muckraking journalist joins the safari, Roosevelt faces a danger even more threatening to his political career: a ruined reputation. With beautifully written detail, author Jim Ross seamlessly chronicles the hunt, draws attention to the political conflicts and human atrocities of the time, and paints a lush picture of the African wilderness, while presenting Roosevelt as both larger than life and touchingly, vulnerably human."

– Susan Coventry, author of *The Queen's Daughter*

HUNTING TEDDY ROOSEVELT

James A. Ross

Regal House Publishing

Published by
Regal House Publishing, LLC
Raleigh, NC 27612
All rights reserved

ISBN -13 (paperback): 9781947548961
ISBN -13 (epub): 9781646030231
Library of Congress Control Number: 2019941548

Interior and cover design by Lafayette & Greene
lafayetteandgreene.com
Cover images © by Andrzej Kubik and Kyryloff/Shutterstock

Regal House Publishing, LLC
https://regalhousepublishing.com

The following is a work of fiction created by the author. All names, individuals, characters, places, items, brands, events, etc. were either the product of the author or were used fictitiously. Any name, place, event, person, brand, or item, current or past, is entirely coincidental.

Printed in the United States of America

For Anne, with heartfelt gratitude and love.

Prologue

"I won't change my mind, Teddy. You must see that." Maggie Ryan laid her small white hands in the lap of her ankle-length woolen skirt and braced herself for yet another flood of words, clinging to the hope that if she remained firm, her beau of twelve months would accept the hopelessness of their romance. Grey clouds gathered above the park's fountain, mirroring Maggie's unhappy mood.

"I believe women deserve the same opportunities as men, Maggie. You know that. The same education and the same right to pursue a profession."

Her energetic suitor paced back and forth in front of the bench where they had stopped to rest beneath a bronze statue of the Italian soldier Giuseppe Garibaldi. Turning toward her, he spread his arms like a Hyde Park orator, straining a yard of fine woolen cloth across shoulders that had been widened from hours of tossing Indian clubs and pounding leather boxing gloves into canvas bags filled with sand. It was impossible to look at his manly figure and imagine the sickly, asthmatic child he claimed to have been before being cured by a punishing regime of strenuous exercise. He exuded the force of nature and machine combined, as if he were some new form of human locomotive. But Maggie Ryan would not allow herself to be run over.

"So you say. But your family doesn't know you've been courting a Five Points grocer's daughter for over a year, do they? And now you're off to Boston."

"I'll be back by Christmas."

"And gone again come January. Four years of it, you said. Gone and back, gone and back. And at the end, what?"

Her mutton-chopped beau raised his eyes to the canopy of sycamore leaves overhead and pressed fists to his waist, where white shirt

1

met creased grey trousers. Not some loose, old-fashioned frock and bowler for him. Today he'd come courting in a new sack coat with a fine matching waistcoat—a dandy as well as a talker. In her black woolen skirt and white cotton shirtwaist, Maggie felt like a dull brown sparrow beside a flamboyant cockatoo.

"Maggie, I can't support us if I don't go to university. If I told my father now, he'd insist that I stop seeing you. I don't want to do that. But I couldn't disobey him, either. So I'm being practical. Principle that ignores fact or hasn't the patience to wait for strength, can't succeed in the long run. Even Abraham passed off his wife, Sarah, as his sister when he couldn't protect her."

Maggie waved her hand in dismissal. Teddy was always quoting scripture and foreign books she hadn't read. "I won't be your fancy girl," she pressed. "I've told you that."

"Maggie! I have no intention of ever touching a woman who is not my wife. Surely you know me better than that by now."

"Don't be telling me you're different from other men. Anyone can see that. But it doesn't matter. There's a life ahead of you, and anyone who's known you for more than five minutes can see that, too. But not if you're tied to a Catholic grocer's daughter, there isn't."

There, I've said it. She rose from the bench and strode toward the park's central fountain. Teddy matched her stride for stride.

"I don't care about religion, Maggie, or where you come from. I don't believe anyone should." He leapt ahead on the path, folded his wire-rimmed glasses, and shoved them into his jacket pocket, limbs moving every which way like a steam calliope. A broad-shouldered bystander in a Prince Albert coat stopped to stare.

"I've been thinking about going west after college, Maggie. The Dakotas, maybe. People don't care what religion you are out there, where you come from, or how much money your family has."

"The place where those red Indians killed that General Custer a few weeks ago? Don't be daft." She walked faster, looking ahead toward the park entrance. Her suitor kept pace without apparent effort, talking and gesticulating without pause while walking backward.

"Montana, then. Or California."

A breath she'd been squashing behind pursed lips escaped in an angry burst. "Sufferin' Jesus, Teddy. Are you deaf as well as dumb? I'm telling you plain, if you go to Boston and leave me behind, I won't wait for you."

They'd been churning the paths round the park for nearly two hours. Da would be missing her at the store if she didn't get back soon. Her handsome beau with teeth as large as tombstones could talk the ears off a brass monkey, but he was no good at listening.

"I have to earn a living, Maggie." He hooked a finger over the rim of his boiled collar and tugged it away from his throat. "But I'm not much good at anything yet."

People were staring. A man in a grey frock coat and piped trousers tapped a thick hickory cane across the palm of his hand and looked crossly at Teddy. The air smelled of rain. It was time to finish this.

"You can read and write and do your sums. That's enough for most men."

"Not where I come from."

The granite arch over the entrance to the park came into view beyond a row of sycamore trees. Teddy picked up a tuft of downy feathers from the edge of the path. "Gnatcatcher. They'll be heading south soon." He let the tuft fall from his hand. "I've always loved natural history, Maggie. I've told you that. Father let me start taxidermy lessons when I was ten, and I've collected over a thousand specimens. I think I might study botany in college." His words trailed off as if the sense of them had finally sunk in. His vision of college and hers of proper romance were as different as chalk and cheese.

"Well then, that settles it." She stopped beneath the granite arch and extended a small white hand wrapped at the wrist in a tight cotton sleeve. "Good luck to you, Teddy."

He took her hand in his and tried to lift it to his lips. She pulled away. "This isn't right, Maggie."

"No, it isn't. But maybe you'll have a chance to make it right when you've finished your schooling. A man of your principles can't expect a girl to lay aside her own plans for years while he goes off chasing his."

Her indefatigable suitor opened his mouth. But for the first time in all the months she'd known him, the torrent of words trickled to a halt. Surprise tugged at the corners of his lips and brow.

She nodded her head in dismissal. "Goodbye, Teddy Roosevelt."

Chapter One

A man always has two reasons for what he does—
a good reason, and the real one.

- J. P. Morgan

NEW YORK CITY
WINTER 1908
THIRTY-TWO YEARS LATER

J. P. Morgan stood at a window of his Manhattan townhouse and watched his two guests alight from separate horse-drawn carriages. Neither was aware he was about to help plan the assassination of the outgoing president of the United States.

Andrew Carnegie, aging steel tycoon and the wealthiest man in the world, emerged from his plain black coach accompanied by a grey-coated footman who brushed snow from the old man's cape and lent an arm for support. Behind him, William Randolph Hearst emerged unassisted from a gold-trimmed carriage as large and gaudy as Carnegie's was plain. Ignoring the wind and the cold, the newspaper publisher lifted his chin toward lower Manhattan as if to survey a tiny portion of his rapidly growing dominion. Then turning toward the townhouse, he mounted the snow-covered stairs two at a time.

Inside, a uniformed butler ushered Hearst and Carnegie into the library, while another brought hot cider in a silver pitcher to the teetotaler Carnegie and a Cointreau to the newspaperman Hearst.

"Gentlemen," said J. P. Morgan when the butler had finished serving libations and closed the twenty-foot high mahogany doors behind him. "Our esteemed and soon to be ex-president, Theodore Roosevelt, has decided to follow George Washington's example and not run for a third term. When he leaves office in a few weeks, he will lead an expedition to Africa to collect specimens of various game animals for the Smithsonian Museum and the New York Museum of Natural History."

4

"Hear, hear," said Hearst.

Carnegie fixed a rheumy eye on Morgan and said nothing.

"The museum sponsors will be content if our beloved president slaughters a sufficient number of beasts to fill their exhibit halls, but we, the financial and journalistic backers of the Roosevelt safari, have different measures of success. I've asked you here so that we might discuss what we hope to gain from our respective investments of money and newsprint, to help each other if possible, and, at a minimum, to avoid working at cross purposes."

Carnegie put down his cup of hot cider and waved a bony finger at Morgan. "We know what you want, Pierpont—Roosevelt out of the country for a year so you can work with his successor to undo all that trust-busting nonsense. If he should take up with some African princess and never come back, so much the better!"

Morgan inclined his head. "Indeed, Andrew. I believe our cowboy president to be a fool of the worst kind: capable, energetic, convinced of his own myopic wisdom, enormously popular, and damn near unstoppable. But as long as he intends to gift the country with a temporary respite from his overbearing personality, I would like to use that gift to good purpose. As do you."

Carnegie drove the tip of his mahogany cane into the Persian rug at his feet. "Yes. To put those fine qualities you just listed to work for a higher purpose—peace and progress." Morgan cocked his head. "Unlike you, Pierpont, I'm fond of our presidential cyclone. He doesn't understand business. We all know that. But he's a force of nature. Unstoppable. Once he's out of office, I want to harness that force on behalf of progress."

Hearst placed his Cointreau on the small rosewood table at his side. "What did you have in mind, Andrew?"

"World peace. As I've said and written."

Hearst laughed. "Theodore Roosevelt? Cowboy, Rough Rider, Builder of the Great White Fleet? He's a warmonger, sir."

"You should talk!" Carnegie snapped.

The self-assured young publisher seemed to enjoy provoking the older Carnegie, but Morgan needed both for what he had in mind.

Carnegie ignored Hearst and addressed himself to Morgan. "The Swedes gave Roosevelt their Nobel Prize for helping the Russians and

Japanese mend their differences after Port Arthur. I want him do the same with the kaiser, the French, and the British. To talk them out of their disastrous arms race. In exchange for my paying half the safari's costs, our peace-loving president has agreed to stop in Berlin on his way back from Africa to meet with the German kaiser. What I want, since you ask, are arrangements for his protection. I don't care to spend a small fortune financing the largest safari in history, only to have some savage put an end to world peace with the point of a spear."

Morgan exhaled a cloud of cigar smoke and watched it rise toward the Mowbray mural overhead. "U.S. Steel has the Pinkertons on permanent hire. I can arrange for them to guard President Roosevelt while he's on safari. But is another European war such a bad thing? For America, I mean."

Carnegie choked on his cider, glaring sideways at Hearst and then at Morgan. "Don't tell me you've become a warmonger, too, Pierpont! I've spent half my life making steel and watching the god-awful things people do to each other with it. Do you know that there's a cannon now that can hurl a hundred-pound shell thirty miles and level a whole city block? Guns that can fire a thousand bullets a minute? Modern war is insanity!"

Morgan exhaled a cloud of smoke and watched it rise toward the ceiling. "You misunderstand me, Andrew. I've read your books and I admire your principles. But the American economy is now as strong as any in Europe. If England, France, and Germany get into another war and America stays out, that may be our nation's chance to finally fulfill its destiny: to become the dominant global power and reap the rewards that go with it."

Carnegie shook his head in disappointment.

Hearst rolled a cut-glass tumbler between his palms and smiled. "An interesting point, Mr. Morgan. But I must confess that my newspapers are more experienced at promoting foreign wars than keeping us out of them."

"A legacy I wouldn't want to defend when my time came," Carnegie muttered.

Morgan raised a hand. "What does Congressman Hearst see as a satisfactory outcome to the Roosevelt safari? Or Publisher Hearst, if you prefer."

The newspaperman put down his drink. "They're the same. Congressman and publisher both want an African version of the *Buffalo Bill's Wild West* show. Ivory-fanged lions and dark African maidens. Not a word on domestic politics or global affairs. Theodore Roosevelt returns from Africa as famous as ever but as a gaudy adventurer, not a serious politician. My newspapers will sell a million copies, and no one will consider Roosevelt a serious candidate if he decides to run for president again in 1912. Remember, his pledge was not to run for a third *consecutive* term. He left the door wide open for another *nonconsecutive* term."

"Do you have someone else in mind for the position, Randolph?"

Hearst smiled and remained silent. Morgan knew perfectly well who the Hearst newspapers planned to promote as the next president of the United States—their owner and publisher, William Randolph Hearst.

Lighting his twentieth cigar of the day, Morgan tossed the cutting into a fifteenth-century Italian marble fireplace deep enough to roast several of Roosevelt's African big-game animals together. "Well, gentlemen, our views of a successful African safari may differ, but our actions needn't interfere with one another. I will arrange protection for Citizen Roosevelt to see that he comes to no harm before he can meet with the German kaiser on behalf of world peace. I will use the coming months to educate the incoming administration on the benefits of a less hostile relationship with business. Mr. Hearst's newspapers will provide ample coverage of African animal slaughter, but not a drop of ink about our former president's idiotic views on global economics or business regulation. As long as we get what we want, Mr. Carnegie and I will continue to provide the Smithsonian with funds to pay for this enormous undertaking. Are we agreed?"

Hearst raised his tumbler. Carnegie nodded. Morgan suppressed a smile.

Elliot Cashman waited a minute to be sure that Morgan's guests were gone before he entered the library through a small concealed door in the wall next to the fireplace. He carried a pen, a notebook, and the flushed, pained look of someone in need of fresh air.

Morgan pointed to the wingback chair that still held the imprint of Andrew Carnegie's bony frame. "Could you hear everything, Elliot?"

"The acoustics are fine, sir. But it's an inferno in there with that fire going."

Morgan waived an eight-inch cigar, dubbed Hercules' Club by his detractors. He didn't mind the heat or that Cashman did. It was time to find out if this latest protégé had the stomach for the more sanguinary side of capitalism, or if, like his predecessors, he would balk at putting skin in the game. "What do you think of Carnegie's plan to have Roosevelt bully the kaiser into backing off from another European war?"

Cashman mopped his forehead with a pressed linen handkerchief. "It's worth a try, sir. General war will bankrupt every country that gets in, but a thousand years of European history says they'll do it anyway."

"What if Roosevelt decides to run for president again in 1912, and tells the kaiser so? What if he threatens to play spoiler by having the United States come in on the side of England and France if it comes to war?"

"Then Germany can kiss its dream of an empire goodbye. Roosevelt will win in a landslide. And the American economy will be in the toilet within a year."

"You think it will take that long?"

"No."

Morgan fixed a calculating eye on his young assistant. Cashman's father had been a prominent Wall Street speculator, leveraged to his eyeballs in railroad holdings during the Panic of '07. His was the all too common story of rags to riches to rags again in one generation. There would be no inheritance for young Elliot. The man, whose sandy-blond hair had already begun to thin, carried an enormous chip on his shoulder about his family's lost fortune. How large? Morgan was about to find out. "I've risked one fortune cleaning up after that bucktoothed madman. I'll be damned if I wind up playing this country's central bank again if he gets us into another mess."

"No one expects you to, sir."

"Of course not. But who else can or will?"

Cashman had no answer. No one did.

"Do you know what angers me most about that so-called *hero* of San Juan Hill?" Morgan glared. "That he's a coward. When the banks were falling like dominoes in '07, I sent my man to Washington with a message for *President* Roosevelt that I'd lend the government whatever funds it needed to stop the run, just as I did in '93. Or that I'd do it myself. But I warned him that it would require consolidating and re-capitalizing the banks that were still solvent before they all failed. The only thing I asked in return was that our trust-busting leader not attack me later for putting together an illegal bank trust." Morgan paused to catch his breath. "That squinty-eyed socialist never even bothered to answer! He had no plan of his own. Even if he had, he wouldn't have had the funds to carry one out. Since, unlike the rest of the civilized world, the United States still has no central bank!"

"We were all scared to death."

"What could that madman have been thinking? With half the bank-ers on the East Coast jumping out of office windows and the shop-keepers on Main Street certain to be next? Did he think that a general financial panic stopped on its own? Or that the country could wait forever? Criminal idiocy!"

Sweat covered Cashman's forehead. "The rumor on the trading floor was that you invited the surviving bank owners to this library and then locked the doors until they all agreed to throw their shares in a pot."

Morgan nodded and blew a cloud of cigar smoke in Cashman's di-rection. "And I pledged every cent I had to get them to do it."

"Thank God it worked."

"Oh yes, the consolidation worked. The Panic ended. Wall Street called me a savior. But a subpoena from Roosevelt's Department of Justice landed on my desk within a week. If our beloved president couldn't be the hero, he was going to make damn sure nobody else was either. The man can be childishly vindictive if he's not the bride at every wedding and the corpse at every funeral."

"I understand why you must hate him."

Morgan hurled his unfinished cigar onto the pile of burning logs and then lowered his bulbous nose until it loomed within an inch of Cashman's sweating face. "Do you think I'm telling you this so that you can appreciate my feelings?" Cashman shifted his weight in the chair and tried to hold Morgan's gaze without flinching. "I'm confiding in you, Elliot, because another panic like the one in '07 will destroy the prosperity of this country for a generation. If that financial ignoramus, Teddy Roosevelt, is allowed to set foot in the White House again and pits government against business, another panic is inevitable. Every European country has a central bank to provide liquidity in a crisis. The United States has nothing. Or it had me until that madman decided to bite the hand that saved him. The new president may be more reasonable. But if he's there just to keep the seat warm for a Roosevelt run in 1912, I intend to spare no effort to prevent that from happening." Morgan paused. "I need to know if you agree."

Cashman swallowed. "I do."

Morgan's eyes bore into his assistant's—a silent, savage stare notorious for turning an opponent's bowels to jelly. "And what, if anything, would you be willing to do to see that Teddy Roosevelt never became president again?"

Cashman's eyes shifted to something in the far corner of the room. His voice was wary and flat. "Anything that won't put me in jail."

Morgan thought for a moment. "We'll talk later."

Morgan called next for the man in charge of security at the conglomeration of steel mills the Morgan syndicate had bought from Andrew Carnegie to create U.S. Steel. Jack Ketchel's reputation for ruthlessness was legendary—earned by hunting outlaw gangs who had made the mistake of believing E. H. Harriman's recently completed Union Pacific Railroad would be easy pickings. Ketchel never asked *why*, and he didn't need to be told *how*. Morgan had secured his services by the simple expedient of offering Ketchel four times what Harriman was paying. Failure to adequately reward excellence was rampant among Morgan's competitors. He enjoyed taking advantage of their shortsightedness whenever the opportunity presented.

Spreading a map of the safari's planned route across the library table and holding it down with a heavy Degas bronze on one side and a Frederick Remington on the other, Morgan called Ketchel to his side and traced the safari's proposed route with a wide, fleshy finger. West from Mombasa to the East Africa Highlands, south through the Serengeti to Mount Kilimanjaro, west again to Lake Tanganyika and the border of the Congo Free State, and then north through Uganda and the Sudan to Khartoum.

"I'm told that it should take nearly a year for two hundred and sixty men traveling on foot to reach their final destination. During that time, the fellow leading the safari may well succumb to malaria, snake bite, lion attack, or some other natural hazard of the kind that abound there. But if he doesn't..."

Ketchel smiled. "He should meet with the unnatural kind."

Morgan blew a fat ring of smoke and looked hard at the former Pinkerton. "I expect every lion to do its duty."

Jimmy Dooley boarded the SS *Hamburg* minutes before it pulled away from the Hudson River Terminal at Twenty-Third Street. He had to use his duffle more than once to batter through the crowds that had arrived to give Roosevelt the big send-off: brass bands, a parade of veterans from the Spanish War, coppers, pickpockets, and thousands more who hadn't a clue what kind of shit their hero really was. The scrum had rendered Dooley overheated, sweaty, and foul.

He'd nearly got stuck at Twenty-Fifth Street, but he managed to join a phalanx from the Italy-America Chamber of Commerce, who had formed a flying wedge to get to Roosevelt and present him with a hideous bronze cup with a pair of flying horses for handles. Hauling his kit up the gangplank, Dooley handed his ticket to the white-uniformed purser and went straight to the ship's saloon, hoping to find a corner suitable for nursing a bottle of Jameson, organizing his thoughts, and extracting the unspoken from what he'd just agreed to.

A steelyard head breaker named Ketchel had sent a message to Dooley's lodgings that morning, instructing him to meet at McSorley's Ale House on Seventh Street. Since he was temporarily short of the ready, and Ketchel always paid fair and promptly, Dooley decided to go. The last job he'd done for Ketchel was to gather a gang of Five Points toughs to break up a group of Wobblies who'd pulled a strike at a steel mill. Making the union leader disappear with no one the wiser required a combination of brains, discretion, and the casual violence Ketchel seemed to have the occasional need for.

Except for the jungle part, which made the son of the New York slums uneasy, the job Ketchel laid out wasn't much different from some of the others. Dooley was to make sure a man getting on a boat for Africa didn't return alive and to make it look like an accident. Piece of cake. But the pay was three times what Dooley had gotten for similar jobs and more than he'd heard of anyone getting for something so simple—even if the target was a big knob politician. The easy money made him wary. He knew his chances of getting his hands on that much cash were slim. Ketchel could either welch on the amount once the job was done, or he could have some other hard case see to it that Dooley met with his own fatal accident once the safari leader met with his. But even at the risk of a double-cross, he didn't have to think twice about taking the job. There was reason other than money to jump at it.

Dooley looked around the *Hamburg's* second-class lounge, taking in its unfamiliar luxury: a pair of plush velvet couches, a half dozen marble-topped tables on fancy iron pedestals bolted to the deck, floors and paneling of dark polished wood that somehow didn't stink of spilt beer, and not a lump of sawdust anywhere. Rapping his knuckles on the bar, he growled, "Jameson." The barkeep looked more like a bellhop than a saloon keeper, and when he took his sweet time finding a bottle, Dooley said he'd take that too. At a corner table, he poured himself another two fingers and allowed the door to painful memory to open for the first time in a decade.

He had been five when Da died falling out of a tree picking nuts in the Bronx. Ma passed in the typhoid epidemic a year later. Older brother Mickey kept them together by digging ditches for the Third Avenue El until he was old enough for Tammany to put him on the police force. That was a happy day. The Dooley boys ate well for the first time in ages. But the cozy nest feathered by a policeman's honest graft came tumbling to the dirt when Mickey got snared in the new police commissioner's anticorruption campaign against Tammany and its connected cops. As the newest member of the force, Mickey had to take the fall for the others—a multiyear vacation upriver to Sing Sing Correctional Facility. *Boom!* Just like that, Jimmy was on the street. He'd just turned thirteen. It wasn't easy to get from Five Points to Sing Sing, even with Tammany springing for the train ticket as far as Ossining. When some unlucky fellow died in a prison yard fight, they added ten years to Mickey's sentence. There was no point making the trip upriver after that.

Jimmy had forced himself to forget his brother and to get on with building his own life—which for the past few years had consisted of managing a fighter named Kisby and breaking heads for money with the policeman's sap Mickey had given him as a going-away present. Then came this fellow Ketchel saying his boss can get Mickey out of prison if Dooley will do a job just a bit out of his usual territory.

He didn't fancy the idea of the heat and mosquitoes. Too much like the Bronx. But other than that, there wasn't much to think about. The police commissioner who put Mickey in jail was the same fellow those idjits out on the street were loudly hailing with bon voyage and wishes for a safe return. Well, the joke was on them, wasn't it? Because as soon as Ketchel showed him proof that brother Mickey was out of Sing Sing, former New York City Police Commissioner Theodore folking Roosevelt was a dead man.

Dooley broke out of his reverie when a tall, weathered man in a long woolen dust coat entered the ship's lounge, bits of confetti paper stuck to his shoulders and half a foot of black polished boot showing below the coat. The man scanned the room until his eyes adjusted to the light. Then he strode over to the table and stared hard at the half-empty bottle and at Dooley, whose hand was wrapped around it. "Are you Ketchel's man?" he demanded.

Dooley looked him up and down. "Maybe. Who are you?"

"Elias Thompson, Pinkerton Detective Agency. I was told that someone named Dooley was to join my crew here. We're the protection for Colonel Roosevelt." He looked again at the half-empty bottle.

Clever boots, that Ketchel, thinking to stash a killer in with the bodyguards. How many other tricks did he have?

"You Dooley or not?" the Pinkerton growled, thumbs tucked beneath his leather belt. Dooley inclined his head. "You know anything about keeping people alive?"

Dooley smiled. "I've been around."

"You speak wop?"

"*Va Fungu*," said Dooley in a fake brogue.

Thompson lifted the bottle from the table and dropped it in his coat pocket. "There's a pair of Italian anarchists in steerage. You stick close to them until we dock in Naples. They like to blow things up. Or to knife them."

Chapter Two

Once he has left office [a President] cannot do very much;
and he is a fool if he fails to realize it…

- Theodore Roosevelt

Roosevelt stood at the rail of the SS *Hamburg* waving to the crowd of well-wishers as the transatlantic liner pulled away from the pier. A reporter's shout lifted over the noise of the crowd. "Any farewell words for the American people, Colonel?"

Roosevelt laughed. "Not yet!" He turned his attention to the parade of tugs and small watercraft streaming down river alongside the luxury liner, whistles tooting and washdown hoses spraying prismed arcs in all directions. A three-story banner on the river side of the Singer Building wished him a safe return, and a volley of cannon fire from the batteries at forts Hamilton and Wadsworth saluted the German liner as it passed the mouth of the harbor. What a bully send-off from a wonderful people for whom he felt as much love as they seemed to feel for him!

One hand resting on the ship's rail, he watched the bustling activity in the harbor, inhaled the fresh salty air, and allowed it to dissipate the accumulated exhaustion of eight hectic years and a frenzied morning. The journey from the Roosevelt home at Sagamore Hill on Long Island to the Hudson River Terminal at Twenty-Third Street, with well-wishers jamming every carriage, train, ferry, and automobile transfer point in between, had been exhausting. But now that the ship was heading out of the harbor, he could feel the fatigue begin to lift and his normal state of exhilaration return. Several of his Dakota Badlands pals had made the trip east to see him off. So had many of his Rough Rider regiment. A fifty-member delegation from the Italy-America Chamber of Commerce had somehow pressed through the crowds to present him with a bronze cup for his help in raising funds for the victims of the Calabrian earthquake. He would have liked to spend more time with them all. But Senator Cabot-Lodge, the French ambassador, and a host of New York politicians had arrived to demand their time as well. The Hearst reporters...well, they had to be entertained, too. He had no answer to their persistent question of whether he was going to run for president again in 1912. But that didn't stop them.

His nineteen-year-old son, Kermit, stood beside him, holding tight to the rail with both hands and adjusting his feet to maintain balance. "Why so glum, Pop?" he asked, wrapping a lean arm affectionately around his father's shoulder. Trim and dashing in a military coat identical to Roosevelt's own, except for the insignia of rank, he had somehow managed to retain its brass buttons while the crowd, in its enthusiasm, had stripped Roosevelt of his.

He was grateful that his eldest son had agreed to take a year off from Harvard to keep his father company on safari. It would be the young man's first adult adventure and Roosevelt was eager to witness the growth it might bring. Especially as a growing number of signs seemed to point in another direction. An accomplished sailor, Kermit's white-knuckle grip on the ship's rail and occasional unsteadiness were telltale symptoms of too much bon voyage champagne rather than faulty sea legs.

"Not glum, son. Just thoughtful. Following George Washington's example of not running for a third term was either the noblest thing I've ever done or the stupidest. I can't decide which." Turning away from the Manhattan skyline, he thought about the changes that would inevitably take place in his beloved country before he would see it again in a year. He hoped they might be for the better but feared they might not.

Kermit laughed. "Well, getting out of Washington made Mother happy. She really missed Sagamore Hill."

Ah yes. A lively little town with plenty of opportunity for a man to put the powers that God gave him to best use. He and Edith had fought bitterly about his moving their family to Washington after he accepted McKinley's offer to be his vice president. She missed the social life in New York, and she complained loud and often that Washington was too hot and too provincial. When McKinley was assassinated and Roosevelt became, at age forty-two, the youngest U.S. president ever, she performed her role as First Lady with grace. But she made it plain that she could not wait to get back to New York. Eight years in Washington had been more than enough for Edith.

But what a bully eight years! As president, he had reversed McKinley's pro-business, high-tariff policies in favor of the trust-busting, conservation policies of the Progressives. He'd had high hopes, too, of breaking the stranglehold that Carnegie, Morgan, and Rockefeller had on American business, and of giving the working man a square deal. But there hadn't been enough time to get it all done. Eight years was simply not enough. He tried to make Edith understand the necessity of one more term to finish what he'd started, but every time he mentioned it, she threw a hissy fit. She told him plain that she'd done her part for twice as long as he'd promised, and that if he ran again it would be without her.

Before Kermit arrived, he had been gazing out to sea, brooding on one of the few ultimatums he had ever given in to. Not even the most popular president since George Washington could hope to get reelected if his wife took up a separate residence. The Hearst papers would see to that. He understood Edith's unhappiness, and he wished there was something he could have done about it. But tarnation! He was president of the most powerful country on the planet, and he'd done marvelous things in eight years! Couldn't she tolerate the *hardship* of being First Lady for another four?

The salty breeze on his face and tangy air in his lungs were a welcome distraction from the unease he felt over the long list of things he'd left undone at the end of his term—the Panama Canal was not yet open; business monopolies still maintained a stranglehold on basic industries; a tariff that enriched manufacturers but penalized nearly everyone else needed drastic reform; the army and navy were not yet up to the standard of the great European powers. He had made the public aware of the value of the country's natural resources, but the exploiters were still running rampant. He was counting on President Taft to finish the job. But he was afraid that Taft, despite his three-hundred-fifty-pound girth, might not be a big enough man for it.

He watched Kermit sway unsteadily at the rails. These were not thoughts he could share with a nineteen-year-old outdoorsman who showed little interest in politics. His eldest child, Alice, had inherited the political gene. It would have been grand if she could have joined them on safari, just as she had on the round the world tour of the Great White Fleet in 1907. What an education that had been for a young woman, and what an adventure! He had hoped she might enter politics on her own someday. But she was married to Senator Longworth now, and her budding sense of adventure had found new territory in the drawing rooms of Georgetown.

Kermit was more of a loner, though very much a man's man. He had strength, courage, coolness in a crisis, and a gift for friendship and languages. His was the action package, not the political one. Sadly, it came with a growing fondness for drink, reminiscent of his deceased Uncle Elliot. Roosevelt hoped the African adventure might provide Kermit with the opportunity to overcome that weakness, just as in boxing and athletics Roosevelt had found the means to overcome a physical frailty brought on by childhood asthma. His son would have to find his own way to tame his affliction. What better place to start than Africa?

"You could invite some reporters to the captain's table tonight and ask them what they think of your decision not to run for a third term," said Kermit, shading his eyes against the ascending rays of the setting sun. "They've all got opinions."

Roosevelt shook his head. "I can't. I promised President Taft that I'd stay out of politics for a year to give him a chance to be his own man. That's one of the reasons I decided to make this safari. I have to keep my word."

"Then invite them to dinner to talk about hunting. You need a party, Dad."

Roosevelt knew it was his son who needed the party, but he agreed nonetheless. "All right. But only invite one. They hunt in packs, you know. And make sure he knows which end of a gun is which."

Margaret Dunn walked into her first-class cabin and smiled in satisfaction at its accommodations. Rather than struggle through the mass of humanity that had gathered to give Teddy the big send off, she'd boarded ship early, intending to enjoy the luxury of her cabin and to listen to the bands and crowds at a buffered distance. Mr. Hearst had wanted her to travel third class or even steerage as she had the previous spring for a story on German immigration. But getting close to her quarry would be difficult, if not impossible, unless she had access to the dining rooms and salons where he would be spending most of the voyage. Mr. Hearst had finally agreed to pay for a first-class ticket, though it cost more than he had promised to pay for the stories she hoped to write—a fact that made neither of them happy.

All she wanted now was to relax and enjoy. Luxury had been no part of Margaret Dunn's upbringing. Though she'd gotten a brief taste of it during her marriage to a Midwest steel mill owner, whose business had failed a year after their nuptials. Finding herself once again in opulent surroundings felt strangely sad and bittersweet. But the crossing to Europe would last only ten days, and she was determined to enjoy it.

The goose down mattress on the teak four-poster bed felt heavenly against her pale skin. The stuffed chaise and wingback chairs in the adjoining room looked soft enough to sleep in. The bathroom tub was…well, a bathtub—on board a ship! The *Hamburg* line boasted theirs was the only one to have such a luxury and then only in its finest first-class cabins. Maggie immersed herself in its enameled luxuriance and remained there for most of the afternoon. There would be no tubs on the African savannah, and no hot water other than what could be boiled in an iron pot over an open fire.

The man for whom the bands and the crowds clamored so exuberantly could have no idea that she intended to join his safari and chronicle its adventures for the Hearst newspapers. He could have no idea that she was even on board this ship. But when they met again for the first time in more than thirty years, she was certain he would invite her to join him. How could he not?

As if in answer, she felt a sudden flutter of nerves, something she had not experienced in decades. Or rather, the fifteen-year-old grocer's daughter who had fallen in love with a seventeen-year-old boy named Teddy felt the flutter. Would he remember her? Of course he would. A week after he'd walked into her uncle's gymnasium to learn how to box, she and Teddy had become each other's first kiss. When she ended their adolescent romance a year later, they were each other's first broken heart as well. You don't forget such things.

Still…would he know her story since then, as she knew his? Maggie Ryan, grocer's daughter, who had turned herself into Margaret Dunn, muckraking Hearst reporter, famous in her own right for exposing the horrific conditions in New York's garment district sweatshops and countless other stories? Of course not. Not even her two deceased husbands knew all the hows and whens. The boy with whom Maggie Ryan had exchanged that forever-imprinting first kiss was in for a shock.

When Maggie approached their table, Teddy was trading guffaws with the ship's captain. The young man at his side, presumably the son, saw her first and rose to take her hand. He was taller than his father, but as lean and hard as Teddy had been when he first stepped into the ring with Flynn, the boxing master.

"Dad, may I introduce Mrs. Dunn, one of Mr. Hearst's mad-dog journalists? She assured me she knows which end of a gun is which. You might want to ask her how."

Note for later, Maggie thought, *Jaw-dropping* is not just a figure of speech. The hero of San Juan Hill, ex-president of the United States, et. al, ad infinitum knocked over his chair and a glass of water, fumbled his pince-nez onto his plate, and wrenched himself upright to acknowledge the introduction. *He remembers, all right.*

"Ma—Mag...?" Teddy stuttered.

"Margaret Dunn," she said, allowing the son to pull out her chair. Teddy suppressed a quizzical look and struggled to regain his composure.

"Mm...my son suggests I ask you about your experience with firearms," he managed to gasp. "When did you learn how to shoot, Mag... Mrs. Dunn?"

"My late husband was an avid outdoorsman, Colonel. He taught me to shoot a rifle and a pistol, and I accompanied him on several hunting expeditions."

"Any as dangerous or exciting as an African safari?" asked Kermit.

She smiled at the handsome young man who seemed to have inherited his father's natural exuberance. "Getting caught up in a revolution in Panama was rather exciting."

Roosevelt fumbled his pince-nez and polished it with his table napkin. His support of the Panamanian rebels had been controversial at the time, as had the rebels' quick and generous show of appreciation once they gained control of the country.

"My husband and I were in Panama to shoot jaguar. Somehow the local authorities thought we might be involved in the revolution, as there were rumors that the U.S. was supplying rebels with guns and money. The local police confined us to guest quarters until things could be sorted out."

The *Hamburg's* captain leaned back in his chair. "Your embassy did not aid you?"

"They were busy negotiating a canal treaty with the rebels."

Teddy played with his napkin. "A refreshingly progressive government for that part of the world."

Maggie smiled. "One that knew how to show its gratitude, certainly. Even before they took power, they gave the United States a hundred-year lease on land to build a canal. I understand that they gave very generous terms."

Teddy tried to change the subject. "Shall we talk about shooting lions?" He rubbed his hands together and cast a hopeful gaze around the table.

"But you haven't shot anything yet, Colonel."

Kermit choked on an ill-timed mouthful of wine.

"Don't let my presence be the cause of dull conversation," she reassured them. "I promise to put my pen away for the evening."

Teddy turned his gaze toward the porthole behind the captain's chair.

Maggie gestured toward the water view that seemed to have his attention. "I may be able to shoot, Colonel. But I've never learned to swim."

"Ha!" He turned his attention back to the table. "I never thought of having a reporter walk the plank before. I've imagined everything else, I assure you."

"Dear me!"

Salacious laughter erupted around the table. Maggie remained cool, at least on the surface. But underneath she felt as warm and flustered as Teddy appeared to be. Having successfully maneuvered the discussion away from how best to kill ferocious animals, she encouraged a lively debate on trust busting, conservation, social reform, and the animus and admiration inspired by their ex-president's global activism. When the ship's captain gave an impassioned plea for America's support for Germany's thwarted colonial ambitions, Teddy became visibly uneasy.

She rescued him with a timely challenge to his public views on women, war, and race. He recovered to make some conciliatory remarks to the German captain in his own tongue. But his eyes did not leave her for more than a few seconds. By the end of the evening, her long-ago love was visibly unnerved and obviously charmed. *Good.*

After dinner, Roosevelt went below deck to collect his thoughts. The smell of straw and manure led him to the forward hold where his former Rough Rider aide-de-camp, from the short Spanish War ten years earlier, was busy caring for the expedition's half dozen horses. Roosevelt picked up a wood-handled brush and worked in silence beside his companion. After a few moments of silent brushing, the man took the brush from his hand. "You're going to get us kicked," he warned. "This one's a prima donna. You're not paying attention to her."

Roosevelt lowered himself onto a bale of hay and watched his friend work. "I've got the damnedest story, Johnny, and I have to share it with someone. Do you mind listening?"

The former Rough Rider nodded and continued his methodical grooming as Roosevelt shared the tale of his adolescent romance with a Five Points grocer's daughter; how she'd exposed the sheltered son of the New York Protestant elite to the people and values of his immigrant city; how she'd broken his heart and changed his life. The cowboy listened as an old and trusted friend would. But when Roosevelt was finished, his friend was blunt. "So you're out of the country twelve hours and already you've broken your promise to President Taft?"

"The promise was not to speak publicly."

"She's a reporter."

"Who put her pen away for the evening, Johnny. I can trust her. That's not what troubles me."

John Potter laid the brush aside and sat down on the bale next to Roosevelt. "There's trouble here, all right."

Roosevelt picked up the brush and ran the bristles absentmindedly against the horse's flank. Potter snatched it back. "You want to hear what I think? Or just what you want to hear?"

"Give it to me straight, Johnny. And the brush, too. I listen better with something to do."

"Take it cold." Potter stood. "You're fifty years old, and we've known each other half your life. You came out to the Dakotas after your first wife died, and you tried to make yourself into a cowboy. You figured out soon enough you weren't one, and you went back east to try your hand at politics. Then the Hearst newspapers cooked up that cocka-mamie war with Spain, and you sent me a telegram to come fight with you in Cuba. You were going to be a soldier! Like a fool, I went with you. And by some miracle we survived that lunatic charge up San Juan Hill that newspapers made you a hero for. You knew after that you weren't meant to be a soldier either, so back to politics you went. You got yourself elected governor of New York and then somehow ended up on McKinley's ticket. He got shot, and you became the youngest president of the United States ever. Cowboy, soldier, politician, and president of the United States! Just like that. Takes a man's breath away."

Roosevelt uncrossed his arms and laced his fingers behind his head. Behind him, the horse they'd been brushing loosed a timely volley of wet turd. "I'm familiar with the story, Johnny. Whatever's choking you, spit it out."

"All right, Colonel. Here it is plain. Good as you made yourself at some of them false starts, you weren't put on this earth to be a cow-boy, a soldier, a police commissioner, or a big-game hunter. The Lord didn't put you here to do some job another man can do just as well or better. He put you here to do the one that, by all accounts, nobody since George Washington has done as good. And you walked away from it."

"It's not that simple, Johnny."

"It never is. But let me ask you this. Suppose that circus fat man you picked to be your successor turns out to be a bust? Will you just go off on another safari? Climb some other already climbed mountain? Or will you go back and finish the job you never should have left in the first place?"

"I don't know, Johnny."

Potter waived his hand and spat onto the straw-covered deck. "Well, I do. And so does anyone who knows a thing about you."

Roosevelt shrugged and passed his palm over the horse's flank.

Potter put down the brush. "While you're chewing on that, let me ask another. Do you remember those rustlers we caught and hauled down to the territorial jail in Red Rock City?"

"Who could forget?"

"Then I'll tell this to you straight, too. You go getting yourself mixed up with some female reporter and the crowd may not tar and feather you. But they won't ever let you be president again."

Restless after his purging with Potter, Roosevelt went to pace the upper decks and wallow in poignant memory.

The woman who had transformed herself into Margaret Dunn, muckraking Hearst reporter, was even more fascinating than the petite Five Points grocer's daughter of his youth. Chance and social convention were the orchestrating factors in most marriages of his time and class. They rarely acknowledged the existence of women like Margaret Dunn. What a foolish waste!

On his second turn around the deck, lost in thought, he failed to notice the hollow-eyed figure in the threadbare coat and cloth cap step out from behind a lifeboat and spring forward with an upraised knife.

Chapter Three

Dooley had been following the anarchist for most of the evening. When he saw the knife, he didn't hesitate. If Roosevelt died before Mickey was out of prison, Mickey would never get out. The rich were stingy enough about paying for what they needed. They never paid for what they didn't.

He thumped the little man's head with Mickey's sap, crumpling him like a rag doll. A bone-handled knife skittered across the deck and into one of the scuppers. The genuine Pinkertons, who had been trailing Roosevelt at a distance, closed, swarmed, and snapped the helpless man's arms before you could say Bob's your uncle. They'd have thrown him overboard, too, if that female reporter hadn't shown up.

The swift and ruthless action gave Dooley the wind. If Ketchel wanted Roosevelt dead, why give him such first-class protection? How was Dooley supposed to see to it that Roosevelt didn't come back from Africa alive, when there were three tough Pinkertons around all the time, and their job was to keep him safe?

The Pinkerton boss locked the door to Roosevelt's cabin and stood inside with his back against the wood. "We need to talk about your security."

Roosevelt moved across the cabin, grateful to be alive but too full of unfocused adrenaline to sit still. "First I need to thank your young operative for saving my life."

"Potter wanted a quick word with him. He said he'd bring him around when he's done. We've been watching that little anarchist since he got on board in New York. He should never have been able to get that close."

Roosevelt turned at the porthole. "Don't be too hard on yourself, Mr. Thompson. Three U.S. presidents have been killed in my lifetime. I'm sure I've inspired as much animus as any of them. I might even have joined them today if your man hadn't been so quick off the mark. I need to thank him personally, before I do anything else."

"I wouldn't advise..." They were interrupted by a knock at the cabin door.

"It's me and your Pinkerton," said the voice on the other side. "Let us in."

Roosevelt brushed past Thompson and yanked opened the door. "Dee-lightful!"

A tough young man with slick dark hair, blue eyes, and a muscular build stood in the doorway, twisting a cloth cap in his hand and shifting his weight from one foot to the other. Roosevelt tried to put him at ease. "Come in, my young hero, come in. Now what's your name and where are you from?"

"Jimmy Dooley. I'm from New York."

"City? What part?"

"Five Points."

Roosevelt paused. A long-ago scene in a New York City park bubbled into consciousness—a young girl on a park bench beneath a statue of Giuseppe Garibaldi. He shook his head to dismiss it. "I know that area," he said. "I was the New York City police commissioner in '95, and I recognize that thing you used to disarm my attacker. How did you ever get hold of a New York policeman's sap?"

"It was a going away present."

The tone of the youthful voice was neutral, but a professional politician's practiced ear told Roosevelt that he had never had the young man's vote and never would. It didn't surprise him. The poorer neighborhoods of New York City, those that should have benefited the most from his anticorruption efforts as police commissioner, had also resisted them the most. "I guess Five Points still has a few outhouses with my name on them."

"None of them spelled right."

Roosevelt guffawed. Potter winced. Thompson glared, making note to have a word with the employee he'd been forced to take into his crew at the last minute.

"Well then, I should be doubly grateful that neighborhood loyalties didn't prevent you from saving my life."

"I came to do a job."

"Well, you just keep doing it." He held out his hand. The young Pinkerton hesitated before taking it. Thompson glared again and then hustled the young man out the door before resuming his interrupted lecture about the need for additional precautions.

"You should take your meals here until we dock in Naples. Stay away from the crowds when we change ship for Africa. Ditch the reporters and camp followers before we steam south and allow only members of the safari to go inland with us after we land in Mombasa."

Roosevelt's tone betrayed his irritation. "The Marconi operator told me to expect ten thousand people on the wharf when we arrive at Naples harbor, plus the mayor of Naples, the German consul general, and god knows who else that may have arrived by then. I have to talk to the German, and if I talk to him, I have to talk to the Italians and everyone else."

Potter pulled a paper from his shirt pocket. "We dock in Naples's harbor at noon and leave on a steamer for British East Africa at midnight. You've got six hours."

"And Mr. Thompson wants me to hide in my cabin? How am I supposed to do that without insulting ten thousand Italians and the kaiser? Be realistic, gentlemen."

Potter put the paper back in his pocket. "Better for your image if you're gored by an African buffalo than trampled by a mob of Italian well-wishers. But if you need to meet with the German consul, that settles it. Thompson's right, though. Ditch the riffraff before we get to Africa."

Roosevelt's voice continued to convey ill-disguised annoyance at the attempt to coddle him. "A year is a long time for a group to shut itself off from all outside contact, Johnny. I'd rather risk fleas from a stray than have the pack snapping at each other's throats out of boredom after a few months."

Potter stared at him hard. "It'll be more than fleas you'll have to worry about, if the stray's a bitch."

Ouch!

Johnny's cowboy humor could raise a welt quicker than a hot branding iron, but he was spared the embarrassment of a weak response by another knock at the door.

Thompson snorted. "There's my point! This ship carries almost three thousand people, and any one of them can get within five feet of you simply by walking down the hall and knocking on your door!"

Roosevelt stepped in front of Thompson and moved to open it. "Just keep that Dooley boy nearby. I feel safe with him around."

Irritation at the Pinkerton's excess of caution lasted no longer than the seconds it took to reach the cabin door and open it. Roosevelt hardly noticed the woman standing there, hands clasped, fingers laced, face pinched in distress. All he saw was the silver pendant dangling from her neck. Thirty years had passed since he'd last seen that little trinket, and he couldn't take his eyes off it now.

"Are you all right, Colonel?" Maggie's voice seemed to come from an enormous distance. His head swelled with the vivid memory of a bright spring day in 1875, when a nervous young man walked into Fleishman's jewelry store on Forty-Seventh Street and spent a month's wages on that little silver locket. The last time he'd seen it was a year later on an overcast afternoon in Washington Square Park, when Maggie Ryan told him their romance was over. How had she held onto it all these years? And why? Thoughts and emotion came in torrents, but words failed.

Teddy did not appear at the captain's table that evening, and when Maggie went to look for him, she found two unsmiling Pinkertons guarding the corridor leading to his stateroom. One checked his list of first-class passengers who had cabins on that side of the ship. The other recited something rehearsed about her name not being among them. Someone, it seemed, wanted to keep her from Teddy.

Holding tight to temper and dignity, she backtracked to the end of the corridor and climbed the stairs leading to the promenade deck where Teddy sometimes took his afternoon exercise. He wasn't hard to spot on the sparsely populated deck, arms pumping and legs churning in rapid stride toward the ship's stern. There was no chance of catching up to him now, even if she broke into an undignified run.

But their paths would cross if she went in the opposite direction while he completed his circuit of the promenade deck, as his pace seemed to promise.

A chill breeze from the bow of the ship blew strands of unpinned hair across her face and threatened to send her toque hat flying into the ocean. She must remember pins and a travel wrap for the next sea voyage. Rounding the bow and holding tight to her hat, she lifted her head to look for her quarry. *May I join you?* was all she could think of to get things started. But he could hardly say no.

Maggie had already covered a third of the deck when a figure in cowboy boots and a canvas ranch coat detached himself from behind a cowl vent and stepped into her path. The voice was neither harsh nor compassionate. Though the crossed arms and wide stance said clearer than words that the cowboy would have ridden her out of town on a rail had they not been surrounded by water.

"Stay away. He's married, and you're not kids anymore."

The salty breeze helped cool the blood that rushed to her face. Her reporter's practiced control kept the heat from her words. "The colonel has many admirers, Mr. Potter, myself among them, but that does not make me Lily Langtry. His virtue is safe, I assure you." She lifted her chin and tried to walk past him. He blocked her way. Two burly Pinkertons came up behind her.

"See that Mrs. Dunn doesn't run into any trouble on her way to her cabin."

Swallowing a litany of pithy observations, she smiled at Potter and followed the silent Pinkertons. *Never argue with the help.*

She did not get near Teddy again during the rest of the crossing. Potter made sure of that. She watched from the *Hamburg*'s upper deck as the ship entered Naples's harbor under a bright blue sky, a strong southwest breeze, and a mild sixty-four-degree temperature. Bands from the bunting-draped *Grossen Kurfurst* and *Moltke* saluted their arrival with a brassy version of the "Star Spangled Banner." A parade of tugs and small craft followed in the *Hamburg*'s wake.

As they neared the docks, an open tender pulled alongside the transatlantic liner and collected Teddy and his escort. A waiting crowd at the arsenal dock cheered the former American president as if he were royalty. By the time Maggie disembarked with the rest of the commoners, the mayor of Naples was finishing his speech praising Roosevelt's global leadership and American generosity in providing aid to the Sicilian and Calabrian earthquake victims. The German consul general then delivered a personal invitation from the kaiser to the former American president to visit Germany on his return from Africa. Formalities concluded, Teddy shook hands through the cheering crowd and stepped into a waiting car.

Maggie closed her empty reporter's notebook and began walking toward the offices of *La Corriere Della Serra*. She had no intention of writing nonsense about speeches and parades. Her readers expected Margaret Dunn to deliver news and commentary of substance on issues of global politics and social justice. Hearst had agreed to pay her way to Africa and to print whatever she chose to write about the conditions there, provided she also delivered regular copy on the Roosevelt safari. Fine. He was paying the bills, but she wasn't going to write drivel.

Before leaving New York, she had cabled *La Corriere Della Serra*, requesting a meeting with one of the newspaper's overseas correspondents who had recently been expelled from the British East African Protectorate after attempting to cross its border into the Sudan to investigate rumors about the resurgence of slavery there. That was the kind of story her readers expected Margaret Dunn to write.

Twenty minutes of twisted streets crowded with revelers brought her to the newspaper's offices. She gave her name to the *addeto* and asked to see *giornalista* Morini. An office boy came to the lobby and escorted her to a large conference room overlooking the street. He handed her an envelope marked *Urgente e Privato!* that had clearly been opened, no doubt as a courtesy. Its single line of text was smudged with fingerprints: REQUIRE ROOSEVELT STORIES AND REPORTS SOONEST. HEARST.

She crumpled the flimsy paper and tossed it through an open, ceiling-high window, watching it fall into an empty vegetable wagon in the street below. Another office boy arrived carrying a wooden tray laden with biscotti and a small pot of espresso coffee. A lean, well-dressed man walked in behind him, offering a tobacco-stained smile and a kiss on each cheek in lieu of a handshake. "Signora Dunn, I am reading your journalistic in the *Herald International* and have much pleasure to meet you."

She returned his smile. "I admire your work, as well, Signore Morini. Especially your efforts to expose the return of slavery in the Sudan. I am traveling to Mombasa with the Roosevelt safari, and I hope to continue the investigations you began in East Africa, if opportunity permits."

The Italian journalist lifted his hands and held his palms forward. "Sit. Please." He gestured toward the olive-wood table in the center of the room. When she had seated herself in one chair, he took the other and held her gaze for a moment before speaking. "*Perdono*, I do not know how to say this without being offense. But the Sudan is a lawless desert, signora. The tribesmen there do unspeakable things to those not of their kind. I cannot describe what they should do to an infidel female who makes the trouble for their business of slaves. You must not voyage there."

"I'm aware of what happened to Mrs. Tinné," said Maggie, referring to the Dutch adventuress who had recently sailed up the Nile as far as Bahr el Ghazal and then disappeared into the desert without a trace.

The Italian reporter placed his palms on the polished wood and held her gaze. "Her guides say Tuareg attacked her caravan. Her hands they cut from her arms and she leaving to die in the desert. Why must you voyage to such a place?"

Why indeed? And would an honest answer trigger Signore Morini's support, or simply his pity and a misguided impulse toward protection? "Are there many female reporters on *La Corriere Della Serra*?"

He smiled. "So you would be another Nellie Blye? For this, you would lose your hands and your life?" He took his palms off the table and folded his arms across his chest, the information she had come for hidden behind them.

"I am not interested in balloon travel or amusing my readers, Signore Morini. I would expose injustice. Women in our profession are sometimes able to go where their male colleagues cannot and expose what is hidden to them. I would use that opportunity."

Morini nodded. "Yes, yes. The stories of New York sweatshops and asylums. The filth of immigrant steerage? As I am say, I have much admiring your journalistic in the *Herald International*."

"Those are the kinds of stories I would write."

30

The Italian journalist unfolded his arms and leaned forward once again. "But you cannot have the success in Africa, having the tender heart only."

"I spent twenty-one days in an insane asylum, signore. Cold baths, rotten food, chained to a wooden bench twelve hours a day."

"Yes, yes. You have the courage. But this is not madness or illness. You ask informations that could make you death. Why must you make this voyage?"

She was not unmindful of the dangers she would face in Africa. But without the benefit of Morini's information on where to go, who to talk to, and where and who to avoid, her chances of succeeding where he had failed were slim. He was asking her to confide what she had rarely admitted to herself. Why would she risk her life for a story? The answer was far from simple. In truth, she wasn't sure that she would. She had risked health and liberty many times to expose injustice. But she had yet to risk her life. Would she?

Not all injustices are equal. It was difficult for a woman to find meaningful employment. That Mr. Hearst would pay less for her journalism than he would pay for her travel expenses was certainly unjust. Should the opportunity present itself, she would risk health and liberty again to do something about either. But the injustice that loosed a truly Vesuvian fire in her was the abuse of the weak by the powerful. She might risk anything to expose and thwart that. But why?

She spoke as if to explain it to herself, as much as to the Italian reporter. "My first husband was a journalist and also my teacher. I was a shopkeeper's daughter with little education when I met him. With his encouragement, I started to read and to educate myself. He encouraged me to write about the New York that I knew, its sweatshops and poorhouses. His newspaper began to print my stories as well as his. We were happy. Then one day he went to report on a steel mill strike. Men hired to fight the strikers shot into the crowed. He was killed.

"I gave up journalism then. I couldn't write. Fortunately, my writing and education put me in a place to meet the man who became my second husband, a mill owner. A year after we were married, a larger steel company offered to buy his mill at a low price. He refused. The larger company then bought the mine that supplied his mill with iron and immediately stopped its deliveries. Without iron ore to make steel, the mill went bankrupt, and two thousand men lost their livelihoods in the middle of one of the coldest winters that region had ever seen. My husband took his own life.

"Twice widowed and again poor, I went back to journalism to support myself and to poke a stick in the eye of the powerful who abuse that power. I have no desire to risk my life foolishly. I would take every precaution. But whatever I can do with my pen to thwart the strong who prey on the weak, I will do gladly and without hesitation. Now you know why."

Morini stood and walked toward the window overlooking the street. "I am sorry for your difficulties, signora." He raised his head. "But the slavers they are not industrialists."

"I will have the protection of the Roosevelt safari," she assured him. "And the slavery will not stop until the colonial powers are confronted with proof and public outcry compels them to act."

Morini turned and nodded. "Yes. The slavery will not end until someone with power ends it. But you must not be foolish. You have this Roosevelt's protection? Truly?"

"I will. He will not refuse me."

"*Bene.*"

After further remonstrance and assurances, Morini shared the details of his Sudanese travels and contacts, routes to take and avoid, guides to trust and not trust. They talked for several hours. Only when the office had emptied for the day, and she realized that her host must want to return home for his evening meal, did she finally take her leave and head back toward the harbor. Hustling through the crowded streets, she considered how she might use the Italian reporter's information while also pursuing the safari stories that Randolph Hearst would pay for. Might she persuade Teddy to take his safari into the Sudan?

Darkness had fallen by the time she arrived at the harbor, though enthusiastic well-wishers still jammed the surrounding streets. No one, it seemed, wanted to go home. Teddy had probably boarded the steamship already. She would catch up with him on the promenade deck or in one of the first-class salons, if she could avoid that pesky Potter. Her bags would have been transferred from the *Hamburg* earlier. But as she needed to collect her ticket at the steamship line office in person, she quickened her pace.

At the Hamburg-American ticket office, she joined the short line of latecomers, several of whom, it seemed, had spent the afternoon in portside revelry. A trio of German military officers exited the ticket office arm in arm, singing in slurred voices. The tallest of the three stopped to address her. "I look forward to seeing you on board, Mrs. Dunn," he said, in slightly accented English. She raised her eyes to meet those of a lean, clean-shaven army officer, perhaps as old as forty, handsome and with the kind of ease that reflects either a well-earned self-confidence or an afternoon's imbibing.

"You have the advantage of me, sir. You know my name. May I know yours?"

"Paul von Lettow-Vorbek," he answered, swaying as much as bowing. "I viewed your name on the passenger manifest. I hoped to make acquaintance with the woman journalist whose courageous stories improve much the *International Herald.*"

It was her turn to smile and bow. Vorbek was almost ten years her junior. But military men of any age could be useful. Particularly the well-read and chivalrous. "Are you and your companions returning to your stations?"

He frowned. "To Zanzibar go my lucky friends. To the garrison in Moshi I go."

"I suppose I should know where Moshi is?"

"It is nowhere. Though one can see the snow at the top of Mount Kilimanjaro when the charcoal burners take a holiday. Many kilometers of waterless scrub separate our little outpost from the beautiful mountain."

Maggie nodded a polite commiseration. Vorbek touched his cap and rejoined his fellows. When her turn came at the ticket desk, the ticket master asked her name and ran a thin, broken-nailed finger down the first-class passenger list. He shook his head. "Signora Dunn?"

"Yes."

He ran his finger down the list again. "I am sorry, signora. There is no first-class reservation in that name."

"That can't be," she protested. "That German gentlemen who just left said he saw it on the manifest. The Hearst office in New York booked a first-class ticket in my name through to Mombasa."

"As I said, signora, I have no such reservation here."

"Then I'll buy another ticket."

"Very good, signora. For what date, please?"

"Date? This one, of course!" Her voice rose in volume and decibel with each incredulous word.

The ticket master shook his head. "This boat is full, signora. I have no cabin to sell to you." He raised his hand and gestured for the next person in line to come forward.

She stood to one side and searched her bag for something to show that her newspaper had, in fact, paid for her ticket. But, of course, she had nothing, since the Hearst office had arranged her passage. Was the man looking for a bribe? She didn't think so. Her offer to buy another ticket was his chance to make that clear. Her hands trembled. The only thing in her bag of any use was a large hatpin that she might use to skewer the unhelpful dolt. But while a night in a Naples jail might produce a readable story, a ticket to Mombasa with the Roosevelt safari was the only ticket that would enable her to write a story that Mr. Hearst would pay for and allow her to write the others she had come so far to get.

A whistle sounded across the quay, signaling that the steamer to Mombasa would leave in an hour. She stepped outside the ticket hut to steady her breathing and organize her thoughts. She needed a ticket or a way to get on board without one, and she had an hour to make that happen. Glancing around the harbor at the ships and groups of people gathered at spots along the quay, she spotted a familiar figure standing under an arc lamp near the harbor master's office, his arms folded, his eyes scanning the quadrant nearest the *Hamburg* ticket office. Their gaze met. Potter's face registered nothing.

Had Maggie known earlier, she would have cabled New York from the *Herald* and had one of the Hearst connections in Naples undo the cowboy's shenanigans. But there was no time for that now. Her employer had no tolerance for failure. Randolph Hearst would leave her stranded in Italy without a penny if she didn't manage to get on board the Mombasa-bound steamer carrying Roosevelt to Africa.

She would have to find a way to get on the boat without a ticket. There was no alternative. Hoisting her bag and stepping onto the lamplit quay, she placed the bulk of the ticket master's shed between her and the interfering Potter while she tried to come up with a plan. She had no doubt he would follow her every move until the ship departed and he was certain she'd been left behind.

If that German officer hadn't boarded yet...perhaps she could persuade him to invite her on board to do an interview about German colonial ambitions in Africa, and then when the ship's whistle blew all ashore, stay behind. The problem of where to sleep and what to eat would resolve itself in due course once the boat was underway. Standing on tiptoe and peering over the masses of steerage passengers and their belongings, she tried to locate the German officer. But the quay was too crowded for her to see more than the tops of heads. She hurried in the direction he must have taken and caught a glimpse of uniformed caps and epauletted shoulders progressing toward the gangway. She shouted, "*Herr* Vorbek!" But he was impossibly far off. Families crowding the steerage entry hemmed her in on every side. Most, she knew, were German farmers heading for the newly opened lands around Kilimanjaro. She tried to squeeze through their bodies and belongings, but her progress was glacial. She climbed a pushcart, its owner yelling at her to get down. She watched Vorbek and his companions move arm in arm up the gangway and disappear into the ship. Her heart raced and sank at the same time.

Now what? She thought about buying a second- or third-class ticket. But Potter would have thought of that. He would have paid whomever was necessary in order to ensure there were no tickets for her. Even if he hadn't, she couldn't chance that someone might tell him of her purchase before the ship set sail and give him the opportunity to stop her again. No, she had to get on board without anyone knowing.

The crowd began to surge in the direction of the steerage entrance at midship. She had no choice but to move with it. In a few minutes, it had brought her near a flushed young man waving his arms above his head and bellowing toward the sky. A heavyset young woman squatted on a cloth sack at his feet. Two children hovered nearby, holding tight to each other. The woman's hands covered her face. A bright red welt throbbed at her neck. The vein that bisected her husband's forehead worked like a bellows keeping time with his hopeless wail. When he finally paused for breath, a figure in a brown priest's robe stepped from the crowd and placed a hand on his shoulder.

"She's lost the family's tickets," said someone in the crowd. Maggie knew no German, but like any child of Five Points, she'd been exposed to enough Yiddish and Italian to get the gist of what her playmates were saying to each other, and the word *ticket* was the same in German and English.

The man lost some of his steam under the priest's restraint. He dropped onto a pile of bags and held his head in his hands. The woman wrapped her thick white arms around her children and stifled a sob. A third child stood to one side, eyes wide and mouth shut.

Maggie approached the husband. *"Sprechen Sie Englisch?"* When he didn't respond, she raised her voice and tried to project it into the crowd. "Does anyone here speak English?"

The short, brown-robed priest who had restrained the young man answered. "I speak English," he said. "But I am busy, as you can see."

"Please," she said. "If these people have lost their tickets, I'd like to help."

He stood and smiled. "An angel of God!" He extended his hand. "Pere de Clercq." Maggie extended hers, but the priest had already turned his palm up. "Three thousand lira. One adult ticket and two *enfants*."

She looked toward the end of the quay where Potter had taken a position at the top of the gangplank. The crowd was thinning rapidly. Families entered midship one by one. She stepped to one side, so that a wall of bodies remained between her and the ship.

"You are a priest?" she confirmed, removing bills from her bag.

"Yes, yes. I return to the Congo, but if you are an angel from God, *s'il vous plait* show God's speed. The ticket office will close very soon."

She counted out half the amount he had asked for. "I want you to take the woman to the ticket office. Help her buy one adult ticket and one child's ticket. Bring the tickets to me, then return to the ticket office with the husband and have him buy another adult ticket and another child's ticket."

The priest shook his head. "They have need of one ticket only for one adult. And the bureau will close *tout suite*, as I have said."

She suppressed a smile. "Yes. But if you get lost looking for it, I'll only have lost half my money."

The priest shook his head in irritation, took the bills, and hustled off toward the ticket office with the woman in tow. When they returned, Maggie collected the first two tickets and gave the priest money for the other two. The line at the midship entrance was rapidly dwindling to a trickle. The figure beneath the Rough Rider slouch hat remained vigilant at the top of the first-class gangplank.

When the priest returned with the remaining two tickets, she asked to see the priest's ticket. He looked confused but hurried to produce it. Examining his ticket and the adult ticket she'd just paid for, she asked, "Does it say anywhere on these whether the holder is a man or a woman?"

His eyes lit with understanding. "No."

She put the priest's ticket in her pocket and gave him the new one. "Would you accompany the woman and her children on board and tell the husband to accompany me? Caution him not to make a fuss."

The priest smiled. "Perhaps you should also wear the *chapeau* if you do not wish to attract attention." He turned to the couple and conveyed her instructions, then disappeared into the crowd, returning a few minutes later with a woman's cotton cap and wool shawl. By then, only a few dozen passengers remained on the quay waiting to board.

Maggie fought an urge to look up at the bow or scan the gangplank for Potter or another lookout. The priest stood in line with the wife and children, hastily covering his clerical robe with a brown traveling cloak. Maggie adjusted the borrowed hat and shawl and went to stand with the dazed husband. "*Danke*," he whispered, staring straight ahead, his face a mask of emotional exhaustion. She walked beside him to the midship steerage entrance, placed her hand in his, and nudged him forward when their turn came to board.

Chapter Four

Toward the close of one afternoon we changed our course slightly and swung in on a long slant toward the coast…[and]…the fine, big groves of palm and the luxuriance of the tropical vegetation. Against the greenery, bold and white shone the buildings of Mombasa; and after a little while we saw an inland glitter that represented her narrow deep bay, the stern of a wreck against the low green cliffs, and strange, fat-trunked squat trees without leaves. Straight past all this we glided at half speed, then turned sharp to the right to enter a long wide expanse like a river, with green banks, twenty feet or so in height, grown thickly with the tall coconut palms. These gave way at times into broad, low lagoons, at the end of which were small beaches and boats, and native huts among more cocoanut groves. Through our glasses we could see the black men watching us, quite motionless, squatted on their heels.

- Stewart White, *African Camp Fires*, 1913

Maggie patted her mouth with a remnant of a once white handkerchief, hoping to blunt the miasma of below deck steerage with the memory of the luxurious bath in her cabin aboard the *Hamburg* just ten days before. Summoning the images of soft white towels to obscure the oppressive tableau of cramped, hot bodies, she turned from the stench and noise of seasick babies and mothers. A perfumed memory of lavender soap momentarily disguised the aroma of overfilled slop buckets. It didn't last.

The stench of unwashed bodies, human waste, and triple-digit temperatures refused to be banished by daydream or act of will. The only thing was to push through the humanity below deck to find a passage leading to the cargo deck above, though it simmered under a tropical sun as hot and lethal as the cramped oven it covered.

Pushing her way through huddled families and into the stern compartment set aside for single men, Maggie moved toward a metal ladder that rose behind a group of shirtless men arguing over a hand of cards spread on the deck. The players looked up when she tried to pass. One stepped in front of her. *"Wo gehen Sie?"*

Ignoring what sounded like an offer of company, she reached toward a ladder that seemed to lead to the deck above. The card player laughed and wrapped a fist of crusty-nailed fingers around her wrist. *"Komm hier."*

Dear God. The sight and sensation of rough, unwashed flesh against the thin cotton sleeve of her shirtwaist made her stomach lurch. Instinct drove her heel hard on top of the man's foot.

"Scheiße!" One of his fellows grabbed the card player by his suspenders and laughingly hauled him back to the game. Maggie mounted the metal ladder two rungs at a time.

The glare of tropical sun forced her to shut her eyes and open them only at intervals, and no wider than necessary to avoid falling overboard. Heat from the unshaded wooden deck seeped through the soles of her boots, forcing her feet into a self-protecting arch. On top of the mid-deck cargo hatch, a Swahili lay on a thin rush mat, unwinding several yards of white turban from his head so that the narrow cloth fluttered in the breeze and covered him from head to foot as he lay down. Others lay nearby in similar repose. There was no shade anywhere and, it first appeared, no Europeans.

"You must cover the head." The voice came from a mound of dark cloth topped by a wide-brimmed hat.

"Pere de Clercq?"

"Yes. Sit. You must take my chapeau." The priest removed his black felt hat, placed it on the deck next to Maggie, and simultaneously extracted a folded piece of paper from the sleeve of his traveling cloak. "I have this for you since two days. *Je m'excuse*, but I cannot make the visit to the compartments of the women and children."

"Of course, Father." Maggie took the paper and disregarded the travel-soiled hat. Require Copy Soonest. Keep Quarry Close and Me Informed—WRH. "Where did you get this?"

The priest seemed agitated, and his speech condensed to a halting hodgepodge of schoolboy English and French cognates. "My superiors send the urgent informations of perhaps troubles. The Marconi bureau has paper for you, also, but you are not on the passenger list. I tell the responsible that we are friends and I will carry it."

Maggie crumpled the note.

"You are running from the difficulties?" The priest's voice was both kind and curious. "An angry husband?"

"An impatient employer."

"Please?"

Maggie shaded her eyes and looked toward the sound of distant surf and bursts of spewing foam, as if whales were breaching. She hadn't realized the boat had come so close to land.

"I'm a newspaper reporter, Father. My paper sent me here to write stories about a safari. Unfortunately, its leader doesn't want papers writing about him. And, frankly, I'd rather write about things that matter, not catalogues of animal slaughter. So, yes, I have the difficulties, as you say."

"A serious journalist? *Vraiment?*"

"Quite serious."

The priest looked at her closely. "*Bon.* Would you write the serious story of the Belgian king who makes the slaves of natives who cut the rubber? Or the British who take land from the blacks to give to white farmers? Would an American newspapers permit such?"

"My newspaper will print whatever I send them, as long as I can verify the facts. Though I've seen no reports of what you're referring to in any European paper."

The priest waived a dismissive hand toward the distant African shoreline of white sand with its solid wall of green behind it, fading gradually into a pale blue sky. "They have not the courage. On holiday, I speak with an English journalist of what happens in the Congo. But he will not write."

"Tell me what you told him, and how you know it. If it's an injustice I can verify, I will write about it."

The priest's eyes scanned the deck, taking in the sleeping Swahili and several other shapeless bundles of inert humanity. "Not here. We must pass first the customs at Mombasa. If there are no difficulties, I will tell you everything then."

Maggie waited until all the passengers had disembarked before setting foot on the quay at Mombasa. Teddy and his companions had passed through the customs house hours before, while she remained on board the German steamer until it was ready to take off again with passengers heading for Dar es Salaam. She had not yet come up with a plan to convince Teddy to invite her to join his safari, and until then it was best that no one connected with the safari know she was in Africa. If that cowboy nursemaid, Potter, thought she was still in Naples or that she had gone back to America, so much the better. When she crossed Teddy's path again, somewhere out on the savannah if need be, surprise alone might prompt an invitation. In the meantime, she would pursue her own stories and try to keep within stalking distance of her uncooperative quarry.

Pere de Clercq was not on the quay or in the customs shed when she disembarked, but he had given her the name of a Goanese guesthouse on the hill above the port where they should meet if he was not detained at customs. A narrow street led inland from the waterfront, bordered by low structures of limewashed coral that radiated heat in the afternoon sun, their interiors blocked from view by ornately carved wooden doors. A few Hindu shops open to the street sold cloth, spices, and simple trade goods watched over by thin men in dirty *kikoys* and plump women wrapped in bright silks and massive bangles. The food offerings that day were limited to dried fish and withered ears of stunted corn.

After an hour's walk, she found the guesthouse where the priest had said it would be—two stories of limewashed coral stucco with deep verandas at each level, *punka* fans swinging back and forth in lazy hypnotic rhythms and barefoot native servers in white *kanzu's* and knitted skullcaps serving drinks. She found the priest alone on the upper veranda, collapsed in a teakwood chair with a blood-soaked handkerchief pressed to his cheek.

Maggie dropped to his side and placed a hand against his swollen face. "Pere Emil, what happened?"

"An interview with *la Force Publique*."

"Dear Lord." She took a cloth from her sleeve and used it to wipe the blood from the priest's face.

He grimaced and gestured for her to stop. "Sit."

She took the chair beside him and placed a hand on his arm. "Tell me what happened, if you can talk."

He removed the bloody cloth from his face. "I anticipated the difficulties, as you know. Perhaps with an entry permit, some things like

41

that. A British official attended the dock. He and his *askari* took me to the customs house where a *membre* of his Majesty's Force Publique was waiting. Perhaps the British official thought it would be a diplomatic caution. A stern warning, something like that. Twenty years of having their way in the Congo Free State makes the Force Publique forget their *politesse*. This type did not even introduce himself. He said sit. Then he *m'approche* and hit the face."

"What!"

"Oh yes! Three times! The British was taken aback, yes. *L'Anglaise* do not support such, in their official capacities. Not white to white, *bien sur*. He had strong words for King Leopold's messenger, and then the black soldier marched him to the *porte*. But the message was delivered, oh yes."

"Message?"

The priest forced a smile through bloody teeth. "*Ne rentre pas*. Do not return."

Chapter Five

Throughout East Africa the lions continually take to man-eating at the expense of the native tribes; and white hunters are continually being killed or crippled by them. At the lonely stations on the railroad the two or three subordinate officials often live in terror of some fearsome brute that has taken to haunting the vicinity; and every few months at some one of these stations, a man is killed or badly hurt by or narrowly escapes from a prowling lion.

- Theodore Roosevelt, *African Game Trails*, 1910

Roosevelt sat on a makeshift bench above the locomotive's cowcatcher, his sunbaked face cooled by the late afternoon air as he watched the fading sun descend toward a dusty horizon. Perched since dawn over the nose of the slow-moving train, he marveled at the myriad birdlife and scattered pockets of hartebeest, impala, and gazelle, utterly fascinated by the British East African Protectorate's establishment of a nature preserve covering the vast track of scrubland to the south of the newly completed railroad linking Nairobi and Lake Albert. Within that preserve, hunting and white settlement had been outlawed. What a bully idea! Had the United States done the same during the construction of the Transcontinental Railroad, there might still be bison on the American plains!

From his seat above the cowcatcher, Roosevelt watched the enormous orange orb of equatorial sunset melt into the horizon like the closing curtain of a silent play. Then began the overture of African dusk, with rustlings, growls, and screeches—as if an orchestra leader had gently tapped the podium to signal to predator and prey alike to shake off their daylight stupor and prepare for the evening's drama. No cloud had appeared during the day to filter the heat and glare. Only the occasional acacia tree, which had somehow survived the predations of the hungry giraffe, provided any semblance of shade. Slowly, the evening sky repainted itself a brilliant pink and then faded through smoke to inky black. The darkened canopy gradually became studded with points of winking light, and just that quickly, taking only fifteen minutes, it was night. Not even from the empty upper deck of a German ocean liner in the middle of the vast Atlantic had the nighttime sky appeared so large or so close.

Roosevelt had been told that on the Victoria Nyanza train, and in the preserve it traversed, sunset meant dinnertime. And he had been warned that if he remained exposed in the open after dark, he might become dinner for some hungry lion. But he hesitated to leave his perch above the cowcatcher just yet. From beneath his seat, he retrieved a leather case containing star charts the Smithsonian had prepared at his request. As a child, he had been fascinated by the constellations, as indeed with almost everything in nature. He knew the nighttime sky of the Northern Hemisphere by heart and he hoped to learn the Southern as well before the end of this African adventure.

As Roosevelt unrolled the waxed chart, Kermit appeared above the cowcatcher with a reminder about dinner and not becoming one. Roosevelt motioned for his son to join him. "Let me show you the Pleiades."

Kermit placed a flat-bottomed gourd on a corner of the unfurled map. "The natives call them the 'digging stars.' When Pleiades first appears, it means the rainy season's coming soon and it's time to plant."

"Wherever did you learn that?"

"Back there in the flatcars, bargaining for this." He tapped the side of the calabash now holding down a corner of the chart. "There are a bunch of Kikuyus hitching a ride to the end of the line. I traded a pocketknife for a couple of gourds of something they call *pembe*. I think it's beer."

Potter appeared at the top of the cowcatcher to deliver the same message about dinner. Roosevelt slapped the wooden slats by his side. "Sit with us. My boy has picked up some of the lingo already. He's telling me their words for the stars."

Potter stepped onto the platform. "I heard someone talked him into trading a Barlow that'll last a lifetime for a gourd of hooch that'll be empty by morning."

Kermit held out a handful of cheap penknives and tin whistles. "Not a Barlow," he said. "I paid ten shillings for a dozen of these in Mombasa." He raised the calabash to his lips and took a long, deliberate swallow before pressing the wooden plug into the neck of the gourd and climbing the ladder to the narrow catwalk on the side of the locomotive. "I'll save us a table." Jumping from the catwalk with the speed and grace of a silent hunter, he disappeared into the train.

Potter took his spot. "Your boy's got an ear for languages."

Roosevelt frowned. "And a thirst for beer. He's taller, stronger, and better looking than the old man, and he can pick up twenty words of a new language in twenty minutes bargaining over a gourd of hooch. Every time I look at him, I want to be nineteen again."

"I thought you were done mooning over your lost youth."

Roosevelt smiled. "Mrs. Dunn rekindled some innocent memories, Johnny. Boyhood nostalgia. A timely word from a plain-speaking friend was all I needed." The words came easily, though they felt incomplete.

"Glad to hear it."

Roosevelt rolled the star chart and put it back in the leather case. "Do you know the British government doesn't allow shooting from this train? Or white settlement of any kind for hundreds of miles to the south of these tracks? They've declared it all a nature preserve."

Potter swatted at something hovering near his ear. "Easy enough to set aside ground that's all sand and termite hills, where the grass can cut a cow's mouth to shreds and the water holes are filled with tsetse, rinderpest, and ten dozen other awful diseases. No one can live here permanently. That's how they could put it aside."

"Spoken like a true rancher."

"I'm glad you got Yellowstone for us, Colonel. But I wouldn't count on President Taft adding more."

"He gave me his word, Johnny."

"And maybe he'll keep it. But lots of people don't see the good in leaving land idle when it can be put to good use."

"I know the argument, Johnny. We have a growing population that needs to be housed and fed. But we should be wise about it, don't you think? Do we have to plough up every square inch of the Great Plains and slaughter every last bison? The people who put this land aside know the answer. They come from an island that was covered in forest not so long ago. Now their citizens have to pay to sit on a park bench to admire a single tree, and their cities are filled with tenements that make New York's look like German health spas!"

Potter swatted another unseen tormenter. "And Alaska would have had tenements that made New York's look like *re-sorts* if the gold hadn't run out so fast. All I'm sayin', Colonel, is if a piece of land can be mined, farmed, or logged, then no one's going to leave it alone for some animal to pee on. You know that and so do I."

Roosevelt laughed. "You're a cornucopia of common sense, my friend. It was a lucky day for me when our paths crossed all those years ago." Potter looked away, and Roosevelt's voice lowered and softened. "Do you remember that young greenhorn who went out to the Dakotas not knowing which end of a rope was which?"

Potter smiled. "Fondly."

"Might that same old cowhand guide another greenhorn over some of the same rough patches? Look the other way at his youthful foolishness? But pull sharp on the reins when he's too green to see or understand genuine danger?"

"I could put your boy in charge of the trackers, I suppose, if he picks up more of their lingo. He shoots as well as you do, and he rides better."

"Thank you, Johnny."

Potter grinned. "We meet up with our guide, Cunninghame, and his porters tomorrow at Kapiti Station. It'll take a few days to get four tons of supplies and equipment sorted into forty-pound bundles and figure out who's carrying what. Those beer-trading trinkets might get lost in all the confusion."

"I was going to suggest the same thing."

"And Mr. Cunninghame has invited us to stay at his sisal farm in the Aberdare for a few days while his boys are sorting everything out. The local tribe wants to put on a ceremonial lion hunt in your honor. He says they use spears, zebra skin shields, and not much else."

"They sound like brave men."

"Well, don't be thinking about borrowing a spear and joining them."

"What if they insist? It sounds like bully sport!"

"You better hope they don't. I'm told they hunt in the nude, or damn near. Try keeping that out of the newspapers! Or away from these cartoon fellows."

Roosevelt laughed. "I don't care about newspapers anymore, Johnny. I'm not running for office again. I'm Citizen Roosevelt now."

Potter spat. "And I'm Prince Albert."

Dooley felt the train begin to climb. He laid his cloth hat against the back of the wooden bench to keep his head from lolling. The nobs in the front slept in bunks, but back here, you snored where you sat. The moon and the wild shadows it painted made sleep impossible. When Ketchel said the job would take him to Africa, Dooley had pictured a hot, sweaty jungle. There had been plenty of sweat, heat, flies, and mosquitos. But so far, no jungle. Central Park had more trees than he'd seen since they'd gotten off the boat in Mombasa. In the three hundred miles they'd covered that day, he had counted maybe ten trees. The land was practically a desert. How anything lived here, he couldn't figure. There were some things alive. He'd seen them up close. When the train stopped to take on water, a pair of giraffes as tall as a Coney Island fun ride came from nowhere and slid their clown hat heads through his window to have a look inside. He'd nearly peed himself.

The memory made him smile for the first time in a month. Mickey would never believe half of what he'd have to tell when he got home. That thought, and the certainty, that Mickey would soon be free made him smile. Dooley lay his head on the back of the hard wooden bench, while the African air settled warm over his chest and the clickety-clack of the metal wheels lulled him to sleep. By the time the moon disappeared behind a passing cloud, he had started to snore.

By midmorning, the train had arrived at a low mud-brick building with the words Kapiti Station painted in blue across a galvanized tin roof. Two men in pith helmets paced the platform. Roosevelt's kid had been telling anyone who would listen that the rains would start soon. He said the dry ground that stretched for miles on both sides of the track would bloom overnight into some kind of green grass ocean. Herds of animals, whose names Dooley had never heard of, would arrive by the thousands to eat the grass and be eaten themselves by the lion, cheetah, and hyena that followed the herds. He didn't believe a word of it. The only wildlife he'd seen that morning were the ticks clustered around the legs of the native cattle that pawed the dirt behind the station, and the flies that settled around the eyes of the small boys who guarded them.

He pushed his way past the Smithsonian boys fiddling with their scientific gear and made toward the front of the car for a better look. Behind the station, two lines of canvas tents stretched a quarter mile toward the horizon. He counted thirty-four to the row. Between them, piles of supplies and equipment for what the Roosevelt kid claimed was the largest African safari ever assembled, lay baking in the sun. Crates of rifles, ammunition, small animal traps, foodstuffs, and medical supplies lay everywhere in jumbled piles, as well as mounds of salt, borax, and cotton bunting. He had never seen such an abundance left unattended. Didn't people steal here? As if in answer, a chorus of chanting voices boomed from somewhere behind the whitewashed station. He understood none of it, except the word *bwana*, which he'd heard more than enough of already. Then a dozen brown, bare-chested bodies appeared in the open space between the tents, moving in single file toward the station. Roosevelt hopped from the train steps and two men in puttees and pith helmets, who had been pacing the platform, scurried to meet him. The three shook hands. Chanting natives formed a circle around the trio, stomping naked feet and grunting. It looked like something out of a newspaper illustration.

"There's your new challenge," said Thompson, stepping off the train behind Dooley. "Two hundred sixty porters, gun bearers, animal trackers, horse boys, and cooks. You going to check them all for knives?"

The Pinkerton boss didn't hide his irritation at being forced by Ketchel to take a stranger into his crew. It was obvious he had no idea of Dooley's true purpose. The fact that it was Dooley, and not one of the real Pinkertons, who had saved Roosevelt from the knife-wielding attacker made the head Pinkerton even pissier. Too bad. Mickey's sap would be teaching the smug copper manners if he wasn't careful.

Thompson waved a torn brown envelope at Dooley's chest. "This was with the wires the consulate was holding in Nairobi for the colonel. It's addressed to you." *Letters usually meant someone was dead.* Dooley held out his hand, but Thompson ignored it. "How did something with your name on it end up in Africa, less than a month after we left New York, in a pile of correspondence addressed to the colonel?"

Dooley shrugged and tried to keep all emotion out of his voice. "I don't know. Ask whoever put it there."

Thompson widened the tear and shook out the envelope's contents. The tear was big enough for him to have done it already, and Dooley was certain he had. Out came two pieces of cardboard with a sheet of colored paper sandwiched between them. The paper looked like one of those cheap boardwalk tintypes that the cart pushers in Atlantic City make for a dime. A man's face grinned through a cut-out image of a circus strongman. Pasted to the back was a label from a bottle of cheap rum: 100 percent proof. The face on the tintype was his brother Mickey's. *Sweet Jesus, Mickey was free!*

"Friend of yours?" Dooley's mouth felt as dry as the sun-parched ground beneath his feet. He shook his head. Thompson put the tintype back in the envelope, and the envelope in his pocket. "Must be someone else's." Dooley suppressed an urge to yank the envelope out of Thompson's pocket. "One more thing." *What now? Mickey was free.* All Dooley wanted to do was go someplace and shout. "The colonel wants you with him when he goes out hunting." Dooley tried to hold his hands and features steady. *Sweet Jesus, was it Christmas?* "I told him no."

"What!" Dooley could hardly control his voice.

"Steady! The colonel plans to hunt on horseback whenever the terrain allows. As far as I know, the only horses where you come from are the nags that pull the ice wagons."

"I can learn."

"And lame one of them fine animals the colonel brought all the way from New York? Go chase yourself." *Don't argue with the man. Wait.* Thompson scowled. "The boss man wants you with him. So that's that for now. When he goes on foot, you'll go with him. Otherwise you guard the camp. Can you shoot a rifle?"

"Yes," Dooley lied. Thompson smirked. Dooley tried to steady a twitch that had suddenly gripped one side of his face. Mickey was free. The pompous politician wanted him out there at his side in the weeds. The fool was even going to give him a gun! Ha! The job would be done, and he'd be home by the New Year. Happy days!

Thompson broke into his thoughts. "Don't think I have the same opinion of your skills as the colonel does. There aren't any pipsqueak anarchists out there in the tall grass. Just big animals with sharp teeth. So when it's your turn to guard the boss man, see to it he doesn't get eaten by one."

I'll push his fat arse into the first set of hungry teeth I find.

49

Chapter Six

The boys told us, with much excitement that there was a large snake nearby; and sure enough a few yards off, coiled up in the long grass under a small tree, was a python. I could not see it distinctly, and using a solid bullet I just missed the backbone, the bullet going through the body about its middle. Immediately the snake lashed at me with open jaws, and then, uncoiling, came gliding rapidly in our direction.

- Theodore Roosevelt, *African Game Trails*, 1910

Dooley marched through the tall savannah grass behind Roosevelt, his son, and a gun bearer. He would have preferred to be alone with his thoughts, but the colonel was a relentless talker. His topic of the morning was his "accomplishments" as New York City police commissioner: clamping down on gambling and prostitution, punishing corrupt cops, confronting "that epicenter of all evil," Tammany Hall.

Dooley struggled to hold his tongue. Mickey was free! That's all he wanted to talk about. But there wasn't a soul, black or white, among the safari's two hundred sixty men with whom he could share his joy and relief. He'd only been able to glance at the tintype before Thompson took it back. Nine years of prison had taken its toll on Mickey. The once handsome face was sallow and lined. He'd lost weight as well as teeth. Dooley would have given anything to keep the printed image, but Thompson's copper's eyes were on him like a two-dollar hooker, and he had no choice but to play dumb. Sleep that night came hard.

All he'd been waiting for was proof that Mickey was out of jail. Now he had it. It was time to finish the job and go home. But his mind resisted the obvious need to come up with a plan. Instead, it spun daydreams about a reunion with Mickey and the things they would do together. The kid brother Mickey left behind had come a long way from shaking down pushcart peddlers for nickels. He'd grown to manhood in the years since Mickey went to prison; his older brother might have a hard time believing it was little Jimmy who got him sprung. And how.

But there would be time enough for Mickey to get used to the truth. Tammany would put him back on the police force once he was out, and Ketchel's money would keep the brothers fat until then. Happy days were coming!

"You said you're from Five Points," said Roosevelt, breaking into Dooley's thoughts. "What do you think of what I did there?"

The fat man hadn't quit jabbering since they'd left camp at first light. Until now, all Dooley had to do was listen. He didn't want to talk; he wanted to dream. "I was a kid," he answered, trying to avoid conversation.

"What did your parents think?" Roosevelt pressed.

"They're dead."

"I'm sorry." But his sorrow didn't stop the blather. "There was a lot of resistance to what I tried to accomplish as police commissioner. It often seemed like the citizens of Five Points didn't believe I was trying to make their lives better."

Dooley felt an urge to raise his rifle and be done with it. Never mind Ketchel's instructions to make it look like an accident. A bullet to the back of the head, and everyone could go home. He reminded himself that Ketchel would never pay for Roosevelt's death unless everyone believed it was an accident. Mickey might even end up back in prison if there was a stink. He took a deep breath. If the pompous old fart wanted to know what the people of Five Points thought, he'd tell him. Why not?

"The poor don't understand why the rich have such gas about women and cards," said Dooley. "They's a necessity, ain't they? And if they make some happy, where's the harm?"

"Need and desire are different things," said Roosevelt.

"Indeed they are." Dooley struggled to hold his temper. "And the poor need money, same as the rich. But a poor man out of work has only two ways of getting it: win it or steal it. Why make a crime out of the only one that doesn't mean bashing someone with a cudgel?" Roosevelt lifted his brow as Dooley warmed to his pitch. "And the do-gooders what bawl about the bawdy houses aren't living ten to a room with half the babies dying before they're out of the crib. If they were, they might know it's the bawdy houses what keeps the rosebuds safe and what gives the old gal a break from breeding."

Roosevelt mopped his forehead with the crown of his campaign hat. "I've heard that view on gambling, of course. But for every lucky man who puts together a stake throwing dice, how many more gamble away the food and rent money? Who protects the young women when the man of the house loses his pay month after month, while she and the rest of the family go without food and shelter?"

"Why not take everyone's boots because some use them to kick cripples?" Dooley answered. "If you want to lead people's lives for them, Colonel, give a meal and a roof to them that's lacking. They'll thank you for that."

Roosevelt shook his head. "No city has enough money to remove all struggle from life. I don't believe it would be in the people's best interest for government to try."

"But it is to take away the fun that helps some get a leg up and others to forget their troubles?" Dooley shook his head, too, consciously mimicking Roosevelt. "The poor don't understand that kind of thinking, Colonel. Have a go at the gangs and good luck to you. But leave the cards and the girls alone."

Undaunted and undented, the politician continued to pit platitude against common sense, until Dooley was ready to put the gun to either Roosevelt's head or his own. He'd never thought the rich deserving. But he had assumed they had common sense. Forced to listen, he was dumbfounded to discover this one had none.

Perhaps because Roosevelt talked so much and so loudly, the hunting party didn't see any animals that morning. The midday heat sent them to the shade of a lone acacia tree where they shared a boxed lunch of impala jerky, bread, and marmalade wrapped in waxed cloth. Kermit slipped a gourd of something from his rucksack and the gun bearer went to fill canteens from a nearby stream. Dooley cut into the coarse native loaf with the blade of one of the flimsy pocketknives Kermit had been trading around camp. The cheap piece of trade goods wouldn't have cut butter when Dooley lifted it from a porter who left it carelessly lying about. He'd sharpened it as best he could, though the inexpensive steel wouldn't hold much of an edge or take any kind of pressure. He spread the marmalade across the bread as gently as if he were trying to slip a wallet from a policeman's pocket.

As Roosevelt's oration moved from Tammany to the American

bison, Dooley's eyes scanned the heavens for deliverance. Back in Five Points, there were a dozen ways to get rid of a man with no one the wiser: shove him under a horse cart or off one of them new elevated trains. If the silly bugger liked to walk the streets, like this one did when he was a police commissioner, there were a hundred alleys to lure him down and a dozen places to put the body. If he was partial to girls, there was them what would help for a fiver. Killing a man wasn't difficult in Five Points. Maybe that's why there was so much of it. But here in the open, with dark eyes watching, and nowhere to wait in ambush that didn't already hide some other four-legged killer, it would be hard to do the deed without getting caught. But the temptation to shoot the blowhard and be done with it grew stronger with each irritating minute.

A line of freight train clouds crossed the sky, giving temporary relief from the glare of the African sun. Overhead, a tangle of thorn-covered limbs and fernlike leaves rustled in a movement of warm air. Then, as quickly as it had arisen, the cloud-cooled breeze disappeared. But something silhouetted against the pale blue sky continued to move after everything else had returned to stillness.

Dooley stared and held his breath.

While Roosevelt droned on and on, a snake as fat as a man's arm and three times as long slithered down the trunk of the acacia and along a limb a dozen feet above the politician's head. Dooley looked away, not wanting to call attention to the lucky danger. He couldn't hear Roosevelt's words for the pounding of blood in his temples. He looked up again and then quickly away. The snake had wound its body around the limb above Roosevelt's head and probed the hot dry air with flicks of its forked tongue. Dooley suppressed a grin. Africa was going to do the dirty deed for him, and he wouldn't have to lift a finger. Bully! Wasn't that the fat man's word?

The smoke-colored serpent lowered the upper half of its body into the air above Roosevelt's head, its forked black tongue darting from side to side to the beat of Dooley's heart. Then its tail relaxed, and the whole scaly length of it eased from the tree limb and onto the dirt, the last few feet of it falling to the ground with a heavy plop.

Topped by a head the size of a man's fist, the front half of the snake rose and swiveled toward Roosevelt and then toward his son. Both men froze, and then the snake turned its head toward Dooley. *Shit.* Before he had time to worry whether the flimsy blade would hold together, or if it could possibly hit the mark, the penknife slick with jam flew from Dooley's hand toward the slithering target. End over end it tumbled until the tip of it nicked the serpent's back a yard away from anything vital. The snake lifted its fat triangular head and arched its back toward the superficial wound. Dooley leapt to his feet. The gun bearer saw the opening and rushed forward, bringing the butt of Roosevelt's Winchester down on the serpent's neck.

Roosevelt found his voice quick enough, but the hearty tone was as false as a policeman's promise. "Where did you learn that handy trick, son?"

Dooley let loose a pent-up breath in a long, loud *whoosh.* "Mumbly-peg," he said, mimicking the politician's bravado. "It's a kid's game."

Roosevelt shook his head. "Never played it."

"I wouldn't think so."

Dooley was glad to be left alone when Roosevelt and his son went off to cool down in a nearby stream, and the gun bearer went with them to discourage any animal that might object to the two white men sharing their watering hole. Dooley would have gone, too, if only for the chance to shove the fat politician's inflated head under water. But he didn't know how to swim, and he wasn't in the mood for more smarmy nature lessons.

Hours of marching and jabbering had left him dopey with fatigue. He checked the tree for signs of more slithering wildlife and then placed his back against the smooth grey trunk, willing his brain to slow. But all it wanted to think about was the fluke of hitting an inch-wide moving target with the blade of a penknife and how close he'd come to meeting his own fatal accident.

He tried to shove the thoughts away. Every inch of his flesh itched or oozed from insects that bit through his clothes day and night, with his gut knotting or leaking, depending on what strange food or drink he'd put in there last. Africa was more pestilent than the Bronx, and they hadn't even entered the jungle yet. He didn't want to think about that. But he didn't know how to stop. Pulling the brim of his cap over his eyes, he willed slumber. But it didn't come.

Instead came an image of Mickey on a Coney Island roller coaster pursued by do-gooders intent on shutting that down, too. The politician was a pious ignoramus. How many times had Dooley seen his da come home stumbling drunk with his pockets all turned out, and Ma taking a skillet to him if he wasn't working? Though she could be all lovey-dovey when it was green bills pouring from his trousers. The fat man didn't know half what he thought he did. And Christ Jesus could he talk! Maybe he was right about more men losing the rent money than making it to easy street. But it beat robbing folks, didn't it?

Smiles and frowns took turns twisting Dooley's resting face. He hadn't thought of Ma and Da in a long time. Too many struggling todays on top of fading yesterdays. He tugged the cap toward his chin, enjoying the sensation of warm breath on rough fabric and ignoring the twig that fell from the tree overhead. The supply of things to swipe at in Africa was endless. Flailing at it all was a path to exhaustion. He'd learned to ignore most of it. Though he couldn't be like those kids who let the flies sip at the corners of their eyes without a bother. The sight made his stomach flip.

He tried to recall an image of Ma, Da, Mickey, and himself all together, but nothing came. Had he forgotten what they looked like already? That was a sadness. Perhaps there might be something to lift his spirits in that gourd the colonel's boy was careful not to share. Though that meant getting up, and he was feeling too comfy for that. If the colonel or his boy killed something, there would be a long bloody march back to camp. The blacks would cut up the carcasses and carry the meat and hides on their heads. But the flies would follow and torment them all, black and white alike. He wouldn't want a dozy head for that.

Something landed on his shirt and scurried south. Instinctively, he swelled his belly to close the gap between skin and belt. *Can't have anything wandering down there.* Stymied, whatever it was paused at the belt line and began to move in circles. Dooley opened his eyes.

Mother of God! There on his belly sat a nasty-looking creature an inch and a half long and nearly as high on account of a thin tail curved up over its back and coming to a point over its head. He strained to get a clearer look. But the pictures he'd seen were proof enough. Scorpion!

The weight he'd lost these last weeks was no longer there to keep gap between belly and waistband closed. *Sweet Jesus!* If he swatted the thing, it would sting him sure. Pores opened in his scalp and rivulets of sweat carried salt to his eyes. He held himself still. What else was there to do? Filmy-eyed, he watched the creature pause at an open shirt button just above his navel.

Don't go in there. It wasn't a prayer. He didn't believe in prayers. But he was whispering them in bunches now as a second creature dropped from the tree, landed on his chest and squared off, tail held high, in front of the first.

This can't be happening. The two filthy creatures raised their tails and circled each other on the mound of Dooley's stomach. Poisonous appendages raised and lowered as they moved clockwise around the gap in his shirt. The sensation of mincing feet made his stomach flutter. The sound of arterial blood whooshed in his ears. One of them was going to lunge at the other, sure. And what if it missed?

Breathing slowly through his mouth, he tried to still a sudden itch in his nose. Sweat poured into his eyes, and his chest struggled to heave while he tried to hold still. Through the slits between his eyelids, he watched the scorpions slow to a halt, wary dancers, poised for a finale. His itchy nose felt ready to explode. The scorpions were ready to strike. He couldn't hold the sneeze.

"Ahaaaa...choooo....!" The last thing he would feel on this earth would be excruciating pain. He knew it and braced for it. But it didn't come. The Roosevelt kid had talked about a missionary who'd been mauled by a lion that picked him up in his mouth and shook him like a rat, and how the missionary wrote that he'd felt nothing and supposed it was God's way of sparing the victim from horrible pain. Maybe that was it. Maybe God was kinder to animals than to men, or kinder to men killed by African animals? Who cared? He looked down toward his crotch, expecting to see a pair of poisonous barbs buried in his midsection. But he saw nothing. *Christ, I didn't blow them down me trousers, did I?* He lay still. Nothing moved. Carefully turning his head to each side, he saw nothing. He forced himself to look between his legs. Through a film of terror and sweat, he spied the victor standing triumphant, its mouth around the head of the vanquished and its prismed eyes staring right into Dooley's.

Spreading his legs as slowly as humanly possible, he raised his torso and removed the cap from his head. Then, while the winner was devouring what was left of the loser, he brought the cap down softly on both, leapt to his feet, and with his prize inside, started down the trail left by the two bathers and the gun bearer.

His heart pounded like a native drum, and he was lucky he heard the bathers before they had a chance to spot him. Maybe it was a good thing that the colonel was such a talker. At the top of the watering hole, the gun bearer stood with his back to Roosevelt, facing open terrain. Father's and son's boots and belts lay under a thorn bush on the opposite side of the water. Dooley approached carefully, keeping a clump of thorn bushes between himself and the lecturing politician. When he reached the bush where the two had left their clothes and footwear, he chose the boot beneath the longer of the two belts and emptied the contents of his cap into it.

Chapter Seven

As I stepped to one side of the bush so as to get a clear aim…the rhino saw me and jumped to his feet with the agility of a polo pony. As he rose I put in the right barrel, the bullet going through both lungs. At the same moment he wheeled, the blood spouting from his nostrils, and galloped full on us. Before he could get quite all the way round in his headlong rush to reach us, I struck him with my left-hand barrel, the bullet entering the neck vertebrae. Ploughing up the ground with horn and feet, the great bull rhino, still head toward us, dropped just thirteen paces from where we stood.

- Theodore Roosevelt, *African Game Trails*, 1910

"Your bodyguard dislikes you," said Kermit, submerged to the waist in the tepid waters of the stream-fed watering hole.

The generously spaced words and flushed face reminded Roosevelt that his son had declined the gun bearer's tea for something out of a gourd in his rucksack. "I don't need Mr. Dooley's vote. I don't need anyone's anymore. What I need from our young Pinkerton is his quick thinking and fast reflexes."

Kermit laughed. "That was some knife trick."

"You might learn something from my prickly bodyguard."

"Such as why he dislikes you?"

Roosevelt leaned back on his elbows so that the water cascaded around his neck and shoulders. "Oh, that's no mystery." But the look on his son's face said otherwise. "All right, let me explain. When one person dislikes another, it's usually because of something the other person's done or stands for. Our Mr. Dooley didn't seem to have strong feelings about our topics of conversation this morning: the kaiser and the national parks. So my guess is, like many who come from humble beginnings, he has strong feeling about those, like us, who don't."

"Can you blame him?"

"I can and do. I judge people by what they do, not where they were born. I expect the same courtesy."

From his post overlooking the watering hole, the gun bearer shouted something and raised a lean brown arm toward the horizon. "What's he saying?" asked Roosevelt.

"*Faru*," said Kermit. "That's Swahili for rhino."

"Oh, bully! Our first."

Kermit leapt to his feet and ran toward the far end of the water hole. "I'll get our clothes!"

Unwilling to wait, Roosevelt sprinted to the top of the rise, where the gun bearer's outstretched arm guided Roosevelt's vision to a sight to fill any hunter's heart. Four hundred yards to the south, an enormous grey animal stood pawing the ground in front of a dust-covered thorn bush. The gun bearer smiled broadly and handed Roosevelt his Winchester. "*Piga*," he whispered. *Shoot*.

Roosevelt shouldered the lever-action rifle and held its iron sight behind the rhino's shoulder. The prehistoric-looking beast with the scimitar nose horn looked to be more than four hundred yards away. A clean kill at that distance would challenge anyone's marksmanship. The last thing Roosevelt or any right-minded hunter wanted was to wound an animal when a careful stalk might lead to a clean and merciful shot.

The foraging beast stood rooting the ground with its great wide horn, unaware or indifferent to the hunter's presence or plan. This prehistoric species had few natural enemies, and the thickly armored adults had none. Roosevelt gestured toward a clump of thorns midway between the watering hole and the animal. The gun bearer nodded.

Even allowing for the combination of equatorial sun and noonday beer, Kermit should have needed only a minute or two to collect their discarded shirts and boots. Where in tarnation was he? Roosevelt looked at the gun bearer's calloused feet, as hard as the hooves of the animal they were about to stalk. His own looked more like bread dough. But he'd be damned if he was going to let the animal get away. With a glare toward the far end of the water hole, he signaled the gun bearer to begin the stalk.

The first fifty yards provided little cover, but the rhino paid no attention to the hunters, lifting his great head only once before resuming his digging. The tick birds that rode the great animal's back and picked insects from between its armor plates paid no attention, either. At two hundred yards, Roosevelt and the gun bearer reached a thin screen of thorn, where the wind was in their faces and the rhino feeding in their direction. The native pointed to another group of thorns a hundred yards to the animal's flank. Crouching low and moving slowly, they covered the ground in a little more than a quarter-hour. Roosevelt looked back to where they had started. Where was Kermit? The rhino stood broadside less than a hundred yards away. The gun bearer mimicked the act of shooting. "*Piga*," he hissed.

Wrapping the leather sling tightly around his forearm, Roosevelt placed the iron sight on the center of the rhino's chest, just behind the shoulder. He sipped a shallow breath and squeezed the trigger. The explosion of a .405 Winchester cartridge was deafening and the recoil just as powerful. The rhino didn't budge.

"*Refu!*" The gun bearer raised his hand above his ear. Roosevelt adjusted the rifle sights to just below the rhino's spine and squeezed the trigger again. *Thwat!* At a hundred fifty yards, the impact of bullet on flesh was unmistakable. The rhino whirled and charged. "*Piga!*" the gun bearer shouted.

The angry animal tore up the ground between them at a gallop. At fifty yards, Roosevelt put two more shots into the rhino's plated chest. The animal stumbled but didn't stop and bore down on the two hunters with frightening speed. At twenty yards, Roosevelt put in another round. Then he and the gun bearer dove for the dirt, and the rhino, apparently unaffected, lowered its great horn to skewer them both.

The lethal horn tip descended a crucial inch and, catching the dirt like an iron plow on a Kansas plain, cleaved a fifteen-yard furrow in the packed ground, coming to a halt as the great beast collapsed a mere thirteen paces from where the hunters lay prone and gasping.

Dooley was startled by the sound of rifle fire. He'd returned to the acacia, expecting Kermit or the gun bearer to appear dragging the stricken Roosevelt. But who was shooting? And where was Roosevelt?

More gunfire followed. He ran to the watering hole and found it deserted. The bathers could not have gone far. Not without their boots. He ran to where they'd left their clothes, and there under the thorns lay Kermit flat on his back oozing sweat and breathing like a blacksmith's bellows. One foot was booted, the other naked and swollen. A khaki shirt and second pair of boots lay nearby. "Something bit me," the boy gasped.

"Where's your old man?" The stricken boy rolled over, shivering. "Shit!" Dooley ran to the watering hole and scrambled up the hill behind it. From there, he could see the shirtless politician a hundred yards away posing with his naked foot on the back of a beast the size of a trolley car. *Sweet Jesus!*

He ran back to the shivering boy and pulled him to his feet. Dooley knew nothing about scorpion bites. But he knew that if a man passed out and puked enough, and in the right direction, he could drown in his own vomit. If the kid died, the safari would be finished, the politician would go home alive. Then god knew what would happen to Mickey. Wrapping the boy's arm over his shoulder, he shouted, "Move your ass!" Kermit hopped gingerly on one booted foot. Dooley gripped him by the belt for support and urged him in the direction of the watering hole. "Walk!" When the boy didn't move, he slapped him on the back of the head. "Move!"

"Something bit me."

Dooley grimaced. "I didn't think it was the hooch."

The gun bearer found them first, kneeling to examine Kermit's foot and then running off to get help. Dooley wished he could have put the boy down and waited. But he didn't like the look of him. He'd lost all color and his tongue hung from the side of his mouth. They were both sweating like coolies, though the boy was shivering like a cold, wet dog. He gripped the kid's belt and propelled him forward.

Potter and Thompson arrived on horseback an hour later. Potter loaded the kid onto his horse and galloped toward camp. The natives, who arrived on foot, went to find Roosevelt and take care of his dead animal. Dooley started to say something about the politician likely needing a pair of boots but stopped. *Screw it.* Neither Potter nor Thompson had said so much as a thank you. Exhausted and over-heated, he felt himself shivering just like the kid. That made no sense. It was hotter than Hades and he hadn't been stung by anything. But his legs felt as weak as porridge and he couldn't stop shaking. When they reached camp, one of the cooks looked at him and grunted, "*Homa.*"

Later, someone told him that was the Swahili word for malaria.

He knew he was dreaming. But that didn't make it less real. Ketchel held Mickey by the scruff of his neck and strapped him to the Edison chair, put a wet sponge to the top of his head, and pressed on a metal cap. A thick wire cable connected the cap to a wall-mounted junction box where a guard stood with his hand on a wood-handled lever waiting for Ketchel's nod. They'd tied Dooley to a chair facing his brother and shoved a sock into his mouth to keep him from yelling.

"Which is it going to be?" asked Ketchel, not bothering to remove the sock. "Your pissant brother or the politician?"

"Roosevelt!" Dooley screamed through the cloth. "Roosevelt!"

Roosevelt and others took turns frog-marching Kermit around the campfire to sweat the poison out of him. The boy remained conscious and eventually tried a few jokes. When it was clear that he was out of danger, Roosevelt went to find the young Pinkerton who had saved his son's life. "It's some kind of fever," said Heller, the taxidermist who doubled as the camp doctor. Dooley lay on a canvas cot in a corner of the mess tent. Grey moths and rust-colored beetles swarmed the paraffin lantern hanging from the tent pole above his head. "I can't find any sign that he's been bitten by anything. He's been calling your name, though."

"Mr. Dooley!" Roosevelt leaned over Dooley's cot. "What have you done for him, so far?"

"Quinine. That'll help, if it's malaria."

"What if it's not?"

"That's all we've got."

Roosevelt pinched the bridge of his nose, paced the tent, and returned to the side of the stricken man's cot. "There's a danger of brain damage with fevers, isn't there?"

"If they go on too long."

"Kermit mentioned something the natives use."

"A powder from a kind of pepper plant that grows around here." Heller placed two fingers on Dooley's jugular and timed his pulse with a steel pocket watch. "The cooks had some in Kapiti, but the head horse boy made them get rid of it. Said it can make a horse go nuts, even a whiff from a cooking pot. Kick a man right through a wall."

Roosevelt placed a hand on Dooley's forehead. "Get some. Break this fever."

Chapter Eight

*The Congo Free State is unique in its kind. It has nothing to hide and
no secrets and is not beholden to anyone except its founder.*

- King Leopold II of Belgium

Maggie started back toward the Goanese hotel, feeling tired, sweaty,
and frustrated. The chalk-white road leading inland from the port radiated like ashes of coal in the afternoon sun. A pair of laborers, naked
except for small loincloths, passed her, pushing a cart piled high with
salt. There were no draft animals in Mombasa, on account of the tsetse fly, and no water, other than what could be pumped by hand from
an underground source that became perilously low in the dry season.
Maggie had learned all this and more in her morning wanderings.

At the customs shed, she discovered that Teddy and his party had
left almost immediately for Nairobi, and from there, they intended
to travel by train across the Athi plains to meet up with their guides
and porters at a place called Kapiti Station. An Indian trader at the
central market claimed to have sold the safari organizers enough
supplies to feed and equip an army. He volunteered that the safari
would likely march south toward Kilimanjaro, as he had been asked
for references to Indian suppliers there. A helpful clerk at the British
consulate opined that the former American president would not upset
his hosts by venturing south into German territory, and, therefore,
the safari would most certainly head north from Kapiti into Uganda.
A white hunter at the Thika Club disagreed with both, declaring that
a competent guide would hold the safari on the Kapiti plain until the
herds arrived with the rains. Other than the fact that Teddy had already
left Mombasa, no one had any firsthand information, though they all
had opinions.

When she reached the hotel, a native in a white kanzu and embroi-
dered skullcap handed her a glass of mango juice and guided her to
the farthest corner of the veranda, where Pere de Clercq and another

man dressed in ecclesiastical traveling attire sat talking. Both men stood. "Madame Dunn, I would present my *bon ami*, Father Slattery."

"Pere de Clercq has been telling me of your adventures together," said the other in a soft brogue that reminded her of the cadences and rhythms of her Five Points childhood, when she was still Maggie Ryan. "Would you care to join us?" He offered his chair and dragged another from a nearby table. "It seems the Congolese intend to prevent my friend from returning to their secretive little colony."

"Hardly little," she said. "It's twice the size of the British and German colonies combined."

"And the world knows little of what goes on there," said Slattery. "The only whites permitted to travel inland are employees of King Leopold's personal trading company. And no journalist can obtain an entry permit."

She inclined her head toward the visibly bruised Belgian priest. "I've seen some of their more direct efforts to suppress publicity."

Slattery sipped his mango juice. "King Leopold doesn't like to overlook anything. Last year, an American missionary in Kasai was put on trial for slander after writing home about how all the able-bodied men in his parish had been taken as forced labor to cut rubber in the jungle."

"Congolese government, ha!" said Pere de Clercq. "There is not such. It is *le roi de Belge* himself, and no other."

"What will they do if Pere de Clercq ignores their warning?"

Slattery glanced at his friend. "Something unpleasant, I'm sure. But my friend was telling me you have an idea that might help him avoid further unpleasantness."

A barefoot servant approached noiselessly and replenished their glasses from an earthen pitcher. Maggie emptied half of hers in one long swallow. "Which he resists because it might delay his return to the Congo until after the rains."

Slattery turned to his fellow priest. "The horrors of the Congo will not be ended between one planting and the next, Emile." Pere de Clercq frowned and remained silent. "Our order is not without resources when it comes to threats of violence against men of God. But we would avoid confrontation wherever possible."

"I must return to the Congo as *rapidement* as possible," Pere de Clercq insisted. "That madman slaughters innocents each day, I tell you."

Maggie leaned forward and placed a hand on the Irish priest's arm. "What I suggested to Pere de Clercq was that he act as my guide and translator while I write stories for my newspaper. I don't speak the native languages or know the territory. I have to hire someone who does. If Pere de Clercq were to assist me, he might leave Mombasa without hindrance from the British, and convince whomever is watching that he's engaged in something that has nothing to do with the Congo Free State and is of no threat to King Leopold."

Pere de Clercq waved his hand like a flag in a breeze. "We have discussed this. I cannot be wandering East Africa, while the Force Publique is murdering my children in the Congo."

"Which is over three thousand kilometers away," said Slattery. "If the Force Publique thinks you've ignored their warning, they'll waylay you before you get ten kilometers out of Mombasa. When they're through, there won't be enough of you left to feed a mongoose."

"God will protect and provide."

Slattery leaned forward. "Perhaps Mrs. Dunn is His way of doing that, Emile. Or of creating a Congolese martyr, if you ignore Him. Free will does sometimes require the Almighty to have a backup plan."

Maggie chuckled. She liked the blunt priest. His humor and patience were a refreshing contrast to the sometimes truculent Pere de Clercq. "I didn't mean to suggest that we would be wandering around the countryside looking for colorful stories," she offered. "I hope to investigate Pere de Clercq's reports of colonial atrocities in the Congo and rumors of the revival of slavery in the Sudan. I need a guide and translator, but I may also need physical protection at some point. A large safari set off from Kapiti a few weeks ago to collect animal specimens for several American museums. It's led by a former American president. Have you heard anything of it?"

Slattery smiled. "We get precious little news here. But we did get that."

"Then you know it must be the largest group of armed men in East Africa, outside of the colonial military. Would King Leopold's men dare attack anyone enjoying its protection?"

Pere de Clercq fanned air with the back of his hand. "We have discussed this also. You do not know where this Roosevelt *marche*. We could spend months to find. This famous person, would he put a king's nose from his face to befriend a journalist and a penniless priest?"

Maggie smiled. "He might for me." *If I can find a way to get past that pesky Potter.*

"Oh?" said Slattery, his tone both curious and cautious.

"Colonel Roosevelt and I were childhood friends. I am hoping that he will feel obliged to offer his protection once our paths cross."

"I see. Well then, you may be interested in something that will be taking place not far from where the Roosevelt safari should be at the end of this month."

It was Maggie's turn to be curious. "How do you know where Colonel Roosevelt will be?"

"The white hunter leading the Roosevelt safari is a neighbor of mine. He has a farm near the Samburu reserve, close to my mission. My parishioners tell me that they have been asked to conduct a *simba kuwinda* in honor of a *Bwana M'Kubwa* at the end of this month."

Maggie spread her palms. "A what?"

"A lion hunt in honor of a Big Man. Presumably, your former president. The irony, of course, is that as soon as the hunt is over, the village will be relocated to Murang'a as part of the government's program to free arable land for white settlement. The headman told me if they kill a good lion for *Bwana M'Kubwa*, they won't have to leave. He wouldn't say who told him. And it may be that no one did and he simply wants to believe it. But the truth is that once your president is there and gone, the relocation will start. The colonial office wants to hold a land auction for prospective white famers before the next rains."

The Belgian priest seized the opportunity to lecture his friend in turn. "The British are not so brutal as le *roi de belge,* my friend. But if you interfere with their natives, *bien sure* they will deport you."

"Perhaps." Slattery raised his glass as if toasting the idea. "But the most effective antiseptic for the sore of injustice is printers' ink, or so I'm told. I've just informed an American reporter of where injustice and a former American president will soon be in proximity. The rest is up to God and to her."

Maggie wasn't sure how to interpret the priest's information about a lion hunt to be held in Teddy's honor. "Are you saying that Colonel Roosevelt knows about this forced relocation?"

"Of course not. And even if he should learn that the natives providing his entertainment will be forced from their homes within weeks after his departure, there is little, if anything, he can do about it. But it is a story that deserves witness. Perhaps President Roosevelt's attendance is God's way of getting that story to a wider audience. In any event, a *simba kuwinda* doesn't happen every day. I leave it to you to decide, Mrs. Dunn, if it's something that your readers might find of interest."

"They will, I assure you."

Chapter Nine

One by one the spearmen came up, at a run, and gradually began to form a ring around the lion. Each, when he came near enough, crouched behind his shield, his spear in his right hand, his fierce, eager face peering over the shield rim. As man followed man, the lion rose to his feet. His mane bristled, his tail lashed, he held his head low, the upper lip now drooping over the jaws, now drawn up so as to show the gleam of the long fangs. He faced first one way and then another, and never ceased to utter his murderous grunting roars. It was a wild sight; the ring of spearmen, intent, silent, bent on blood, and in the centre the great man-killing beast, his thunderous wrath growing ever more dangerous...

Rearing, the lion struck the man, bearing down the shield, his back arched; and for a moment he slaked his fury with fang and talon. But on the instant I saw another spear driven clear through his body from side to side; and as the lion turned again the bright spear blades darting toward him were flashes of white flame. The end had come. He seized another man, who stabbed him and wrenched loose. As he fell he gripped a spear head in his jaws with such tremendous force that he bent it double. Then the warriors were round and over him, stabbing and shouting, wild with furious exultation.

From the moment when he charged until his death I doubt whether ten seconds had elapsed, perhaps less; but what a ten seconds!

- Theodore Roosevelt, *African Game Trails*, 1910

After the hunt and native celebration, Roosevelt returned to Cunninghame's farm in the nearby Kitanga hills, accompanied by Potter and Kermit, who had survived his scorpion sting with only a daily diminishing limp as evidence of his ordeal. The farmhouse was a simple one-story structure of mud bricks, fitted comfortably with homemade furniture and packed-earth floors covered in animal skin rugs. The men gathered for celebratory drinks on the stone veranda, which ran along the front and sides of the house, shaded by trellises of frangipani and plaited palms. A pair of modest outbuildings, used for cooking and storage, occupied a small space behind the house. The entire compound covered no more than an acre.

Roosevelt stood at the edge of the veranda looking eastward toward the Samburu village, where thatched-roofed huts spread across a lush green hillside. A column of sparks rose high in the air from the bonfire at the village center. According to their host, the dancing in celebration of the successful lion hunt would go on until sunrise. Roosevelt felt nothing but awe and admiration for the skill and courage of the Samburu warriors, who had slain a full-grown lion in a traditional hunt using only animal hide shields for protection and metal-tipped wooden spears as weapons.

He confided to his host, "I haven't experienced such an exciting afternoon since Cuba! That lion shook that Samburu spearman like a cat would a rat! The courage of those men! Bully! Just bully!"

"The Samburu is a fine man with a spear," said Cunninghame. "Not so much with a hoe."

Kermit raised an arm and pointed toward an ox wagon passing through a stand of flame trees at the edge of a sisal field a few hundred yards away. "We've got visitors."

Cunninghame squinted into the fading twilight. "Word must have spread of your arrival. That's the mission wagon."

"Look in the back, Pop." Roosevelt squinted, too, until Kermit added, "Put a hand over your bum eye."

Roosevelt suppressed annoyance at his son's indiscretion. Few people knew about the boxing injury that had rendered his left eye nearly useless. He preferred to keep it that way. But he took the boy's advice and immediately felt the corners of his mouth lift.

"I think we're going to have a party," said Kermit.

Potter made a face as if he had swallowed something bitter.

Cunninghame identified the visitors. "That's Father Slattery from the Catholic mission at Masii. A bit of a complainer about government policy toward the natives but an educated man. You'll like him. I don't know the other two. One seems to be a priest, as well, judging from his attire. The other is clearly a lady. Always welcome, those."

Maggie... When Potter mentioned that Maggie had stayed behind in Naples, Roosevelt had felt both regret and relief. He'd attributed his feelings then to boyhood nostalgia. But as he watched the ox wagon draw closer to the farmhouse, his excitement and discomfort were unarguably of the present.

A pair of grey oxen strained at the yoke of the two-wheeled open wagon as they slowly hauled it up the packed earth drive. At the top of the veranda, Roosevelt waited to greet the unexpected visitors. How had Maggie managed to secure passage from Naples and find them out here in the middle of the African nowhere? The girl he knew those many years ago had been uncommonly strong-minded. The woman she had become was uncommonly resourceful as well.

A hand pressed on his shoulder. "I don't know why you don't like reporters, Pop. But this one's got spunk to track you down out here."

"I'll be darned if I know how. No one knew our planned route, other than you and Mr. Cunninghame. This side trip wasn't even on the itinerary until ten days ago."

The wagon pulled up to the foot of the veranda. Roosevelt descended the steps to greet the passengers.

"Hail the house!" called the priest, who Cunninghame had identified as Father Slattery.

Kermit stepped to the back of the wagon and helped Maggie alight. She smiled and gave him her hand. "How nice to see you again, Kermit. And you, Colonel."

"A pleasant surprise, indeed," said Roosevelt.

A native servant, dressed in a long-sleeved, ankle-length cotton kanzu, rolled out a cart containing a single unopened bottle of whiskey, two half-full bottles of gin and rum, and a pitcher of fruit punch made of mango, orange, and banana. Another servant brought three additional hide-covered chairs for the newly arrived guests.

Roosevelt was careful to keep a proper distance from Maggie, though his eyes couldn't help wandering in her direction. Potter coughed and grunted each time they did. No doubt he meant well, but Roosevelt refused to be rude and pretend he was not pleased to see her. When everyone was settled and had been offered sufficient libations, he returned to the discussion of the Samburu lion hunt.

"The bravery of those men! Not one of them flinched or gave ground. Even when the lion grabbed one of them and dragged him down. If the Spanish had defended San Juan Hill with half the discipline I saw today, I wouldn't be here talking to you."

"You're fortunate to have seen what you did," said Slattery. "It may be the last *simba kuwinda* to be held in this part of the colony. The constables come next week to supervise the relocation of the host village to Murang'a." Cunninghame opened his mouth but then seemed to have second thoughts. "Any sign of trouble?" Slattery asked.

Cunninghame shook his head. "The village is being compensated for its land."

"In farm implements and cloth."

"It's not my decision, Father. I've lived among the Samburu as long as you have, and I'd be happy to end my days among them. But we both know why they have to move."

Roosevelt noticed the houseboys listening from just inside the doorway a few yards away. He would follow their example. Listen and keep his thoughts to himself.

"I know the colonial office's explanation," said the priest. "British East Africa must be opened to white settlement. Settlers need to be fed. The hunters and gatherers who live on arable land nearest the settlements must learn to farm or make way for those who will."

Cunninghame wrapped his sun-browned hands around his drink. "Hard to argue with the logic."

"If you accept the premise that British East Africa *must* be opened to white settlement," said Slattery. "Even if you do accept it, relocation in *advance* of that settlement seems extreme."

Cunninghame turned to Potter. "I remember you telling me, Mr. Potter, that your grandparents rode West on a covered wagon when the American frontier was still occupied by Indians. How often were they attacked before they reached their destination? How many killed?"

Potter held up a hand and stood. "This cowboy is going to go check the horses."

Cunninghame smiled. "My apologies. I shouldn't use my guests to make a point. What I mean to say, Father, is that the British East Africa colonial office hopes to avoid the American experience of violence between natives and settlers. The same thing happened between the Boers and the Zulu. They'll never say it that plainly, of course. It's a delicate business. But I applaud the sentiment and wish them luck."

"And the natives?"

"God has a plan, or so I'm told, even if we don't always know what it is or why."

The other priest, who had been silent until then, erupted. "Blasphemer! The brutalities of kings are not God's plan!"

"Emile," said Slattery in a soothing voice. "My friends," he continued, addressing the others, "Father de Clercq has a mission in the Congo Free State. They don't relocate villages there. They burn them, take away the men to be used as forced labor to gather wild rubber in the jungle, and then cut off the hand of anyone who doesn't meet his quota."

Cunninghame's face tightened. "I've heard rumors like that. So have the Samburu. None of them will go farther west than Kigoma."

"Is that why you plan to take us north into Uganda instead of west when we reach Lake Tanganyika?" asked Kermit.

Roosevelt winced again. That was Kermit's second indiscretion of the evening. Cunninghame was the only other one supposed to know the safari's planned route.

"There's good hunting in the Congo," said Cunninghame. "Better elephant and a kind of white rhino we don't have here. But you can't find a native guide or a porter who will cross Lake Tanganyika."

Maggie sat quietly in a zebra-skin chair between Kermit and Father de Clercq and said nothing. Though, Roosevelt was acutely aware of her eyes when they turned toward him, which was often. The others cast glances in his direction, too—some openly, and others, like Slattery, with more discretion. It was obvious that all were waiting for him to speak. He reminded himself that he must avoid getting involved in political discussions—especially with a newspaper reporter present—but to remain silent any longer would be rude in this company. He turned to the priest with the French accent and the mission in the Congo. "Tell me what you've seen with your own eyes, Father."

The priest folded his hands, as if in prayer. "The soldiers come to my mission at the end of the rains. They take the men. The women *reste* to plant the crop. Some small boys, also. Ten months, when the rains come again, the men return. But not so many. Three have hands cut. I leave the mission and *porte* the Kasai. I see villages burned. Everywhere no food and men without hand. All for the rubber."

The priest spoke for twenty minutes. When his English failed, the other priest interpreted. No one interrupted. When he was finished, the only sounds on the veranda were the distant drumming from the Samburu village and the buzz of insects lured to the paraffin lanterns Cunninghame's houseboys brought to illuminate their conversation.

"You're a brave man to go back there," said Roosevelt when it was clear the missionary had finished speaking. "An American Negro missionary named Sheppard came to President McKinley with a story like that when I was in the White House."

"We know of him," said the priest. "He returned to Congo and *Les Belges* put him on trial for writing lies about the king."

"I heard something of that."

"And you do nothing?"

Roosevelt sat upright in his chair and crossed his arms in front of his chest. "Dr. Shepard's missionary society has employed an excellent French lawyer. He will make the Congolese officials understand the consequences of an unjust conviction. If Dr. Shepard is convicted and sentenced to a term in a Congolese prison, I have no doubt President Taft will send the Marines to bring him home, as I did for the American businessman, Perdicarus, when he was kidnapped and held for ransom in Morocco."

"Yes, yes," said the missionary, shaking his head. "The world knows the freedom of one American is worth more than a pile of severed African hands. But there is no justice in this."

"It's a beginning," said Roosevelt. "And an excellent example. If you harm an American citizen, white or colored, anywhere in the world, you can count on the Marines to come and kick down your door. It doesn't matter who or where you are. Belgian king or Moroccan bandit—the result will be the same."

"Bully!" said Maggie, mimicking Roosevelt's trademark expression of enthusiasm. "I think I'll lead with that quote."

Roosevelt felt as if he'd been hit in the head. He hadn't meant to get involved in a political discussion, and then he'd gone ahead and done just that. Damnation! "I had assumed this was off the record."

Maggie stood. "I'm going to get some air. Would you care to join me, Colonel? Perhaps we might talk about your lion hunt. On the record. If I'm to lose my recollection about your views on how and when to use the U.S. Marines, I must give my readers something of interest.

Was the lion hunt terribly frightening?" Potter stood. Roosevelt shook him off. Kermit chuckled.

"Maggie!"

"Margaret Dunn," she replied. "Or Mrs. Dunn, if you prefer. Mr. Hearst thinks that it sounds more journalistic than Maggie Ryan."

"Damnation, Maggie! I promised Taft I wouldn't talk politics for a year. I came halfway around the world so if I shot off my mouth, there'd be no one to hear but the elephants. You can't print what I said about the Marines. Not with war in Europe coming."

"*Former President Theodore Roosevelt says European war imminent.* Perhaps I should lead with that. What do you think?"

"Maggie!"

"You'd be wise to quit shouting that name, or you'll have some explaining to do."

"Damnation, Mag… Damnation!"

"Tell me about your lion hunt, Colonel. My readers will want to hear about that as well."

Roosevelt felt his pulse throb in his ears. "I can't do that!" He suppressed the urge to shake her. "I signed a contract with *Scribner's* to write a book about the safari to cover Kermit's and my expenses. They have exclusive rights. The Smithsonian is paying for everything else, but I didn't think it right for them to pay our way, too."

"I also make my living with my pen, Colonel."

"And I must keep my promises." He turned to see if Potter was lurking, or if the sudden chill he felt was just his friend's telepathic warning wafting from the farmhouse veranda.

"Then what *shall* we talk about, Colonel? On the record. I've traveled halfway around the world—the hottest part of it in steerage—to find and interview the most popular president since George Washington; the one who left office of his own free will when he could have had a third term just for the asking; the one who instead disappeared on a self-imposed, yearlong exile into darkest Africa. Well, I've found you. I've talked to you. And I'm ready to write. What would you have me write about?"

Roosevelt closed his eyes and lifted his face to the star-filled sky.

Maggie folded her arms across her white cotton blouse. "You're the professional politician, Colonel, skilled in the art of compromise. You won a Nobel Peace Prize for helping the Russians and Japanese find a face-saving way to end their hostilities. Tell me what I should write about. Or, to use a hunting metaphor, tell me why I should holster my pen when the quarry is broadside in front of me."

He felt himself smile. "Because it's a one-shot story, Maggie. And if I deny it, it's a miss. Hearst won't forgive that. Especially if you could have a better shot, and more of them, if you hold your fire." He watched her gaze lift upward and to the right—the gambler's tell for a bluff.

"How much better? And when? Would you take me with you to the Congo to write about the atrocities Pere de Clercq described? Or to the Sudan?"

"I can't let a journalist accompany the safari, Maggie. That would violate my agreement with *Scribner's*. But I can talk to you about politics as much as you want while we're here, if you promise not to publish for a year."

"I'll be out of work and starving by then."

"It's the best I can do, Maggie."

"It's nothing at all! It's not compromise; it's sleight of hand."

"Maggie…" he paused. "I'm happier than I should be comfortable admitting to have the chance to enjoy your company again, even if it's only for a few days. But if the price of rekindled friendship is breaking my word to President Taft or my promise to *Scribner's*, then I must forego it."

She looked at him, mouth half-open. "You're being a priss, Teddy. That's not the boy I remember."

He held his breath. They were neither of them children anymore. They were adults, in the prime of life, alone with the love of their youth under a starlit African sky. If he stayed any longer, he was going to make a fool of himself. He had no idea what she felt.

"Teddy?"

Light-headed and uncertain, he whispered, "I'm sorry, Maggie." Then he turned and walked slowly back to the farmhouse.

Chapter Ten

It was an unceasing pleasure to watch the way of the game and to study their varying habits. Where there was a river from which to drink, or where there were many pools, the different kinds of buck, and the zebra, often showed comparatively little timidity about drinking, and came boldly down to the water's edge, sometimes in broad daylight, sometimes in darkness; although even under those conditions they were very cautious if there was cover at the drinking-place. But where the pools were few they never approached one without feeling panic dread of their great enemy the lion, who, they knew well, might be lurking...

- Theodore Roosevelt, *African Game Trails*, 1910

Dooley lay on a sweat-soaked cot inside an airless tent, his head a web of nerves cradling a hive of fire ants. Sweaty palms pressed matted temples, but they could not stifle the throbbing inside. The taxidermist, Heller, had told Roosevelt about a powder the natives used to break fever. But he didn't say the effect was like boiling the patient's brain over an open flame. The clothes that clung to Dooley's skeleton, and the canvas beneath, were a sponge for the bilge that oozed from his pores and orifices over the last hours. Or was it days? Bodies came and went. Light alternated with darkness. Time stopped.

In a merciful moment of pain-free consciousness, he realized that he must kill Roosevelt soon, before a continent where nature specialized in human torment robbed him of the strength to try. But the insight was quickly overwhelmed by a bowel-voiding convulsion that narrowed his mind to surviving the next few seconds. His fingers clutched the sides of the cot, as though his body were being swept to sea. His lungs heaved foul air, and his body toppled to earth, tasting dirt.

Hours later, maybe days—he had no way of knowing and no energy to move or inquire—he opened his eyelids and looked down upon a body surprisingly dry and shockingly naked. The torturer with the brain-boiling powders stood at the foot of the cot, a candle in one hand, though it was broad daylight, and a sharp, pointed needle in the other. *What the folk?*

"You're awake!" said the taxidermist. "Good! Colonel's gone off to Cunninghame's farm. He'll back in a few days. He had me give you some native medicine to break your fever. Seems to have worked. But I had to burn your clothes and bedding. They were infested with bot fly larvae. A few more minutes and I'd have been done with this, too."

"Done with what?"

"Removing the chiggers from under your nails."

"Get away from me!"

"Steady, man. The larvae are small. I can remove them now, or leave them to get bigger and eat their way out." He held the needle over the candle flame. "Trust me, this is less painful."

"I said get away!"

The taxidermist put down the candle. "Listen to me. You've got malaria as well as bot fly larvae under your skin in a dozen places. Weren't the boys putting a hot iron to your clothes?"

"I don't need my trousers creased in folkin' Africa! And I'll not have you sticking needles under my toenails either!"

The taxidermist stood back from the cot but did not lower the needle. "I understand this is unpleasant. But the fact is bot flies like to lay their eggs in wet cloth. The boys put a hot iron to the washing to kill the eggs before they hatch. Or they're supposed to. If they don't, the eggs hatch and the larvae burrow into the skin of whoever puts on that cloth. Then the larvae eat their way out. Or in… No parts excepted." He gestured toward Dooley's midsection. "I'll remove the ones you can't reach. But you can do the others yourself, now your fever's broken and you're awake."

Dooley glared.

The taxidermist put the needle down next to the candle. "I can help you, you can do it yourself, or you can do nothing. But if you're going to have them out, I'd be quick about it. They're eating their way into you as we speak, and they're getting bigger by the hour."

Some things are best forgotten quickly. When the taxidermist left with his instruments of torture, Dooley grabbed a bottle of Jameson's and stumbled out of the tent, hoping to march his pincushion carcass around the camp until the pain receded and he came up with a plan to do to Roosevelt what Africa was trying to do to him. For that, he needed two things: a way to make the politician's death look like an accident, and a fall guy to take the blame in case the accident wasn't sufficiently convincing.

He knew now that his city-honed tricks were of little use on the African savannah. There were no alleys to lure a man down or horse carriages to shove him under. He didn't have the language to befriend the horse boys, gun bearers, or cooks in the hope of finding one careless enough in his job to allow the occurrence of an innocent accident, and in any event the African staff seemed to have been well chosen. There seemed little chance of slipping something into Roosevelt's food unnoticed by those dark, watchful eyes, or of loosening a shoe on his horse, or setting fire to his tent. But he had to find a way to kill Roosevelt while he still had the health and strength to complete the task.

The following afternoon, Roosevelt, his kid, and the cowboy nanny returned from their visit to the safari guide's farm. In the clearing beside the mess tent, the natives put up a tripod of stakes and hung the head and skin of a black-maned lion from its top. The thing was damn near as big as a horse. Every native in camp came running to see it, shouting and pushing to get a better look. Sweet Jesus, it was only a dead animal.

Egged on by his horse boy buddies, the little *sais* that took care of Roosevelt's horse pushed his way to the front of the crowd. Dooley had never seen all three of the horse boys anywhere together, except with the horses. There had been other celebrations over dead animals—rhino, elephant, gazelle, and wildebeest—but if one or two of them left the horses for any reason, the third always stayed behind. He'd checked, lots of times. They never left the animals alone.

The boy put his hand in the lion's mouth, and the crowd hooted. Dooley looked around for anyone who might not be caught up in the carnival. All eyes were locked on the boy and the dead lion. Backing away and walking rapidly toward his tent, an idea began to form in Dooley's mind. The taxidermist had told Roosevelt that even the smell of that fever powder could make a horse go nuts. If the sadist was right, a bit of the stuff could come in handy, sooner or later.

Back in his tent, he ran a wet finger across the top of the trunk where the taxidermist had prepared the potion. He put finger to tongue, and his nose swelled like he'd been hit by a brick, his eyes filming over like on bath day. This was the stuff, all right. He scraped the visible flakes onto a piece of paper and then wiped the top of the trunk with a dirty sock that he wet from a canteen hanging from the tent pole.

Outside a pair of drums led the crowd in a chant of, "Simba! Ah! Mmmm. Simba!" He opened the canvas flap and looked down the row of tents. There was no one in sight. Making his way toward the edge of camp, he skirted the clearing where the Roosevelt kid, standing on a box next to the hanging lion skin, was saying something to the crowd in their native lingo, his head no more than halfway up the animal's back.

Dooley moved quietly past the crowd. No one gave him a second look. The horse picket was on a bit of high ground behind the camp, next to a fat ugly tree as big around as a trolley car. No one was watching the horses. When he entered the picket, one of the animals pawed the ground and shot a wad of snot out of its nose. He waved a hand at it. "Get away! I'm not here to feed you." The horse stood his ground. Opening the paper and spilling a few of the red flecks into the cloth, he took one of the horse brushes lying between the tree roots and rubbed the cloth across its bristles. The drums and chanting stopped. Then he put the brush back between the tree roots and walked rapidly toward camp.

The impromptu celebration over the lion skin was over, and the cooks began their evening fires. When he passed the mess tent, Roosevelt came out and hailed him with a toothy grin. "Glad to see you up and about, young hero. I trust Mr. Heller didn't mistreat you too badly."

"He tried."

"Ha! Well you don't look any the worse. I wanted to thank you, again. This is the second time your quick thinking saved the day. Keeping Kermit on his feet and sweating kept that scorpion venom from reaching his heart, according to Mr. Heller. Did you know that before you did it? Or was it just instinct?"

"I know a sick man will drown in his own puke if you leave him lying."

"Well, I'm grateful. We both are."

A barefoot native wearing a thin red blanket draped over one shoulder, and not much else, ran into the clearing, jabbering and pointing down the path behind him. A bunch of his fellows shouted in reply and ran off in the direction he'd pointed. Dooley tried to suppress his excitement. "I wonder what's gotten into them."

"Shall we go see?"

Roosevelt led the way down the narrow path that led to the picket. As they got closer, Dooley could hear hooves pounding on packed earth, wild neighs and whinnies, and shouts of excited natives. Two of the horse boys had hold of the reins of a wild-eyed horse, and the third was trying to fling a cloth over its head. The animal reared on its hind legs and lifted the two reins holders off the ground. The third let out a scream, threw down the sack, and ran. Potter stepped forward and added his weight to the boys' to restrain the horse, and so did Kermit. The frightened animal threw its ass in the air and kicked at the sky. The third horse boy reappeared with a burlap sack. Maybe he thought to sneak up on the horse and pull it over his head. It was a dumb idea. The horse spun like a weathervane and caught the kid square in the chest with a backward thrust of his hooves. He fell to the ground and didn't move.

Roosevelt drew his sidearm and approached the animal from the front. "Hold him steady, Johnny, best you can."

Potter grunted.

Kermit wheezed, "Go ahead, Pop."

Roosevelt aimed the pistol at the horse's head and fired. The animal collapsed. A native ran forward and cut its jugular with a curved knife.

Dooley left the clearing and returned to his tent. When no one was near, he took the powder from his pocket, stuffed it inside a dirty sock, and crammed the ball of cloth into the bottom of his saddlebag. The powder made horses go nuts all right, just as Heller had warned. Now, how to give it to a horse with Roosevelt in the saddle and no one the wiser?

Roosevelt watched the short dry grass disintegrate into puffs of chaff beneath the feet of two hundred forty men, each carrying a forty-pound bundle on his head. The rains were late, but the hunting opportunities had become plentiful as the safari made its way north across a dry country where the animals were forced to concentrate around the dwindling watering holes. So far, they'd collected a variety of zebra, kudu, impala, giraffe, gemsbok, warthog, wildebeest, and eland, totaling almost a third of the plains animals the Smithsonian had requested.

From behind the trunk of a dead mimosa tree, toppled and left to wither by a passing elephant interested only in the sweet bark around the base, Roosevelt and Kermit had a clear view of a muddy water hole. Half a dozen animals had already come to drink that morning—several gazelles, impalas, and a lone wildebeest. The blind was far enough away from the water that the hunters' presence did not seem to bother the animals, whose sense of danger seemed primarily a function of distance and daylight.

The party had occupied the blind since dawn, in hope of ambushing a lion. But nothing had approached the water hole in the last hour, and Roosevelt thought it safe to converse in a whisper. The day was too beautiful to go unremarked, and his mind teemed with ideas that, even in the middle of Africa, demanded an audience.

"What do you think of that Belgian priest's stories of what's happening in the Congo?"

Kermit shrugged his shoulders. Roosevelt struggled to suppress his annoyance. At nineteen, and more interested in killing rhinos than saving the world, Kermit was proving an unsatisfactory audience for a father's spontaneous homilies on subjects other than blood sport. To be fair, the naïve Smithsonian scientists and the burly Pinkerton bodyguards were not much better. Around the nightly campfire, where he longed to hold court on world affairs, political corruption, and the evils of concentrated wealth, he found himself badly missing the bully pulpit and the audience it attracted. Long, hot marches gave him plenty of time to second-guess his selection of Taft and to brood about his promise to Edith not to serve more than two terms, which he was now convinced was the biggest mistake of his life. But he had no one with whom he could share these and other thoughts.

Surrendering the reins of power at age fifty had proved harder than he would have imagined. Shooting lions was thrilling to a point, but it was not the same as kicking the Columbians out of Panama and building a canal to the Pacific Ocean. On the savannahs of Africa, he was discovering that life could be tepid without a suitable challenge and an appreciative audience.

Kermit broke into his melancholy musings with an urgent whisper. "Kudu!"

A hundred yards away, a large kudu bull, supporting an impressive set of wide spiraling horns, stood with his harem of cows and yearlings, contemplating the approach to the water hole. Roosevelt lifted the Holland & Holland 450 to his shoulder and held the iron sight steady behind the animal's muscled foreleg, waiting for the bull to turn broadside. When it did, he gently squeezed the trigger.

The animal crumpled like a poleaxed steer and then toppled to its side and lay still. *Bully!* Though one of the yearlings that had been standing next to its mother a dozen yards away seemed to have also fallen. The small herd stampeded.

"*Mbili kupiga?*" said the astonished Kikuyu gun bearer. *Two kills?*

The three men trotted across the hundred yards of ground to where the large kudu lay dead on the parched grass. The entry wound in the bull's chest was high, but the Holland had done its work. Roosevelt was happy that the power of the 450 made up for his sometimes erratic marksmanship caused by fatigue in his one good eye. The big gun's impact was lethal at long distances—even if the animal weighed more than a thousand pounds and the shot was less than perfect.

By the time they reached the fallen bull, the sun had completed its morning climb across the cloudless sky, and the short grass was alive with the sound of buzzing insects. Twenty yards beyond the lifeless bull lay what proved to be an equally lifeless yearling a fraction of the bull's size. Roosevelt gripped the tiny animal's stiffening foreleg and turned it over easily. There was no bullet hole or any other evidence of what had killed it.

The gun bearer placed a hand to Roosevelt's shoulder and gestured toward a movement in the short grass. Two khaki-clad figures approached the watering hole—one, stout and sandy-haired with the lower portion of his face covered by a scraggly Van Dyke beard; the other, younger, taller, slimmer, and clean-shaven.

"*Dit is myne,*" said the older of the two, coming up to the dead yearling and placing a dusty boot on its slender neck.

Roosevelt had no knowledge of the Afrikaans dialect, but the man's language was close enough to German—which Roosevelt spoke fluently, and to Dutch, of which he had acquired a smattering from his grandmother—for Roosevelt to well understand his meaning. He answered the Boer in a hodgepodge of the two. *"Mijne ist groter."* Mine is bigger.

The man said something too rapidly for Roosevelt to understand, and the other prompted in English. "My father says he doubts it." The Boers laughed and Roosevelt joined them.

When the skinners arrived, having heard the blast of the Holland, they proceeded to cut up the big bull and salt its hide, while Roosevelt and the Boers traded questions and answers in a mix of English, Dutch, German, and gestures.

What had killed the young kudu? The young Boer, who had introduced himself as Jans, smiled proudly and pointed to a small hole almost in the center of the kudu's ear. Then he held out his rifle, which wasn't much larger than a Springfield .22 and hardly formidable enough to bring down a rabbit, much less a sizeable herd animal, if the shot was anything other than a bull's-eye to the head or the heart.

His father, who said his name was Jakobus, wanted to know why Roosevelt had taken such a large animal when the meat would be old, tough, and too much to consume before it spoiled. And what were the *kaffirs* doing with the skin?

"I have two hundred sixty men to feed every day," said Roosevelt. "Nothing goes to waste. The hide will go to a museum in New York, where the children will see the African game animals they've read about in books."

Answers followed questions until the skinners finished their work. Then the Boers tied their little kudu to a pole and lifted it to their shoulders.

"Kom na ons kamp," said Roosevelt, inviting the Boers to visit the safari camp.

The elder Boer smiled and nodded. "We come," his son promised. "With meat and beer."

The Boers arrived at sunset. One carried a large wooden box and the other a string of calabashes, which he set down next to the campfire. *"Biltong en bier,"* said Jakobus. *"Is al wat 'n mens nodig het."* Dried meat and beer is all that men need.

Roosevelt removed a Rough Rider slouch hat and campaign blouse from a satchel behind his canvas camp chair and addressed Jakobus in German. "If you and your son would ride with us, I would ask you to honor me my by wearing these in the hope that some might mistake your hunting skill for mine." Then he handed Jans a wooden box that contained a sharpshooter medal he'd won some years ago at a policeman's fair in New York, and which he had brought along on the safari for luck. "I've never seen a better shot than the one you made this morning on that young kudu. If there is to be a sharpshooter medal in this camp, it must be worn by you."

"*Dankie,*" said Jans as he and his father settled around the campfire and ate the kudu meat stew and drank beer.

Communicating in a hodgepodge of German, Dutch, and English, Jakobus turned to Cunninghame, who seemed to follow the polyglot conversation, though he spoke only in English. "*Jy was in die oorlog?*" he asked. *You were in the war?* Cunninghame, nodded. "*In die kampen?*" Jakobus continued. *In the concentration camps?*

Cunninghame shook his head. "No, thank God."

The elder Boer turned to Roosevelt and waved an instructional finger. His son translated for anyone who might need it. "When America fought the British, they didn't have machine guns and artillery. They didn't put your women and children in stockades like cattle and feed them next to nothing until they died of starvation and disease."

Cunninghame intervened. "Was your family in the concentration camps?" he asked in halting Afrikaans.

"My mother and sister," said Jans.

Roosevelt thought of his promise to Andrew Carnegie to meet with Kaiser Wilhelm on his way back from Africa. The German leader would be contemptuous of any appeal to forbearance or humanity. His country's motivation to rearm had complex roots. But they included a deep national outrage at Britain's brutal treatment of the Germanic-speaking Afrikaner civilians during the recently ended Anglo-Boer war in South Africa.

He gazed across the fire at the native boys roasting hunks of kudu meat on sharpened sticks, bits of bright cloth wrapping their loins and brass rifle cartridges filling decorative holes in their earlobes. The peoples of Europe's colonial "empires" would someday rise, as America had, and throw off their masters. The Afrikaners failed. But others would not, even if that day of reckoning seemed impossibly far from here. He tried to lighten the conversation by recounting the details of the attempt on his life on board the *Hamburg*, and Kermit helped with the story of his encounter with the scorpion.

"I would meet this man who is always around when there is trouble," said Jakobus.

Roosevelt laughed. "My young protector is practicing his horse craft with the *saises*. He's trying to learn to ride."

Jakobus cocked his head. "You follow the herds on horse?"

"And foot. We'll collect jungle specimens, too, when we get there."

"West of Tanganyika?"

"And north."

Jans looked at the sharpshooter medal Roosevelt had given him. "Bad men there."

"We are two hundred sixty strong."

The old Boer shook his head. "Men who carry bundles are not fighters. And you have fewer than a dozen rifles. I count them." He smiled apologetically, as if to say "old war habits die hard."

"Yours are the only other guns we've seen in two months," said Roosevelt. "What could be out there that might cause us trouble?"

Jakobus raised his hand and pointed toward the rising moon. "Bad men from the Sudan. When the sirocco winds blow, the Fulani ride to take slaves and loot."

"Slaves?" asked Kermit.

"*Ja*," said Jans. "To trade, and for their *kraal*."

"Two hundred sixty unarmed men with bundles on their heads will excite the hearts of such men. You must stay south of Tanganyika. The Fulani won't cross into German territory, but they have no fear of British."

Roosevelt tried to keep the surprise and concern from his face. He had not yet told anyone of his intention to exit the safari north through Khartoum rather than return to Mombasa. Nor had their guide, Cunninghame, advised that they might encounter armed bandits in the northern British territories. The Boer was right. They were a scientific expedition and not organized for a fight. They would be easy pickings for any armed force they might encounter.

Chapter Eleven

There is no surer sign of advancing civilization than the advanced respect paid to a woman, who is neither a doll nor a drudge.

- Theodore Roosevelt, 1913

Maggie gave up trying to bludgeon conversation from a subdued Pere de Clercq or to find a spot on the narrow wagon bench that didn't send bolts of pain up her spine whenever a wagon wheel crossed a rut. She tried instead to enjoy the forest tapestry of muted yellows, browns, and greens while the mission wagon rolled through wooded hills sparsely covered in jackalberry and sausage trees. But her mind remained restless, returning again and again to her unsatisfactory conversation with Teddy.

She had no desire to chronicle how many wild animals her former beau had killed. She would write about the British East African colonial government's high-handed experiment with eminent domain. But more importantly, she would enlist the full scope and stature of the Hearst newspaper empire to ignite popular outrage and force world governments to put an end to a European monarch's enslavement of an entire native population. If the story remained the private grievance of Pere de Clercq and his fellow missionaries, the Congolese were doomed. At the very least, Teddy could provide a Hearst journalist the protection of his safari, even if he mistakenly believed that in his current capacity he could do nothing else to help.

She was not surprised that he didn't immediately invite her to join his safari. His cowboy guardian's early efforts to prevent her from even reaching Africa were warning enough. But his mealymouthed excuse for not acting like a gentleman was unworthy. The assertion that some obligation to President Taft or *Scribner's Magazine* obliged him to keep her at arm's length was nonsense. The worldly politician, who her former beau had become, and the pioneering journalist Maggie Ryan had forged from her own modest circumstances were not to be satisfied with shooting wild animals and writing about it. Another encounter should soften his timid resistance. Two would surely bring it down, though first she had to find him.

The driver slowed the wagon at the edge of the wood where it opened onto a plain of low scrub, bristle grass, and thorns. "*Chakula,*" he announced, producing a basket of goat meat and cassava wrapped in palm leaves and oiled paper. Maggie noted the heavily patched trousers and faded cotton shirt and presumed these were worn in deference to his passengers, as the few young men they had passed that morning wore little more than strings of beads around their waists and long iron-tipped spears across their shoulders. Native nudity neither shocked nor offended her, though the only male organs she had seen prior to this trip were the ones belonging to her late husbands. She had been both surprised and pleased to discover their variety.

The driver attempted to make fire for tea, but his sulfur matches failed to cooperate. Retrieving a pair of foot-long sticks from the chop box beneath his seat, he rapidly assembled a bow and spindle by wrapping a string around one stick and tying its two ends to the other. Bracing the spindle on the wagon floor in the middle of a clump of dry grass, he worked the bow until the grass began to smolder. Then he added a few dry twigs to the smoldering grass and in short order had a pot of steaming tea ready for their consumption. "Chai," he said proudly.

She and Pere de Clercq ate the *chakula* and drank the chai in companionable silence. The priest had not said a single word since they left the Samburu mission that morning, and he remained silent even after they'd finished their meal and the driver cracked his whip to signal the oxen to resume their journey. She contented herself with watching the passing landscape and the scattered processions of women carrying large grass baskets of yams and corn on their heads, and iron and copper jewelry around their upper arms and necks. The wagon didn't encounter another group of young men until it reached the outskirts of Nairobi. And there, both sexes had added a loose draping of cotton blanket, worn in a way that conveyed an unmistakable lack of enthusiasm for the superfluous city garment.

When the sandy track widened and became hard-packed dirt, Pere de Clercq broke his silence and spoke to the driver in Swahili. A half hour later, the wagon arrived at a small tin-roofed building, where a dozen rooms clustered around a central courtyard, and a long veranda faced the sandy street. A mix of military and commercial travelers sat at several tables that were set for afternoon tea. "*Les Belges* do not come to this place," said Pere de Clercq as they entered the building. "We must leave our bags and return later. I go to the *bureau* of *Les Freres Blanc* for information about the *contrôle des frontiers* at Bujumbura. The wagon will take you to where you may telegraph your lion stories." With that, he set off on foot, and she did not see him again until that evening.

The smile of the Indian telegraph clerk turned to a wail of despair when she laid the stack of pages on the wooden counter.

"Never, *Sabu*, has anyone tried to send such a mountain of paper from this office. Surely, it is a book not a letter!"

Maggie didn't know whether the clerk was worried for the wear on his fingers or his machine, but an extra twenty shillings addressed his concerns. Two fretful hours later, he punched the final key on the story of her encounter with the Roosevelt safari and the Samburu lion hunt held in Teddy's honor. Almost immediately, the machine came alive with an emphatic reply from Randolph Hearst. "More, more, more!" the clerk said, reading the transcription. He looked at her with an expression of despair. "Please, *Sabu*."

"Of course. Not today."

But Hearst's impatient command underscored the challenge of her next step. She had no choice but to keep stalking Teddy's safari until he invited her to join him. But she had no idea of where he might be or where he might be going next. She thought to make inquiries at the British consulate, among the Indian merchants who sold safari supplies, and with the Arab traders who assembled gangs of porters. Surely one of them would have some useful information. But all that would have to wait until tomorrow.

Returning to the hotel, she found Pere de Clercq pacing the veranda. "The White Fathers have a boat at Kigoma," he announced in a low, hushed voice, standing to offer her a teak chair. "They would take me across the Tanganyika to Kalemie. I should not have to pass the Force Publique at Bujumbura."

She tried to process what this meant, both for the Belgian priest and for her own travel plans. "I can tell that must be good news, Father. Though I don't know where or how far away any of those places are."

He opened a small travelers' map and spread it on the table between them. "Kalemie is on the Congo shore of Lake Tanganyika. Nine hundred kilometers, perhaps more. Three month's journey, with luck."

Maggie frowned. "Is there a Mount Kenya between here and there? I know Colonel Roosevelt intends to collect elephant, and I overheard the *Hamburg* captain say that the best specimens in British territory are near Mount Kenya."

The priest put his finger on the map, near a blotch of concentric circles to the north of Nairobi. "Mount Kenya rests here. Two hundred kilometers." He put the index finger of his other hand on a point halfway across the map in almost the opposite direction. "Kalemie there."

Maggie tried to hide her disappointment. The priest's journey would not take him anywhere near where Teddy was likely to be.

Pere de Clercq tugged at the lobe of his right ear with his thumb and index finger and spoke rapidly. "I would go tomorrow."

She was startled but not surprised. The priest's virtual silence since leaving Cunninghame's farm did not bode well for their continued association. Still, she must try to dissuade him. "What about the warning that King Leopold's men gave to you in Mombasa? If you head to the Congo border directly from here, won't they be forced to stop you?"

He resumed his pacing in silence.

Maggie tried another tack. "King Leopold's men didn't try to stop you when you left Mombasa with me and headed north to Meru. Perhaps it was because they believed you'd heeded their warning. Wouldn't it be best if they kept thinking that way? If you come with me to Mount Kenya as a guide and translator, we could head west from there toward the Congo. It won't be a direct route, but it might be a safer one. I fully intend to write your story if we can get there alive to gather proof."

Pere de Clercq lifted his chin and spoke firmly, though his breath came fast and shallow as if he were running instead of pacing. "I must be with my children before the end of rains, when the Force Publique returns to the villages to take the men for the rubber."

"But how will you stop them, Father? Alone? You need to think this through."

As do I, she thought. It didn't make sense to linger in Nairobi. Teddy would return, if at all, only at the end of the safari, which could very well take another year. There was a small chance that if she remained in Nairobi, she might run into someone who knew his whereabouts. That might be better than heading west across the savannah and simply hoping for the best. Especially since her guide was being watched by thugs who would have no compunction about leaving them both for the hyenas if they believed the priest was heading back to the Congo. But if they left Nairobi without knowing Teddy's location, shouldn't they go to a place where they knew he *might* be?

Pere de Clercq shook his head stubbornly. "It is God's will that I go. Tomorrow."

Maggie stood and began to pace as well. "What about provisions? And please don't tell me God will provide." He shrugged. "Suppose I give you funds to buy provisions for a month. For both of us. If we don't find Colonel Roosevelt at Mount Kenya, we can go on to the Congo from there, or I can return to Nairobi alone."

"The rains."

"May be late. We'll walk fast."

When the following afternoon came and went, and Pere de Clercq had not yet returned, Maggie remembered the instinctual caution that had led her to give him only half the funds necessary to purchase four steerage tickets when they met on the dock in Naples. She knew him better now. But as the hours passed, it occurred to her that it might have been prudent to give him only a portion of the cash necessary to supply and equip the next leg of their journey. She did not believe that a priest would abscond with her funds, but to some men of God, Robin Hood was no sinner.

The fading orb of equatorial sun was slowly painting an orange glow over the city rooftops when she spotted the little priest marching up the street in front of four shoeless natives, each with a canvas bundle on his head. "We must hurry," he announced.

"Now?"

He nodded. "There were men in the market. *Belge.* I must go."

"Father, it will be dark in an hour. We don't have time to get out of the city and find a place to camp. We might get eaten!" The priest had told her once that they needed to make camp and a fire before sunset each evening, before the night predators came out looking for their evening meal. Had he forgotten?

Pere de Clercq said something to the native beside him, who shifted the load on his head. The others remained seated and silent. "My children suffer. I must get back to them."

She tried one last time. "Your children need the help of someone more powerful than the despot who's exploiting them, Father. That someone may be near Mount Kenya right now. You had his sympathy at Cunninghame's farm when you told him of the horrors going on in the Congo. You need to move him from sympathy to action. When Colonel Roosevelt is president again, he'll act. He'll have to. That's how you can help your children, Father. Alone, you'll just get yourself killed."

The priest removed a small black book from inside his cassock and pressed it into her hand. "God sent you to help his servant escape Mombasa. I am certain His plan for me is to return to the Congo. If His plan is for you to find this Roosevelt again, He will send someone to you. *Bonne chance, madame. Et soyez prudent!*" He folded her fingers over the notebook and said something to the nearest porter. The native placed his bundle on top of his head and led the way down the street toward the outskirts of town. The three other porters remained seated in the dirt.

Fatigue and a sudden sadness washed over Maggie. She told the natives to come back in the morning. They remained silent and seated in the dust. "English?" she asked.

"*Hapana.*" All three shook their heads in tandem. One pointed to the book in her hand. She opened it, expecting it to be some sort of religious tract. But it was a travelers' phrasebook consisting of about two dozen pages of basic Swahili/English phrases and a simple fold-out map of the British East Africa Crown Colony. The porter must have seen Pere de Clercq referring to it during the afternoon's negotiations in the market.

A tabbed page and a penciled arrow in the margin pointed to the phrase he must have known she'd need first. "*Karudi katika asubuhi,*" she read out loud. *Come back in the morning.*

"*Ndio.*" They spoke, nodded their heads in unison, and then hoisted their bundles and walked off down the street, leaving her to ponder what she was going to do next.

The three porters returned at daybreak, balancing what remained of Pere de Clercq's purchases on their heads. A boy of twelve or so accompanied them—or perhaps followed, since the older men paid him no attention. The boy stood by the cloth bag that contained her personal possessions. When she didn't chase him away, he lifted the bag to his head. The older men waited. "*Twende,*" she said, using the first of a dozen words she had committed to memory from Pere de Clercq' phrase book. *Let's go.* The tallest of the three, lean and muscled in an ankle-length *kikoy* and a buttonless shirt that may once have been white, held out his palm. "*Posho.*"

His meaning was clear. He wanted to be paid before they started. But Maggie resisted the idea of beginning the day with tedious negotiations in phrasebook Swahili, while the sun rose higher and hotter by the minute. In any event, Pere de Clercq had always paid at the end of the journey, not the beginning. "*Twende,*" she repeated. "*Posho usiku wa leo.*" *Pay tonight.*

The porter shrugged and led the way down Government Road to where tin-roofed wooden structures gave way to mud-thatched huts and then finally to patches of scrub and grass. There were no roads marked on the priest's map, nor did they encounter any once they were beyond the town. A wide sand track led through a landscape of scrub and thorn, crisscrossed here and there by narrow paths made by foot or hoof. She wondered what the animals Teddy planned to shoot found to eat in such a sparsely vegetated landscape.

The porters' chatter and occasional rhythmic chanting passed the time. Near midday, they left the path to rest in the shade of a lone acacia tree that rose from the horizon a hundred yards away. One of the porters made a fire and placed an enameled cup from his bundle in the flame, filling the heating cup from a calabash at his waist. A few minutes later, he presented her with the steaming brew. "Chai," he said.

She answered with one of her newly acquired phrases. "*Aksante sana.*" *Thanks much.*

Food, it seemed, was not part of the midday break. She hesitated to inquire, as in her haste to leave Nairobi, she had not thought to check the contents of the bundles that Pere de Clercq had left behind. Presumably one contained nourishment, which they would eat in due course. But how much and how long it might last, she could only guess. She thumbed the phrasebook, finding its contents more suited to the commercial traveler than the poorly prepared bush explorer. When she deemed herself and her companions sufficiently rested, she gave the order to leave. "*Twende.*"

No one moved. The native who had demanded to be paid before they left Nairobi, held out his hand. "*Posho.*" Tribal scars carved into his face and the row of strong white teeth filed to points for cosmetic effect gave a certain presence to his demand. She'd paid them no attention before.

"*Usiku wa leo,*" she repeated. *Tonight.*

He shook his head and scratched a dust-covered shin with a yellow fingernail.

"*Twende,*" she said again. *Let's go.*

He reached into the waist of his *kanzu* and retrieved a thin, bone-handled knife. "*Posho.*"

Dear God. She looked around at the trackless terrain and at the three half-naked men who held her possessions and demanded money. Was this what the *Corriere Della Serra* reporter had warned her about? Guides who robbed their lone female employers and left them to die in the desert? Acquiescence seemed called for. But her temperament recoiled at negotiation under duress, and experience warned that extortionists rarely stop once they've achieved success. Her attention was drawn to the boy who was watching the nearly wordless confrontation, his face intent and wary. Her instinct said to do something quickly, as dithering could lead to as much trouble as dickering. She pointed to the bag beneath the boy's skinny legs. "*Twende.*" He looked at the men. The one who had demanded pay shook his head and pointed the blade in the boy's direction. "*Hapana.*" *No.* The boy hid his face.

Now what? She wondered if they could hear her heart beating. It sounded so loud in her ears. Did they see a weak, defenseless woman? To rob if they wished, or worse. Or did they see a *mzungu*? A white. Alone at the moment, but certain to be followed by others who might order a swift hanging if she were molested. She pulled the bag from beneath the boy's legs and started back toward the trail. The one with the knife shouted, but she did not answer or turn around. She listened for the sound of running feet, knowing she had no plan and no chance if he should pursue and assault her. But the only sound was the buzzing of insects and the pounding of blood in her temples. She walked until she came to the trail they had left and then turned south toward Mount Kenya, fighting the urge to look back.

Damn that priest! She pulled Pere de Clercq's traveler's map from her waistband, its cheap ink and coarse paper already smeared and spotted. Other than a few crude lines of geography and a handful of place names, it showed no other markings. Certainly none that referenced where food or water might be found. The priest had said that the mountain was a seven-day march from Nairobi. Surely there would be food and water at one of the places named on the map. And people who spoke English! She held the cloth bag in one hand and wiped sweat from her brow with the other. Overhead, the bright yellow orb in a cloudless sky seared any hint of moisture from the plain of scrub and withered grass. She looked back along the trail. The acacia and the Africans were gone.

Thoughts of returning to Nairobi fought with those of hunger and fatigue. Surely if she returned, she could make better travel arrangements than the mess bequeathed to her by the Belgian priest. Wasn't that more sensible than wandering the savannah alone, without food, water, or shelter? She tried to suppress such thoughts, but they refused to be banished. Suppose she returned to Nairobi and relaunched with proper preparations? Would Teddy still be near Mount Kenya by the time she got there? And suppose she crossed paths with the larcenous porters on her return? What unpleasantness might result from that unhappy encounter?

Folding the map and tucking it into her shirtwaist, she resumed her trek, though her thoughts remained frenzied and untamed. *This is madness. Where will you sleep? What if you don't find food or water?* She scanned the barren landscape while her sun-roasted brain mocked her. Did the world really need one more newspaper story about misbehaving monarchs? Was a chronicle of how many wild animals a former American president killed worth getting her killed, too? Danger was the inescapable bedfellow of ambition in her profession, and as elsewhere, one chose wisely or suffered the consequences.

Raising a shaky hand to her dust-caked brow, she looked back along the trail and then up ahead. Perhaps just over the horizon there was a village with food, water, and people who spoke English. She had not come this far, nor made her living and reputation, guided by sensible concerns. Or by quitting.

Maggie recalled a conversation she'd had with an American sailor when Mr. Hearst sent her to the Philippines to write about the sinking of the battleship *Maine*. She had asked the sailor about the chance of finding survivors, and he'd shared something he called the rule of three: three minutes without air, three days without water, and three weeks without food. Whether it was as true for an African trekker as a shipwrecked mariner, she wasn't sure. But if so, she had at least until midday tomorrow before it might be too late to turn back, though she would need shelter and fire before then.

She paused to take her bearings. Pere de Clercq had warned about the necessity of making camp before sunset and of building and maintaining a fire throughout the night to ward off predators. If she didn't come upon a village soon, she would spend the night in the open where she had neither a tent nor means of making a fire.

Opening her bag, she inventoried its contents in the hope of finding something useful: two long-sleeved, high-necked blouses; a heavy skirt that covered her limbs to mid-calf; toiletries and notebooks; pens and currency. Nothing for present needs. Facing a landscape seemingly devoid of water, shelter, or life, she put one foot in front of the other and resumed walking.

Pieces of geography that had been invisible in the afternoon glare began to reveal themselves as the sun dropped into the lower quadrant of sky. Mounds of earth and clumps of thorn appeared as shadows on the sparse terrain. She headed for a spot that had both and decided to spend the night there, though a column of ant-like creatures with transparent wings and thick bodies called the mound home. Christ had eaten locusts in the desert, she reminded herself. Crushing one of the winged ants between her fingers, she placed it hesitantly on her tongue. Her stomach heaved. In three weeks she might be ready for such a meal, but not now.

Holding the edge of her palm against the horizon, she measured the distance between earth and sun with her fingers. According to Pere de Clercq, each finger width equaled approximately fifteen minutes, though she didn't know why that should be when people had such differently sized fingers. Two of hers fit between sun and horizon. If Pere de Clercq was right, it would be dark in thirty minutes. The seaman's rule and the Belgian priest's manual timepiece led her thoughts back to the Samburu wagon driver and his method of making fire for tea when his white man's matches failed. Like liquid under pressure, her mind searched out hidden cracks that might lead to helpful connections. Time was running out. It was worth a try.

She stripped a branch from a nearby thorn bush and fashioned a spindle and bow like the wagon driver's fire starter. The lace from her petticoat provided the string. The other parts, as best she recalled, were two pieces of wood to hold the spindle, top and bottom. None of the thorn branches were wide enough for the task and the trunk of the bush was clearly too thick to break. *Damn!*

As the belly of the sun slipped below the horizon, darkness began to fall with it. Sitting with her palms to the sides of her head, she exhorted calm and inspiration. The touch of her hands on her hair made Maggie think longingly and irrelevantly of a hot bath and a brush. The connection appeared at once. *A brush. With a wooden handle. In her bag.*

As the light began to fade, she broke the brush in two and laid the wooden handle and backing beside the thorn bow and spindle. A handful of grass fit into the concave brush backing, and the handle held the spindle. She pulled the bow slowly so that the string spun the spindle against the wooden base. When nothing fell apart, she pulled harder and faster.

Darkness fell. The night orchestra of the semi-desert commenced its overture with creaking and chirping, while things unseen passed through the cooling air. Her neck tightened and her hands spasmed from the tension of pressing the broken brush handle against the top of the spindle and from sawing the bow. Minutes passed, but she dared not pause to flex her hands. When she thought she smelled smoke, she pressed harder and bowed faster. Stars appeared and then a sliver of moon. Finally, she smelled smoke and waited anxiously for the grass to ignite. She bowed until her hands lost all feeling.

Then *twang!* The string broke.

Dear God! She re-tied it and started again. The spindle turned like a spinning jenny, and after several tense minutes, she smelled smoke again. She pressed harder and pulled the bow faster. Then the spindle cracked, and pieces of the bow flew off into the darkness. A curse as loud and as foul as any ever heard in Five Points erupted from her throat. She gave it voice until she had nothing left.

"*Sabu?*"

The sound reached her ears when she finally paused for breath. She peered into the darkness, every sense alert, feeling the ground for a rock or other weapon.

"*Sabu?*"

A slim form, lit from behind by ghostly starlight, stepped toward her and placed a bundle on the ground. "*Jambo, Sabu...*" The rest was a jumble of unintelligible Swahili, but the tone was kind, cautious, and unmistakably scared. She let out a breath. It was the boy who had shown up with the porters that morning and insisted on carrying her bag. "*Jambo, mtoto. Aksante sana.*" The boy gestured for her to untie the bundle. Inside was a small canvas tent, a sack of rice, a tin pot, and a box of sulfur matches. He handed her the calabash of water that hung from his shoulder on a leather thong.

Thank God.

The boy made a fire, pitched her tent, and boiled a cup of rice. Of his chatter, she understood only the word thief—which she presumed referred to his fellow porters—and *Babba de Clercq*, which clearly referred to the Belgian priest and explained both the boy's presence and his perseverance. Pere de Clercq must have had doubts about leaving her to the mercies of his market hires and had sent along a boy from the Nairobi mission to look after her.

Snuggled inside the canvas tent with a fire glowing outside, she slept without dreaming. In the morning she woke to the smell of dry earth and boiling tea. She and her new companion resumed their march, and by midmorning they found water. They found more two days later. But they passed no villages and saw no animals.

Her companion was uncomplaining, though he had many questions. Where were they going? Did she have friends there? Would they have food? He knew some English, after all, and her Swahili phrasebook helped fill the gap. She told him they were going to a mountain where she had many friends and where there would be much food. By the sixth day, however, the rice was gone, and by the seventh so was their water. They saw no mountain, and each day the air tasted more and more of sand.

When darkness fell that night, she retreated to her tent, parched, hungry, and exhausted. She had no expectation of sleep, but she did not want the boy to see her worry. For most of the day, she'd been working the sailor's rule of three like a string of worry beads. There was still time to retrace their steps to the last watering hole, assuming they could find it. But a return to Nairobi would take at least a week, and they had no food. If they went on, they might find food and water at any time. But if they didn't find any? She wasn't just risking her own life. Outside, an innocent boy lay huddled by a fire, tired, hungry, and uncertain. He had trusted and followed her. Damn that priest!

Signore Morini's question and admonition wove a web around every other thought. *Why must you make this voyage, signora? You must not be foolish.* Well, she had been foolish. She wasn't pursing a story of injustice. She was lost, hoping to stumble upon a safari that might help her find such a story, with no guarantee that it would, even if she located it.

She fell asleep exhausted and woke up terrified.

Screams and shouts filled the predawn air. Dashing outside, she feared that she might find her young friend being disemboweled by a pack of hungry hyenas. What she found instead were a dozen gun-toting natives dressed in khaki, three-quarter trousers, dark blue puttees, and red felt fezzes barking commands at her prostrate companion. She raised her voice over the din, wincing at its obvious tremor. The shouted phrase was another of the tabbed and underlined nuggets from Pere de Clercq's travelers' guide. "*Una taka nini?*" What do you want?

The uniformed natives ignored her. She shouted again to no avail. Then a tall white man in military khaki stepped through the phalanx of darker men and extended his hand. "The honor of your company only, Mrs. Dunn." He raised his other hand, and the native soldiers fell silent.

Thoughts raced, though her tongue remained stuck to the roof of her mouth.

"We met outside the *Hamburg* ticket office in Naples harbor," he prompted. "My companions and I had been celebrating the end of our home leave."

Brushing a clump of matted hair from her face, she caught sight of a white cotton sleeve that reminded her she was covered only in her petticoat. "A moment, please." Slipping back into the tent, she threw on a skirt, blouse, and boots and tried to harness thoughts and breath scattered by days of hunger and sudden surprise. She couldn't remember the officer's name. But she remembered the rumors in Nairobi about Germany arming native soldiers. The soldiers in khaki and red fezzes must be those recruits.

When she came out of the tent, the officer was standing beside his small camp table on which he had placed a metal canteen, a jar of what looked like preserves, and a loaf of dark bread. The morning sun was just breaking above the horizon. He poured the contents of the canteen into a brass cup and handed it to her. "Welcome to German East Africa."

The life-giving liquid coursed through her body and refilled her parched cells. Energy returned to her limbs and clarity to her head. "*German* East Africa?"

"Since three days, I would imagine. May I ask what brings you here?" His smile was cordial, but his eyes and mouth were serious.

"Mount Kenya."

The smile disappeared. "And your companions?"

"I'm traveling alone."

The officer shouted something over his shoulder in German and one of his native soldiers brought over the young porter. She assumed he, too, had been given something to eat and drink. But he looked scared and dazed. The German officer quizzed the boy in Swahili for several minutes, with an occasional sidebar in German with a nearby soldier. When he was done, the soldier took the boy away, and the officer returned his attention to her.

"You are in German East Africa, Mrs. Dunn. The mountain that you say you are looking for is in British territory, four hundred kilometers north of here." He raised his hand and pointed in the direction she'd come. A metallic imperial crown on the side of his Südwester hat glinted in the first morning light. "Has no one told you there's a war coming?" It was a question, but the tone was that of suppressed accusation.

"Many hope not."

"Do you have travel papers?"

"I didn't know I needed them for where I thought I was going." She tried a flirtatious smile but the officer's face retained its military formality. "I'm sorry. So much has happened since Naples. I've forgotten your name."

"Paul von Lettow-Vorbek." He inclined his head. "Commander of his Imperial Majesty's *Schutztruppe* at Moshi."

She turned toward the now silent and waiting soldiers. "Are these your *Schutztruppe*?"

"They are *askari*. Foot soldiers of the *Schutztruppe*."

"I've heard about them. Your neighbors are quite concerned at the prospect of armed natives."

Vorbek's face betrayed controlled annoyance. "The British will use Irish and Sepoys in the coming war. Germany has no such sources of expendable manpower."

A lost traveler without papers might have changed the subject. The trained journalist persisted.

"The British colonists seem most concerned at the prospect of disarming that native manpower once the war is over—if it comes. They say the Masai are formidable enough with just iron spears and skin shields."

"Yes, yes. Like lions who have feasted on human flesh, the blacks may not wish to go back to their old ways once they have guns and have used them to kill whites."

"Pandora's box is the analogy I've heard most often."

The German smiled. "The British Empire is large. They must everywhere use small white populations to control much larger native ones. Such methods require strict control of weapons and monopoly on the use of force. Such will not be possible in the future. It is the price a greedy people must pay for refusing to share the hegemony."

All this was said with a confident voice and a polite smile, illuminated by a rising sun in a blue cloudless sky. Though the ground beneath them would soon begin to bake, Maggie felt chilled. Did the genial man sitting in the White House have a thought for the war that everyone in East Africa seemed to think was inevitable? Did anyone but Teddy Roosevelt have the force of character to stop it?

A moment passed before either of them spoke again. Commander

Vorbek was obviously waiting for her reaction to his little homily on statecraft. She regretted giving him the opportunity and thought it time to change the subject. "I don't know how much longer we would have lasted out here without food or water. Thank you for finding me, feeding me, and pointing me in the right direction." She took Pere de Clercq's travelers' book from her cloak pocket and opened it. "My guide gave me this before he left for the Congo. Can you show me where we are and how I might make my way back to Nairobi?"

Vorbek shook his head. "You are in German custody, Mrs. Dunn. Once the *Schutztruppe* has returned to the garrison, I will send a letter to your embassy in Dar es Salaam."

"Am I your prisoner, *Kommander?*"

"My guest. Please."

"For how long?"

"Until your embassy responds to my letter."

She tried to keep her voice from betraying her alarm. "But I've done nothing wrong. I've just gotten lost."

"You have no papers. You are traveling alone in an area that has no civilian population and, as you now know, no food or water to support any kind of travel. However, this path lies on a direct line from Nairobi to the German garrison at Moshi. Knowledge of that route will be of the highest military value once hostilities begin."

"I'm not a soldier, *Kommander*. I'm a reporter for the Hearst newspapers. And if I remain out of contact for much longer, Mr. Hearst will send the cavalry to find me."

Vorbek waved a hand across the barren landscape. "Then he will need a better map than yours." Then he shouted something to his *askari*, who began to break camp. "Can you ride a horse?"

"It's been some years."

"You must try. The *Schutztruppe* will follow on foot."

A few minutes later, an *askari* appeared leading a dusty brown mare. With a word from Vorbek, he cupped his hands to help her into the saddle. She felt awkward, alarmed, and strangely excited at the same time.

"How long will it take for us to get to Moshi, *Kommander?*"

"A few weeks. First we go to Kilimanjaro. A runner brought news this morning that an *Ngoma* will be held there tomorrow night. My men were not pleased when we came upon your camp and they thought that we might be delayed here."

"Well, I'm glad not to be the source of further trouble. I attended an *Ngoma* at a village near Meru where the African hunters surrounded a big male lion and killed it with spears. Lots of singing and dancing afterwards. Quite charming."

"This should be much larger. A safari has killed two elephants and the *Wakamba* have called an *Ngoma* so the meat may not be wasted. Every young warrior and woman in the district will come."

"A large safari?"

"I am told it is enormous."

Chapter Twelve

It is a formidable task, occupying many days, to preserve an elephant for mounting in a museum, and if the skin is to be properly saved, it must be taken off without an hour's unnecessary delay...porters, gun-bearers, and 'Ndorobo alike, began the work of skinning and cutting up the quarry, under the leadership and supervision of Heller and Cunninghame, and soon they were all splashed with blood from head to foot. One of the trackers took off his blanket and squatted stark naked inside the carcass the better to use his knife. Each laborer rewarded himself by cutting off strips of meat for his private store, and hung them in red festoons from the branches round about. There was no letup in the work until it was stopped by darkness.

- Theodore Roosevelt, *African Game Trails*, 1910

Roosevelt had been writing in his tent all morning and his article for *Scribner's* about the elephant hunt was coming along wonderfully. Tomorrow, after the Ngoma, he would give the *Scribner's* article to the Boer boy, Jans, to take back to Nairobi with a load of salted animal skins. The Boers had agreed to stay on as far as Uganda—the father as guide, and the son as driver of the occasional ox wagon, hauling the salted hides to the coast and replenishing their stores as needed. They were bully company, and Cunninghame didn't seem to mind.

The tent was a comfortable place to write in the morning. The narrow flap let in enough air to keep him from sweating, and the light was sufficient, so long as no one stood in the opening and blocked it—as someone was doing now. Roosevelt took off his pince-nez, turned to see Cunninghame, holding a faded bush hat in his spotted hands, an I-told-you-so look on his face. "There's a German officer outside who wants to see our papers. He's got thirty armed *askari* with him."

The rains had spoiled the elephant hunt near Mount Kenya, and, according to the planners at the Smithsonian, the next best place to find a trophy-size bull was at Kilimanjaro. Cunninghame didn't have a license to take hunters across the border into German territory, and he claimed that the British colonial office would be furious if he allowed their honored guest to slip away and visit their unpopular neighbor. He'd also predicted that the Germans would be just as alarmed to see two hundred sixty able-bodied men, many of them armed, crossing their border uninvited and unannounced. Roosevelt reassured him all would be well. He knew the German kaiser.

The officer who waited for them outside was dressed in a neat khaki uniform with six white metal buttons down the front, blue piping along the trousers, leather ammunition belt and shoulder straps, and a comfortable felt hat—not unlike the Rough Rider campaign hat—pinned on one side with a metal Imperial cockerel. An orderly row of armed natives dressed in khaki short pants and puttees stood behind him. Kermit, Potter, and a dozen or more cooks and porters stood off to one side, the natives jabbering excitedly at their countrymen dressed in military attire and carrying rifles.

Stepping into the sunlight, Roosevelt addressed the officer in German with appropriate reference to the insignia on his shoulder. "*Guten tag, Major. Ich bin* Colonel Roosevelt."

The officer's chin moved abruptly back. "*Die amerikanischen präsident?*"

"*Ja.*"

It was a moment before the officer spoke again. The native soldiers stood at attention and looked at no one. "Your professional guide says you have no papers," he said at last in careful English. "This is correct?"

"We should talk in my tent," said Roosevelt, speaking in German.

"We stand here," said the officer, in English.

Kermit stepped out from the crowd of onlookers. "You've got that letter from the kaiser, Pop."

"That's right. Would you bring it here so I can show it to the major? It's in the pigskin library inside Carlyle's book on Frederick the Great."

While Kermit ran off to fetch the letter, Roosevelt began to relate the stalk of the two massive bull elephants that would feed the *Ngoma* that evening.

"We should speak English," the officer responded. "Your companions must understand my orders."

Kermit returned with a fat cream envelope bearing the seal of Imperial Germany. Roosevelt handed it to the officer. "There's a bit up front," he said in German, "about Russia and so forth. You might want to skip that. The kaiser probably didn't mean for anyone to see it but me. The part about coming to hunt in Kilimanjaro is there toward the end."

The German read the letter and examined the Imperial seal. When he had finished, he pinched the bridge of his nose between thumb and index finger and looked off toward the border to the north. "So... with this you march three hundred armed men into German territory with no notice of any kind..."

"It was spur of the moment, Major." Roosevelt switched to English. "Americans don't use travel papers. We have many states and friendly neighbors."

"I must send to Dar es Salaam for instructions."

"Better to inform than to ask. I would tell your superiors that Colonel Roosevelt took Kaiser Wilhelm up on his invitation, that he had a successful hunt, and that he's on his way back to British East Africa."

The German shook his head. "I cannot allow ..." he began, but he was interrupted by a soft female voice from behind the line of *askari*.

"May I come with you?"

Potter, who had been silent till then, blurted, "What...? Hell, no!"

Maggie pushed through the row of *askari* and extended a small dust-caked hand. "How nice to see you again, Colonel."

Roosevelt laughed, both surprised and delighted. "You are relentless, Ma...Mrs. Dunn."

"You are companions?" The German's tone betrayed confusion as well as suspicion.

"Since childhood," said Roosevelt.

"But you are not traveling together?"

"No," said Potter. "And they're not going to be."

Then Cunninghame spoke. "None of my business, but we're three hundred miles from the coast. That's ten to fifteen days for your runner to make it to Dar es Salaam, Major, and whatever extra time for someone to make up their minds. After the *Ngoma* tonight, there's not going to be enough food around here to feed two hundred sixty men for a month. We'll eat the district into famine if we don't move on."

The officer took a small black notebook from the leather pouch attached to his shoulder strap. Roosevelt and the others watched as he wrote. When he finished, he tore the pages from the book and gave them to one of his *askari*, who put down his rifle and took off at a trot. Then he turned to Roosevelt. "I am Paul von Lettow-Vorbeck. Tonight we enjoy the *Ngoma*. Tomorrow, we talk."

To Maggie's relief and Potter's obvious chagrin, Teddy seemed to have forgotten his reluctance to talk on substantive matters, pleased as he was to have her company and happy to resume the spirited conversations they'd had at their last meeting. He continued to insist, however, that she not quote him in print. Alone in the heart of Africa with a cultured German officer and the most outrageous and erudite politician of her era, she was reluctant to relinquish the opportunity of chronicling Teddy's bonfire homilies on world affairs, corrupt domestic politics, America's manifest destiny, and whatever else the yeasty combination of German and American braggadocio might serve. His eagerness for her company was so transparent that she declined his conditions. His response, over the next several hours, was to speak mostly German, which she could not understand. After listening to a lively twenty-minute exchange between him and Vorbek, that grew increasingly animated the longer it went on, she finally interrupted and agreed to his condition that she not write anything of their conversation.

"You win. I won't quote you. Though if it wouldn't be presumptuous, might I contribute as well as listen?"

Vorbek looked grim. "We were discussing British atrocities in the Cape Colonies."

"The Boer War," Teddy clarified.

"And their new war tactic of putting civilian non-combatants in open-air prison camps behind barbed wire, where they die by the thousands of disease and starvation."

Teddy's brow compressed and his face reddened, betraying the emotions for which she, and his public, most admired him: empathy for the oppressed of all classes or nations, and a righteous anger toward those who misuse their power.

Vorbek turned to Maggie. "It is this criminal war tactic, Mrs. Dunn, that is the real Pandora box. Not my country's defensive training of African soldiers."

106

Maggie glanced at Teddy. "War itself is Pandora's box," Roosevelt said. "No one who opens it can completely control what comes out. The crime is opening it in the first place. Except, of course, in self-defense or on behalf of the oppressed."

Vorbek grimaced. "It is open already, I think."

The Ngoma began with the lighting of an enormous bonfire, accompanied by rhythmic drums, a cappella vocals, and single gender dancing. Most of the porters, cooks, and horse boys had arrived early for the night's festivities. The unlucky few who had to remain to guard the safari camp received generous allotments of *pembe* to ease their sorrow. Dooley watched the Germans and Americans mingle amid the colorful goings on and, seeing them happily occupied, took the chance to slip away and return to camp.

Roosevelt's tent was easy to find when the camp was occupied, as there were always people and activity around it. But the camp was nearly empty now. Two rows of darkened tents, thirty-four on each side, squatted silently under pale starlight and reflected moon. Moving quietly between the rows, he watched and listened for the guards who were supposed to have remained behind. But other than the distant glow of the bonfire and the sound of drums and dancing, he saw and heard nothing. Roosevelt's tent was in the middle of the two rows, about halfway down. Dooley had to pull aside a dozen tent flaps before he spotted a telltale pair of wire-rim glasses lying on an open book on a small writing table. Standing outside, he listened for the sound or sign of roaming guards. Seeing and hearing no one, he stepped into the tent.

The Boer kid had given him the idea, with his story about a widow who'd lost three husbands to plugged guns that had exploded when fired, and how none of the local eligible bachelors were keen on being the next. Several guns lay about the otherwise orderly tent. Two he recognized as being those that Roosevelt used most often, and those that his gun bearer cleaned frequently. Others he hadn't seen used at all, including a big, nasty-looking one with a pair of side-by-side barrels and a lot of fancy carving. Perhaps it was a backup for elephants and other outsized beasts. It didn't look like an everyday weapon. which might mean the gun bearer didn't clean it very often.

Picking up a handful of pebbles, Dooley dropped them one by one down each barrel. The Boer's story made it sound like a few stones or a clump of dirt would do the trick, but the pebbles just rattled through and came out the other end. Maybe the widow's guns had been smaller. He stuck his thumb in the end of the gun and wiggled it around with room to spare. A plug would have to be the size of a fat cigar. His eye went to the candle on the cot-side chop box.

Before Dooley could retrieve it, two things happened almost simultaneously. The ambient light inside the tent began to fade, and voices came from outside. He suppressed the urge to bolt. Maybe the moon had gone behind a cloud. Maybe someone was back from the party, or off to it. A boyhood of petty larceny had taught him the wisdom of patience. Stumbling around in the dark was what woke the sleeping grannies and the drunk night watchman. The voices came closer. Native jabber. The big gun would make a good enough club, if it came to that. Though it would be better to slip away, if he got the chance. The voices stopped outside the tent. The moon reappeared from its hiding place.

Two native soldiers had a third by the arms and, passing the tent, dragged him in the direction of the central campfire. Dooley waited until the voices and footsteps faded. Then he took the candle from the writing desk and pressed it into the gun barrel as far as it would go, poured dirt and grass on top of it, and tamped the whole mess tight with a stick. Then he put the gun back where he found it and stood at the tent flap, listening. Patience. He counted to one hundred, keeping time to the sound of distant drumming. Hearing nothing else, he opened the tent flap, looked around, and stepped outside.

The first shout was in the native lingo and came from twenty yards away. The next, even closer, was in German. Dooley pretended not to hear and started to walk between the tent rows in the opposite direction. The shouting followed until it caught up with him. A fez-topped *askari* stood in his path and raised a gun to his chest. Dooley lifted his hand in a friendly gesture. "*Jambo*," he said, using the common Swahili greeting.

The *askari* barked something in German. Looking around for the other *askari* and failing to see him or anyone else, Dooley decided that action would be better than talk. Balling his fist, he hammered it into the astonished man's face, knocking him to the ground. Then he pulled Mickey's sap from his hip pocket and laid it into the soldier's skull until he was silent. Permanently.

Awake in the predawn light, Dooley listened to the commotion outside his tent. He didn't understand a word of it. But the natives were pretty excited about something. Likely some bleary-eyed porter had stumbled over the dead *askari* on his way back from the *Ngoma*. Hearing English voices join the commotion, he got up to see what had brought them.

Cunninghame stood next to the dead *askari*, talking to Roosevelt. "Fights aren't uncommon at these big affairs. Pour enough *pembe* into young men from different tribes and disputes are bound to happen. But I've never seen one result in killing."

Roosevelt took a moment to respond. "I thought the locals were all Wakamba."

"This village and the others nearby are Wakamba. But the *askari* aren't. And neither are our people: the porters, cooks, and *saises*. You also have other young fellows from other parts of the district come for the big *Ngoma*—Masai, Ndorobo. Too many excited young men, and only a handful of local girls. Fights are bound to happen."

The German officer, Vorbek, arrived then, accompanied by his native troops. Dooley stood at the edge of the crowd and listened. The German officer questioned the porters who had found the body, and then he consulted with one of his men before approaching Roosevelt. "I must question the members of your camp immediately. Beginning with the whites. Please gather them now."

The Boer guide, Kruger, who was standing with Kermit and Potter, said something sharp in German or Afrikaans. Dooley was never sure which was which, though he recognized the word "*kaffir*," which seemed to be a snotty word for native.

The German turned to Roosevelt. "You should know, Colonel, that when an African kills, he usually uses a *panga*—a long knife for the cutting of brush and crops. If they have no *panga*, they kick. They do not fight with fists, as we Europeans do." He pointed to the body lying on the ground with its head bashed in. "No *panga* was used in this fight. The face is much bloodied. And the head is *kaput*. Bashed in."

"Are you accusing one of us of killing a *kaffir*?" Kruger demanded, this time in English.

The German directed his response to Roosevelt, while pointing to Kruger. "I will start with him."

Dooley jammed his swollen right hand into his pants pocket and went to look for a pair of gloves.

When he returned and it was his turn to be questioned, Dooley was asked how he had spent the previous evening, after he had left the *Ngoma*. While he was spinning his tale, the German pointed to Dooley's gloves. "Why must you wear those?" Dooley's heart fluttered. No words came. "Remove them."

There was no choice but to comply. Dooley pulled off one with his teeth and then, wincing, used the free hand to pull off the other. "Fell off a horse," he said.

"When?" asked the German.

"This morning."

Kruger stepped forward. "He falls a lot, *ja*." There were a few laughs from those who had witnessed Dooley's painful progress in riding and shooting. The German, however, didn't laugh, and neither, Dooley noticed, did Potter. Roosevelt looked distracted.

"When did you leave the *Ngoma*?" asked the German.

"Clock time? I don't know. It was going strong when I left. Came back here to get a bottle from my tent."

"Did you share it with anyone?"

"With me," said Kruger, stepping forward again.

"I understood you were with the horses," said the German.

"Later, *ja*. Before that we drink."

Dooley was thankful for the Boer's unexpected help. Though it was not out of friendship, since they hadn't exchanged a dozen words. More likely, the Boer didn't like the idea of whites being held to account for a native's death. The German was having none of it. He turned to Roosevelt. "I would speak with you alone."

Chapter Thirteen

The leader works in the open, and the boss in covert.
The leader leads, and the boss drives.

- Theodore Roosevelt

J.P. Morgan and his assistant, Elliot Cashman, stood at the window of Morgan's New York City townhouse library, trying to escape the August heat. Sixteen-foot windows, angled to catch whatever breeze might survive the crosstown baking, funneled nearly drinkable air into a room as hot and damp as a Chinese laundry. Morgan's favorite armchair lay covered in chintz, while the rest of the library furniture had been hauled off to the basement until the heat wave was over. Clipping his tenth Hercules' Club cigar of the day, Morgan flicked the tobacco leaf cutting into the street to join the others he'd tossed there over the past several hours. Andrew Carnegie and Randolph Hearst had stopped by earlier that morning to go over the first reports they had received from their employees on the Roosevelt safari. There was much to digest and act upon. Carnegie's taxidermists had catalogued an astonishing inventory of animals killed by Roosevelt and his son, together with a warning that additional taxidermy supplies and equipment would be necessary for all the animals to be adequately preserved for the exhibits at the Smithsonian and Museum of Natural History. The museum halls themselves might have to be razed and expanded.

Hearst's newspapers continued to churn a steady stream of articles poking fun at the gargantuan Roosevelt animal slaughter. But the newspaper publisher had also managed to put one of his reporters in the path of the safari where, despite Roosevelt's pledge not to entertain the press or talk about politics for a year, the reporter had managed to get him to talk about more than killing animals.

"What do you think of the reports from that female reporter who managed to track down the Roosevelt safari?"

Cashman shrugged. "Nothing we can use yet. Rumors about the

mistreatment of natives in the Congo Free State; speculation about German colonists getting ready for war; but nothing about Roosevelt running for president again when he gets home. Nothing about his physical health or psychological disposition. She only managed to cross paths with his safari twice, and both times he didn't let her stay."

"A report from that phony Pinkerton that Ketchel planted with the safari is what we really need. Did he get the tintype we sent of his brother on that carnival ride, and does he believe it means he's out of Sing Sing? How's Roosevelt's health holding up to the rigors of the safari, and what are the prospects for a convincing accident? Has he even tried yet?"

Morgan glared at the distant Hudson River, as if impatient for a breeze. "I doubt our man knows how to write. And it's probably safest if he doesn't try. What did the governor say when you went to see him about releasing our man's policeman brother?"

Cashman ran a finger behind the wilted band of his boiled collar. "Ten thousand dollars to the governor's re-election fund to let the brother out of Sing Sing for a day so Ketchel could make that tintype of him outside the walls. For a full pardon, Governor Hughes wants complete financing for his re-election campaign and a federal judgeship if he loses."

"What are your thoughts?"

"I'd want more than a tintype as proof that my brother was actually out of prison for good. But Ketchel seems to think this Dooley will buy it, and that the Hearst papers will be headlining the tragic and accidental demise of our former president sometime soon."

"I meant give me your thoughts about Governor Hughes."

Cashman wiped his forehead with a damp handkerchief. "Rockefeller and Gould watch your every move, looking for a potential weakness they can exploit. If you let yourself be extorted by a pipsqueak politician like Charles Evans Hughes, they'll look for a way to use that. Giving in to the governor could be costly in the long run."

Morgan chewed his cigar. "Agreed. Throw another ten thousand at him, but that's it. Tell him if that Irish policeman isn't out of Sing Sing by the end of the month, I'll support his opponent in the upcoming election, and in every election the *former* governor might enter after that. When the rest of the political money finds out, Charles Evans

Hughes won't be able to raise a dime from a shoeshine boy." Cashman looked away. The blunt conversation seemed to make him uncomfortable. Morgan licked the end of his cigar. *You're about to become even more uncomfortable, laddie. Time to see what you're made of.* Morgan hurled a lungful smoke in Cashman's direction and advanced, waving his cigar. "Have you secured that loan we spoke about?"

Cashman lifted his shoulders, as if poked in the spine. "I told Father that you offered to let me in on a new syndicate you were forming. He expressed some concerns. A million-dollar loan secured by everything our family has left is… Well, it's everything we have left."

Morgan nodded. He knew the senior Cashman would be nervous at first, but that in the end he would likely agree. At heart, the senior Cashman was a gambler, not an investor. His son was more cautious, though smart enough to know that fortunes were made by taking chances, not avoiding them. Was he smart enough to know that this was his chance?

"Did he agree to put up the collateral for your million-dollar loan?"

"In the end."

"Good. Now I want you to go down to the exchange this afternoon and use it to buy five million dollars of Comstock Lumber on margin."

Cashman's face, which until then had been flush and moist, suddenly lost its color. "Margin? All of it?"

"Five times. More, if you can get it. I want you to control at least five million dollars' worth of Comstock common stock by close of the market today."

The front of Cashman's shirt looked as if he'd just stepped from the bath. "That's a lot of leverage, J.P. And I've never heard of Comstock Lumber."

Morgan smiled. "Neither has anyone else. Not yet. Comstock has no assets or operations at the moment."

"A shell company?"

"Temporarily. Next month, the Department of the Interior will announce that it intends to permit logging in Yellowstone National Park. When they announce that Comstock Lumber has been awarded the exclusive logging concession, your borrowed million will become twenty or more overnight."

Cashman looked, if possible, even more uneasy. "What if the award to Comstock isn't announced? Or if it's delayed? Or if Roosevelt comes back from Africa alive and holds President Taft's feet to the fire on conservation and all his other promises?"

Morgan shrugged. "If Roosevelt comes back alive, President Taft will have to delay the logging contract until after the Republican Convention. The deal to give an exclusive concession to Comstock won't hold that long."

Cashman took a deep breath. "And I'll owe a million dollars on worthless stock. With no way to pay it back."

"That's what it means to have skin in the game, Elliot."

Water flowed from Cashman's brow as if it were being expelled from a clothes wringer. His eyes remained closed. Several seconds passed before he spoke. "If I've learned anything from you, J.P.," he said, lifting his head and gazing thoughtfully at his employer, "it's never to put all your eggs in one basket. Even if it's a sure thing, something can always go wrong. The treasurer could run off with his secretary. Congress could declare your sure thing unlawful. I've never heard of you betting it all on one throw."

Morgan glared. "I did it in the Panic of '07. And this is every bit as important as stopping a run on the banks." Cashman's face fell in disbelief and despair. "Not the Comstock piece. That's a sideshow. I mean keeping that squinty-eyed socialist out of the White House. Permanently. There's nothing more crucial to the survival of this country."

"And you want me to gamble more on this sideshow than I can ever pay back? Even if I live to be a hundred?"

"I do."

Cashman's body began to quiver. His skin had the color and texture of trout belly. "I don't understand, J.P. Why?"

Morgan brought his bulbous nose to within inches of Cashman's face. "Because I need to know that if something goes wrong in Africa, I can send you there to fix it. I need to know that you'll do whatever is necessary to make sure that Roosevelt does not come back from Africa alive, not because you believe it's in the best interest of the country, but because you *personally* cannot afford for him to live. I need to know that for you, this means riches or the poorhouse. That's the only way I can be sure that I can rely on you absolutely if something unpleasant needs to be done."

Chapter Fourteen

Kusema laini, lakini kubeba fimbo kubwa.
(Speak softly, but carry a big stick.)

- Swahili proverb

Roosevelt tightened the cap on his bottle of Waterman's ink and placed it on top of the loose papers comprising the elephant hunt article he had just written for *Scribner's*. The delay, on account of the native soldier's death, had given him time to add an account of the *Ngoma*. But the article was done, and it was time to get back to the business of the safari—collecting specimens of flora and fauna for the Smithsonian and the New York Museum of Natural History.

Together, he and Kermit had collected nearly everything the museum required for its planned Africa exhibition, but the Smithsonian wanted more. Presumably they had their reasons for wanting two of everything, even if they could never exhibit it all at the same time. But he had made both museums promise to lend to others anything not on display, so that citizens of cities other than New York and Washington might see the magnificence of the African plains animals.

He and Kermit had so far collected more than two hundred and fifty specimens of the major big game species: lion, elephant, Cape buffalo, rhino, wildebeest, hartebeest, impala, giraffe, zebra, and gazelle, plus many more birds, reptiles, and lesser mammals. But there were several score more animals on the Smithsonian manifest, and to bag a white rhino they might have to march as far east as the Congo Free State, or as far north as the Sudan. It was time to get back to what they came to Africa to do.

Leaving his tent, Roosevelt headed down the avenue of trampled grass between the rows of canvas that housed the safari staff. He waved to the cook at work in the open-sided mess tent, one of the several working venues that formed a semicircle around the camp's main cooking fire. The supply tent had walls and a guard. The taxidermist and others used tarps hung over a scaffolding of cut poles to protect the workers from the sun and allow air and access from all sides.

Stopping outside one of the tarps, he observed the Smithsonian workers scraping and salting an elephant hide and packing its de-mar-rowed bones in labeled wooden boxes. The taxidermist stood at a table littered with dry bones while he inserted a spoon-topped rod into a six-foot long femur and pulled out a sausage string of thick white marrow. The man looked hot and distracted; he and his fellows labored in virtual silence.

Roosevelt hailed him. "Why the grim faces, Mr. Heller? You can't all still be recovering from the native festivities!"

The taxidermist grimaced, wiped the sweat from his eyes, and then took off his apron and stepped out from under the tarp. "We're out of salt. This is the last hide we'll be able to work until we get more."

Roosevelt was surprised. "How? We left Nairobi with twenty tons."

"We did. But it takes more salt to cure one elephant than it does fifty lions or buffalo. We've captured five already—a bull, a cow, and three youngsters."

"Do you have enough to finish?"

"If we dry the bones instead of salting them. I told Mr. Cunning-hame last week that we needed more salt. He said we could get some in Dodoma. I guess he thought we'd be there by now."

Damn that German. "Do what you can with what you've got. I'll see to it you get your salt."

Continuing his impromptu inspection, Roosevelt poked his head into the supply tent. Inside, a Kikuyu guard sat cross-legged on the ground in front of a stack of ammunition boxes and, at the tent flap's movement, slid his hand toward a spear propped against the boxes. Roosevelt remembered the greeting that Kermit had used on their previous visit. "*Jambo, walinzi.*"

The guard returned his hand to his lap. "*Jambo, Bwana.*"

All seemed to be in order. Roosevelt left the tent and walked to the top of the ravine that separated the safari camp from the Wakamba village and the German bivouac beyond it. Regardless of the German's orders, the safari could not stay indefinitely in a camp with dwindling supplies and nothing to do. It was a formula for disaster. He would not preside over disaster. Looking up, he spotted Potter passing the last of the work tents, his head turning from side to side. Someone must have told him that the boss was on the prowl.

"Over here!" Roosevelt shouted. Potter hurried over and stood beside his boss at the edge of the ravine. "Do you know about the salt?"

"And flour, sugar, and oats."

"I'm going over to chat with our host."

"Do you want me to come with you?"

Roosevelt thought for a moment. "No. That may get the major's back up. But tell Cunninghame to have the boys ready to go in the morning."

"He'll shit. That limey's scared of these Germans."

"Tell him after he's had his tea."

The German camp was separated from the safari by a wide, dry ravine that would likely run torrents in the rainy season. Roosevelt hoped he might run into Maggie, who he had not seen since the morning after the *Ngoma* when Vorbek closed the German camp to casual visitors. He missed her company and was sorry not to have had more of it.

At the top of the ravine, he was met by a pair of armed *askari*, rifles at the ready, presumably posted there to prevent casual wanderings between the two camps. He addressed the soldiers in German and asked to be taken to Haupt Vorbek's tent.

The German officer's accommodations were no less spacious than Roosevelt's own, with room for cot, desk, and what appeared to be a canvas tub. Two men could easily stand upright within the tent, though the design tended toward the tepee rather than the square favored by the British.

"I came to thank you for your hospitality," said Roosevelt as the *askari* motioned him inside, "and to let you know that my party will be leaving in the morning."

Vorbek was seated at his campaign desk and did not stand when Roosevelt entered. He shuffled some papers, pinched the bridge of his nose, stared out the open tent flap, and then finally looked at his visitor. "I might be persuaded to overlook your lack of travel papers, Colonel. But you don't seriously expect me to ignore the murder of one of my *askari*?"

"Major," said Roosevelt, with what he hoped was the right combination of firmness and understanding, "if you have evidence implicating one of my men, then, by all means, arrest him. You'll have my full support. But there are two hundred sixty others out there twiddling their thumbs and eating their way through what's left of our stores."

"I've sent to Dar es Salaam for instructions."

"Which might arrive in a month or not at all." Roosevelt squared his shoulders. "No, Major. We'll have sickness and desertion by then. I won't have that. My men and I will return to British territory tomorrow."

Vorbek stood. He was half a foot taller than Roosevelt, and the vein that ran up the side of his neck throbbed like a beaten animal. "You are now in German territory, Colonel. Under my authority. There are thirty armed men outside sworn to ensure that you respect such authority."

"You're not going to shoot me, Major," said Roosevelt in a soft, determined voice.

"I don't need to," said Vorbek. "I can arrest your guide and porters and leave you to wander the desert like Moses."

Roosevelt removed his pince-nez and stood at the tent flap, looking out at the ordered German encampment. His voice remained soft and measured. "I imagine you love your country, Major. And that you hope it prevails in the coming war with England and France."

"No soldier wants a war," said Vorbek. "But if God is willing, Germany will assume its rightful place in world affairs."

"And if you shoot a former American president? With a Hearst newspaper reporter chronicling the slaughter for worldwide distribution? Where do you think America will stand in this coming war? Neutral, do you think?"

"I am not going to shoot you, Colonel."

"That's up to you, Major." Roosevelt's muted tone adopted the unmistakable growl of a fellow predator. "But *I* intend to shoot *anyone* who attempts to stop my safari from leaving here in the morning. Your men can shoot back, or not, as they are instructed. But either way, the Hearst newspapers will have a field day printing stories about little Cuba over here on the African savannah. And the first casualty of that skirmish will be Germany's hope of fighting England and France alone in the coming war." Roosevelt folded his pince-nez and put it in his shirt pocket. "You can avoid a meaningless confrontation with a group of harmless sportsmen, or you can single-handedly lose a war for your country before it even starts. Patriot or egotist? The choice is yours."

Vorbek smiled. "So this is the 'speak softly and carry a big club' I have read so much about?" Roosevelt returned the smile. "Follow me." Vorbek led Roosevelt to an area of trampled grass beyond the encampment where a German sergeant led his unit of khaki-clad *askari* in a close-order drill. Two dozen African soldiers performed the twenty-minute exercise without a hitch. As a finale, the sergeant dragged a grass-filled scarecrow, draped in a British khaki uniform, across the field and set it up at the perimeter. On his command, the *askari* fired into the dummy until its grassy chest disappeared in a cloud of chaff. Then they charged with fixed bayonets and tore what remained of the scarecrow to shreds.

Vorbek gestured at the carnage. "You have fourteen hunting rifles, I think."

Roosevelt bared his teeth. "I took San Juan Hill with fewer."

"Not from German-trained troops."

Vorbek led Roosevelt back through a spotless encampment a quarter the size of the safari camp. When they reached the ravine that separated the two camps, he stopped. "I am persuaded by your analysis, Colonel. But I would have difficulty acting as you wish. A white member of your safari has undoubtedly murdered one of my *askari*. If I release you without penalty, I will lose the loyalty of the men I must lead in the coming conflict, and that of the Wakamba, upon whom I rely for porters and other support."

"That's a personal difficulty, Major, not a national one."

"Of course," said Vorbek. "As is yours with food and salt. But somehow you would turn it into an international one. Must I do the same?"

Roosevelt knew better than to ask how. But Vorbek didn't wait for an invitation.

"Sadly, Colonel, I must inform you that I intend to arrest one of your men for the murder of my *askari*."

"Who?"

"Your son, Kermit."

Roosevelt's hand went automatically toward the empty holster on his hip. Vorbek's eyes followed the movement. "It is crude, yes. But you give me no time and I have few alternatives."

"What are your alternatives," asked Roosevelt, barely controlling his temper, "besides falsely accusing my son of murder?"

"There is only one, actually. And you will not like it, either."

"I'm listening."

Vorbeck took a deep breath. "The Wakamba have a custom they call *matabish*. In situations where a powerful person has committed an offense, he may be allowed to pay a *matabish* in lieu of the usual punishment meted to others. If you wish your safari to leave without incident, you might offer to pay *matabish* to the dead *askari*'s family, and to the tribe that hosted the *Ngoma*. If they are both satisfied, you may go."

"You want me to pay a bribe?"

"Call it what you wish, Colonel. I understand the Wakamba view the custom as acceptance of responsibility without admission of guilt. 'When in Rome' is the English saying, I believe."

A pair of *askari* came to Maggie's tent and barked something in German, gesturing with their rifles for her to follow. Was this to be her release? She wanted to ask about her traveling bag, but she knew no German, and Major Vorbek had kept her travelers' phrasebook with its crude map. If this was not her release, what else might it be? She had seen Teddy and Major Vorbek exchanging heated words the previous afternoon, though the *askari* had prevented her from joining them. Both camps had been unusually busy all morning.

Led by one *askari* and followed by the other, she hurried along a path through the ravine that separated the German camp from the safari and both from the Wakamba village. Beyond the camps, the path climbed out of the ravine and around a seemingly depopulated Wakamba village, before ending at a packed-earth clearing where hundreds of natives had gathered in ceremonial finery under a bright midday sun. Young warriors stood on one side of the clearing, holding iron-tipped wooden spears and hide-covered shields decorated in patterns of white lines and dots. The women gathered on the opposite side, dressed in lengths of dark cotton *kanga* cloth similarly decorated.

Maggie felt underdressed and overheated in her dark ankle-length skirt and white cotton blouse.

Parting the crowd of women with their rifles, the *askari* brought her to the front and stood on either side to keep the curious at bay. Teddy and Vorbek sat on wooden stools in the center of the clearing facing a grass hut at its edge. The noise and animation increased as the minutes passed, and then gradually subsided to near silence, broken only by the sound of flies and of dry wind whistling over parched grass.

Clearly, this dressed-up gathering had nothing to do with her release, Maggie thought. Was it the start of another Ngoma? An elderly man, dressed in bark cloth, emerged from the grass hut. His right hand held a length of dark wood attached by hide strips to what looked like a lion's tail. Two young warriors stood by his side, gripping their own shields and spears.

Teddy and Vorbek stood at the old man's approach. Maggie was too far away to hear what was being said, but it seemed that Vorbek did most of the talking. Or perhaps it was translating. Then, on a word from Teddy, one of the safari's gun bearers entered the clearing, leading a dark brown mare, followed by a dozen porters carrying sacks of mealie and other miscellaneous bundles. Teddy spoke again and then Vorbek. The old man flicked his lion's tail whip in the direction of the horse and trade goods, and, as if on signal, the crowd broke into a rhythmic chant, of which she understood only the word, *M'waAmerika*.

What was she witnessing? Ever since the murdered *askari* had been found the morning after the *Ngoma*, Major Vorbek had restricted her to the German camp with the excuse that there was a murderer on the loose and courtesies, such as intercamp visits with her countrymen, must be suspended. She had twice tried to cross the ravine to the safari camp to see Teddy and demand that he secure her release, but the ever vigilant *askari* blocked her way each time, crossing their rifles across her path in the universal symbol of "do not pass."

When the old man returned to his hut, the warriors led the horse away and the several dozen women carried off the bundles of trade goods. Teddy and Vorbek left the clearing and the *askari* escorted Maggie through the remaining crowd and back to the German camp. The safari camp, when they passed it, was abuzz with porters striking tents, assembling bundles, and loading wagons. *My god, they're leaving!*

She shouted Teddy's name across the ravine, though it was clear that her voice was not strong enough to carry over the noise or the distance. On the village side, a Wakamba mother with a baby slung in a *kanga* cloth at her hip stopped to look. The *askari* gestured with their rifles for her to move on, and she cinched the child tighter to her hip and hurried away.

For a moment Maggie thought of trying to grab one of the *askari's* rifles and shoot it in the air. But the soldiers watched her closely, and the idea that she might overpower one of those powerful dark men was absurd. That Teddy was clearly leaving without so much as a fare-thee-well was crushing as well as maddening. She wanted to scream.

As soon as the *askari* returned her to her tent, she packed her kit and made ready to leave. But when she stepped outside, they appeared almost immediately to block her path. Snatching the nearest breakable object—a string of calabash water containers—she smashed them one by one over the firestones. The *askari* tried to herd her back toward her tent, but she refused to budge. One of them trotted off, presumably for help or orders, and the other remained.

How could Teddy leave? How indecent and cowardly! Were all great men such self-centered bastards? The man wasn't fit to lead a Salvation Army band, much less the United States of America!

The *askari* returned with the German officer, his schoolmaster-like scowl a perfect match to his curt admonition. "A lady must not destroy the property, Mrs. Dunn."

"Nor a gentleman detain a lady on the absurd pretext that she poses a potential military threat! What exactly are your intentions, Major?"

"As I have explained—"

"You've explained nothing! You've concocted flimsy excuses for un-gentlemanly behavior, and you should be ashamed."

"Mrs. Dunn!"

"Why wasn't I permitted to leave with Colonel Roosevelt?"

Vorbek sighed. "Because among the American scientific expedition you are not. You came through a militarily sensitive area. He did not. Colonel Roosevelt brings an invitation from our kaiser. You...claim to have gotten lost. My superiors, for this, must make the instructions."

"And I am to stay with you until then? Here?"

Vorbeck shook his head. "We stay nowhere for very long. The

German colony is large and we who administer it are few. In the morning, we journey to Moshi for the supplies. There is a helio-telegraph there. Perhaps instructions from Dar es Salaam also."

Maggie fumed. Teddy was undoubtedly returning to British territory. If she didn't follow soon, how would she find him again? "And what do you propose to do with me, Major, if there no instructions waiting for you at Moshi?"

Vorbek shrugged. "Next we go to the garrison on Lake Tanganyika, our frontier with the Congo Free State. There will be much for you to write about along the way."

Hearst expected copy on the Roosevelt safari, not the meanderings of a German East Africa military patrol. But if Vorbeck could get her to the Congo Free State, perhaps she might yet find evidence to back up Pere de Clercq's atrocity story. A German military escort could even be better than a safari. Safety without the animal slaughter. "Have I a choice?"

"You have several, Mrs. Dunn. You may choose, for example, to accept my invitation to dine this evening *a la Wakamba*. It's not very tasty or nourishing, I must warn you. Cassava paste wrapped in banana fronds and dipped in palm oil. But the British will blockade our port at Tanga once the war starts, so I acquire the custom. From the land we must forage after that."

"And my other choices?"

"We can break the bread and discuss them. You may choose perhaps to share the story of your journalism. How one disguises herself as a madwoman to write about the horrors of a mental institution. I have read your stories in the *International Herald*. I would know how such a woman comes to wander the African desert in search of a mysterious mountain. I am curious, as well, about your friendship with Colonel Roosevelt. He acts as a boy with you and his adjutant would keep you at some distance. I am guessing your friendship is not from childhood only."

Dear God.

"Or you may choose the silence and the loneliness. Such would be a timid choice for one who has come so far by courageous action. We may be companions for some time, Mrs. Dunn. We should enjoy each other's company."

Chapter Fifteen

Black care rarely sits behind a rider whose pace is fast enough.

- Theodore Roosevelt

Roosevelt made his way through the half-mile tunnel of dust raised by two hundred sixty men riding and marching barefoot across sun-seared soil that hadn't felt rain in five months. Midway through the column, he found the young Boer, Jans, and Dooley, walking beside an ox wagon piled with salted elephant hides. An eight-foot rod in the Boer's hand snapped rhythmically over the head of the lead oxen when it wasn't resting on the animal's back.

"Good afternoon, gentlemen." The Boer touched his wide-brimmed hat. Dooley looked startled but said nothing. The soiled bandana covering Roosevelt's mouth and nose made him feel like a cowboy bandit, but lungs scarred by childhood asthma dictated the precaution. "Has Mr. Dooley been entertaining you with stories of the big city?"

The Boer pointed to the clear sky. "Buildings that touch the clouds, *ja*. But then I tell him the story of Mrs. Schmidt and four husbands and he say it a lie!"

Roosevelt laughed. "You should tell that story to the rest of us when you get back from Nairobi. Mr. Cunninghame believes we may have crossed the border an hour ago, and if he's right, I want you to take these skins to Selous and Company for shipment back to the United States and pick up whatever supplies Mr. Cunninghame says we need."

"Since this morning we cross, *baas*."

"Ha! Well, you seem to know where we are. Our taxidermist says we need salt before we can hunt again, too. Bring back as much as you can. We'll be heading toward Tanganyika from here, and supplies of anything are going to be hard to get from here on."

"*Ja, baas*."

"And bring this to the American consulate." He handed Jans an envelope with his article for *Scribner's* on the Kilimanjaro elephant hunt.

"If Dr. Keller is there, ask if he can spare some quinine and McPhersons' pills. The other Pinkertons don't seem to be doing as well with the food and climate as our Mr. Dooley." The Boer took the package and slipped it inside his shirt as Roosevelt turned to Dooley. "I see that you're making progress with your riding. Bully! I want you to join me and Kermit when we hunt on horseback as soon as Mr. Potter says you're ready."

The Pinkerton tucked his chin and muttered into his chest. The words were indistinct, but the tone sounded pleased, if not deferential.

The Boer returned in three weeks with fresh supplies of salt, dry goods, outdated newspapers, and a sack of mail forwarded from the American consulate at Mombasa. "Tell Kermit I bring something for him, too."

Roosevelt took the sack of mail while the porters unloaded the rest of the wagon. "That's thoughtful of you. He's reading in his tent." Returning to his own dwelling, Roosevelt emptied the consulate bag on his campaign desk and called to one of the *totos* to bring a cup of hot chai. The newspapers and political mail could wait. The fat cream envelope addressed in his daughter Alice's distinctive violet-colored ink had his immediate attention. There was nothing from his wife. He read through Alice's letter twice before air moving through the open tent flap announced the arrival of company.

"Sorry to interrupt," said Potter. "Happy news?"

He lifted the sheet of cream stationary covered in Palmer script. "According to my eldest daughter, the one married to Senator Longworth, Randolph Hearst has sent some crackerjack female newspaper reporter to Africa at the same time as us. His newspapers have been carrying fascinating stories about the resurgence of slavery in the Sudan, the arming of native soldiers in German East Africa, and reports of colonial atrocities in the Congo Free State. According to my daughter, the Hearst reporter's stories are even more popular than mine! She wants to know if there's any chance I might cross paths with their fascinating author, a Mrs. Margaret Dunn."

"She's the Germans' headache now."

"I don't know. Perhaps Vorbek let her go. How else could she be sending out newspaper stories?"

"Maybe she charmed him into sharing his government telegraph."

Roosevelt snapped his teeth and pinched the bridge of his nose.

"Just so long as she doesn't show up here," Potter added.

In truth, Roosevelt was pleased at Maggie's success. He didn't mind sharing the front page of the newspapers, and he wouldn't mind terribly if their paths crossed again. Though somehow he chaffed at the idea of her charming the German.

Potter remained just inside the tent flap, shifting his weight from one foot to the other and tugging at his right earlobe. "Well, I'm sorry to add bad news. But what I came to tell you is that another porter deserted last night."

"What!"

"That's three since Kilimanjaro."

"How many guns are missing?"

"None. That's the first thing I checked. They took enough mealie to make it back to Kapiti, but nothing else that we can find."

Roosevelt recalled that the outfitter they engaged in Mombasa to recruit the native labor had insisted that desertion among the porters was rare, as the natives weren't paid until the safari was over. As long as they felt safe, well-fed, and not overworked, they stayed to collect their pay. But if chance put money in their hands before that, they'd leave in a flash. Why carry forty pounds on your head for a year if you can get any amount quicker and with less effort?

"I've asked your boy and that young Boer not to give money to the porters. But they're so fond of that *pembe*, they can't help themselves."

"Damnation!"

"I'll send the Boer kid back to Nairobi right away with more hides. That'll take care of half the problem for a while. By the time he catches up to us again, we'll be in the Congo. None of the porters will desert there, no matter how many shillings the boys put in their pockets. They value their limbs too much."

Several maimed young men had appeared together at the *Ngoma*. Kermit said that they were escaped rubber workers from the Congo, and their gruesome injuries certainly gave credence to the missionary's stories.

"That Belgian king is going to hell."

Potter stepped toward the tent flap.

"Unless he gets there soon, that's not going to help the Congolese."

Roosevelt rousted Kermit from his cot before sunrise. The hungover boy couldn't swallow a cup of sweet chai or chew a slice of bread. When they left camp to begin the morning hunt, he quickly lagged behind, and Roosevelt had to send the gun bearer to the back of the column so that Kermit would not become separated from the group.

The trackers forged ahead and Roosevelt followed, though his thoughts were far from hunting. It was time to confront Kermit about his unfortunate weakness for alcohol. Many believed that how much a man drank, even a nineteen-year-old man, was his own business. But porters deserting because Kermit and Jans put enough *pembe* money in their pockets was safari business. As leader of the safari, he needed to address that. He hoped Kermit would listen.

The bully pulpit and the head of the family table were identical in at least one respect. Each could be used to inspire as well as to castigate. Though he knew of few instances where the latter achieved anything of value when it was not combined with the former. William Jennings Bryan lost three presidential elections because he didn't understand that fundamental aspect of human communication. But how did one chastise a teenage tippler so as to inspire him to moderation?

He thought about how the safari's sponsor, Andrew Carnegie, was vilified for decades as a bloated malefactor of wealth. In later years, something made the robber baron see the error of his ways and inspired him to distribute his immense fortune for the public good. Presumably the change came about by the same process that seemed to work in most men—by experiencing a chastening truth and envisioning a compelling alternative. Kermit needed to undergo the same transformation if he was to overcome his affliction. But how could a father help him begin? Every man was different. Teenage boys and girls, the most different of all. As a father and leader of the largest safari Africa had ever seen, he was at a loss.

Shortly before noon, the lead tracker spotted a herd of Cape buffalo grazing on the side of a low brown hill covered in wild fig and thorn. Cunninghame had warned repeatedly that Cape buffalo were among the most dangerous of all the African big game animals and must be approached with great caution. Intelligent and without fear of man, even when fatally injured, a wounded buffalo would lie quietly in ambush for any predator foolish enough to pursue it.

The gun bearer scooped a handful of dry earth and allowed it to fall to the ground, its drift revealing a small movement of air from the direction of the herd. The hunters were downwind and the herd couldn't smell them. A large bush willow between the men and the buffalo provided favorable conditions for a stalk. Proceeding cautiously and in single file through the short grass, they kept the bush willow between themselves and the herd and, once past it, dropped to hands and knees and crawled. The gun bearer led the stalk, motioning the others forward only when the buffalo had their heads down or were hidden behind brush.

The sun marched slowly across a cloudless sky as a layer of sweat and dust basted the hunters' bodies. After an hour, they reached the edge of a small rise some eighty yards from the herd. The gun bearer pointed to a large male buffalo grazing close to a thicket of thorns. Roosevelt removed his pince-nez from his shirt pocket and tried unsuccessfully to clean the sweat and pollen from the lenses with his damp shirttail. Finally, he whispered to Kermit, "You take it."

The boy's skin was the color of bacon fat and his breath came in slow, deep swallows. Roosevelt looked away, feeling sick at heart. What parent wants to see his child hungover, and not for the first time?

Kermit lifted the Winchester to his shoulder and wrapped the leather sling around his forearm. The black walnut stock slid in his moist palm. His hand shook. He slipped the custom double safety, pulled the trigger too hard, and watched the barrel of the gun jerk to the right.

Roosevelt licked the lens of his eyeglass clean in time to see the shot and the puff of dust that rose from the animal's midsection. Whirling toward the source of its pain, the bull's dark and angry eyes bore into the grass in their direction. The herd scattered. Then the bull whirled again and plunged into a heavy thicket of thorn.

The gun bearer looked away. *Bwana M'toto* had made a bad and dangerous shot. A belly wound. Now they would have to hack their way through dense thorns where a gut-shot buffalo waited, angry and in pain.

Roosevelt tried to keep his voice even. "We'll give it time before we go in."

The three men stood and retraced in a few minutes the ground that had taken them an hour to cover on their hands and knees. The bush willow that had provided cover for the stalk gave them shade to rest.

"I'm sorry, Pop. That was an awful shot."

Not trusting himself to respond immediately, Roosevelt tried to remind himself of his son's many fine qualities—among them physical courage and a flair for friendship and languages. But troubling weaknesses had come to the fore in Africa. Prone to fits of melancholy when the safari was stuck in camp for too long, the boy had turned quickly and often to drink. Roosevelt worried about his son's increasing resemblance to his deceased Uncle Eliot, a self-destructive drunk. An African adventure might have been an opportunity to halt that unhappy progression. But so far, it had only made it worse.

Leaning back against the willow, Roosevelt gazed toward the thicket of knobthorn where the buffalo lay waiting. "You've read Socrates, haven't you? You know his maxims?"

"An unexamined life is not worth living?"

"Know thyself was the one I was thinking of." He removed his pince-nez and searched for a clean square of shirt to clean the other lens. "I've always thought that one of the best things about going off to school and becoming independent of your family is that, at last, you get to work on creating who you want to be. Or if you don't know what that is yet, and most people don't, you at least get the chance to take stock of who you are and decide what changes you'd like to make now that you're in charge."

Kermit remained silent.

"I remember having to face the fact that I'd been born with a puny body and asthmatic lungs and accepting that if I didn't do something about them, I wasn't going to have much of a life. That's not your challenge, of course. You've got a fine body and an even better mind. But we all start by looking at the hand we've been dealt and deciding how to fix it or play it. Have you done that yet?"

"I think so."

"And what have you found?"

"Well, at the risk of being immodest, I'm fit and strong as you point out, good at languages, and I believe I've inherited your gift for writing."

"Any weaknesses?"

"Well, I wish I had your *joi de vivre*, Pop. Sometimes I get awfully down."

"Black care rarely sits behind a rider whose pace is fast enough, son." Kermit looked away. "What else?"

"I wish I had a girl."

"Ha!" Roosevelt smiled. "Wishes aren't weakness. Only failing to act on them, if they're worthy." His son's expression remained unreadable. "Let me get you started. What about your fondness for drink and your habit of not stopping when you've had enough? You've noticed those, haven't you?" Kermit bowed his head. "They're not character flaws, son. A character flaw would be noticing and not doing anything about them. But they are weaknesses."

Kermit sighed. "I drink too much, at times. I know that. I try to be moderate."

"Has it worked?"

"I guess not."

"So what do you intend to do about it?"

"I don't know, Pop. Try harder? What else is there to do?"

Roosevelt returned the pince-nez to his shirt pocket. "You could lay off it altogether. Some men do."

"I don't know, Pop. I get awfully blue sometimes. A bit of the vine keeps me going."

"But it's not *a bit*, is it?"

"No."

"Is there anything else that keeps you going, beside the drink? What about riding and shooting?"

"One can't ride and shoot all day and night."

"But one can fill the days and nights with things that excite. It's boredom and lack of purpose that sap a man's strength."

Kermit fell silent again.

"Look, son, I don't mean to lecture you. But I would like to help, if I can. Perhaps by pointing you in a worthy direction. Sickness and infirmity were the weak cards I was dealt. You've pulled a different hand, and, frankly, I have no advice on how best to play it. But melancholy and a fondness for drink are common enough. Others have found ways to overcome them. If you want to have a bully life, or any kind of life at all, you'll do the same."

Kermit took a deep breath. "I know, Pop."

"Well, that's a start." Roosevelt put his arm around his son's shoulder and leaned against the bush willow. Closing his eyes, he felt the young muscles beneath his arm begin to relax. Only then did he allow himself to drift off.

Kermit was relieved that they didn't need to crawl the two hundred yards back to the thorn thicket. The wounded buffalo wasn't going to leave there voluntarily any time soon. Though once they arrived at the imposing wall of brush and thorn, his worries came in waves. A wide hole ringed in broken brush showed where the buffalo had entered. Stepping through it felt eerily like entering a horror story where the hero was about to open a door he shouldn't and step into a space where no good awaits. Only this wasn't Pop reading a story to the Roosevelt children around a Sagamore campfire. This was Africa. The door was real, and there was an authentic monster waiting on the other side.

Kermit was aware, as well, that prey and predator rely on the same three senses: sight, sound, and smell. As between man and beast, the animal held the advantage in all three. When prey had the opportunity to become predator that discrepancy in sensory acuity was often fatal to man. He should not have taken a shot at such a distance. His head, that morning, had felt as big as that buffalo's ass, and he hadn't a chance of hitting the broad side of a barn from anywhere but close range. The only hopeful aspect of the dangerous path they were now forced to follow was that when they finally came face to face with the beast, the engagement would be at so close a distance that any shot could hardly fail to find its mark.

Lost in a whirligig of unhappy thought, it was a moment before Kermit felt the gentle tug on his shirt. The gun bearer pointed to his nose and then to a crushed section of thorn ahead. Kermit tapped his father on the leg and conveyed the signal. Each man dropped to a crouch as the sound of bovine nasal clearing wafted through the thorns. The sound reminded Kermit of a giant troll under a bridge as in Mr. Grimm's fairy tales—something huge, angry, filled with snot, and waiting to tear human limb from limb.

The thorns shook and the three men raised their guns in the

direction of the movement. Roosevelt stepped to the right and laid his Fox twelve-gauge double-barreled shotgun in the crook of a jack-alberry tree. Kermit hadn't seen his father use the double-barreled gun in months, but he was glad to have the extra firepower now. The gun bearer propped his Springfield on an upraised knee. Kermit slipped the Winchester's safety and raised the rifle to his shoulder. Those who remembered to breathe, did so silently. Then the thorns suddenly parted, and an animal the size of a Minotaur filled the opening. A black boss of thick rippled horn extended across its skull and for half a yard on either side. The animal looked directly at the hunters, dipping first one horn and then the other, hooking them left and right like a boxer at a training bag. Then it pawed the ground with its front hooves and dug in the hind ones to gain leverage for the charge.

The gun bearer filled his lungs and shouted, *"Piga!"*

As if on signal, the animal surged in the direction of the sound, looking like nothing so much as a locomotive bursting out of a tunnel. Kermit squeezed the trigger and saw an inch-wide hole open in the animal's chest. The gun bearer fired next and then leapt to the side as the beast charged past, skidded to a halt, and turned with its head already lowered for another charge. His back against the wall of thorns, the gun bearer wiggled left and right as he tried to force his body through the foliage. The buffalo charged, knocking him through the brush and pinning him to the ground with his boss. With the tips of its massive horns, the buffalo hooked the earth on either side, trying to skewer his helpless prey.

Then came the roar of Roosevelt's twelve-gauge side by side and an explosion of red between the buffalo's shoulders, just behind the head. The animal whirled. Kermit put another round from the Winchester into its chest. Then the double-barreled Holland exploded again, though the animal didn't react and the sound wasn't that of a high-powered cartridge slamming into its target. It was a flat-out explosion. The gun bearer recovered his feet and rifle, while Kermit put a final volley into the beast's chest, which sent it crashing to its knees. The gun bearer shot again, sending the animal to its maker. There was no further sound from the Holland.

Kermit collapsed to the ground in nervous exhaustion. Then he looked for his father. "Pop?" He crawled to where he'd heard the

Holland and found what was left of the gun hanging like a twisted shepherd's staff from the crook of a jackalberry tree. The right barrel had been blown out the side and bent nearly in half. Beneath it lay his father, spread-eagled on his back and covered in blood.

Dooley watched Kermit ride into camp, leading a horse with a groaning Roosevelt draped over its saddle. The taxidermist, Heller, had the porters carry the big man to the mess tent and lay him on top of a wooden table where Heller cut away what was left of Roosevelt's shirt, poured a bottle of something through a funnel into his mouth and a bottle of something else over his wounds. Over the next hour, the taxidermist removed what was left of Roosevelt's eyeglasses and the splinters around them, using a variety of needles, tweezers, and a thin brass rod with a nasty-looking hook at the end.

When he was done, Heller sat with Kermit, who had remained at his father's side throughout. Dooley waited for both to leave, thinking he might have an opportunity, with everyone gone, to finish what he had started. Eventually it became clear that the boy intended to sit there all night, so Dooley went back to his tent but couldn't sleep. Roosevelt wasn't dead, and Ketchel, the bastard, wasn't going to wait forever. The next tintype might well be of Mickey swinging from a rope.

The safari had been in the field five months, and Roosevelt father and son had surely slaughtered half the beasts in Africa. Suppose, with that buffalo, they had everything they'd come for? With his face all stitched up, Roosevelt would want to go home, wouldn't he? Dooley didn't like the idea of finishing the job under an open tarp, next to a pair of dozing coppers and a kid who looked like he was going to stay up all night. But would he have another chance? He left the tent and went back to the mess where Roosevelt lay on the table. Taking a spot on the other side of a nearby guard fire, he waited for Kermit to fall asleep.

Just before sunrise, a hand on his shoulder shook Dooley awake. "Bwana Potter," said the horse boy, as if that were a sufficient explanation for being awakened before the cock crowed. Too late, he thought about going back to his tent for a jacket. It was warm near the fire, but beyond it a chill lay over the ground that would not burn off until sunrise. The horse boy led the way through dew-wet grass to a clearing outside camp. Potter was waiting there with a pair of saddled horses.

"We need fresh meat," Potter said, which didn't make sense after the enormous buffalo they'd brought into camp the day before. But that was all Potter said, and he wasn't smiling. Dooley felt the hair on the back of his neck lift like a porcupine's quills. Had Potter figured out the who and the how of the busted gun? Was he going to take the man who had nearly blown off his boss's face out into the bush and put a bullet through his head? Call it an accident?

When Potter kept his rifle at the ready across his saddle and made Dooley take the lead as they rode through the tall grass, it seemed clear that over the next hill, or the one after, the pious cowboy was going to shoot him. Dooley had no gun and no idea of how to stop what was going to happen next.

As they came to the top of a rise, Potter told him to halt. A lone Thompson gazelle stood a hundred yards away, grazing in the yellow grass. Potter pulled a Springfield from its saddle scabbard and tossed it to Dooley. "Show me what you can do."

Surprised and unprepared, he pumped a cartridge into the chamber, shouldered the rifle, and pulled the trigger. Nothing happened.

"You forgot the safety."

More angry than scared, Dooley snapped back the piece of metal that kept the rifle from firing accidentally, gripped the barrel, and jerked the trigger. The gazelle looked toward the sound and then trotted away unharmed.

Potter shifted his own rifle, which, for most of the ride, had lain across his lap, and pointed the barrel toward Dooley. "That German officer seemed to think you might have killed his native soldier." There was no anger in his voice or any other hint of how he might feel about the German's suspicions. Air seeped from Dooley's lungs and blood rushed to his head. "Tell me what happened."

So this wasn't about Roosevelt? Or the exploded gun? That should have been good news, but the cowboy's attitude and vigilance told him to remain wary. He had made up a story, just in case he needed it. But would it work?

"I was havin' a bit of spark with one of the native girls. She ran off when her soldier boy showed up. Me and him had a tussle."

"You killed him." Potter's voice remained flat, without expression.

"He had a rifle. All I had was me fists." He pulled Mickey's sap from his hip pocket and waved it at Potter. "And this. It was a fair fight." Potter remained silent. "Maybe if somebody came along and said, Now, boys, stop it. All polite like that. Well, things might have ended different. But there wasn't anybody there but us, and I wasn't going to let him shoot me, now was I?"

"Anything else?"

Else? What else? He didn't expect me to tell him I'm sorry, did he? Dooley raised his chin. "That's it."

Potter spat. Then he gestured for Dooley to get back on his horse. They rode in silence. Every gully looked like a spot to dump a body and leave it for the hyenas. Potter might not shoot him for killing a native in a fight, but that didn't mean he wouldn't turn him over to the Germans. How would he kill Roosevelt then? His thoughts were a blur of what-ifs and escape plans, all ending with him dead and Mickey rotting in Sing Sing.

When they came upon a herd of impala, Potter told him to try again. Dooley stilled his breath and tried to remember the Boer's catechism of shooters' dos and don'ts. Dismounting, he wrapped the leather sling around his upper arm, assumed a three-point stance, steadied his breath, and gently squeezed the trigger. The impala dropped where it stood.

They rode over to where the animal fell and Potter got down from his horse to begin gutting it. "The colonel's going to recover," he said, cutting open the animal from throat to crotch and pulling out its insides, either reluctant to trust Dooley with the knife, or knowing without being told that Dooley had no idea how to field dress a large game animal. "The tree the colonel used as a gun rest took most of the explosion, and his glasses saved his eyes. That gun bearer thinks something must have gotten into the barrel when they busted through the thorn. Kermit blames himself for wounding the buff and making them go in after it." Dooley suppressed a smile. "The colonel's made of tough material. Heller says he can hunt again as soon as his face heals. Maybe a week. But from here on in, I want you with him." Dooley's heart skipped a beat. "You've got no morals, Mr. Dooley. But you think and act fast. That gun bearer is just out looking for animals. The colonel and his boy are just looking to shoot them. Someone needs to be there looking out for everything else. So when the colonel is healed up and ready to hunt again, you're going with him."

Dooley struggled to keep the elation from his voice. "What about the other Pinkertons?"

"You're the only one who's healthy right now. Thompson's got malaria again and the other two have the bubble shits. Until any of them are up and about, I want you with the colonel wherever he goes. I don't care if it's into the bush to answer a call of nature."

Dooley's heart kicked into high gear and he tried not to smile. *I'll watch his ass, like a mother with a newborn babe.*

Chapter Sixteen

To gain all, we must risk all.

- General Paul von Lettow-Vorbek,
My Reminiscences of East Africa, 1920

J.P. Morgan and his assistant sat on opposite sides of Morgan's twenty-foot-long rosewood desk in his office on the thirty-six block of Madison Avenue. Images of Socrates and Galileo looked down approvingly from the Mowbray mural overhead. The Hudson River breeze that wafted through the tall windows overlooking Madison Avenue stirred some loose papers on the desk but cooled no one. He and Cashman had spent an hour that morning with William Randolph Hearst and Andrew Carnegie going over the latest communication from the reporter Hearst had planted with the Roosevelt safari. What they heard made them all uncomfortable, though each for different reasons.

"If that Belgian priest is telling the truth about what's going on in the Congo Free State," said Cashman, "Leopold is a bigger scoundrel than the Borgia Popes. Does he think England, France, and Germany are going to let him ruin the colonial game for everyone? It's one thing to exploit natives. but it's quite another to exterminate them! He'll wake up one morning to find his neighbors crossing Lake Tanganyika to carve up his precious little colony for themselves."

Morgan waved his cigar in dismissal. "They're too busy preparing for war against each other."

Cashman fell silent.

"That reporter claims Roosevelt hasn't ruled out running again for president in 1912. There's nothing about his being on his deathbed or even close to it. A close call with a snake—nothing else! That socialist cowboy is above ground slaughtering animals and plotting his political comeback!" Morgan picked up a copy of Dunn's report and began reading numbers. "Two hundred sixty-nine animals for Roosevelt, and the same for his boy, including seventeen lions, eleven elephants, ten Cape buffalo…"

Cashman continued to sit in silence.

Morgan put down the paper. "Where's Comstock trading this morning?"

"Fifteen cents per share. Down a nickel. The stock you had me buy with that million-dollar loan is now worth less than twenty thousand dollars."

"When is the loan due?"

"June first."

"That's cutting it close, Elliot. The Yellowstone logging contract can't be awarded to Comstock before mid-May now." Cashman swallowed.

"Carnegie says the plan is for the safari to end up in Khartoum sometime in late March. If Roosevelt is still alive, he'll hear about the Yellowstone logging as soon as he sets foot in the consulate." Cashman looked ill. "Do you think he'll keep quiet when he hears that?" Cashman shook his head. "Do you think Taft will have the gumption to stand up to Roosevelt and keep his promise to Comstock?"

Cashman went over to Morgan's sidebar and poured himself a tumbler full of Armagnac. He looked at the ninth-century Ptolemaic map of Africa on the wall above the bottles and raised his glass in mock toast. "Guess I'm going to Africa."

"It's your choice, Elliot."

"Oh yes, poverty or riches."

Morgan shrugged. "Or jail. Some little fish always gets caught when a new *reform* administration comes in."

Chapter Seventeen

Nine tenths of wisdom consists in being wise in time.

\- Teddy Roosevelt

"Where the blazes have the hippo gone?" Roosevelt demanded.

They had marched twenty days from Nakuru through sweltering heat and clouds of tormenting black flies, finding little game along the way and less water. Cunninghame had promised all would change once they reached Lake Victoria, but he he had only been right about the flies.

After fourteen days of leaving camp before dawn and hunting hard until dark, they'd seen just one hippo worthy of a shot. Kermit had kept his promise to stay away from the native hooch, but he remained anchored by a stupor of body and spirit that long marches and fatherly counsel did nothing to lift.

"It's a big lake," said Cunninghame. "The only one bigger is your Lake Superior. Hippo can be tucked in anywhere along the shore from here to Bija."

"Then let's cross and try there."

Cunninghame looked pained. "It may not be any better over there, Colonel. And there aren't enough boats to cross us all, or the right kind. We could buy a few of the shallow-draft canoes the locals use to fish near shore. But I wouldn't put two hundred and sixty men and their equipment in them and try to cross fifty kilometers of open water. Flash storms come up over the lake every afternoon this time of year. We could end up like the Spanish Armada, drowned like rats."

"A few of us could cross, couldn't we? With the rest following along shore." Roosevelt never liked to do another man's thinking. But if a man wouldn't do his own, he'd do it for him.

"I wouldn't advise it, Colonel. You're looking at two days and nights of hard paddling with sore arses all around. Anything you shoot before the column catches up will rot, unless you carry a few hundred pounds of salt and manage to keep it dry. If you land anywhere south from straight across, you'll be in German territory again."

Roosevelt patted his shirt pocket. "I still have my letter from the kaiser."

"I can't stop you, Colonel, but you'd be going against my professional advice."

"Understood. But it is doable?"

"Only by a madman."

Seven men in five dugout canoes pushed off from shore just after dawn the following morning. Supplies and equipment filled the three largest canoes, each manned by a single paddler. Roosevelt and Kermit shared the next, and Dooley and the gun bearer Kashama the smallest. Roosevelt imagined they'd progress in something like a V-shaped goose formation, with himself and Kermit in the lead. But after a few hours, the three heavier boats had fallen back and the two smaller ones struggled to maintain a consistent line. Each boat took the waves and the frontal breeze differently, as the canoes carrying himself and Kermit had a pointed bow, and the one with Dooley and the gun bearer was rounded.

By afternoon, the wind had begun to shift from west to north and to increase steadily in force. Masses of dark clouds appeared over the horizon, filling the sky and moving fast in the direction of their little boats. Then the sun disappeared behind a charcoal sky, the wind increased, and water poured through the darkness into and around their shallow crafts in a surge that would have frightened Noah. The boats foundered, separated, and disappeared into grey sheets of impenetrable rain.

The storm only lasted ten minutes. Then the sun reappeared and steamed their clothes as they watched the phalanx of massive grey clouds march down the lake. Roosevelt put two fingers to his mouth and gave a sharp whistle, knowing that sound carried clear and far over calm water. The other boats could be anywhere. But if they could hear each other, they might be able to follow the sound and converge. He whistled for half an hour without result.

Kermit picked up his paddle.

Roosevelt held up his hand.

"We can't leave. We have to gather everyone first."

"I know, Pop. But if we paddle a square—five minutes west, five south, five east, and five north—we'll run into any boats in that area. If we don't find any, we'll be back where we started, more or less, and we can expand the square another five minutes, and so on. No one will find anyone if no one moves."

Roosevelt was doubtful. "What if everyone picks up a paddle and starts off in a different direction?"

Kermit frowned. "I don't know. I guess the result would be the same as everyone staying put—no one reconnects. But if one of us moves systematically the way I described, at least there's a chance of that boat finding another."

Roosevelt was far from convinced, but he couldn't think of a better plan. "All right. We'll give it a try." He picked up his paddle and leaned into the stroke, the wind at his back, and his mind filled with thoughts of command. Would each of the boats stay put, waiting to be found? And if so, for how long? Would one of them eventually do the next best thing and paddle for the nearest shore, which was east, the way they had come? Or would one or more continue in their original direction, where the shore was two days distant? Surely no one would paddle south. But did that city boy Dooley know which way was which?

There would be time for recrimination later, though he hoped not the need. How stupid not to have planned for a possible separation! Neither he nor Kermit carried a timepiece, but he guessed they were making thirty strokes a minute. They started south, the direction the storm had blown, counting three hundred strokes, then east, north, and west again, pausing occasionally to whistle and wait for a response. At the end of a circuit, they expanded the perimeter to six hundred strokes, starting west and pausing every three hundred strokes to whistle and listen. On the next circuit they expanded the grid to nine hundred strokes and started east.

By late afternoon, Roosevelt's fifty-year-old arms were numb with fatigue, though his brain remained charged with the adrenaline of combat. For that's what it was. Combat with an adversary for whom he was ill-prepared, with the possibility of disastrous consequences for those he led. Hour after hour, they paddled in silence, ignoring the fatigue, the wet, and the chaffing. They stuck to Kermit's plan, as it seemed the best option to pursue. If one of the paddlers in the supply canoes had thought of unpacking one of the rifles, matching it with the right ammunition, and firing off a shot, they hadn't heard it.

The sun slipped inexorably toward the horizon as they began their thirteenth circuit. They'd been paddling since dawn. Roosevelt's whistle was a feeble echo of what it had been a few hours before. But Kermit's stroke was indefatigable. Watching his son's broad, youthful back lift and lower the narrow-bladed paddle hour after hour without pause or complaint, filled Roosevelt with pride and comfort. He was sure that the young man was observing him, too, knowing his father was in a pickle and waiting to see what he'd do. Would he think straight? Lead? Would he get them out of this self-made disaster?

Do what you can with what you've got where you are, had been Roosevelt's motto in public life. What he had was a canoe, a paddle, and a bright young subordinate who'd come up with a rational plan. What he could do was carry it out until it worked or until they came up with something better. Where they were, however, was separated from their companions in the middle of an inland ocean, the second largest body of fresh water on the planet. There was no point sugarcoating the facts. He had led men into battle and to victory. Few human experiences rivaled that. Now he would do what he could with what he had to avoid leading them to defeat on account of his own stupidity and poor preparation. *Though it might well still come to that.*

In the middle of these dark thoughts, Kermit raised his paddle and cupped a blistered hand behind his ear. "Did you hear that?"

Roosevelt heard nothing. The shotgun implosion seemed to have added another layer of muffling to the hearing damaged by his youthful foray into pugilism. He turned to give range to his better ear.

"You don't hear that?" Kermit asked again.

Roosevelt shook his head. Kermit gestured with his paddle and then pulled hard in that direction, his stroke like a frenzied brewer at a mixing vat. A few minutes later, Roosevelt heard the sound, too, and laughed. "That's one of those tin whistles you were trading for beer, isn't it?"

Kermit turned and grinned.

The whistle proved to be wielded by one of the African paddlers, whose excitement in seeing his fellows led to gyrations of celebration that threatened to capsize both their boats. He and Kermit jabbered in Swahili, and Kermit translated that the paddler had not seen or heard anyone since before the storm and believed himself destined to end his days in a crocodile's belly. Kermit assured him that all would be well, then retrieved his Springfield and ammunition from the paddler's boat and fired off three rounds in succession. After half a minute, he fired another three and after a short interval a final three. There was no response. "Guess we should keep going."

"Agreed," said Roosevelt. "Minus whatever we've drifted since we found this fellow, we've come about eighteen hundred strokes north and west of where we started. This boat is heavier than ours and seems not to have drifted as far as we did. The other one is lighter and may have drifted farther."

"That sounds about right, Pop. Why don't we do a tight grid of a hundred strokes starting from here? The other supply boats should be somewhere close by. When we pick them up, we can go back to where we started and look for Mr. Dooley and Kashama."

"Excellent plan!"

It was another hour before they found the next boat and another two before they found the third. The only fuel they'd had since dawn was adrenaline. After picking up the third boat, they retraced the grid to where Roosevelt and Kermit had begun that afternoon, and from there, navigated by the stars southwest two thousand five hundred strokes (Kermit did the geometry in his head), and began the process all over again. Kermit fired the Springfield every five hundred strokes, and the native paddler blew the tin whistle more or less constantly. The sky had begun to lighten when they heard the drum of paddles against wood and finally rendezvoused with Dooley and the gun bearer.

Exhausted and exhilarated, they tied the five boats together and shared strips of impala jerky with loaves of cassava wrapped in palm leaf. The food replenished their strength and restored Roosevelt's voice. He leaned forward and put his hand on his son's shoulder. "You did well, son. Immeasurably well. I'm more proud of you than I know how to say. Without your intelligence and strength, I would have certainly lost these men."

Kermit grinned. "It's wonderful when a plan works exactly as you pictured it, isn't it?"

"And rare. Most of us improvise with what life dishes out. A few reflect and correct course when they realize they've gone astray. I can think of few better examples of intelligent improvisation than what you did here today. I couldn't be more happy or proud."

"Thanks, Pop."

"How do you feel?"

"Pretty darn good."

"Well, now that you know what that looks and feels like, you should be able to find it again when you need it. Not a bad day's work!"

The first *askari* appeared an hour after Roosevelt and his party beached their canoes and set up a lakeshore camp. Major Vorbek and a dozen more African soldiers arrived an hour later. "Colonel Roosevelt, I presume," he said as he entered their modest camp, echoing Henry Morton Stanley's famous greeting to his fellow explorer David Livingstone.

As it seemed appropriate to his own recent experiences, Roosevelt replied with Livingstone's heartfelt, "I feel thankful that I am here to welcome you."

The impromptu homage to the great age of African geography reminded Roosevelt of the profound influence that epoch had had on his youthful imagination. The vast inland lake that he and his party had just crossed had yet to be circumnavigated when Stanley met Livingstone near the shores of Lake Tanganyika fewer than forty years before. The source of the Nile was still a mystery. No white man had seen the great Congo River or traveled its length across the width of Central Africa to the Atlantic Ocean. When Roosevelt was a boy, the map of Central Africa was as blank as it had been in the time of Ptolemy.

As a teenager, Roosevelt had devoured *Scribner's* serialized accounts of Stanley's horrific and wonderful expedition. Young Theodore used to spend hours in his father's East Twentieth Street library, lost in Stanley's exotic descriptions and *Scribner's* lurid illustrations. Now that boy was here and quoting the explorers' dialogue verbatim. Life was indeed bully!

"I apologize for wandering into your backyard again," Roosevelt said to Vorbek, when he'd recovered from his reverie. "We ran into a little trouble crossing the lake."

"And the rest of your expedition?" asked Vorbek. "Scientists and sportsmen on a peaceful mission to gather specimens for your national museums?"

"They're coming by land. To Bija."

"So." Vorbek's face looked pinched and his voice sounded suspicious. His next words were terse. "Bija is fifty kilometers north of here, Colonel. Once again, I find you in a militarily sensitive area with war coming."

Roosevelt's eyes surveyed the sandy loam and scraggly brush. "Here?"

"Whoever controls these lakes, Colonel, controls Central Africa."

"You are not at war, Major. And let us hope it remains that way. In any event, one middle-aged man crossing this lake in peace time with his teenage son and a few native paddlers is hardly a threat to any nation's opportunity at postwar riches."

Vorbek's back stiffened. "What are you doing here, Colonel?"

"Hunting hippo."

"There are no hippo here."

"I was misinformed. I was told there might be hippo near Bija, where we had intended to land."

Vorbek shook his head. Suspicion gave way to peevishness and then to resignation. "You present me once again with the difficulties, Colonel."

"We'll be on our way then."

"That I cannot allow."

"No need to make things complicated, Major. Bija is fifty kilometers north of here, you say. We can be there in three days."

Vorbek raised his brow. "Perhaps with…how you say: *verbundenen Augen*?"

"Blindfolded?" Roosevelt surveyed his surroundings, anger and incredulity rippling across his face. "I won't try to guess, Major. But I don't intend to put on a blindfold or allow my party to be led stumbling sightless through rough terrain for three days. If the newspapers ever got hold of that image, neither my professional future nor yours would be worth a *pfennig*."

"Ach, the newspapers! I cannot let you or your men survey this area. And I myself cannot remain. If you refuse the *verbundenen Augen*, you must remain here until I receive instructions."

"Do you have telegraph facilities near here, Major?"

"I cannot say."

"Well, how long will it take for you to receive instructions?"

"I have not yet an answer to my inquiries from Kilimanjaro."

Roosevelt looked up and down the pebbled beach, calculating how long before Cunninghame and the rest of the safari reached Bija, and whether they would have the spunk to march south and look for their castaway companions.

Vorbek followed his gaze. "You must not think that you can shoot your way past my *askari*, Colonel, like one of your Western cowboys and their red Indians. You are seven now. Not two hundred sixty."

Kermit, who had been listening quietly, interrupted. "Excuse me, Major. Your reference to America's cowboy heritage gives me an idea that might be helpful."

"Good," said Roosevelt. "Because mine are not fit for uttering."

"Do you have a large wagon?" asked Kermit.

Vorbek shook his head. "I cannot say."

Kermit looked toward the horizon. "Well, while we were out scouting for hippo, we came across fresh wagon tracks. The ruts were deep, so I'm assuming it was a large wagon." Vorbek stiffened. "I don't know if you've ever seen illustrations of the wagons used by our American pioneers, Major. But if we cut up our canvas tents, make a frame, and put that on a wagon, you could transport the seven of us to Bija without the need for blindfolds."

Vorbek smiled. "So no fear for the newspapers then? Is it so to you, Colonel?"

Roosevelt smiled. "'Blown off course by a vicious storm on a turbulent African lake, former President Roosevelt and his small party of sportsmen hunters were fortunate to arrive safely on German shores, where they met with a gracious hospitality and a comfortable transport back to their anxious fellows.' I could write the article myself. We'll be fine with the newspapers. Though they'll want photographs. You wouldn't happen to have a dry plate or one of those new box cameras?" Vorbek spread his hands. "Ah yes, you can't say."

"My adjutant, Sergeant Fussner, was with the Boers at Mafeking. They had such wagons. I will send him to collect your canvas in the morning, as you suggest. The work will be complete by afternoon."

"Bully, Major. Just bully. See what men of goodwill can do when they put their minds to it?"

"Yes, yes. We will make the necessary modifications for the sleeping as well."

"No need to trouble yourself, Major. The seven of us can sleep fine under one canvas."

"There will be eight of you, Colonel."

"We'll squeeze him in."

"Her."

Roosevelt's heart fluttered like the wings of a startled grouse burst from its hiding place by a stalking hunter.

Chapter Eighteen

Listen to the yell of Leopold's ghost
Burning in hell for his hand-maimed host.
Hear how the demons chuckle and yell.
Cutting his hands off, down in Hell.

- Vachel Lindsay, *The Congo*, 1915

Threadbare khaki did little to protect Dooley's bony ass from the pounding wooden flatbed or the politician's stream of blather that added more hot air to an already stifling wagon. Dooley felt like he was going to puke, collapse, or both. Only the Africans seemed oblivious to the dark, dank, and discomfort. The gun bearer blew snores from a hairless face propped on scabby knees, and the paddlers jabbered in the dark like kids at a church picnic. So did Roosevelt and the female reporter, sitting so close that their knees and foreheads nearly touched. Neither seemed to notice the jolting or the rank smell, though they had managed to grab a spot nearest the canvas flap and fresh air. They'd been talking since dawn. Dooley wondered what the Roosevelt kid thought about his dad's mooning like an infatuated schoolboy.

Closing his eyes, he tried to quell the growing dizziness and nausea. The realization that he'd missed another chance to kill Roosevelt made him feel even more ill. When the boats first got separated, he'd hoped that he might come upon the politician's canoe, ram it, and drown him. The fat politician couldn't have stayed afloat for two hours, much less two days. But the other boats had found each other first. And now, packed like sardines in a canvas sweat tent, he didn't see another chance coming any time soon. His gut churned not knowing how long Ketchel would wait.

Sweat clouded Dooley's eyes and drenched his clothes. The others seemed not to sweat as much or breathe as hard. Could he have the malaria again? His face felt puffy and swollen and the fingers that touched it tingled. If he didn't get some air soon, he was going to vomit. Grabbing the wooden frame that held up the canvas, he hauled himself into a bent crouch and turned his body toward the back of the wagon. *Too fast.* He could feel the blood drain from his head. His knees buckled and his body pitched to the floor.

"Cut another!" someone ordered. Dooley's mind returned from wherever it had gone. Blue sky and white clouds hovered in a triangle above his eyes. Someone's lap cradled his head and a wet cloth slid over his face. Nearby voices argued in an unfamiliar tongue.

"Cut a row of them," the politician demanded.

The boy stepped across Dooley's view and cut a row of *V*s in the top of the wagon canvas with a small pocketknife. Warm blessed air seeped into the confined space. Someone outside pulled open the flap at the rear of the wagon and shouted something in German. The politician shouted back. Dooley didn't understand a word. It didn't matter. His lungs cleared and breathing came a little easier.

Hovering faces blocked his vision. The woman again. "You've upset Sergeant Fussner."

Roosevelt's face swam into view. "He wanted Kermit's pocketknife. Called it a weapon! I told him it's the same blue sky and white clouds on both sides of the border. No military significance whatsoever. But suffocating the former president of the United States and his party might prove disadvantageous."

From the back of the wagon, the son asked, "Did you tell the sergeant that we already know his big secret?"

"Best to save that."

Dooley reached for the wooden canvas frame and pulled himself upright. The reporter peered in his face like a brooding hen. "Feeling better?"

He nodded warily.

The politician piled on. "Fit for duty? I may need your brawn, if that fellow decides to shoot me for making a few air holes."

Dooley almost whispered a thank you. He felt in no position to quarrel now.

The reporter turned to the politician. "I don't understand. What big secret justifies keeping us cooped up in this canvas sweatbox?"

Roosevelt shook his head, but the voice at the back of the wagon came from someone who either didn't see the silent instruction or chose to answer anyway. "This wagon stinks of machine oil. It's packed with eight grown adults, but it makes tracks only half as deep as the others we saw near the lake, which presumably were made by this same wagon. You heard Major Vorbek's comments on control of the lake. There's your answer."

"Where?"

Kermit moved forward, nearer to Maggie. "Major Vorbek's patrol had a wagon when you were with them, right?"

"Yes. But it was filled with sacks of flour and other supplies."

Roosevelt held up his hand. "We owe Major Vorbek a confidence, son. He didn't have to let us go."

"Oh, please!" said Maggie. "You mean there was some piece of military equipment under those sacks?"

Roosevelt looked stern. "You don't want to write about this. If war comes, the last thing you want is for one of your articles to be the match that lights the keg."

"I don't see—"

"The next war between industrialized nations will be the first fully mechanized military conflict in human history," Roosevelt lectured. "Carnage on the scale of industrialized war will be something straight out of Dante."

"You're talking politics, Pop."

Roosevelt let out a breath of hot air and pulled at the cut strips of canvas overhead. "For all the good it will do out here. Let's give Mr. Dooley more air."

Yes, let's, thought Dooley.

Maggie was first out of the wagon when it pulled off the track near a stand of thorn trees just before sundown. The *askari* cut the thorns with their *pangas* to widen the clearing, and then piled the cut thorns into a circular hedgerow eight feet tall and four feet deep around the wagon, its passengers, and escort. Kermit stood beside her and commented on the preparations. "It's called a *boma*. A thorn fence to keep the lion and hyena from dragging off the wagon ox during the night if the party isn't large enough to post an all-night guard."

Maggie shivered. "It feels like a cage."

"It is. But to keep the predators out, not us in."

The *askari* cook came around with cold porridge. Maggie picked at the unfamiliar fare and watched the sun, which had kept the wagon baking most of the day, dip below the horizon. Darkness fell quickly and with it came the cold.

"It's funny," said Kermit. "Sun up and sun down usually kick off a chorus of birds in the morning and insects at night. I don't hear a thing, do you?"

Maggie looked up at the stars that had begun to appear in the vast, cloudless sky. "Maybe a storm?" Then she heard the sound that no human being could ever mistake for anything else—the sound of an infant crying. Silent figures appeared out of the darkness just outside the barrier of thorns.

"*Chakula, mtoto!*" An emaciated brown arm pushed through the prickly hedge. Behind it, a gaunt figure stood holding a baby in a piece of ragged cloth slung at her hip.

Maggie didn't need a translation. She stood, intending to push her cup of gruel through the thorns. But the German sergeant barked something to the *askari*, who blocked her way with crossed rifles. The sergeant said something in a tired voice, but she didn't understand his German. By then, other figures had appeared, other hands pushed through the thorns, and the whole circular hedge began to move inward toward the wagon from the collective pressure of the crowd.

"*Aufhören!*" shouted the German, firing his sidearm into the air.

"Dear lord, what's happening?" Maggie shouted. No one answered. The sergeant shouted an order, and the *askari* fixed bayonets to the ends of their rifles and began thrusting the pointed weapons into the hedge. Shrill cries pierced the night air and the thorns quit their inward march. But for how long?

One of the paddlers shouted. Voices in the dark responded.

"Who are they?" she asked. "What are they saying?"

"I don't know," said Kermit. "They're not speaking Swahili."

"These are people from Congo," said the gun bearer. "Soldiers burn their *kraal*. They have no food. Some have no hand."

Roosevelt and the German engaged in a hurried consultation, apparently in agreement for once.

"Do something, Te…Colonel!" Maggie pleaded.

Teddy's demeanor conveyed clearly that her outburst was neither timely nor helpful. But his response was thorough and his voice patient. "Sergeant Fussner says these people come from the Iruti forest, from villages that haven't met their rubber quota. Their *shambas* have been torched and the survivors are fleeing east into Uganda. When they get there, the British push them south into German territory."

"Oh, Teddy! I mean do something now! These people are starving."

Teddy said something to Fussner, who responded with a shrug and what sounded like an apology. "He has only enough provisions to get us to the border and his men back to wherever it was we started."

"Surely he can spare something!"

"Not without starting a riot he won't be able to stop unless he's ready to shoot people. These folks are desperate. They'll kill each other and us for a scrap of bread. If that fence doesn't hold, he'll have no choice but to use his weapons."

Maggie was awake before first light. Teddy had insisted she sleep in the wagon while the others bedded down outside with Sergeant Fussner and his *askari*. But who could sleep with the wailing and moaning of hungry mothers outside the *boma*, and the cries of the desperate ones who tried and failed to push their way past thorn and bayonet? She left the wagon at first light and peered through the *boma* at a steady stream of women and children shuffling south along the sandy track. The bolder ones cast pleading glances at the thorn barricade while keeping a cautious distance from the armed *askari*. Teddy conferred with the German sergeant while several of his *askari* cut a wagon-sized hole in the thorn wall, and the rest stood behind them with rifles and fixed bayonets. No one asked about breakfast.

When the time came, Maggie took her place in the wagon on the slat bench opposite Teddy. The *askari* led the oxen to the opening in the *boma*, stripped off its canvas and stood aside for the wagon to pass through. Maggie was confused by the removal of the canvas. "I thought we weren't supposed to see anything."

Teddy answered in a low voice. "The mob outside will swarm us if they think this wagon is carrying food. We have to show them it's not. I told the sergeant we don't want this blindfold nonsense to be the cause of his having to shoot a bunch of starving refugees."

"What about his big secret?"

"I told him we already know it and I gave him my word that we'll keep it. I also told him that it's better for his country to get us to Bija alive so we can expose what their neighbor, King Leopold, is up to, rather than have us die at the hands of a mob while in German custody."

Maggie shuddered. "I'm sending this story from the first telegraph we come to. I'll walk it out, if I have to."

His eyes rested on her face. "That won't be necessary."

Later that day, Roosevelt spotted a flock of black ungainly birds circling the cloudless sky up ahead of the wagon. The gun bearer saw it, too. He raised his arm and pointed. "*Ndio. Tai.*"

"Vultures," Kermit translated.

Dooley shuddered.

A half hour later, they came across the bodies. Some lay in the middle of the dirt track; some in the bush near where they'd tried to hide. Each of the adult bodies was missing its left hand. Roosevelt felt a sudden urge to send the Great White Fleet to bombard King Leopold's palace in Brussels. The paddlers and several of the *askari* began to wail.

"They are Tutsi," the gun bearer explained. "Like these dead."

"Who killed them?" asked Maggie.

"Hutu, who work for a white king. The men do not want to cut rubber, so the Hutu burn the Tutsi villages and the women run away."

"Why did they cut hands off the bodies?" asked Roosevelt.

The gun bearer shook his head. "They are *nyama*." Animals.

"It's more calculating than that," said Kermit. "The missionary at Mr. Cunninghame's farm told us about it while Mrs. Dunn was interviewing you for her newspaper article. He said that Leopold only allows the *Force Publique* to use their guns to shoot runaway rubber workers. They can't hunt or do anything else with them. At the end of the rubber season, when the *Force Publique* return the rubber workers to their villages, each soldier has to account for the bullets he was issued. If one is missing, he has to produce a human hand to prove he used it to shoot an escaping worker. If he can't, he's given a hundred lashes with a rhinoceros hide whip. The missionary said few survive the punishment. A hand for a bullet is Leopold's way of making sure the natives don't stockpile ammunition until they have enough to use on him. Brutal but effective."

"Dear God!" said Maggie.

"Has a lot to answer for," muttered Dooley.

Roosevelt felt maddened by what he had seen that day and by the knowledge that Leopold's neighbors would do nothing about it. Dead and starving Congolese lay everywhere along the track the wagon had to follow. When they stopped for the evening, the *askari* didn't bother making a *boma*. Any predator hunting for an evening meal was unlikely to enter a firelit camp when easy meat lay everywhere for the taking.

He had heard European diplomats justify African colonization as an act of enlightened civilization by cultures pledged to bring primitive peoples out of savagery and into the modern world. But one dyspeptic European ruler, allowed to despoil a land larger than the United States east of the Mississippi and exterminate the people in it, made a mockery of that justification and of the great powers that preached it. It seemed clear that the Europeans would do nothing about the rogue among them while they were busy preparing for war with each other. Until that score was settled, no one would pay attention to the odious Belgian king and his collection of severed human hands. *Damn it! The man had to be stopped.*

Roosevelt looked at the grim faces around the campfire. Each appeared as troubled as he, but none gave voice to his thoughts. He had seen the same thing in Cuba after battle. Shock and horror fueled the mind but stifled speech. Thoughts galloped uncontrolled or remained stuck on the horror just witnessed. He tried to engage the taciturn Sergeant Fussner to see if he could learn something useful. "I know you're not a man of politics, Sergeant. But your neighbor needs a good, thorough... Kermit, what's the word for 'hiding'?"

"*Ein gutes Versteck.*"

Fussner shrugged. "With Major Vorbek, you should talk. He has the much ideas. I, not so many."

"Well...do you think Germany would govern the Congo differently if it were hers?"

"*Ja.* Of course."

"Is that Major Vorbek's view?"

Fussner shrugged again. "*Herr* Vorbek is not a politician. He speaks from the heart. I hear him say that no German can treat the African as the Belgian kaiser does, or as the British treat the Afrikaners."

"Being less brutal than Leopold doesn't set the bar very high," said Kermit.

Fussner shook his head. "Ach, the politics. You see us with our *askari*. You see the farms and schools at Kilimanjaro. If Germany came to the Congo, would it not be the same?"

"German East Africa has no rubber," said Kermit. "Neither do the British or French territories."

"But we have the sisal. We pay wages to Africans who help us harvest. We do not burn villages and cut off hands of those who keep their own ways. If they do not make trouble, we do not trouble them."

Maggie caught his eye. "May I ask what you're talking about?"

"Politics," said Kermit.

"I'm sorry," said Roosevelt. "Today's events need venting. Sergeant Fussner doesn't speak English."

"Oh, please. Let me join. It was beastly, what we saw today."

"This can't appear in your newspaper."

"If it means doing something about those miserable refugees, you have my word that I won't quote you."

"All right then!" Roosevelt clapped his hands. "Kermit, you translate for Mrs. Dunn." He turned to the German sergeant. "Sergeant, suppose I give the Congo to the kaiser?"

The German looked startled. "You cannot give a country."

"Germany can take it," said Roosevelt. "Leopold has no army. He'll have no choice but to step aside. If England and France can avoid war in Europe by letting Germany have a colony in the Congo, that's best for everyone. England and France already have more colonies than they can administer. If Germany took over the Congo, your kaiser would have what he wants without plunging Europe into war. And the rest of the civilized world would have peace."

"*Ja*, with the Major Vorbek you should speak."

When Kermit had finished his translation, Maggie spoke up. "Does the kaiser want the Congo?"

"He should," said Roosevelt. "It's what every German leader since

Bismarck has wanted: land for his growing population and a piece of the global pie. The kaiser is just more belligerent than his predecessors. I'm going to talk to him."

"And say what?"

"That he can take the Congo from Leopold, or gamble the future of his country on an all-out European war that Germany will lose if the U.S. comes in on the side of France and Britain. The facts speak for themselves."

Maggie frowned. To his surprise, her voice was curt and almost disrespectful. "Such as the fact that the president of the United States is named Taft, not Roosevelt? Or that it takes an act of Congress to go to war?"

Kermit paused in his translation. "She's got a point, Pop."

"A minor one. What do you think of my idea?"

She took a dismissive swing at it. "More importantly, what will President Taft think? Or aren't you planning to tell him?"

He tried not to give voice to his irritation. "I haven't decided."

She continued to press. "And why should the kaiser pay attention to an offer that comes from someone who hasn't got the power to deliver? The president of the United States can do that. But as you told those priests back at Cunninghame's farm, private citizen Roosevelt has no such power."

Kermit held up his hand to stop the conversation while he tried to catch up with the translation. When he had finished, Fussner shook his head. "With the Major Vorbek you should talk. To this sergeant you give just the headache."

Roosevelt stood and walked away from the fire. He felt angry and frustrated. The ambivalence and uncertainty that had weighed on his soul upon leaving office was gone. Not running for a third term *had* been the biggest mistake of his life. His successor didn't have the gravitas to bully the kaiser to prevent war in Europe or to coerce the colonial powers into quashing the Belgian rogue in their midst. But having once held the throttles of power, would President Taft willingly step aside after a single term and let the better man retake the helm? Would the party bosses allow him? The answer was obvious. Not a chance. *Damn it!*

Chapter Nineteen

While still over a hundred yards from the hippo, I saw it turn as if to break into the papyrus, and at once fired into its shoulder, the tiny pointed bullet smashing the big bones. Round spun the great beast, plunged into the water, and with its huge jaws came straight for the boat...

— Theodore Roosevelt, *African Game Trails*, 1910

Maggie stood in the shade of an umbrella thorn and listened to Teddy confer with the German sergeant in measured voices, while the sergeant drew lines in the sand with a stick. Not for the first time, she regretted her lack of languages. When they were finished, an *askari* brought over two rifles and a small canvas bundle, and the German sergeant handed Teddy a chit of paper which he signed with the steel pen he always kept in his shirt pocket. Then the sergeant and his *askari* climbed into their empty wagon and turned south, heading back the way they'd come. Maggie had been in the Germans' custody for nearly four months, but her long-sought release didn't feel like freedom. It felt like abandonment.

Before he left, the sergeant admitted that he was not entirely sure where the border lay, though he thought it should be less than a day's march away. She hoped he was correct. Beneath the unwashed hand that shaded her sweaty brow, an unbroken vista of *mswaki* scrub, sickle bush, and dry dusty earth stretched to the horizon. Perhaps she might have a proper bath before too long. How long had it been? Five months? She would ask Kermit about that canvas tub he had mentioned. What a luxury that seemed in the middle of this arid landscape, with only the occasional bucket of water from some clouded hole where anything might lurk.

But there was to be no bath that day. The marchers halted at sunset, having encountered no sign of either the border or of human habitation. Darkness fell quickly. They slept in their clothes on the sandy ground, huddled inside a *boma* around a small fire. Kermit and the Africans took turns tending the flame until dawn. Maggie slept as close as she dared, deciding that filthy and warm was preferable to filthy and cold, though she woke the next morning unaccountably stiff, achy, and chilled.

After a quick repast of hot tea and German biscuits, the eight marchers began their trek through scrub and thorn as a rising sun lifted a grey horizon on a ribbon of vibrant pink. Alone at the head of the column, Teddy's squared shoulders and steady stride showed no sign of fatigue, which she would have found inspirational if she could have believed the unwavering gait reflected a determined mind filled with noble thoughts and plans to act on them. But that was a dream. His was not the stolid pace of a vigorous man committed to act on important goals. It was the walk of a man in a trance, unaware of his body, lost in indecisive thought. She wanted to kick him.

Had years in power made him forget the effort actually required to capture it? Twelve months ago, he could have been president of the United States for a third term. Now, if he wanted to reclaim that power, he would have to persuade the Republican bosses to dump a compliant president in favor of a notorious renegade who had been an unpredictable pain in their backsides for more than a decade. Teddy might have been the only American politician with the force of character necessary to broker a European peace, redress the atrocities in the Congo, and cope with the myriad challenges of this new century. But if he wanted to regain the position necessary to implement those worthy goals, he needed to make up his mind and do what was necessary. Among other things, that meant returning to America without delay and mending fences with William Randolph Hearst. Without the popular frenzy only a newspaper could incite, the Republican bosses would never abandon their comfortable bird in hand for an untamable lion in the bush. Teddy had less than a year to force his way back into the game, and he couldn't start from Africa, or without help.

Lost in thought, she nearly tripped over a native who had stopped to point toward a group of thatched huts spread across a dry hillside a hundred yards ahead. Kermit conferred with the gun bearer in Swahili and then with Teddy. "If it was my village and I saw men with guns marching in my direction," said Kermit, "I'd come out to have a look. Wouldn't you? Where is everybody?"

Teddy held his rifle across his torso. "Take Kashama and poke around." He had spoken little since the previous evening, when Maggie had given her honest reaction to his fantasy of power without position. What words he had, he'd shared with Kermit and no one else.

The two men were gone twenty minutes, returning in the company of a bare-chested old man with the stooped carriage and glazed stare of a blind Homer. Beside him walked a thin, lame, and nearly naked boy. The old man gestured toward the empty huts and the scrub plain beyond them. Kermit translated. "He says those Congolese refugees came through here three days ago. A bunch of men with guns came right behind them. The whole village took to the hills, except him and the boy."

Maggie looked at the boy, who held his weight against a long pole and stood on his one good foot. The other foot, scarred and shriveled, rested against the pole that supported him.

Teddy shifted his gun to his shoulder. "Ask him how far we are from the border."

Kermit spoke first to the old man and then to the boy. "They don't seem to understand the idea of a border. But the *mzee* says there's a town a day or two march to the north. He hasn't been there in a long time, though."

Maggie felt her heart lift for the first time in days. "Might there be a telegraph in this town?"

"You can't write about this," said Teddy, addressing her for the first time since the previous evening.

Her face flushed. *How dare he!* "My promise was not to quote you, Colonel. But I will write about what I've seen here, about atrocities committed by a European monarch. The world must hear about this. And just because you don't—"

Teddy's face turned a splotchy red. "I mean you can't tap this out on a British telegraph. Write anything you want about King Leopold, the maimer. But if you write about the British pushing refugees into German territory, they'll censor it. They may even deport you."

"Pop? There might be a telegraph line in Kampala. I'm guessing that's just a few weeks' march east of here."

"We're not heading east."

Maggie lifted her chin. "Then I must make other arrangements."

Teddy was not skillful enough in the art of deceit to be able to keep the thought from his face, but which he was gentleman enough not to say. *Like the arrangements that got you lost looking for Kilimanjaro? The ones that nearly made you breakfast for a pack of hyenas?* But it was a moment before he spoke again. Time enough for all to notice a pair of grey gulls and some smaller white birds flying east. They must be getting close to the lake again.

"When we meet up with the safari," Teddy said at last, "I'll ask Cunninghame to lend some men to escort you to Kampala. If there's a telegraph there, the British may let you use it. But they won't let you tell the whole story. Not the way you want."

Kermit spoke again. "How about sending Mrs. Dunn's story out with the next wagon of skins we send to Nairobi? It won't get to America as quickly, but if you put it in the pouch with your magazine pieces for *Scribner's*, it will get there uncensored."

Teddy smiled. "If Mrs. Dunn doesn't mind the delay. She can go with the wagon to make sure her article gets out safely."

Maggie returned his smile. "Thank you, Colonel. I'm sure my scribbling will be safe next to yours." She had no intention of leaving Teddy now that she had finally caught up with him. Leopold's atrocities and Teddy's determination to do something about them were stories the world needed to hear as soon as possible. She hoped it hadn't been a mistake to show her impatience. She didn't know what kind of push it would take for Teddy's feet to follow his mouth. But until he realized he must run for president again, and soon, she intended to remain at his side to watch, record, and if necessary, shove.

Teddy opened his mouth and then closed it, as if hesitant to say anything further. "We should talk later."

She started to place a hand on his arm but, remembering Kermit, withdrew it. "If you're worried about your commitment to *Scribner's*, Colonel, you needn't be. My intention is to proceed to the Sudan. I'm told that slavery has made a comeback there. That's a story that needs to be told every bit as much as Leopold's atrocities in the Congo."

Teddy's eyes widened and his mouth opened once again. "The Sudan? Alone? An infidel woman? Ma…Mrs. Dunn, don't be absurd."

"If there's no story I may write about here, Colonel, then I have no choice but to strike out on my own. I must make a living."

"We're heading into the Sudan after Uganda, aren't we, Pop?"

"That's supposed to be confidential."

"Sorry."

Teddy let out a slow breath and his mouth widened to something like a grin. "I suspect that you haven't revealed anything that Mrs. Dunn hadn't already guessed."

The Hearst reporter knew better than to smile, but Maggie Ryan felt no need to suppress her satisfaction.

Dooley was sure they were lost again. The old man in the empty village said a town lay in this direction. But after three days, they saw no sign of it. Then the track turned toward the big lake, and they started to see signs of life: a collection of mud-wattle huts and some fishing boats. Two days later, they found the white hunter Cunninghame and the rest of the safari camped near a weed-choked bay by the shore of the lake.

The porters came running when the marchers were still more than a mile from camp. Chanting and whooping, they lifted Roosevelt and his kid on their shoulders and carried them off. Potter and Cunninghame, looking pleased and relieved, greeted the procession in front of the mess tent. Cunninghame held out his hand and clapped Roosevelt on the back. "I've had scouts out looking for you for a week. I was beginning to fear you'd drowned or been shot by the Germans."

Damn near both, thought Dooley. But he kept his mouth shut.

"There's a fair number of hippo around here. When you're rested, we'll have a look."

Roosevelt grinned. "Why wait? Kermit and I..." He looked around. "Where's my sidekick?"

Dooley had seen the boy go off with one of the natives, but he wouldn't give the lad away. He had earned his drop of the *craythur*. If it was more than a drop...well, that might prove useful, too. The boy was less observant when he'd had a few.

Cunninghame called to one of the natives, who trotted over with a long double-barreled gun. He checked the bore and then handed it to Roosevelt. "There's an island of hyacinth in a cove about two kilometers from here. The hippo feed along its edge in the late afternoon. Mbeki can take you there."

Roosevelt took the gun and turned to Dooley. "Since my son seems to have deserted me, would you care to come along on another boat ride, Mr. Dooley?"

I'd rather have me teeth pulled!

Potter spared him the need to answer. "He'll join you in a few minutes, Colonel. I need a word with him first."

The politician shifted his weight from one foot to the other, seemingly anxious to get going. "When you're ready." Then he marched off with Cunninghame, whistling some silly tune.

Dooley shook free of Potter's grasp. "I'll not be getting in a boat with that madman again!"

"You'll do what you're told, or you can walk back to New York from here."

Dooley reached for the sap in his back pocket but stopped before Potter could notice. He'd have no chance to kill Roosevelt if he gave in to the urge to teach this arrogant cowboy some manners. Potter could keep his teeth for now.

"Tell me what happened out there, and make it quick."

Dooley spat into the sand. "Your man nearly got us killed is what happened. Tiny boats in a lake as big as an ocean? Waves as tall as trees, and wind like the end of the world? We're lucky to be here and not at the bottom of the drink."

"How did that female reporter find you?"

"It was Germans what found us, washed up on shore like a bunch of drowned rats. They put her and us into a wagon and dumped us out in the middle of nowhere and told us to start walking."

Potter shook his head. "She was with the Germans?"

"That's right. She was in their wagon already when they shoved us all in and sent us back here."

Potter looked up at the clouds, as if there might be an answer written there. "Catch up with the colonel and see he doesn't get eaten. We'll talk again tonight."

By the time Dooley caught up with Roosevelt, the politician was already off in another tiny boat, heading toward a bunch of floating weeds in the middle of a shallow cove. Cunninghame stood on shore, watching a skinny native paddler maneuver the flimsy canoe in response to Roosevelt's pantomimed directions.

Dooley approached the guide. "You got another one of them little boats? I'm supposed to see himself doesn't get wet."

Cunninghame frowned. "Hippos get testy if you crowd them."

"But not if you shoot at them?"

The guide squinted toward the hyacinth. "Mbeki knows what to do. He'll look for a bull away from the others, give the colonel a clear shot and then paddle like hell for shore. The colonel may have other ideas, of course."

Dooley wondered how they planned to haul three thousand pounds of dead hippo into a little canoe. But the thought was interrupted by a native shouting and waving his arms toward the island of weeds in front of Roosevelt's canoe.

Sweet Jesus.

Two heads the size of pushcarts broke the surface a dozen yards behind Roosevelt's canoe. Before Dooley or Cunninghame could speak, a half dozen more hippos' heads rose from the water on either side of the flimsy boat.

"Dear God." Cunninghame barked an order in Swahili and a native came running with a gun. Shoving a cartridge into the breech, he raised the gun and fired toward the hippos nearest the boat. Roosevelt stood at the front of the canoe and fired at the same time. A pair of heads disappeared beneath the water.

The paddler dug his blade into the water and pushed the boat frantically toward shore. Five more hippos broke the surface behind the canoe, opened their mouths, and bellowed. Cunninghame fired again. One head disappeared. Roosevelt fired next, and a mouth as wide as a meat wagon snapped shut and slipped below the surface. The other hippos moved forward, undeterred and bellowing like a train wreck, mouths ready to swallow Roosevelt and his boat whole. Dooley stifled a cheer. Surely one of them was about to make a tasty meal of the fat politician.

"Shoot, man!" shouted Cunninghame.

Dooley lifted his rifle and fired into the water at the hippo farthest away from the canoe. A half dozen more hippos appeared and joined the chase. He aimed at one, just for show. It didn't matter. Roosevelt was a dead man now. He and Cunninghame couldn't possibly kill them all, and the politician would surely lose his footing at any moment with the little boat rocking back and forth with every shot. Falling into the water would be a fitting end to him, eaten or drowned.

A dozen natives arrived to watch the *mzungu* get swallowed by the *kiboko*. Cunninghame shouted something in their lingo, and they all picked up rocks and hurled them toward the swarming hippos. One animal turned away from the boat and charged the shore. The natives ran to the trees. Roosevelt's paddler turned the boat sharply this way and that, threatening to throw the politician into the trailing mouths with every turn. Cunninghame fired again. Dooley did the same, hitting a cloud. The rock throwers resumed their bombardment with carnival gusto. The paddler rose to one knee, twisting his upper body with every stroke. Then—for no apparent reason that Dooley could see, unless they'd finally had enough of the gunfire and rocks—the hippos slowed and stopped, moving neither toward the fleeing canoe nor toward the rock throwers on shore.

Damn. Dooley fired at the hippo nearest the boat, hoping to goad it into action. The paddler thrust the canoe toward a bed of papyrus. Dooley watched helplessly as the boat disappeared into the fronds, and one by one the hippo heads submerged and were gone.

Chapter Twenty

[The crocodile] got his front paws over the stern of my canoe and endeavored to improve our acquaintance. I had to retire to the bows, to keep the balance right, (It is no use saying because I was frightened, for this miserably understates the case) and fetch him a clip on the snout with a paddle.

- Mary Kingsley, *The Congo and the Cameroons*, 1897

Weeks later, north of Victoria Falls, the safari halted at the edge of a fast-moving stream where yellow grass ran to the water's edge, and a wall of green jungle on the far side shaded a muddy bank littered with sunbathing crocodiles. Dooley watched the porters cut logs of bush willow to make rafts to carry the men and supplies across as he tried to block out the drone of Roosevelt's latest lecture. According to his nibs, the stream they were about to cross came from Lake Victoria and eventually, along with a bunch of other streams, became a mighty river called the Nile. Or so some English man claimed to have proved a few years back. That might interest some, but after the near thing with the hippos, Dooley's attention was on the crocs.

So was the Afrikaner guide's. The old Boer interrupted Roosevelt's lecture to give one of his own. The deeper parts of the river, he said, ran too fast for the big reptiles and also for loaded wagons and men. Rafts and ready rifles were the answer to getting the porters and supplies safely across. The horses, however, wouldn't step foot on the tippy platforms of lashed logs that the porters were cobbling together from nearby scrub, and the wagon was too heavy. Getting the wagon and horses across was going to be a problem.

Roosevelt turned to his kid. "Any ideas, son?"

"A couple." The grinning idjit leapt to his horse and charged off down the riverbank and around a bend. To do what? Find a bridge?

Dooley stared at the enormous open-mouthed reptiles on the opposite bank, basking in the afternoon sun, looking like fifteen-foot turds with teeth.

"They prefer rotting meat," said Cunninghame, catching Dooley's glance. "They store their kill underwater if they have the chance and wait for the flesh to rot off the bone." Dooley suddenly felt a chill. "A big croc nearly killed a boy on my farm a few years ago. He and his friend were casting a net into a stream when the croc came out of nowhere and dragged the boy to his underwater food locker. But he wasn't dead yet. He'd been chewed a bit but wasn't drowned. When the croc went back for the other easy meal, the boy in the hole managed to wriggle out and swim to shore. He was never right in the head after that. Nightmares about rotting flesh and so forth..."

Dooley looked away. He didn't believe it. No man could hold his breath that long, not even a native. But Africa was full of the nasty. He'd seen and heard enough of it by now.

The Roosevelt kid came back an hour later with the breathless news that a horse could outrun a croc in shallow water and could keep its footing in the deeper, swifter parts where the crocs wouldn't go. Dooley didn't want to think of how the kid had figured that out. But no such thought troubled Roosevelt. He declared it bully sport and invited Dooley to help race the horses across the shallows or guide them through the swifter water while the others crossed on rafts.

The man was serious. Potter's eyes flashed a silent reminder that Dooley's job was to keep Roosevelt safe. Dooley's gut began to loosen, then clench. What was he supposed to do? Stop the idjits from being their idjit selves, or just fling his body at any croc that got close? Roosevelt waved him toward the water, taking for granted that Dooley would be happy to join their *bully* sport!

He couldn't back out, not if he wanted to keep his place as the capable lad and solo bodyguard. Clamping his gut, he followed father and son upstream to a spot the boy declared to be too swift for crocs, but not horses. It didn't look any different to Dooley. But neither of the Roosevelts sought his opinion. At least they weren't going to be racing giant reptiles through shallow water. Roosevelt and his son whooped and spurred their horses into the stream. Dooley swallowed a surge of bile and followed. *Don't let go and, suffering Jesus, don't fall.*

Slack-jawed crocs waited downstream for whatever tumbled their way, mouths agape and small white birds hopping with impunity around their exposed yellow teeth. Cloudy brown water surged like a warm bath around Dooley's legs. His breath quickened and his throat tightened. The whooshing sound in his ears was louder than the rush of silty water over his horse's neck.

The Boer's riding lessons had been on dry land, for Christ's sake, and they hadn't included crocs. Though he'd learned to tell when a horse wasn't comfortable and when it was most likely to do something to get its rider hurt—the one under his butt kept trying to face upstream while his ass slid in the other direction. It couldn't get its footing. Eventually, the horse stopped and refused to go further. Dooley dug his heels into the animal's side, with no effect. The horse didn't move. They were no longer facing the opposite bank, where they needed to go, but stood stuck in no-man's-land, head upstream and ass down. Tepid, tea-colored water rushed past on either side.

Dooley clung to the reins and tried not to fall off. Up ahead, Roosevelt's horse seemed to have stopped, too, though the kid had nearly crossed. Roosevelt yanked his reins and kicked his horse until it, too, finally moved. Dooley tried the same, but the bastard wouldn't budge. He kicked harder, and in a flash the horse whipped his head around and seized a chunk of Dooley's thigh between its teeth. *Jesus!* He dropped the reins and grabbed the beast by the ears. In an instant, his ass slid off the saddle and his body rushed downstream fast and out of control.

Mother of God! Tepid water, thick with silt and debris, drenched his eyes and filled his mouth. His feet flailed to find the bottom. Like a tin can in a rain gutter, he was upside down, ass backwards, and every which way but upright and breathing. His mouth and lungs filled with water. They'd taught him to ride; they hadn't taught him to swim. Then something yanked at his arm! *Jesus!* He jerked back, fearing he'd find nothing but a stub at the end of a limb. Whatever had him, let go. He kicked and flailed, struggling to find air. Then something grabbed him again, this time by the hair. His head broke the surface and he felt air and sunlight on his face.

"Hang on!" As if he needed to be told. It was Roosevelt. He grabbed the politician's saddle and felt himself being dragged upstream. When they reached the horse, standing where he'd left it, obstinate and immobile, Roosevelt barked, "Hold on!" Then he dumped Dooley over the saddle like a wet blanket, grabbed the reins, and led the two horses in the direction of the opposite bank, heads high and water rushing over their backs.

Exhausted, Dooley lay draped over the saddle, watching the bags on the horse in front of him flap like leather wings in the strong brown current. It reminded him of that winged horse on the handle of the brass cup those crazy Italians had given Roosevelt in New York. Then something clicked inside his head. *Mother of God!* Inside the lumpy saddlebag, pressed between his gut and the horse's ribs, was an old sock wrapped around a piece of oiled paper. Inside the sock was the last of the *pili pili* the taxidermist had given him to break the malaria fever.

Squeezing a hand inside the saddlebag and holding on to the pommel with the other, he found it. The sock was drenched, but the twist of oiled paper inside was dry and tight. The horse beneath him looked straight ahead, intent on its footing and oblivious to the fidgeting man on his back. Roosevelt looked straight ahead, too. Side by side and staggered by half a length, the rear of Roosevelt's horse bobbed mere inches from Dooley's face. Tearing the oiled paper open with his teeth, he lifted the tail of the politician's horse and shoved in the powder.

All hell broke loose. Roosevelt's horse let out a scream, dropped its ass into the water and rolled. The politician disappeared beneath the surface, his hatless head surfacing twenty yards downstream and moving fast toward a hundred hungry crocodiles waiting with open jaws.

Kermit reached the opposite bank before he heard the whinny of a panicked horse. Turning, he saw the Pinkerton, Dooley, halfway in the water clinging to the neck of an unmoving mount, and a rider-less horse in front of it bucking in circles. Pop was nowhere to be seen. *Dear God!* He dug his heels into his horse's ribs and charged downstream looking for any sign of his father. Ahead, a pair of fifteen-foot crocs rose from the bank and slithered into the water. A thousand pounds of muscle and teeth thrust in tandem toward a large flat bolder in the middle of the stream, where a pair of shaking arms held fast to the rock. Kermit pulled his rifle from its scabbard, plunged his horse into the water, and fired.

Dooley looked around to see who might be watching. The crocs would surely finish the two Roosevelts. But he had to make a show of it. Hauling his mount to the opposite bank, he shouted the alarm and galloped to where the porters were unloading the rafts. Potter, Kruger, and two of the Pinkertons grabbed rifles and ran along the bank. Dooley grabbed a rifle and rode past them. In the middle of the stream, a dozen crocs feasted on what was left of Kermit's horse. Twenty yards away, Roosevelt and his son stood back to back on a flat-topped rock. Kermit held his rifle steady in the direction of the feeding crocs. Roosevelt didn't have a gun, and his face was hidden by his son's back. Late to the horseflesh party, one of the enormous reptiles slipped away from the scrum and paddled toward the meat on the rock. Dooley stopped his horse, lifted his rifle, took careful aim at the swimming croc, and deliberately missed.

The thousand-pound reptile lunged the last few feet toward the two men in the middle of the stream. Kermit lowered his rifle until the barrel almost touched the top of the big croc's head and then pulled the trigger. The croc sank. A moment later, snout and tail reappeared downstream, drifting with the current.

The noise alerted the other crocs. Done with the horsemeat now, one by one they peeled off from what was left of the dead animal and turned toward the rock in the center of the stream. Dooley fired into their midst, aiming at nothing. Potter and the others were approaching fast but were still a hundred yards away. Kermit killed another croc, once again letting it get to almost handshake distance before shooting it in the head. The croc rolled onto its belly, and its pals made a quick meal of him before resuming their assault on the rock. Dooley fired again, aiming for Roosevelt and missing by inches.

The Pinkertons arrived at last. Then Potter. Then Kruger. All opened fire, even before dismounting. Soon a dozen dead crocs littered the steam. When their corpses reached the shallows, a dozen more crocs feasted on their lifeless bodies. Then, suddenly, Roosevelt was in the water. Kermit dropped his rifle and grabbed his father's body before it could drift away. He heaved Roosevelt onto the rock and rolled him onto his back, face covered in blood and body limp.

A dozen natives arrived on foot. The Boer sent them back for a raft. Steady rifle fire kept the crocs at bay while the natives strung a line across the river and hauled a raft over to the rock. Kermit stepped onto the raft, carrying Roosevelt on his back—alive or dead, Dooley couldn't tell.

Chapter Twenty-One

*In a moment of decision the best thing you can do is the right thing.
The worst thing you can do is nothing.*

- Teddy Roosevelt

Dooley stood behind the gawking porters and watched the taxidermist pull twigs and river crap from the gashes on Roosevelt's head, torso, and limbs. He couldn't see any bullet wounds or crocodile bites. Well, if Roosevelt wasn't dead, it wasn't for lack of trying. The man had more lives than a saloon cat.

He turned to leave and felt the iron grip of bony fingers on the back of his arm. "What happened out there?" It was Potter, snarling like a dime-store sheriff spoiling for a fight.

Clamping his jaw, Dooley took a moment to think. From a hundred yards upstream, the cowboy couldn't have seen much more than dead reptiles and live Roosevelts. He should have been happy about that.

"Your idjit boss and his kid walked us into a river full of crocodiles. That's what happened."

Potter squeezed harder. "You're being paid to keep the colonel safe."

"Then next time tell him to have his precious kid build a folkin' bridge." He yanked his arm from Potter's grasp and strode away, not looking back until he'd found a dry spot along the river bank with a clear view so no one could sneak up on him.

This man just won't die. Dooley watched the porters gather wood and make fires up and down the riverbank. When darkness came, they slept beside the embers on beds of green leaves. In the morning, two hundred sixty mostly silent men gathered up their bundles and marched single file into a tunnel of fetid greenery as dark and tall as a tenement stairway, alive with things that bit, stung, and poisoned.

It wasn't easy to stick close to Roosevelt amid hundreds of porters spread out over more than a mile, hacking their way through layers of dense, slippery foliage and prickly poisonous vines as thick as his arm.

Every few hours, the marchers came upon some reptile-infested water that appeared out of the dank greenery and disappeared back into it. They crossed the deep ravines on makeshift footbridges and forded the others. Each had its gallery of basking crocs waiting for an easy meal.

Day after day, they hacked at dense foliage, forded fast-rushing rivers, shot crocs, and watched for things that slithered overhead and underfoot. They didn't hunt anymore; they just endured.

Then one afternoon, wet, bitten, rubber-legged, and exhausted, the column broke out into sunlight and grass. After making camp, the marchers dried their soggy clothes and tents and ate their first hot food in weeks. Dooley kept an eye on Roosevelt, knowing Mr. Ants-in-His-Pants would be off to slaughter some wild animal before anyone's boots had a chance to dry. He and the old Boer had already spread a map, jawing in a hodgepodge tongue of their own. Maggie hovered nearby. Kermit joined her. Dooley moved closer to listen.

"Mr. Kruger says this is the last bit of veld that might hold big game," Kermit told the woman. "There's nothing but sand, scrub, and nomadic bandits beyond here. We'll be going out to look for white rhino in the morning. That's the last thing on the museum lists."

Maggie placed her hand on the boy's arm. "May I come with you?"

The kid's blush was visible from fifty feet away, though his face was tanned half as dark as some of the Africans. "I'll ask Pop. But I'd love to have you."

I'll bet you would.

The two Roosevelts and the woman went out together at first light. Dooley tried to join them, but Potter headed him off. "You're no use out there if you can't keep your ass in the saddle or hit what you're aiming at. Take one of the nags and go practice. Come back when you can hit something without falling off."

Dooley seethed, but there was no point arguing. He hadn't been alone with Roosevelt since before he'd nearly got them drowned trying to paddle across a lake the size of an ocean. Since then, Roosevelt was either off with his kid, adding to their collection of dead animals, or canoodling somewhere with the female reporter. Dooley knew that he needed to get close to the man if he was to finish the job. Time was running out.

Later, he wished he'd just shot the Boer when he had the chance. Jans had been gone two months, driving a wagonload of skins 1400 kilometers back to Nairobi, and no one was expecting him now. Killing him would have been easy. But Dooley didn't think of that until later. Potter had him out practicing his riding and shooting damn near every day, and that's how he spotted the Boer and his ox wagon rounding a *kopje* a few miles from camp, plodding along with its overdue cargo of salt and supplies. Distracted and in a pissy mood, Dooley didn't feel like having his ear bent by someone who hadn't spoken to another white man in months. So he rode on, leaving the Boer to make his way the last few miles to camp alone.

When he returned from his riding practice, Dooley found the porters unloading the supply wagon and Potter, Cunninghame, and the two Roosevelts raising glasses around the campfire, celebrating the Boer's return.

"I'd offer you a whiskey, Mr. Kruger," said Cunninghame from his canvas chair on the far side of the fire. "But we used it all up weeks ago. I take it you ran into trouble?"

The kid nodded, as if he'd been expecting the question. "*Ja*, the ox get the tsetse fly. The axle it broken in a *sloot*. I miss you late by three weeks at Kigoma, I think. Then we meet the *kaffirs* from the Congo! *Gott in himmel.*"

"We ran into them, too," said Kermit.

"*Ja?* Over the wagon they climb and hands under the salt to look for food."

"The ones with hands," said Cunninghame.

"I don't want to shoot them, man. So I take the wagon north."

Roosevelt put down his cup of tea. "How did you find us?"

"The *kaffirs* they ask at the villages. We hear you go into the *reënwoud*. There is not for wagons. So we turn back and think to find you on the *veld.*"

Cunninghame raised his cup. "Well, you arrived just in time. We're out of whiskey and damn near out of salt."

"I bring some both." He pitched a gourd at Kermit. "And this for my friend."

Roosevelt and Potter exchanged glances.

"We've had our own adventures," said Kermit, tucking the gourd under his chair. "Pop's big Holland blew up when we followed a wounded buffalo into some thorns. Then his horse dumped him in the middle of a river full of crocs."

"Kashama thinks the gun got plugged with termite mud," said Roosevelt.

The young Boer cocked his head as if he was trying to remember something. His expression was thoughtful and his eyes turned toward Dooley for a brief moment before slipping away. Dooley slipped his hand into his pocket and touched the handle of Mickey's sap. As Kermit continually added details to the misadventures, Dooley caught Jans looking again in his direction. The first glance was curious, the second one troubled.

When the evening wound down and people drifted off to their tents, Dooley returned to his own but couldn't sleep. His instincts told him to button the Boer kid, find out what was on his mind and settle it fast. He got up from his cot, slipped Mickey's sap into his hip pocket, and slipped down the darkened lane between the rows of canvas tents. Small cooking fires at the outskirts of camp glowed like crocodile eyes on a moonlit riverbank. The sound of voices raised in argument came from the clearing near the mess tent. He approached in silence and listened.

Kermit lifted a gourd to his lips and the Boer kid cut the air with the side of his hand to illustrate a slurred point. "I tell you, Kermit man. He asked me these things, what you tell me from your father's gun and his horse. Even the scorpion, he asked me."

Kermit put down the gourd, spilling some in the process. "They were accidents Jans. I was there."

"No, mate, listen. Kashama's a good boy. They don't give *bwana* a dirty gun. The mare got bit by a snake, maybe. But the other horse would jump, too, not stand."

"What are you saying?"

"I don't know, mate. But not accidents."

Dooley listened from the shadows, his hands moist in the cool evening air and his heart pounding. So the Boer kid remembered his persistent questions on jungle hazards. Maybe he'd also heard the taxidermist's warning about the effect of *pili pili* on horses. Even if he hadn't, it would come out soon enough when everyone started asking questions. Potter already knew that he had killed the native soldier back in Kilimanjaro. If Potter or Thompson put all the pieces together, neither would think twice about putting a bullet in their employee's head and leaving his carcass for the hyenas.

He needed to act fast. He'd come to Africa to kill a politician, not to get killed himself. Though things seemed to be setting up the other way now. He might be able to kill the Boer before he had a chance to share his suspicions. But Potter would never let him near Roosevelt alone if there was another unexplained death. He needed time, and he didn't have it.

Do something, Jimmy. Instinct, that time and again had saved his sorry carcass from jail and worse, screamed at him now. There were too many eyes on him. Potter was smart. Thompson was ruthless. How could he kill Roosevelt and get away with it if the whole camp started watching his every move? He needed time. The only way to get it was to get away.

Leaving the shadow of the fire and making his way back to his tent, he grabbed a rifle and filled a satchel with supplies. Then, when he was sure the camp was asleep, he slipped between the line of tents, found the horse that gave him the least trouble, and led it quietly into the night.

Chapter Twenty-Two

...the leopard didn't wait to be driven. Without any warning, out he came and charged straight at Kermit...

- Theodore Roosevelt, *African Game Trails*, 1910

Sunrise lay like a wafer of gold on a pewter horizon when Roosevelt woke Kermit at dawn the next morning. "There's a horse missing," he said. "And pad marks of a big leopard just outside camp."

Kermit groaned and rolled over in his cot.

Roosevelt tugged the boy's blanket until it slid to the ground. "Get dressed. We're going after it." He left his son fumbling into his clothes and strode off between the tents to the clearing where Cunninghame was questioning the *sais* who had reported the missing horse and the gun bearer who had found the leopard tracks.

"You'll want a shotgun," said Cunninghame. "It'll be close quarters if you find the leopard nearby. He'll either slip away when he gets wind of you, or he'll come right at you. You'll never get a rifle to your shoulder fast enough."

Roosevelt looked at the disheveled and glassy-eyed Kermit shuffling up the path between the rows of tents.

Cunninghame's eyes swiveled toward the boy and then back again. "There's no blood trail, which probably means the horse pulled its tether when it smelled the leopard and before the cat had the chance to attack. The other horses should have spooked, too. But maybe just the one got the leopard's smell and took off, then the leopard followed."

Roosevelt tightened the chinstrap on his slouch hat. "Do we go after it on horse or on foot?"

"Foot, if you've got the stomach for it. A big cat coming from behind can pull a man off a horse faster than he can pull his weapon. They're not afraid of men. We're just two-legged prey without hoof, horn, or claw. Easy dinner, once they've acquired the taste. You'll need to kill this one quickly or drive it off. A leopard hanging around a camp won't leave until it's had its fill."

Kermit remained silent, though he usually had a dozen questions in such situations. His skin looked the color of grease in an unwashed pan, and his eyes barely opened. Roosevelt barked the order. "Let's go."

"*Twende*," the gun bearer repeated for the benefit of the trackers.

Dry grass crumpled to puffs of chaff beneath the naked feet of the two trackers, the rising sun glinting off the metal blades of their spears. Roosevelt and the gun bearer followed at a distance, and Kermit trailed fifty yards behind them. Soft murmurs of excitement and frustration carried clearly in the crisp morning air, as one or the other tracker picked up the leopard's trail, lost it, and then found it again. Roosevelt thought it a nervy and dangerous way to follow an animal capable of fatal ambush. They weren't likely to sneak up on anything by trampling the dry savannah in search of spore. They would push it. And no matter the quarry—Montana grizzly bear or African leopard—a pushed animal's only choices are to run, hide, or attack. He didn't feel good about waiting to see which one this killer chose.

"*Huko*," said the gun bearer a short while later, gesturing toward a thick tangle of buffalo thorn surrounding a tall fever tree a quarter mile away. *There.* He called the trackers back. Kermit, who had been lagging behind, caught up. His face was pale and he sweated profusely.

"Are you okay, son?"

Kermit nodded. The gun bearer pointed to the copse of trees and spoke slowly and deliberately. Kermit's translation came between labored breaths. "He says the leopard is holed up in those thorns. Most likely it's watching us from up in that fever tree in the middle. Kashama wants to lead the trackers around to the other side of the trees to distract the leopard and keep its attention. He wants us to wait an hour and then start crawling toward the thorns. He says cats don't count well, and by then it may have forgotten that you and I are here."

Roosevelt hoisted his gun. "These shotguns aren't going to be much help if the leopard is up a tree."

Kermit gave his shotgun to the gun bearer, who handed him the Springfield rifle in return and said something in Swahili. "He was thinking the same thing."

The three Africans took off on a slow, wide arc toward the opposite side of the copse where the gun bearer said the leopard was hiding. The trackers strode upright, their metal spears balanced across their shoulders. The gun bearer brought up the rear, cradling the twin-barreled shotgun in his arms.

Though they had an hour to kill, Roosevelt decided it was better to remain silent lest the sound of their voices carry to where the leopard was hiding. He also needed time to think.

Kermit was drinking again, a lapse that made a father's heart ache. Roosevelt's younger brother Elliot had died from drink at the age of thirty-four. That Kermit might be cursed with the same affliction was a gut-wrenching nightmare. That he might come to the same end was intolerable. A loving parent could not allow that to happen.

But what could he do to change that terrible outcome? He would talk to the boy, of course. Again. Though talking had not halted Elliot's determined crawl to the gutter—a crawl that eventually became a sprint. Roosevelt looked at his son, snoring beneath a wide canvas hat. Where were the words to convince a nineteen-year-old of his mortality and the need to forgo what, for others, was an innocent pleasure? As a professional politician, Roosevelt knew the rhetorical tricks calculated to tap and stir emotion. Best suited for inspiring a willing crowd to a common purpose, such words had little impact beyond the moment. The passion of crowds, in adulation or anger, was impermanent. Lasting change requires a powerful and personal motivation. With it, one could achieve almost anything. Without it, change didn't last. If Kermit quit drinking on account of his father's words, he would return to it sooner or later in times of tension or ennui. Neither guilt, nor pleasing one's parent could inspire permanent change. Kermit had to find his own motivation. Change would not come or remain until he did.

When he judged that an hour had passed, he tapped Kermit's boot and walked his fingers through the sand in the direction of the trees where the gun bearer had said the leopard was hiding. Kermit nodded. Resting the barrel of the Fox 12-gauge across his forearms, Roosevelt led the way, inching forward on bent elbows and splayed legs. Kermit followed, Springfield rifle slung across his back and canvas hat strapped beneath his chin.

A layer of sweat, stems, and dirt covered the men from head to foot before they had gone a dozen yards. Clothes snagged on thorns and flesh endured the unceasing attack of flies and ants. Above them, the white-gold orb of the midday sun rose above the copse of buffalo thorn, sending every other living creature scurrying for burrow or shade. In stoic silence, they crawled to within a hundred yards of the thicket. Then, feeling a tap at his ankle, Roosevelt stopped. Kermit closed a circle of thumb and finger to his eye, signaling that they should scan the trees ahead.

The most likely place for the leopard to rest was in the branches of the tall fever tree at the center of the twenty-yard patch of buffalo thorn. Roosevelt put a hand over his useless left eye and looked up and down the smooth-barked tree. Straight white spines grew from the branch nodes in pairs. Small compound leaves created a thin green canopy that made the tree look farther away than it was. Every dappled patch of dark and light might be a leopard. He looked for the telltale swing of a tawny tail dangling below a horizontal tree limb, but he saw nothing. Kermit shook his head; he didn't see anything, either.

Roosevelt pointed to his ear. Until a moment ago, the grass and scrub around them had buzzed with the droning cacophony of bird and insect. Now, as a warm breeze wafting steadily from the north shifted in the direction of the thorns, the insect orchestra abruptly ceased. Roosevelt pointed to his nose. *If it's here, it can smell us!* He pointed to his son's rifle and then to the copse. Kermit turned to face the trees. Roosevelt pressed his back to his son's and faced the opposite direction. The small hairs on the back of his neck quivered, as if blown by a chill breeze. From an instinct passed down from prehistory, he didn't just sense the leopard nearby. He knew it was there and that it was close.

Roosevelt pressed his back against Kermit's, propping his forearm and shotgun on a half-bent knee. Kermit lifted the Springfield and held it ready at his shoulder.

The leopard made no sound. Roosevelt peered into the rippling screen of short brown grass. Kermit watched the copse of thorn and the scrub in front of it. The silence was louder than a drumroll. Then a perfectly camouflaged pattern of tan and brown appeared in focus no more than a dozen yards from Roosevelt's outstretched leg. His eyes met the leopard's. The animal's flank quivered just once before it sprang. Rear paws gripped cracked sandy ground. Clumps of dry earth flew to each side. The big cat flew through the air, yellow claws outstretched and gleaming, as sharp as surgical blades, jaws framed in ivory fangs ready to grab its prey and rip out its throat.

Roosevelt aimed the shotgun at eyes the color of burnished amber and pulled the trigger. The airborne leopard slammed into his chest, ripping the shotgun from his hands and twisting the finger wedged in the trigger guard. Kermit leapt to his feet and swung the Springfield like a club, smashing the six-foot leopard where it lay on his father's chest. When the leopard didn't move, and the body beneath it did, he knew which one of them was dead.

Roosevelt wriggled out from under the lifeless predator and struggled to his knees. Kermit stumbled into the dry scrub and vomited. The leopard lay on its side, oozing pink fluid into the sand. The flies returned.

Roosevelt looked at his grotesquely bent index finger and then extended his hand. "Help me with this."

Kermit stared and then turned to heave a second time. Letting go a breath that he'd likely been holding since first sensing the cat, Roosevelt took the bent finger in his other hand and yanked it straight with an audible pop. Kermit just stared.

The gun bearer and trackers showed up minutes later, jabbing the dead leopard with their spears, whooping, snapping their fingers, and chanting something over and over, the only word of which Roosevelt recognized was *chui*. Leopard. Kermit remained vacant-eyed and silent. When the Africans had finished skinning the leopard and had hung its pelt over a carrying pole, they started back to camp. Kermit had not said a word since before they'd left on hands and knees to what had almost been their funeral.

Roosevelt put his hand on his son's shoulder as they walked side by side through the dry grass. "I won't make a joke, like 'cat got your tongue?' We've both got a right to be a little shaken. That was a near thing."

Kermit broke his silence. "I never thought any real harm would come to us out here, Pop. Not when that snake fell out of the tree, not when that scorpion bit me. Not when we went into the thorns after that wounded buffalo, or when you fell into that river full of crocs.

All of that seemed like part of some grand, exotic adventure. But that leopard had murder in its eyes. You killed him, literally, at your throat."

Roosevelt squeezed his son's shoulder. "I don't mind telling you, I was terrified. I guess the Lord has further plans for me."

Kermit shuddered. "We should have had another shooter with us. Letting Kashama go off with the other gun was foolish."

"You're right. Next time, we'll bring Mr. Dooley along. Potter seems to have lost confidence in him after he fell off his horse in that river. But we won't be crossing any more croc-infested waters from here on."

Kermit looked away. "Maybe not him."

"Why? Mr. Dooley's no outdoorsman, but he thinks and acts fast. If he'd been with us, picking his teeth with a penknife, that leopard might have taken a blade between the eyes as well."

Kermit hesitated. "I'm not sure how to say this, Pop. But Jans thinks your gun blowing up and your horse going nuts in that river may not have been accidents."

"The Boer boy? That makes no sense. He wasn't here for any of that."

"Well, that's what he thinks, after I told him about what happened."

"While the two of you were celebrating with that *pembe* juice?" Kermit looked away. "All right," said Roosevelt, annoyed at having broached the subject of drinking in exactly the wrong way. "But I wouldn't encourage that kind of talk. Rumors can spread through a camp like smallpox. Next thing you know, people will be shooting at shadows outside their tents."

"I don't know, Pop. He says your gun wouldn't have blown like that from anything that could have gotten into it in those thorns. He says it had to be plugged."

Roosevelt removed his spectacles and pinched the bridge of his nose. "The gun bearer told me that termites got in there with their mud. How does Jans connect any of that to Mr. Dooley?"

Kermit looked down. "Well, we'd had a few gourds by then, but he says Dooley asked him a lot of questions about accidents on safari. Jans told him about scorpions and plugged guns."

"That's not enough."

"He said something about the horse that threw you, too. But I didn't quite follow. You should talk to him, Pop."

"Fine. Bring him and Mr. Dooley to the mess tent when we get back to camp. Jakobus, Potter, and Thompson, too. I want this straightened out. Fast."

Jans and his father arrived before the others. Roosevelt thanked the boy for his work getting the salt wagon safely back from Nairobi. Then, taking advantage of the others' tardiness, he spoke bluntly. "I need you to stop sharing *drank* with my son."

Jan pulled back his head as if he'd been slapped.

Roosevelt held up his hand. "You have every right to a bit of celebration after your long journey. You did a fine job. But unfortunately, my son is one of those men who can't stop once he starts. That's his problem, of course. Not yours. But I'm asking you not to share any more *bier* or *drank* with him while you remain with this safari."

Jans shrugged. His father remained impassive.

Roosevelt glanced down the row of tents, but there was no sign of Kermit or the others. "I should wait for everyone. But maybe you'll feel freer to speak if we start now. Kermit tells me you have some ideas about the gun that blew up in my face and the trouble I had with my horse."

Jans looked uncertain.

His father nodded. *"Praat, seun."*

Jans let out a pent-up breath. "Kermit, he told me your horse panic in the *stroom* with the *krok*, and the Dooley man stays calm next to it. I tell him that's not the way of horses, *bass.*"

"What else?"

Jans held one hand in the other and looked at his father. "I tell Pa, too, that the Dooley man asks me a lot of questions. How people get hurt on safari, he wants to know. I tell him *skerpioen* find the boot and Frau Botha with four husbands dead from plugged guns."

Roosevelt looked up to see Potter striding up the lane between the tents, followed by Thompson and Kermit. He waited for them to enter and then asked, "Where's Mr. Dooley?"

Potter looked grim. "According to the horse boys, he took off this morning."

"I checked his tent," said Kermit. "His rifle's missing. I'm not sure what else."

"Maybe his horse stepped in a hole," said Thompson. "Or he got lost."

Potter pressed a fist to his hand as if to control both. "The head sais sent a boy out to look for him when he wasn't back by midday. He said the trail leads back along ours and that the horse is moving at a pretty good pace."

Roosevelt looked from one to the other. "What do you make of that?"

"Not hurt," said Potter. "Maybe lost and following our trail in the wrong direction. Or maybe he's decided to go home. In a hurry."

Roosevelt turned to Thompson. "He's your man. What do you make of this?"

"I don't know, sir. He's not one of mine, actually. He was added to the crew by the fellow who hired us."

Roosevelt waved his hand. "Well, we can't be allowing deserters in this outfit. Not white ones, certainly. Mr. Dooley can spend a night on the veld. See how he likes it. But in the morning, we go after him. He can't have gone far."

"I think you should remain here, sir," said Thompson. "Your son explained that some of your accidents might not have been accidents. If this man means you harm, going after him could be riding into an ambush. That may be why he took off."

"*Ja*," said Kruger. "Let the hyenas get his scent. Two months' march to Nairobi, Jans can do. But this Dooley man is no bushman. He won't be alive one week."

Roosevelt fumed. "I don't like this one bit. Either Mr. Dooley is a bad operator, or he's a city-boy who got himself lost. In either case, we should go after him."

"I'll send two men with a tracker tomorrow," said Thompson. "They can follow him for a day or two. But if he keeps heading back the way we came, I'd say we've got a deserter, and I don't want one of my men getting shot trying to pick him up."

"The *veld* will take care of him," said Kruger. "Or the *kroks*, if he goes back into the *reënwoud*."

Roosevelt didn't like it, but Thompson was right to think of his men. Either Dooley was lost and would be happy to be rescued, or he wasn't and the savannah and jungle would do what by training and temperament Roosevelt would have preferred to do for himself—beat the stuffing out of him.

Dooley survived the first week, though finding clean water, edible food, and safe shelter required all his physical reserves, mental strength, and recently acquired outdoor craft. When he wasn't battling hunger, fatigue, and goddamn Africa, his thoughts turned to the balls-up he'd made of his mission to kill Roosevelt and the consequences to Mickey if he didn't finish the job. One whole morning passed as he sat on a rock, head in hands, thinking. Morgan had kept his part of the bargain. Mickey was out of prison. But if Morgan concluded that Dooley hadn't kept his, he'd have Mickey back in jail quick—or killed. Roosevelt had to die. It was that simple. The only way to make that happen was to stick close to the safari and survive.

The first night was a near thing. Bolting from camp into the scrum of the nighttime hunt and hunted might have been the quick path to being eaten alive. But two hundred sixty men carrying four tons of supplies and equipment leave a path of trampled grass that's hard to miss in moonlight. Following it put quick distance between him and any pursuers. Riding all night and half the next day, he stopped only when hunger, fatigue, and looming jungle made the decision for him. He had no intention of reentering that wet, slimy pestilence, veined with croc-infested rivers and snake-draped trees. Sheltering in the shade of a termite hill with a wall of impenetrable green at his back and a wide view of the veld, he remained all day watching for followers.

All he saw were the goddamn animals. A pale orange sun scorched the already withered grass and seared the backs of scattered herds that fed on it. He still had no idea what most of the animals were, but he could name the zebra and the thing that looked like a big deer, which he'd heard the natives called *tendalla*. He'd remembered the name because it sounded as if they were saying ten dollars, and he thought that a ridiculous price for a piece of meat. When the sun began its slow descent toward the horizon, he retraced his trail away from the dripping jungle and its insomniac monkeys and made a fireless camp in the boughs of a smooth-barked tree, high above the coughs and grunts of the nighttime prowlers.

In the morning, Dooley found a muddy water hole, the ground pockmarked with small-hooved animal prints. Most likely they came at night, because there was nothing there now, other than some small furry thing digging at the bottom of a nearby termite mound. It didn't look appetizing. But he was hungry, so he killed it. Then he did what he'd seen the natives do—slit it from ass to throat, pull out the insides, cut off the head, peel off the skin, and stick what was left on a sharpened stick over a small fire. He couldn't risk a fire at night. But no one could pick out a small flame on a shimmering semi-desert in the middle of the day. It was the first warm food he'd had since bolting camp and it made him sleepy. He lay back against the termite hill and thought of nothing.

Another night in the trees and another day of uneventful watching persuaded him it was safe to retrace his steps and try to stay within stalking distance of the safari. He would have to catch Roosevelt outside the camp, and that meant getting close, remaining concealed, and staying alive.

Sleeping in trees at night kept him safe from lions, hyenas, snakes, and fire ants. Riding before dawn and after dusk allowed him to catch up to the safari without being spotted. He found them on day ten at the edge of the veld, where the grass ended and the scrub and sand began. The nights there were chilly, and the trees stunted and few. The air tasted like sand. He hid his horse and kit on the far side of a low hill to the west of the camp, and from there he watched the comings and goings of the safari, cinching his belt tighter while he waited for a chance to catch Roosevelt alone.

The politician rode out of camp early each morning, accompanied by his son and a gun bearer. Sometimes they stayed out all day. Other times they returned to camp at noon and went out again later. Twice, the newspaper woman went with them. During the day, Dooley watched from the boulder-strewn *kopje* near the safari camp. At night, he returned to a copse of trees near a water hole a few miles beyond. After a week of following the daily routine, he decided his best chance of killing Roosevelt would be to attack when the kid went off after some poorly hit animal and took the gun bearer with him. He could use Mickey's sap to lame Roosevelt's horse so it looked like it took a tumble and Roosevelt fell and snapped his neck.

It wasn't much of a plan, but the heat, cold, hunger, and thirst weren't inspiring better. Hot days, cold nights, and poor food were taking a toll on his mind and body. His strength was slipping away, and his thoughts turned more and more toward his own survival. One morning, he awoke spewing from every orifice and crawled to the watering hole to strip and clean himself. Afterwards he lay shivering in the sun, trying to summon the strength necessary to return to his vigil. Eyes closed and shivering, he didn't hear or see the five turbaned men on unshod horses until one got close enough to fling a rope around his neck and yank him to his feet.

Chapter Twenty-Three

It is not all pleasure this exploration.

- Dr. David Livingstone (journal entry made a few days before his death in March 1873 near Ilala, Central Africa)

Rutega Ben Kis and his men made camp on a sandy hill above the wide swath of trampled earth that he and his band of Sudanese bandits had been following for three days. It wasn't a fresh trail, but it was temptingly large. He hoped to catch the caravan that made the trail and steal as many of their animals and supplies as his men could carry. The sickly straggler's horse and gun were a promising start. He wasn't young or pretty enough to fetch a price as a slave, and it cost food and trouble to keep a man alive, especially a sick one. If the wretch had no other value, they would keep his goods, cut his throat, and leave his carcass for the *fisi*.

He ordered his men to tie the prisoner to a thorn bush. Then he questioned the *mzungu* in the simple British he had learned trading horses with the infidels at Khartoum. "You wish food? Water?"

The *mzungu* tried to nod, but hemp around his neck kept his head immobile against the crooked wood. "Yes," he whispered.

"What will you pay?"

The *mzungu* pretended not to understand, so Rutega kicked him. "You wish fire this night? Or *fisi* to eat your belly?"

"Fire," he croaked.

"What will you pay?"

The infidel's words were an indistinct groan. But the bandit leader recognized the name of the white prophet, *Yesu*. Perhaps it was a prayer. "Yes. Ask your *Yesu*." He pointed to the sun and traced its journey to the horizon. "At *juna chini* you will say how you will pay. Or *fisi* will come this night and eat your face!"

Dooley tried to calm his pounding heart and churning bowls. He

lowered his head and glanced sideways at the bandit's tea-colored pro-
file—ritually cut, tattooed, and half-hidden by a faded cotton turban
that may once have been blue. Some of the cutthroat's words sounded
like English. The rest were African gibberish. But the message was
clear; the desert hooligans wanted more from their prisoner than just
his horse and gun. If he didn't give it to them, they'd do him the nasty.

He hadn't had a drink of water since first light. His head felt like a
baking pot and his tongue like a slab of dried fatback. His gut churned
incessantly, but it no longer leaked since there was nothing left to come
out. He closed his eyes and begged his brain to come up with something to save his carcass from the hyenas. *Think,* boyo*! What malarkey
will these dark devils swallow?* But brain and body were past responding.
Sun-tortured limbs trembled as if chilled. Tears fell, unbidden and
unwanted. *We're in a pickle now, Mickey.*

His eyes hurt when he tried to open them, though there was little to
see other than a burning orb in a cloudless sky and shimmering sand
and scrub below it. The heathens lay in the shade of a fat tree, arguing.
About him? The Boer guide had warned Roosevelt not to stray too
far north, that beyond the Uganda grass belt, there was only sand and
bandits. What a pompous ass! After nearly drowning them on that big
lake, you'd think he might have learned to listen to his betters!

Thoughts wandered without direction, irritable and at times in-
coherent. But when the sun touched the horizon, a ribbon of pink
spread across the shimmering sand, and the air began to cool. So, too,
did Dooley's fevered mind. The bandits left their shady place and knelt
in a row to chant their heathen prayers. Never mind Roosevelt. What
he needed now was a simple lie to soothe the filthy bastards so they
wouldn't feed him to the hyenas come nightfall. When the chanting
was over, the one who had spoken in English kicked him again. "Pay
now!"

"Four tons of salt," he blurted, pulling numbers and inspiration out
of thin air. "Six horses. Twelve rifles."

The bandit laughed. "Your prophet made wine from water, *bismillah
al-rahman.* Would he make horses from sand to save your unworthy
carcass?"

"All that trampled grass leads to rifles and horses. I can help you
steal them."

The bandit frowned. "We are only five. A caravan that cuts the earth so wide has a hundred men or more." The bandit squatted so that he was eye to eye with his prisoner. "How can five steal from so many?"

Dooley strained at the cord that bound his neck to the thorn branch. "Only six have guns. Take a white man, like you did me, and a black man. Then send the black man back to the camp with a message for the safari leader. Five guns and three horses for me and the other white man you take."

"Twelve guns and six horses, you say?"

Dooley tried to shake his head, but the cord bit into his neck. "He'll give up five guns and three horses without a fight. It leaves him enough to still defend the camp."

"Twelve guns and six horses," the bandit repeated.

"Two hundred men with bundles on their heads make a folkin' long line. The whites with guns have to spread out to protect them. If you know which ones have the guns, you can kill them easy. I'll show you who they are."

The bandit grunted, "You would steal from your own tribe?"

Dooley smiled and dipped his chin, though it made the cord bite into his throat, choking his words. "The man leading the safari has my brother in jail. My brother goes free if the safari leader dies. So I don't give a rat's ass if you take all his guns and horses. Easier for me to catch and kill him."

The bandit made a face that was half-smile, half-snarl. Revenge, it seemed, was a motive he understood.

Stars glittered in a coal-black sky, indifferent to the fate of things below. Dooley struggled to banish gruesome thoughts of being eaten alive by hyenas, while his captors debated his fate into the wee hours. At sunrise, the turbaned kicker came to deliver their verdict. "You live one more day." He dropped a calabash of water in Dooley's lap.

"Food?" asked Dooley.

The bandit laughed.

Roosevelt leaned forward over his horse's neck and peered at a lone acacia tree, which split the horizon. Something that might have been an enormous rhino grazed behind it, partially blocked from view. He

raised his hand to alert Kermit and Maggie, who had been riding behind him, deep in conversation for most of the morning. He and Kermit usually hunted alone, while the others remained in camp to skin,
preserve, pack, and load. But since Maggie had joined the safari and
they were finally out of the jungle, he had invited her to come on the
morning hunt. Kermit was less moody when she was around, and she
treated his boyish attentions with a maternal affection that gave their
outings the pleasant glow of a family picnic.

Kermit lifted the Springfield from its scabbard and slid off his horse.
"I think it's a white."

Roosevelt squinted. "I don't see any cover for a stalk."

"Trust me, Pop." Kermit raised the rifle to his shoulder, took aim,
and gently squeezed the trigger. A dozen yards in front of the rhino, a
puff of sand lifted from the ground. The animal didn't move.

"That's a long shot, son. Four or five hundred yards."

Kermit grinned, raised the rifle a fraction, and squeezed off another
shot. A long second later, Roosevelt heard the *thwack* of bullet striking
flesh and watched the rhino take off at a gallop. Kermit jumped on his
horse and rode after it. The tracker trotted behind.

Roosevelt fought the impulse to heel his horse and join the chase;
he and Maggie had not been alone since Cunninghame's farm, but he
couldn't leave an unarmed woman unprotected, even though he felt
awkward and unprepared for what might come next.

Neither looked at the other as they slipped from their horses. Puffs
of dust marked Kermit's progress toward the horizon while they
watched in a silence unnatural to both of them. He picked up a stick
and traced lines in the sand.

"If that's a white rhino and Kermit doesn't lose it," he said to break
the awkward silence, "that's the last specimen on the museums' lists.
We can start for home."

He didn't mean to startle her, but his words seemed to have that effect. Maggie opened her mouth, but no sound came out. When words
came, they were strained and awkwardly pitched. "Your family will be
happy to see you."

He looked away. "The Smithsonian is supposed to have a boat waiting for us at Khartoum. The plan was to go down the Nile from there
as far as Alexandria and then pick up a steamer to Europe."

She remained silent.

"I'd like you to join us." The words came without forethought, though he had no desire to take them back. He wanted her to join him. He was not just being polite.

Maggie took a minute before she spoke, and it was a question, not an answer. "Will there be anyone to meet you in Khartoum?" Her voice was a whisper and her eyes would not meet his.

"Reporters, if word has gotten out. The Egyptian consul knows our approximate arrival date, and he can't keep a secret worth a damn."

"Only reporters?"

He knew what she was fishing for. He'd thought of it, too, the instant the words were out of his mouth. "Edith," he said, not wishing to be deceitful. He searched for words, caught by conflicting emotion. "But it's not certain. She wasn't happy with my going on this safari. Or with my taking Kermit. But the plan was for her to try and meet us in Khartoum."

Maggie looked away.

He spoke again because he felt compelled, though the words were not what he wanted. "Cunninghame will be taking the column back to Kapiti. If you prefer, you can return with him."

Her expression was unreadable. Surely it wasn't possible, after all this time…she couldn't still… He shook off the childish thought. The truth was he didn't want her to go. It was as simple and as complicated as that.

Maggie met his gaze. "I must think this over, Teddy, and so should you." She folded her hands and turned away.

He stared at the horizon and frowned. Maggie's words, heavy with meaning, lingered in the air between them. He paced beneath the branches of a knob thorn, trying to think. What was taking Kermit so long? He listened for the shot that would mean that Kermit had caught up with the rhino. But all he heard was the bray of far-off zebras and the buzz of nearby cattle flies. The longer Kermit was gone, the more likely it was that he would not return for hours.

Releasing a cloud of pent-up breath, he stole a glance at Maggie. Her eyes remained fixed on something far away. He shifted his gun from hand to hand, unable to remain still. Maybe it was best the safari ended now. He'd done what he'd come to do. The decision about what path to take next was always going to be difficult and complicated, even without the unplanned opening of a long-healed wound. A deep sadness settled over him, but he felt no urgency to shake it.

The blue-turbaned bandit with the horse trader English kicked Dooley awake and dropped a calabash of water into his lap. "Drink. Then ride." Dooley lifted the gourd and drained it, feeling lightheaded and almost weepy with relief. It was late afternoon, and at the edge of the encampment, the scrub and sand were painted a burnt orange laced with exaggerated shadow. It would be dark in an hour.

The bandits brought Dooley his horse, and the five of them rode until almost sunset before stopping at the crest of a sandy hill that overlooked a wide expanse of grass and low thorn. "There!" The bandit leader gestured with an outstretched arm. "A white has killed a *faro*. The *kaffir* cuts it with a knife."

Dooley saw nothing but short windblown thorn and grass, but his pulse raced at the bandit's words and his throat tightened. If there was a white man out there butchering some animal, it had to be the politician or his kid. "Young or old?" he asked.

The bandit cocked his head. "He is without beard, as you can see."

Dooley squinted. He saw a bit of movement, but it could have been anything. "I'm hungry, and I can't see a damn thing. But a white man with no beard is the son of the boss man. Take him, and the boss will give half his horses and bundles for the boy's return."

The bandit's lack of response made Dooley wonder if his captors, like the weaker gangs of Five Points, preferred the easier pickings of unarmed men. But eventually, four of the bandits rode off in the direction of Roosevelt's kid and his dead animal. The one with the English remained behind.

"Come," he ordered. "There are two whites more. Not far." He took the reins of Dooley's horse and led them down the rise and across the open scrub in the direction of a raised point on the horizon. The sun had nearly disappeared when the bandit slid from his horse and motioned for Dooley to do the same. He started to ask a question, and the bandit silenced him with the back of his hand. "*Aammus!*" He didn't need a translation. "Blind Englishman, we are close."

The bandit tethered the horses to a thorn tree at the base of a small rise and then motioned Dooley to climb quietly to the top of the hill. At the crest, the bandit dropped to his stomach and pointed to a small copse of trees a quarter mile in the distance. Dooley felt his heart clench. There, with his back against a darkened tree and his face half-covered by a slouch hat, slumbered the fattest bull's-eye in the amusement park.

"*Piga!*" he hissed, using one of the few African words he'd learned in almost a year. "Shoot!"

The bandit backhanded him again. "Would you kill a she-goat fat with milk? Is that not the one who would pay with horses and guns?"

There was no time to argue. Dooley reached into his pocket for Mickey's sap. But of course it wasn't there. They'd taken that, too. The turbaned African looked at him hard and then dragged him by the hair down the hill.

"Teddy, there are men with guns on that hill," Maggie whispered.

Roosevelt raised his head and looked toward a low rise of ground halfway to where Kermit had shot the rhino. At first he saw nothing. Then a smear of pale blue moved in the dry scrub. Something beside it moved too. He squinted harder and made out two figures lying prone in the sand. "Can you see rifles?"

"The one with the turban is holding something. But it doesn't look like any rifle I've ever seen."

He squinted again, as the last rays of a setting sun fell on the telltale barrel bands of a Moroccan Snaphaunce musket. Then the figures were gone. "We should move." He spoke calmly, hoping to impart an emotion he didn't feel. Turbans and muskets were the kit of the nomad bandits that the old Boer had warned about. Roosevelt led the horses to a copse of knob thorns and Maggie to the gully behind them. From there, with his back against a termite hill, he held his Winchester on the rise, where the two men had disappeared, and waited until the metal bead at the end of the rifle blended into darkness.

Maggie had said little since she'd told him to think things over. He had to admire her calm and poise. But with darkness nearly upon them and nothing left to watch, the silence once again felt uncomfortably awkward. "We'll have to stay here the night," he apologized, wincing at the words as soon as they left his mouth and wishing he could take them back, or at least rephrase them. His pulse throbbed. Not at the danger, which was real enough, but at the reality of their aloneness. Where was Kermit?

Maggie's face was obscured by darkness, but her voice was clear and oddly modulated. "Won't your Mr. Potter send some men to find us when we don't return?"

"If Kermit made it back to camp, yes. Otherwise, he'll assume we're all together and have decided to bivouac in a safe place rather than trek back across unfamiliar territory in the dark."

"Then we're alone for the night." It was a statement, not a question.

"We are." It came out a whisper.

"Should I be alarmed?"

Yes, he thought. But he didn't want to frighten her. "I imagine those fellows out there are much like our cowboy rustlers—poor men looking for easy pickings. They'll be happy with a horse and a saddle, if they can get it easily. But they won't risk a gunfight. We'd be in more danger from lions and hyenas if we try to make it back to camp in the dark."

Her voice drifted through the darkness, light and almost flirtatious. "I didn't mean alarmed by them."

Blood rushed to the places it does in such moments. He, of the inexhaustible supply of words, found himself once again without any.

"Should we climb one of those trees near where you tied the horses? Pere de Clercq told me that if you can't make a fire, you should climb a tree."

That wouldn't stop a lion or a leopard. But there was no point mentioning it. "Good idea. We'll be safer off the ground." He led the way to a mopane tree next to the copse of thorns, made a stirrup of his hands, and watched Maggie gather her skirts and climb into the branches. Then he hoisted himself up and settled into the crook beside her, trusting its thick limbs to hold their combined weight.

Points of distant light began to fill the inky sky. He squinted into the starlit shadows and listened hard. Maggie resumed her silence. He didn't think she was scared. Her poise, under the circumstances, was remarkable. A hyena called to its fellows. The tree rustled as Maggie adjusted her weight.

"Teddy, what if someone who wants to harm you sent those men?"

The thought had occurred to him. Especially on account of that fake Pinkerton deserting the camp in such a hurry. But he tried to reassure her. "I don't think so. How would someone find us out here? And why would they bother?"

The hyenas cackled again, closer this time.

"There's something I must tell you." At her words, his breath stilled and his other senses tuned to her presence. He had no premonition of what might be coming. "When I sent my stories with yours in the wagon to Nairobi, I also sent a report to my employer, Randolph Hearst."

Roosevelt felt cold and deflated. "About what?"

"Those poor, maimed Congolese."

"And?"

"Your sympathy for them."

The icy fingers of an invisible hand gripped his heart and squeezed. "Did you tell him what I told Sergeant Fussner about letting Germany take the Congo from King Leopold?"

"No, Teddy. I promised not to do that. But if Mr. Hearst shares my reports with others and it's believed that you'll help the Congolese if you regain the White House…if that got back to King Leopold…"

Roosevelt expelled a breath and lied, not to spare her feelings but to conceal his own. "I'm sure those were just a couple of local brigands out there."

Thompson had insisted that the knife-wielding attacker on board the *Hamburg* was a professional, not some crazed anarchist as they had decided to tell the newspapers. He had not wanted to believe it then. But if true, it would be naïve to think that whoever sent the first assassin would not send a second. Or a third. Hearst would surely share Maggie's reports with his confidantes, some of whom were powerful men whose fortunes had fallen under the Roosevelt presidency and would suffer more if he regained the White House. If those men drew the same conclusions as Maggie and assumed he would run for president again… Well, violence had been a part of American politics since Burr shot Hamilton, and it was not going to change any time soon.

Closing his eyes, Roosevelt tried to recall the blurry image of the two men lying prone on a distant hill. Kruger had warned him about Fulani bandits. If both men had been wearing the Fulani turban, they might have been just a couple of local bad boys. But one was bare-headed and a shade lighter than his turbaned companion.

"Kruger says the locals get busy this time of year. Khartoum is close for fast horsemen, though it will take the safari a month to get there on foot."

"You have to get back to the United States, Teddy. As fast as you possibly can."

Do I? Sitting up a tree, literally as well as figuratively, he felt strongly that it was time to decide what to do next with his life. There was no point putting it off any longer. The familiar path was politics. But providence, or its opposite, had called his attention to another possibility, one outside of politics, class, and everything that had defined his life until then, and it was exerting a powerful, almost tidal pull.

"You have to go," Maggie repeated. "You're not safe here."

"Have you ever been to Montana?" His voice was soothing and uncharacteristically gentle. "A man could live a bully life out there."

"Montana!" Her tone was incredulous and almost shrill. "You have a duty, Teddy!"

The calm that had momentarily enveloped him felt torn as if by a blow. *Balderdash!* He paused to calm himself. Maggie was scared. He hadn't prepared her. In the strangely silent darkness, he closed his eyes and tried again. "What I'm trying to say, Maggie, is that you were right. Threats are meaningless if they're not backed by power. The leader of sixty-five million war-fevered Germans will just laugh at a powerless private citizen who presumes to bully him. If I wanted to bring peace to Europe, confront Leopold, and fix the other ills of this world, I should never have left the White House. But I did, of my own free will. To challenge a sitting president of my own party now would be hubris, plain and simple. I'll get my hat handed to me. Deservedly so."

He paused to let the truth of his words sink in.

"Nonsense!" she exploded. "Europe is about to erupt in war. You can stop it, Teddy. Taft can't. England and France won't. Millions of young men will die if you don't win back the presidency and use it as only you can. A mad despot will continue to enslave millions of Africans, while his neighbors do nothing. How can you turn your back on that responsibility?"

He tried to soothe her and to make her see sense. "Listen to me, Maggie. I'd like nothing more than to stop this war and to kick that Belgian vampire off his bloody throne. But no political party is going to dump their own sitting president for a Cassandra who left by choice and then changed his mind after swatting mosquitoes in the jungle for a year. The party bosses control the convention. They'll have to stick with Taft, or they'll be out of jobs and the party will be out of power. It can't happen."

She wouldn't listen. "Taft is not Theodore Roosevelt. The bosses will take you back with open arms. The Hearst newspapers—"

"Will eviscerate me, Maggie. Randolph Hearst is no friend of mine. Hell, he wants to be president himself."

"You're making excuses."

"I'm facing facts."

"You're quitting."

"No, Maggie. Here in this tree, in the middle of the African savannah, I'm facing them square. I intend to live a meaningful life. Always. But from now on, it will be a life outside of politics. It has to be. President Taft gave me his word that he'd carry out my policies, and I must trust him. I gave him my word, as well. I have to remain worthy of that trust."

Her face was unreadable. He had no idea if his words were getting through.

"Schoolboy nonsense! Taft can't stop the kaiser. Or King Leopold. You can. What else matters?"

Maggie was the *R* in relentless. He'd almost forgotten how stubborn she could be. And how smart. They argued into the night. Everything came pouring out—her impassioned view of duty, his for practical results. She refused to be moved. Then shortly before dawn, she placed her hand on his. It was the first time he had felt her touch since that day in Union Square Park over thirty years before. He felt as if their hands had been fused by one of Mr. Edison's magnetos. Neither spoke. As night turned to morning and the sky in the east turned a soft, promising pink, he held her hand and allowed his mind to take them both to new places.

Chapter Twenty-Four

Far better it is to dare mighty things, to win glorious triumphs, even though checkered by failure, than to take rank with those poor spirits who neither enjoy much nor suffer much, because they live in the gray twilight that knows not victory nor defeat.

- Theodore Roosevelt

Roosevelt and Maggie returned to camp with their tale of ambush and escape. He feared his guilty musings must be writ large on their faces, but what he found instead was a camp in turmoil, unquestioning and overjoyed that he and Maggie were still alive. A tracker, presumed deserted, had stumbled into camp at first light with the harrowing tale of his abduction by a band of Fulani bandits and the news that Kermit and the missing Pinkerton, Dooley, had been captured by the same gang.

Kermit captive! Roosevelt tried to keep the emotion from his face as Kruger translated the tracker's story. The bandits had released him to convey their demands: twelve rifles, six horses, and one hundred thirty bundles of cargo.

Thompson looked worried. "That's almost half our guns."

"*Ja*, and supplies," said Kruger.

Jans looked from one to the other, disbelieving. "We ride now, man! The *kaffir* say they are only five."

Roosevelt held up his hand. "I want an inventory of guns, ammunition, and supplies, Mr. Thompson. Mr. Kruger, I want all the information you can get from this tracker about the bandits and their camp. Numbers, weapons, supplies, and geography. I want to know how their camp is laid out and how it's protected. Then I want you both to meet me in my tent in twenty minutes."

Maggie grabbed his arm. "You're not going to give up a few guns and supplies to save your son's life?"

"Mr. Kruger, do you think this is the only band of brigands between here and Khartoum?"

197

The old Boer shook his head. "Fulani horsemen ride everywhere now the rains end."

"Could we pay off this bunch and retrace our route back to the coast?"

"Without half our guns and goods? First, we starve. Then they slaughter us."

He placed his hand on Maggie's arm and held her gaze. Both heart and head had powerful voice, but only one could lead. Stepping from the mess, he returned to his tent to wait for Thompson and Kruger to bring the information they would need to plan an attack.

Kermit's uncovered head felt like marbled meat broiling under the ferocious equatorial sun. His wrists and ankles swelled on either side of the hemp that bound him and his fellow captive. The toppled fever tree to which they were tied gave little protection from the stinging windblown sand and the bright yellow cauldron overhead. He tried to question Dooley about the bandits' strength, weapons, and routines while their captors rested in the shade of their tents. But the wretch's answers were little more than feeble groans and weary head shakes. If Dooley had observed anything during his captivity, the Pinkerton deserter was in no condition to share it. He was clearly ill and possibly dying.

Thinking to provoke his attention, Kermit shared the camp consensus that Dooley was nothing more than an incompetent assassin. "Everyone thinks you tried to kill the colonel with some jungle tricks you learned from Jans, but that you're too much of a city boy to make them work."

An eyelid parted the width of a blade of grass and a half dozen words passed Dooley's cracked lips in labored puffs of breath. "Idjits...saved his...folkin' life..."

"You took a knife away from a skinny anarchist when you knew the other Pinkertons were right behind you. But when the Boer who told you about plugged guns came back from Nairobi and heard what happened to Pop, you made a run for it. You knew he would figure out what you did and tell us."

Dooley moaned. "Didn't run...got snatched...like you."

Kermit stared at his fellow prisoner. No one had considered the possibility that the Pinkerton's disappearance may have been involuntary. No one had even known the bandits were around. But it hardly mattered now. Pop was alive and Dooley was neither a danger nor a help. The thought that his father and Mrs. Dunn might also be captive or dead was a torment—both were possible. Too much to drink, a bad shot on a rhino, then bushwhacked by a bunch of desert cowboys, leaving Pop and Mrs. Dunn to face god knew what. Could he have failed worse?

When the sun had nearly finished its afternoon torture, the bandits left the shade of their tents and gathered on prayer rugs to kneel and touch foreheads to the ground. One chanted what Kermit assumed was Koranic verse while the others responded. When they were finished, someone started a fire and began cooking the communal meal. Night fell. The temperature followed. One of the bandits brought the prisoners a drink from a calabash of water but no food or fire.

The cold desert night kept Kermit awake while he rocked his body back and forth, hugging his shoulders, trying to ward off the cold. Bandit voices carried clear in the still night air, though he had no idea what they were saying.

The Pinkerton hadn't moved since early afternoon. Only his chest, rising and falling in the rhythm of the not yet dead, gave any hint that he was still alive. How long had it been since he had last eaten, and how much longer would he live? A healthy man might survive weeks without food as long as he had clean water, but the Pinkerton looked like a dying man. If he'd been without food since he disappeared from camp, the end might be close.

Overhead, a tapestry of winking stars threw silent shadows across a broken landscape of rustling grass, gleaming stones, and gnarled twists of thorn and scrub. A sharp, strange noise issued from the tumble of dry scrub a dozen yards away. Kermit recognized with a shudder the eerie donkey bray, dog yelp, and hog grunt sounds of the ventriloquist hyena. His heart began to drum and his mind to race. A dozen yards from where he sat tied to the comatose Dooley, two pairs of eyes glowed with reflected moonlight. The outline of a dog's face, lion's ears, and crippled hindquarters was unmistakable. Kermit drove his hand into Dooley's side.

"Wake up!" Dooley groaned and remained motionless. The glowing amber eyes advanced in tandem. Kermit fanned his palm along the ground, feeling for something to throw. But the bandits had been thorough in removing the loose sticks and stones from around their prisoners' tether. "Ha!" he shouted. The amber eyes paused in their advance. Then a single pair moved forward in front of the other. "Ha!"

An answering shout came from the bandits' fire. Someone stood and peered in their direction. "*Fisi!*" Kermit shouted. The man laughed and returned to the circle of light and warmth. The hyena swung its dog face toward the bandits' fire and then back toward its prey. It advanced another step. "Ha!" There was nothing else to do.

This time, the scavenger didn't pause. Undeterred, it slid one padded foot in front of the other until its hairy snout hovered an inch above Dooley's outstretched boot. Kermit swung his own boot at the animal's side, but it was short by several inches. The hyena skipped to one side and opened a fanged mouth designed by nature to crush bones and extract marrow from animals that weighed half a ton. With a loud, wet clap, its jaws snapped together like matched cleavers over the end of Dooley's boot.

"Ahhh!!" The panicked cry proved that the Pinkerton was still among the living, but it had no effect on the predator. The hyena tore at the poor man's foot until the end of his boot ripped apart, and with it one of Dooley's toes. The Pinkerton's scream brought the bandits from their fire. A line of spears and burning brands forced the snarling animal to retreat. One of the bandits cut Dooley's bonds, dragged him to the fire, and stuffed a dirty rag into what was left of his boot.

The blue-turbaned English speaker came and squatted next to Kermit, lifting his chin with a gritty fist. "Tomorrow you pay. Or *fisi* will eat your stomach." Then he drew a knife, cut Kermit's bonds, and dragged him to the fire beside the groaning Dooley.

Sleep didn't come that night. The bandits' snores and Dooley's moans merged with the cacophony of howls and screeches from beyond the fire that kept the night hunters at bay. Kermit was still awake at dawn. As the sun lifted from the horizon, he saw a dust cloud rise with it and grow larger and closer with each passing minute. There were no herds this far north. It had to be horses. Could it be Pop and the others?

He shook the nearly comatose Dooley. "Wake up! The colonel's coming."

Dust rolled across the broken landscape, accompanied by the sound of hooves pounding dry earth. The bandits emerged from their tents carrying muskets and spears. Half took positions behind scattered boulders, training their muskets on the approaching cloud. The others ran for their horses. The dust cloud stopped a hundred yards from camp, thinned, and drifted away to reveal a line of fifty armed horsemen. Kermit's heart sank. Unless Pop had traded his slouch hat and khaki shirt for a turban and cotton robe, this wasn't a rescue. It was more trouble.

The bandits raised their rifles and greeted the new arrivals with a volley of shots in the air. One of the newcomers dismounted and advanced to confer with the blue-turbaned English speaker. After a short palaver, they came together to inspect the prisoners.

"Son of a king!" the newest bandit barked in guttural English. "Your father must have many sons to put so little value on you."

So Pop's alive.

"I disappoint him," Kermit muttered, realizing too late that no answer was better than the wrong one. *They know who I am.*

The new bandit nodded, as if the prisoner's answer were a missing puzzle piece. "And if thy father dies, who has claim to the rifles and horses he will not part with to keep his disappointing son alive?"

Kermit shrugged.

The bandit kicked him. "You will talk, *abn malak*." He shouted something to the men on horseback and Kermit watched five of them ride off in the direction of the safari.

Roosevelt put the porters to work cutting thorn to create a barricade around the camp while he tried to reassure the others with a bully speech about not being unduly concerned about five poorly armed nomads. He asked Kruger to reconnoiter the Fulani camp and confirm the porter's information about its layout and defenses. He tried to think of everything. There could be no repeat of the near disaster on the lake. The consequences could not be higher.

Kruger mounted his horse, tightened the chinstrap of the slouch hat Roosevelt had given him, and checked the rifle scabbard. "We should attack tonight. When the *kaffir* see the thorns, they know you will not trade. Then they do something to change your mind."

He had the kindness not to say, "To Kermit."

Rutega and the leader of the new arrivals had been debating the division of coming spoils for most of the day and had yet to reach the point of repetition, a measure of both the importance of the matter and the experience of the debaters. They were still at it when the riders who had left to reconnoiter the safari camp returned to report that a barrier of cut thorns had been erected around the camp, and that nothing had come in or gone out for several hours.

Rutega stood at the front of the low cotton tent and looked in the direction of the safari camp. "Two hundred men cannot sit long behind thorns with no water."

His companion nodded. "They'll need meat, and their horses grass."

Rutega called to a sharp-faced man whetting the blade of a long metal spear with a stone. "Ride with your brothers to this wall of thorns. Kill the first white who comes out."

The man bowed his head and then rode with three others toward the safari camp.

Kruger found the *kaffirs'* camp on a small rise about two kilometers east of the safari *boma*. With the sun at his back, he scanned the hill with a pair of field glasses that he'd taken at Mafeking from a numbskull British officer who thought he could face them into the sun and remain unseen. The hill was steep—though no more than a hundred meters long—barren of scrub and grass, and topped by a tumble of chair-sized boulders and broken scrub. Portions of low *kaffir* tents showed between the boulders. Many men moved between the tents. Too many.

The porter had either lied about their number or had been too scared to count properly. There were at least fifty of the rag-headed dogs, not five. He scanned the hilltop for horses. Likely they had been tethered on the far side of the hill in whatever shade might be there. He lowered the field glasses and scanned the slope, memorizing fissures and gullies that might help or hinder the coming attack. A gully rimmed with boulders snaked across the bottom of the hill. Above, the ground was bare. Shadows shifted with the waning sun, revealing what had been hidden a short while ago and concealing what he had committed to memory. The terrain was as bad as it could possibly be—a steep, sandy hill barren of cover. An attacking force in daylight would be slaughtered.

As the setting sun hovered above the horizon, Kruger raised the glasses for a final look at the hilltop camp. Horses that had been hidden in shadow now appeared picketed along the slope behind the tents. Too many to count. Near them, two white men lay tied to a broken tree surrounded by a patch of bare ground. One shifted his limbs from time to time. The other made no movement. Trussed in the open under an African sun, neither would survive very long.

Kruger tucked the glasses into his shirt and made his way back to the tethered horse, then rode as hard as he could toward the safari camp. The report he had to give was grim. A frontal assault would be suicidal. The two white prisoners lay staked in the sun like animals. One might be dead already. A quick trade might be the only way to save whomever was still alive.

It was nearly dark when Kruger reached the barricade. Slowing his horse to a walk, he shouted for someone inside to make an opening. *"Hodi!"*

"Karibu, Bwana." As a dozen porters cut away a section of thorns, the telltale click of a musket hammer sounded from behind a nearby mopane tree. A lead ball whistled past Kruger's ear, followed by a metal-tipped spear that caught him high on the back of the leg. Clinging to the horse's neck, he dug his heels into the animal's ribs and lunged through the opening in the thorns.

Rutega looked up as the three horsemen who had ridden off at dawn thundered back into camp, leapt off their horses, and fired their muskets into the air. He listened to their tale and then went to question the infidel prisoners.

"Oh, disappointing son of a king. What does thy father look like? Is he tall? Short? Fat? Thin? This I would know."

"A newspaper cartoon," said the boy.

Rutega kicked him in the ribs. "We have killed an unbeliever and I would know who he is!"

"What does he look like?" groaned the other *mzungu*.

"Round. With hair on his lip the color of sand and a hat to cover one side of his head only."

The king's son turned pale and began to shake.

Rutega laughed.

Roosevelt helped carry Kruger to the mess tent, where the taxidermist stitched up the wound in the Boer's leg and removed the thorns from his limbs. Potter, Thompson, and Jans arrived while the patching was underway. Between probes and stitches, Kruger described the bandits' camp, the geography around it, and how the raiders were armed—single-shot percussion muskets, spears, and short swords. Jans translated for Potter and Thompson, while Roosevelt switched between German and English, depending on whom he was talking to. Kruger reported that there were at least fifty armed bandits, not the handful the porter had claimed. A frontal assault was impossible.

Roosevelt felt his heart harden. "Did you see Kermit?"

Kruger looked away. "I saw two white men tied to a tree. One not moving."

Roosevelt turned to Thompson and Potter. "I want you two to organize the Smithsonian packers to disassemble the specimen crates. Then show some men how to cut the slats to look like guns." Then he turned to Jans. "I want you to organize the rest of the porters to cut up tents and make vests to go along with the fake guns."

Jans dipped his chin and translated for his father. Kruger, lying prone on the table, said nothing. Potter and Thompson looked blank-faced. Neither moved.

Roosevelt clapped his hands together. "Let's move. We need two hundred sets of guns and vests. I don't want the boys up all night. We attack in the morning."

Potter broke the silence. "With respect, Colonel. Our friend here with the spear in his ass has just seen this bandits' camp, and he says a frontal assault will get us killed. I know they've got Kermit, but wooden rifles cut from busted crate and khaki vests cut from tents? Are you thinking of scaring them off with a parade?"

"Not scare, Johnny. Distract."

The unease of the men was palpable. Roosevelt would lose them, if he didn't conjure the words necessary to inspire and assure. But he was in no mood for calculated speeches. With or without their help, he would rescue Kermit, and his impatience to get on with it was volcanic compared to Potter's caution. He would tell it plain and they would follow or not.

"Before dawn, two hundred and forty porters, dressed in *askari* vests made from tents and carrying wooden rifles made from packing crates, will march to the base of the hill in front of the Fulani camp. When the sun comes up and the Fulani see them, they'll take up defensive positions facing their attackers. When the fake *askari* start up the hill, the Fulani will fire off their single-shot muskets and then have to reload with dry powder, cotton patch, and ramrod. That takes time. At the first shot, any of you who want to ride with me can charge up the hill from the other side and take the camp from behind."

No one spoke.

"Any volunteers?"

Kruger lifted his head from the cutting table. "Wooden guns? Your *kaffirs* will run from the first musket ball."

Roosevelt turned to the Boer's son. "Jans, you saw what the Germans have done with their native troops. Do you think you can make a bunch of dressed-up bundle carriers hold a straight line long enough for us to rescue our men?"

Jans grinned. "For Kermit, I will try."

"I don't like we give guns to *kaffirs*," said Kruger. "Even toys made from wooden crates."

Roosevelt snapped his teeth. "The Germans have given them real guns. If war comes, they'll know how to use them."

There was silence all around and then Potter spoke again. "You're a madman, Colonel."

"I'm taking that hill at dawn, Johnny. Alone, if I have to."

Potter sighed. "I'll be with you."

"And me," said Jans.

"*Ja*," said his father.

"I guess that's what you're paying us for," said Thompson.

Potter gestured toward a *panga* that lay on the mess table next to a piece of butchered meat. "We can use those *pangas* like we did those machetes in Cuba when the army wouldn't pay for sabers."

Roosevelt rubbed his hands together. "Bully idea, Johnny. Now let's get moving."

The three men left to do their tasks. Kruger remained on the table while the taxidermist finished his stitching. Roosevelt went to find Maggie.

Maggie had heard the musket shot and saw Kruger carried into Teddy's tent, but when she tried to follow, Potter turned her away. Every encounter with that interfering nursemaid was a reminder of what lay ahead for her and Teddy. If there *was* anything. Teddy didn't see that, of course. Fueled by passion and undeterred by any obstacle, he moved in one direction and at one speed—straight and fast. But what about sense and principle? Would the Teddy she knew allow passion to ignore one and compromise the other?

He might trample reason to dust, and often did. He was human, after all, as much as any man. But the Teddy she knew was first and always a man of principle. If he was going to be president again, he would have to remain one.

Then he was there, holding the tent flap open with one hand as he stood at the threshold. "I don't want you to go back to Nairobi." He didn't step inside and she didn't invite him in. Pressing her lips, she willed her feet to remain planted. "We need time." He waited for her to agree.

The word she whispered was too soft for him to hear, and it was meant more for herself than for him. "No." She turned her head away. When she looked back, he was gone.

There was no point trying to sleep. Wandering the row of tents, a third of them suddenly gone, Maggie stopped at the mess to watch a group of laughing natives dismantle packing crates and carve them with *pangas* into something resembling wooden rifles. Others ripped apart canvas tents and sewed pieces of cloth into rough approximations of an *askari* vest. Sweaty, chattering black faces worked side by side with silent, grim white ones. If there was going to be a real battle out there in the morning, this stage prop preparation was madness.

Returning to her tent, she fell into an exhausted sleep and awakened before dawn to the sound of porters chopping a ten-foot hole in the thorn barricade surrounding the camp. A pale limping Kruger appeared at her tent, accompanied by Jans and one of his trackers. "*Mev* Dunn," called Jans through the opening. "We bring this boy to take you to a safety place."

She threw on her cloak and stepped outside into the chill early morning air. "Why? Where?"

"To a *jag blind,*" Jans said, answering only the second question. "Not far." The older Boer handed her a leather case containing a pair of British military field glasses. "With those, you will see all what happens. Do not leave the *jag blind* without this boy who leads you. He will know what to do after the fighting." Jans turned and spoke to his father, who nodded and grimaced, his face stretched tight from the pain of his wounded leg.

Thoughts streamed through Maggie's head, chaotic and uncertain. *A half a dozen armed men against five times that many? Untrained natives armed with toys against ruthless bandits? Kermit, captive and helpless?* She wanted to scream, "Stop!" But no one would pay attention. Teddy had no fear. The others would follow, no matter how mad the plan. Kermit would surely be killed. All of them might be slaughtered. And then what? What would happen to her?

Montana! She could just strangle him!

The native tracker led her through the opening in the thorn barricade and along an animal path barely visible in the predawn light. Behind them, the pale grey sky hovered over a faint line of pink where land and sky would soon divide. Walking steadily for thirty minutes, they arrived at a copse of mimosa trees on a small patch of elevated ground sprinkled with patches of low thorns. The tracker pointed toward the safari camp along the plain a half-mile away, then in the direction of a low hill, equidistant but to the north.

Maggie raised the Boer's field glasses and scanned the safari camp. It was nearly empty. Outside the *boma*, Boer father and son had assembled a double line of two hundred men on a patch of clear ground in front of the camp. Each of the porters wore an open vest cut from a canvas tent and each carried a slat of packing crate crudely cut to resemble a Springfield rifle. To what effect, they would soon find out. The Boers appeared to be trying to form the double line of porters into a military square, twenty men long and twenty deep. It was taking a lot of time and much shoving and shouting. The difficulty of what should have been a simple maneuver made her even more fearful.

When the square finally formed, the Boers led the fake soldiers toward the distant hill where the bandits camped. The undulating square appeared and reappeared in the Boer's field glasses as the fake *askari* followed the ups and downs of the broken terrain. Five men on foot, each leading a horse by the bridle, kept close to the back of the formation until it disappeared into a ravine a few hundred yards short of the bandits' hill. When the square reappeared, the horsemen were gone.

Only the largest objects, such as the column of moving men, were visible through the field glasses in the predawn light. The bandits' camp remained hidden at the top of the hill. Closing her eyes, Maggie said a silent prayer for Teddy, Kermit, and the other brave and foolish men who were risking their lives that morning. *God keep them safe.* When the sun broke over the horizon behind her, she raised the glasses again. While she watched the top of the hill, dim forms acquired edge and depth. Soft mounds of meaningless grey became low, horizontal tents. Small dark lines became horses, and the occasional blur that moved between them became men.

Maggie lowered the glasses to where the porters, in their makeshift uniforms, waited at the base of the hill, an undulating hive of fidgeting humanity a hundred yards from certain death should anything go wrong. The Boers stood and faced the square, their backs toward the bandits' camp. Jans held his right hand above his head, palm toward the square. Maggie raised the field glasses toward the top of the hill. A dozen men in dark turbans and light-colored robes moved among the low tents and scattered boulders. Beyond the tents, two trousered men lay tied to a toppled tree. One had to be Kermit and the other the deserter, Dooley. Huddled and filthy, they were unrecognizable.

The sun rose steadily higher and she saw without glasses the bandits' camp and the square of natives below. One was a bustle of activity, the other a silent surprise waiting to be noticed. The wait wasn't long. A single bandit trotted toward the lip of the hill and was quickly joined by several more. Then a score of turbaned men poured out of the tents, rifles and lances in hand. At a signal from the Boers, the square at the bottom of the hill began to move. Slowly, menacingly, it marched across the open ground toward the bandit camp. Then it climbed. A shot reverberated from the top of the hill. A puff of black smoke rose from behind a rock. Then another, and another, and finally dozens.

Suddenly, from behind the bandit camp, a salvo of rifle and pistol fire erupted like Fourth of July fireworks. Teddy, Potter, Thompson, and the two other Pinkertons charged into the camp from the back of the hill, firing into the bandits from horseback. Dust and confusion blanketed the scene. Bandits swarmed. Two turbaned men grabbed the reins of Teddy's horse. He shot one with his revolver and slashed the other with a porter's *panga*. Riderless horses ran this way and that, turbaned men in pursuit.

The next few minutes were dust-choked chaos. Teddy and the other men rode among the bandits, shooting and slashing. The bandits attacked individual horsemen with swords and spears. Clouds of black musket powder drifted across the hilltop, obscuring crucial detail. Bodies fell. The fighting went on for what felt like forever. Then all at once, sound and motion stopped. Dust settled. Clouds of musket powder cleared. Alone astride their horses, Teddy and the Pinkertons possessed the hill. The bandits had fled, leaving behind tents, horses, and prisoners. Through the glasses, she watched Teddy leap from his horse and drop to his knees at the side of one of the bound men and press a canteen to his lips. Her throat closed and her eyes misted.

The tracker touched her arm and pointed toward a dozen turbaned men fleeing on foot in their direction. "*Twende*."

She followed the half-naked tracker through scrub, brush, and thorns as he led her back to the safari camp. Twice she stopped to catch her breath and heard the bandits close behind. The tracker shouted as they approached the thorn barricade. "*Hodi!*" Two gun bearers with genuine rifles stepped through the opening and fired shots over their heads while she and the tracker ran inside. There was no answering musket fire.

Maggie made her way to Teddy's tent and stood in front of his campaign desk, looking down at the hand-drawn map with his notes for the coming battle. Genius, madman, unstoppable force of nature. But to what end now? She paused only a moment before taking an envelope from her blouse and slipping it beneath the map. Then she left the tent, collected her kit, supplies, and the one sorrel horse that remained in the unguarded picket and spurred it hard toward Khartoum.

Chapter Twenty-Five

Don't hit a man if you can possibly avoid it;
but if you do hit him, put him to sleep.

\- Theodore Roosevelt

Roosevelt stripped off his bloody shirt and sat down at his camp desk to write an account of the battle while it was still fresh in his mind. Maggie was off with one of the trackers and would no doubt prepare her own article as soon as she returned. Both would go off in the wagon to Nairobi with the last of the animal skins. Kermit was alive. The Dooley boy might survive. They had bested the same desert brigands that had slaughtered Chinese Gordon and the British garrison at Khartoum fewer than twenty years ago. He hadn't felt this alive since Cuba, and he was damn near bursting!

Filling his steel pen from the bottle of Waterman ink, he looked down at the sketch he had made to illustrate his battle plan. The slope behind the bandits' camp had been steeper than Kruger's report had led him to believe. The horses had not been able to climb it at speed. That and several other corrections had needed to be made. But the map would make a wonderful addition to his article for *Scribner's*.

Lifting the sketch, he spotted the pale envelope beneath it, "Teddy" scrawled in feminine script across the seal. The vein at his right temple fluttered like that of a stunned bird as he opened the single sheet of lined paper covered in tight Palmer script and folded over a thin silver locket. The tightness in his chest that had appeared when Maggie confessed her reports to Randolph Hearst returned with renewed strength. His hands trembled.

Dearest Teddy,

I hope and pray that God will keep you safe in the coming battle, as well as your son and the other brave men who follow you. If you are reading this, then you have won a tremendous victory and I will tell the world of it in the hope that you will soon put to good use the acclaim that must follow. Mr. Hearst may not be your friend, but he has too much ink in his blood to suppress a story that will sell a million newspapers. His readers will proclaim you a hero once again, and the Hearst papers will have no choice but to lend their voice to the crowd. After that, the White House will be yours for the asking, if you pursue it with speed and vigor.

My impractical pragmatist! I know you haven't considered the possibility of defeat, as you seem to have made no provision for me should you lose. Forgive me, then, for making my own preparations, including borrowing your spare horse, supplies for the journey, and your Colt pistol, as whatever the outcome of the coming battle, I shall need all of them and a bit of luck.

I should be angry with you for neglecting all thoughts for my safety, and even more for leaving me once again to make the choice that will free us to follow our separate paths toward what can only be achieved alone. Protest if you must, but would you be looking back today at a life well spent had you tied yourself to a Five Points grocer's daughter in your impetuous youth? Would I have escaped the inevitabilities of such a life, traveled the world, and accomplished what so few of my gender have had the chance to, had I allowed it?

In another time and place, you and I might have had a passionate, accomplished, and meaningful life together. But our fate was not to start from such a place, and the choice we have twice been given is to make the most of our lives apart, or less of them together. Once again, you've left it to me to articulate the choice you know we must both make. You are too principled to pick the other and too reluctant to say the hurtful words required to let it go.

Dearest Teddy, you can stop the coming war in Europe before it begins, free the miserable Congolese from the grip of an evil despot, and do all of the things a leader of the most powerful country on earth should do, but won't, if his name isn't Teddy Roosevelt. Neither President Taft nor any European leader will take up these tasks. You can, once you are president again, and you must. All that I do now is to help you to make that happen.

Please don't follow.
Fondly,
Maggie

He read the letter twice. The little trinket felt like a ball of lead in the palm of his dusk-caked hand. His breath faded and returned in sudden swallows. He tried to stand, but his legs refused to respond. His head fell and his eyes swam unfocused over sand and dirt. Sounds of celebration—happy drums, and deep bass singing—seeped through the walls of the tent. His chest felt inside out.

The letter couldn't be more clear or its message more unwavering, but he refused to accept it. Willing his jellied legs to stand and move, he picked up his gun and strode stiff-legged through the riotous celebration with one thought in his head. *You're wrong, Maggie.*

He found Potter and Heller in the mess tent tending to Dooley. One sat on his leg while the other cut away the pus-soaked rag at its end. "Can he be moved?"

Heller looked up. "In a week. If he lives."

"Or we can just take him out and shoot him now," Potter muttered.

Roosevelt bent over the bloody cloth and sniffed. "Gangrene?"

Heller lay down his knife and stripped what was left of the wrappings. "Not yet."

"Then wrap him up when you're through and get him ready to travel."

Dooley groaned.

Potter pressed a hand over Dooley's mouth. "Now?"

"We're breaking camp. Mrs. Dunn took a horse, and she's headed for Khartoum."

"Good riddance."

"No, Johnny. Every bandit we chased off that hill is licking his wounds somewhere between here and Khartoum. She won't make it alive."

Potter kept his hand over Dooley's mouth. "And every porter we've got is still prancing around that hill with his fake *askari* vest and wooden gun. Even if we could collect them all, two hundred sixty men on foot aren't going to catch a single rider on horseback. Even if you are sure which way she headed and that she hasn't changed her mind."

Roosevelt picked up his gun. "And if the Fulani catch Mrs. Dunn, or any member of this safari, the fake soldiers and wooden gun trick won't work twice. We need to get this safari safe to Khartoum before another band of brigands picks up our trail."

Heller cut away the last of Dooley's rags and poured a solution of carbolic acid on the pus and dried gore beneath. Dooley screamed.

"Dammit, Colonel. We'll break camp as fast as we can, but if we don't have enough rifles to protect them, every one of our porters will be sitting ducks for any Fulani we run into."

"We can't afford any more hostages, Johnny. Mrs. Dunn has only a few hours' lead. I'll take Jans, a tracker, and Kermit, if he's strong enough to ride a horse. The rest of the rifles can remain with the column. Break camp and follow as quickly as you can."

"I don't like this, Colonel."

"Nor do I. But we could end up in a worse pickle if we don't rescue Mrs. Dunn quickly."

He left Potter and Heller clucking like spinsters and went off to find Kermit and Jans. There was no time to talk to Kermit about Maggie. But if he was strong enough to ride a horse, his rifle and Jans's would make a crucial difference if they ran into more Fulani.

He found the boys outside the *boma*, surrounded by dancing porters, trackers, and every other native who could hold a gourd of hooch to his mouth. Pie-eyed on *pembe*, the two young men were clearly in no condition to help anyone, and there was no point in asking or telling them anything. How quickly the prowess and wit that Kermit must have summoned to survive Fulani capture had dissipated in drunken revelry, and along with it, the pride and relief that had filled a father's heart just an hour earlier. Angry, frustrated, and determined to act, Roosevelt mounted his horse and rode off to find Maggie.

Kermit's stomach churned from the first food he'd eaten in days. His head throbbed and his legs felt like lead. Stumbling between rows of tents, he hailed a blue-turbaned porter carrying a Fulani musket. "*Bwana M'Kubwa iko wapi?*" The native pointed toward the mess tent. Willing himself in that direction, Kermit arrived at the tent where Potter and Heller were applying tinctures to a comatose Dooley.

Potter looked up. "This one tell you anything while you were trussed up together?"

Kermit started to shake his head, but the motion made him so dizzy he stopped. "Just that he got picked off while he was out riding, same as me. He didn't run away like we thought."

"I don't believe it."

Kermit felt his gut churn. "It didn't seem to matter much to him when he said it. And who'd lie when he's dying?"

"A liar."

Heller finished wrapping Dooley's foot and called to a pair of porters to carry him to his tent. "The laudanum should keep him knocked out for a few hours. But you'll need to get food in him before you do anything else. He can't travel like this."

The Africans hoisted Dooley like a sack of mealie, arms and legs askew. "Have either of you seen Pop? He's not in his tent."

Potter snorted. "He went looking for you an hour ago. That reporter woman took a horse, and he thinks she's heading for Khartoum."

Kermit remembered then that his father had tried to tell him something before he'd stormed off. But what? And where did he go? "That's a month's march from here."

Potter dipped his hands in an enamel basin and rinsed off the blood. "A week on horseback. And she's got a hell of a story to tell. Former President Roosevelt repeats his famous charge up San Juan Hill to rescue a son held captive by savage tribesman in darkest Africa. The Hearst newspapers are going to have a field day with that."

Kermit put a hand to his head to keep it from pounding. "Alone? The Fulani we just chased off will be everywhere between here and Khartoum."

"That's why the colonel went looking for you. He wanted to take you, Jans, and a tracker to bring her back before the Fulani got themselves another hostage. What was that woman thinking?"

Sweat poured from Kermit's scalp and down his back. He sat down hard on one of the mess benches.

Potter patted Kermit's shoulder. "Get up, son. I don't care how you feel. We'll need every rifle we have if we're going to get this safari to Khartoum in one piece. Find your father and Mrs. Dunn before the Fulani do, and get them back here fast."

Chapter Twenty-Six

*Always when on a long march assume the attitude
you feel most inclined to, as it is less tiring.*

- Mary Henrietta Kingsley,
Travels in West Africa, 1897

Maggie slept during the heat of the day and rode hard under a waning moon to avoid the Fulani bandits. The trackless wasteland held little fodder or water, and random stretches of hoof-slashing stone lay everywhere under layers of drifting sand. By midmorning of the sixth day, Teddy's horse was limping.

She tried to examine the animal's hoof but it skittered away, holding its muzzle high as if sampling the air. *Now what?* She held out her hand to calm it. But the horse turned, nostrils quivering, its thick slab lips pulled high over yellow teeth. *Fulani?*

Teddy's pistol lay at the bottom of the saddlebag, under a half-empty canteen and what was left of the mealie. She reached for the reins. The horse backed away, sniffing the air. She stepped slowly toward it and reached out a hand. "Steady." It looked at her once and then bolted, saddlebags flapping a treacherous goodbye as it galloped toward the horizon. *Dear God.*

She remembered then Pere de Clercq's warning about dehydration and heat stroke that awaited those who challenged the African sun during the heat of the day. But what else was there to do but follow the horse? Any attempt to reach Khartoum on foot without the provisions in the animal's saddlebags was a certain route to a grisly demise. She closed her eyes against the merciless orb hovering like hot death in a sky unmarked by cloud or hint of breeze. Then she started to walk.

That night in the tree, Teddy had said that Khartoum lay ten days north by horse, or a month on foot. That seemed a long time ago now. Leaving the safari had been a calculated risk, and perhaps a reckless one. But it was the kind of risk she told *Signore* Morini she was willing to take for the chance to expose and thwart the exploitation of the powerless by the powerful. No matter the outcome, it was better than a future of soul-sapping regret that she and Teddy would inevitably suffer had she stayed in camp and invited further temptation. At least it had seemed so then.

The horse's trail remained straight and easy to follow and the ground mercifully firm. But within an hour she knew that Pere de Clercq had been right about the rest. Squatting in the sand with her back to the burning sun, she made a tent of her long black skirt and decided to wait for evening to continue her journey. The moon had been nearly full the previous night. If the horse kept a straight path, and if it wasn't too far, then maybe she would find it. If not…well, she prayed there were no hyenas about.

Oh, Teddy… What a useless end. You, dithering about what to do with the rest of your life, and me, dead in the desert. Let that not be!

In her mind, she heard her father's derisive laughter. *Have you asked the good nuns how their loving God allows sickness and misery in the first place, Maggie? "Pray for the Flynn children who lost their ma to the cholera," they tell you. When it was him who let her catch her death in the first place? You're too smart to believe such nonsense.*

But she did, even though Father O'Brien's explanation that pain and suffering were the price man must pay for Original Sin was hardly satisfactory. From the priest's apologetic tone, she had surmised he didn't find it satisfactory, either. The late Mr. Dunn claimed that Eastern religions' ideas of karma and reincarnation provided a more rational explanation of seemingly unjust suffering. But she could never warm to gods who looked like elephants, no God at all, or the idea that one had to earn a place in whatever came next, when so many could barely survive the here and now.

So while the sun sought to broil her skull inside the oven of her toque hat, she implored the God of her childhood to help her survive the next days and to lead Teddy to find the sense and strength to do what only he could.

When the sun finally dipped below the horizon and the air began to cool, she got to her feet, brushed the sand from her skirts, and followed the horse's tracks. Twilight lasted a brief half hour, and the moon rose soon after that. The horse's tracks kept a straight line, never deviating left or right. What could it have seen or heard? How far had it gone? *Please, don't let there be Fulani.*

Humming Christmas carols beneath a tapestry of gemstone stars, Maggie repeated the prayers of her childhood and indulged in silly thoughts of a future with Teddy in places other than Montana and Panama. As the air began to lose its daytime heat, her mind wandered to the woolen blanket she had last seen on the escaping horse's behind, rolled behind two flapping saddlebags. She was too parched and hungry to sustain a pace that might have kept her warm. Her weakened body shook with cold.

Dawn came, and still the tracks led toward the horizon. It would be hot in another hour. Her last drink had been the afternoon of the day before, her last food hours before that. Did the sailor's rule of three operate so far from the sea?

When the sky began to lighten, she saw something ahead that made her hope that her prayers might have been answered—a dry ravine, filled with rounded stones, and a four-legged animal with its head buried in a clump of parched grass. Teddy's horse. The animal looked up once and then lowered its head, continuing to eat. There must be water somewhere underground to sustain that pocket of plant life, she thought. A few yards away, she saw a smaller patch of grass that had been eaten down to the sand. She picked up a pair of flat rocks and started to scrape away the sand and soil beneath the stubble. By midday she had dug a hole the size of an upended steamer trunk, and from its bottom oozed an odorous muck of thin brown liquid. She raised her face to the sky and whispered, "Thank you."

Three days later, dawn spread fingers of light over brown rubble walls that rose from the sand like the ruins of a Crusader fortress. Maggie slid from Teddy's horse and slipped to the ground, holding her knees to her chest and allowing a wave of relief to course through her body. Slitted eyes, parched beyond weeping, stared at a sight she'd thought she might never see. Khartoum.

Teddy, Teddy, Teddy...

Her trembling limbs stilled in the warmth of the rising sun, but her mind remained fogged by hunger and exhaustion. Sipping what was left in the canteen, she tried to think of what she must do first when she entered the city. Her thoughts were stuck in a labyrinth, where dead-end passages were missed opportunities and uncertainty about whether Teddy had read her note or tried to follow. The sun warmed her shoulders and the canteen gave up the last of its foul brown water. She hauled herself into the saddle by an act of sheer will and turned Teddy's horse toward the city.

A dozen urchins dressed in dirty cotton and covered in crusted sores stepped out from the shadows of the city gate and surrounded her. One grabbed the horse's tail and the others tore at the saddlebags. The animal bared its teeth, kicked, and broke free of the grasping hands. Galloping down sandy cart paths and narrow alleys, trailing a tangle of ropes and cloth, the horse stopped beneath an arch of lashed poles that opened onto an acre of stalls and blankets, piled with dates, grains, brass ornaments, colored cloth, and a variety of dry goods. A crowd gathered and stared. Two men approached and eyed Teddy's horse as if it were some sort of desert unicorn.

Money, telegraph. Money, telegraph. Get whatever you can for the horse before someone robs or kills you for it. Find a telegraph.

The men conferred in hushed voices. Then one turned away, lifting his hand in dismissal. The other remained and addressed her. "Here fly kill horse," he said with a sorrowful smile, waving the sleeve of his striped *jellabiya* in a dramatic arc. "Here live only donkey."

Maggie scanned the busy market, noting a handful of underfed donkeys and ill-tempered camels.

The trader touched four fingers to the side of a black *tarboosh* worn smooth of its felt. "Ten *shilingi*."

"The horse is not for sale today. I'm looking for a telegraph."

The trader's laugh exposed a *khat*-stained mouth thinly populated with blackened teeth. She tugged the horse's reins and turned away. "One hundred *shilingi*!" She patted the animal's side and it resumed walking. The trader gathered the hem of his *jellabiya* and scurried behind a row of stalls, emerging in front of her between a table piled with green mangos and a trellis of brightly colored cotton cloth. "Three hundred *shilingi*!" His voice conveyed the deepest measure of oriental outrage, despair, and injustice.

Maggie rested her hand on the pommel. "Three hundred British pounds and you can keep this fine saddle."

The trader lifted a hand. "Rest."

She took that to mean *wait* and watched the man scurry purposefully away. A slim dark boy in a threadbare *kanzu* appeared from behind a spice stall and passed a gentle palm over the animal's nose, allowing himself to be sniffed and licked in return. He did not speak and seemed to require nothing from Maggie other than forbearance. She was too tired to object. Peering over the top of the stalls, she tried to ignore the grumbling in her gut. Twenty minutes passed. Where was that gap-toothed swindler? Turning, she spotted the trader scurrying past a stall of multi-colored cotton clothes, a fistful of currency clutched to his faded *jellabiya*. Bowing, he spread a cloth on the ground and laid some crumpled notes in its center—American dollars, Egyptian pounds, and two Maria Teresa silver dollars. He counted them slowly and with a flourish. She did the arithmetic. "This isn't enough."

The trader gave an exaggerated sigh, no doubt hoping to convey the self-evident futility of seeking more for such a speculative investment in such an unlikely place. She gazed over his bobbing head. No other horse trader appeared poised to emerge from the gallery of dry goods stalls. "Very well." She removed the satchel containing Teddy's Colt pistol from the saddlebag and handed the reins to the triumphant merchant, stuffing his collection of mixed notes and coins into her traveling bag and heading off to find a telegraph.

The waterfront at the confluence of the White and Blue Niles, which was the desert city's reason for existence, must lay somewhere to the south. If she could find a telegraph to send Teddy's story, she could then look for a boat to take her down the Nile and on to Cairo. She might even have a meal and a bath before then. Though the horrors she had seen in the Congo and the ones soon coming to Europe would only be thwarted if Teddy regained the White House and used the power that came with it. Her dash for Khartoum and the other risks and sacrifices of her African adventure would be wasted if distraction delayed her or if obstacles prevented her from getting those stories out in time. More than a bath, she needed a telegraph. Now!

As if in answer, the urchin who had befriended her horse appeared from behind a spice stall and motioned for her to follow.

"Telegraph," she ordered. The boy smiled and trotted ahead,

slithering through the maze of carts and stalls, turning every so often to see that she followed. Passing through a tall stone gate and entering a labyrinth of narrow alleys, she followed him for half an hour. Finally, he stopped, not at a telegraph office, but at a whitewashed inn that served a midday meal.

"*Kadaharan*," he said, rubbing his stomach to facilitate understanding. There was no point in being petulant. She might as well eat.

As the millet and boiled goat settled in her gut, waves of renewed energy and suppressed exhaustion in turn spread through her body. Visions of a steaming hot bath fought all efforts to ignore it. She exited the inn through its sunlit courtyard, where three white-robed men in red felt *tarbooshes* shared a hookah under the shade of a broad-leafed date palm. One rose to greet her. "*Sabu*, a room perhaps? For you and your husband when he arrives?"

"A telegraph."

"Please?"

"A machine for sending messages over wire. Do you know where I can find one?"

"Yes, yes. I must know telegraph, most assuredly. The British at Government House possess this thing, as all the world knows."

"Can you tell me where I might find this Government House?"

"Yes, yes. Near to the *Souq* market. And a room upon your return?"

"Perhaps."

The horse trader's urchin, who had undoubtedly remained for just such a possibility of further employment, led her back through the maze of streets and alleys to a limewashed building where a brass plaque identified it as the British consulate. She knocked on the carved wooden door and waited. After several long moments, a section of door slid to one side and a ruddy white face appeared in the opening. "Consul's in Omdurman today. Can't say when he'll be back."

Maggie passed a sweat-soaked palm over her matted hair. "Can he be reached? I've information about the Roosevelt safari." She gestured at her hard-used clothes and boots. "And I've ridden far to bring it to him."

A pair of freckled fingers scratched the hairless cheek. "A safari, you say? Can't say I've heard of it."

She tried to suppress a mounting impatience. "Do you have a

telegraph? Might the consul be reached that way? I assure you he'll want to hear what I've come so far to tell him."

The soldier frowned. "We have a Wheatstone, ma'am. But Sergeant Jones is the only one what knows the keys. And he's with Mr. Willet at the garrison."

"Sergeant..."

"Corporal, ma'am. Flannigan."

"Corporal. I know something about telegraph keys. Enough to send the consul a message, if you'll allow me." She smiled sweetly, hoping her dusty face didn't look like something from a carnival sideshow.

Flannigan looked doubtful, but his face finally dissolved into a resigned smile. "Suppose it can't hurt. You do look fair worn from your travels, if you don't mind my saying." He lifted a heavy wooden bar and pulled open the door. "I was just about to make a cup of tea."

"If that's an offer, Corporal, I would be delighted."

She followed the friendly young man through a small waiting room, down a narrow hall, and into a central courtyard. He pointed to a wooden staircase across the courtyard. "The machine's round the other side and up them stairs. I'll have to fire the dynamo to get her going. May take bit, if she's being temperamental. Then I'll make that tea."

"That would be wonderful, Corporal."

The young man led her to a windowless room and propped the door open with a brick to let in light and air. "When you're done with your tapping, there's a tub in the residence, if you have a mind. No harm having use of it while the consul's gone. He don't use it much."

She hesitated. "I take it we are alone, Corporal?"

"Indeed we are, ma'am. Mr. Willet's a bachelor. No need of staff when he's out on his rounds."

"I see."

The young man blushed. "I didn't mean offense by suggesting a bath, ma'am."

Maggie smiled. "A woman traveling unaccompanied in Africa meets all sorts, Corporal. Not all of them gentlemen. I trust that I don't need to worry about you?"

Flannigan sighed. "A gentleman it is, ma'am. But I'll be only a shout away, if you'll be needing assistance. Them enamel tubs can be treacherous."

While Corporal Flannigan went off to do his errands, Maggie studied the unfamiliar telegraph machine. It differed from the Western Union device that was standard in the Hearst offices around the globe. Instead of a simple brass key attached to a pair of wires and mounted on a hand-size wooden base, the British machine was the size of a china cabinet—a monstrosity of dials and levers with a Medusa's head of wires pouring from both sides. She would have to decipher its means of operation quickly or wait until the British consul returned and hope he permitted her to send her story out uncensored. The alternative was to press on to Cairo, which could take months.

Corporal Flannigan must have properly coaxed the dynamo, because the cabinet suddenly began to hum and hiss while she tried to puzzle how to operate it. Enormous though it was, and regardless of what might be inside, she counted only six visible moving parts: four dials and two levers surrounded by letters and numbers. Apparently, this British machine didn't use the dot/dash code of the Western Union machine. It seemed the operator must turn a dial to the appropriate letter or number and then pull the handle to transmit.

Easy enough, she thought. Though, it must take forever compared to Morse. She turned the letter dial and pulled the lever until she had spelled out the telegraph address of the Hearst office in London. Almost immediately, the machine sprang to life. As she entered the first words of her story, the second dial spun simultaneously with her transmission, spelling out questions that she had neither the time nor the intention of answering. Jamming the second handle put an end to the distraction.

Letter by letter, the story of Teddy's African reprisal of his cavalry charge up San Juan Hill made its way to the Hearst office in London, followed by a detailed exposé of King Leopold's atrocities in the Congo, and the German colonial government's preparation for war in East Africa. When the transmission was finished, she placed a tired hand on the Wheatstone cabinet. *Sow the wind, reap the whirlwind.* The stories were on their way to a global audience and nothing could stop them now. If governments were to be shamed into timely action, she was proud to be the match that lit the fire beneath them, no matter the outcome.

And now to that bath!

Chapter Twenty-Seven

If you want time to pass quickly,
just give a banker your note for ninety days.

- J. P. Morgan

Ten weeks before his million-dollar loan was due, Cashman stepped onto an Arab *dhow* on the Nile River, just south of Alexandria, Egypt. Nearby, in a lateen-rigged boat piled high with grain and dates, two women clad in billowing black cloth stared from behind sequined veils, whispering in their foreign tongue over the tinkling of copper anklets and bracelets. Cashman had hoped to negotiate passage up the Nile, from Alexandria to the Aswan cataracts, and then hire camels and a guide for the final thousand-mile trek to a place called Khartoum in the Sudan. But there didn't seem to be a soul around, save for the whispering women. "You stay put," ordered Ketchel. "I'll find someone to take this tub upriver. Or we'll take it ourselves."

There was no point arguing with Morgan's security man. Cashman's task was to find and kill Roosevelt. Ketchel's was to see that Cashman finished the job or died trying. According to Andrew Carnegie's informant at the Smithsonian, Roosevelt's safari would disband when it reached Khartoum. From there, he would travel by boat and caravan to Cairo, and then by steamer to Europe. Cashman's task was to get to Khartoum first and do what Morgan's hired assassin had apparently failed to. But how? As he watched a line of camels laden with heavy white stone follow a pair of white-robed men down the face of a sand dune, he admitted he had no idea.

Whether sweating on the open deck of a cold transatlantic ocean liner, or shivering in the hundred-degree heat of the North African desert, Cashman felt more like an invalid than an assassin. He'd never killed anything, or even imagined that he could. If Morgan's professional hadn't been able to do the job, what chance had he, Elliot

Cashman, Wall Street scrivener? He would make a mess of it and get himself killed or thrown into an African prison.

When he'd shared his concerns with Morgan in the banker's office shortly before boarding the ship for Africa, Morgan's response was as cold and unadorned as a hangman's noose. "I understand your concerns, Elliot. Professionals have skills you don't. But when a job becomes more difficult than the professional anticipated, he may be tempted to abandon the task or to give less than his best effort. The man we put on the Roosevelt safari may have done that. I don't know. But there's no point sending someone who might do the same. We don't have time." Dark clouds of acrid cigar smoke wafted across a desk the size of a dinner table. Cashman tried not to gag. "What we need now is someone who doesn't have the professional's option to slack or fail. Someone who has no choice but to succeed...or to die trying. In other words, Elliot, we need you."

Cashman swallowed hard. He couldn't let that be the final word. "Even if what you say is true, Pierpont, I don't know anything about killing. What can I do that your professional wouldn't have already thought of and tried?"

Morgan glared. "You can persevere."

"And if that isn't enough?"

Morgan inhaled through a roll of smoldering tobacco leaf. "Only one of you can return from Africa alive, Elliot. You or Colonel Roosevelt. Your family's money—and mine—are betting on you."

Morgan had been right, of course. Either he would kill Roosevelt and secure for himself more riches than he or his family could ever spend, or he would fail and suffer the kind of ruin and disgrace that would make sticking his head in a lion's mouth the only sensible course of action. Of the two, it was not the prospect of great wealth that had brought him halfway around the world to stand shivering in one hundred twenty-degree heat on the sun-scorched sands of the Nile River; it was the certainty that he and his family would be impoverished and disgraced if he failed. That was the calculus that distinguished Elliot Cashman from Morgan's hired assassin, and Morgan had made that calculation a long time ago. Fear, it seemed, was a more powerful motivator than greed. Cashman knew he was learning a fundamental truth much too late.

In Naples, and again in Alexandria, he'd been tempted to leave the ship, hoping that he might somehow walk away and disappear. But Morgan's man Ketchel was quick to dispel that fantasy. "Don't try to pull foot on me," he'd warned, whetting a folding knife against his shirtsleeve and tossing pieces of dried lamb at the phalanx of reptiles that followed the *dhow* across the river. "If you do, I'll catch you, flay you, and feed the pieces to them lizards. What's left can crawl raw to wherever we're going. Makes no difference to me."

The man was convincing. And in truth, there was no place to go.

Ketchel returned with a café au lait-colored man wearing a striped *kikoy* around his ample waist and nothing above save several bands of faded facial tattoo. "We're off."

"Is he the owner?"

Ketchel spat into the water. "Hell's it matter?"

The boatman unfurled the lateen sail and caught a barely perceptible breeze that turned the craft into the current, the first of many zigzag crossings that would carry them slowly upstream for the next thirty days.

At Aswan, they left the boat and hired a guide to take them by camel beyond the cataracts, riding at night and resting during the day wherever they could find shade. The heat was bearable while they remained near the river. But where a papyrus thicket or an unstable slope of fine white sand crowded the riverbank and forced them to turn inland, the sun was enough to bake a man's brains inside the cauldron of his skull.

Beyond the final cataract, they boarded another dhow, which carried them the last few hundred miles to Khartoum. They arrived on the last day of February, two weeks before Cashman's million-dollar loan was due.

"Safari, sirs? We are desert here. There are no animals." The innkeeper, at what seemed to be the town's only travelers' lodging, looked at Cashman and Ketchel as if they'd been out in the sun too long.

Ketchel leaned a wide, scarred fist on the counter beneath the man's chest. "Okay. Caravan then. Lots of white men. You heard anything?"

The man wagged his head from side to side. "You are the first white men to honor this establishment in many months."

Ketchel brought his other fist to the counter and leaned toward the innkeeper. "What about a white woman? Any of those show up here?"

The man grinned and made a strange movement of his head from side to side. "A *Sabu*, much traveled, honored here, yes. But she did not stay."

"A reporter?" asked Cashman.

The man shrugged. "A white woman. Much traveled. In search of a telegraph. A fine one might be found, I say to she, at the British consulate. If the Fulani have not cut the wires again for jewelry."

"How long ago?"

"This day, *saab*. A few hours past."

Ketchel leaned over the innkeeper and lowered his voice to nearly a whisper. "And where is this British consulate?"

The innkeeper raised a shaky hand toward the beaded curtain that covered an opening in the mud-brick walls. "Near the Souq al Arabi market. A white soldier rests by the door when the consul is there."

Ketchel threw a handful of Egyptian coins on the counter. "Thanks, pal." Then he and Cashman strode into the glare of the white sand street to find the reporter who would lead them to Roosevelt.

Corporal Flannigan's tea was cold and tannic by the time Maggie slipped out of her filthy clothes and into the enameled bath. The tub he had filled with a score of boiling kettles was now delightfully tepid. Propping a chair against the closed door and stepping into the cleansing waters as if they were the holy Ganges, she rested her head against the cool enameled metal and sank into the nearly forgotten sensation of warm water blanketing her body to the neck.

Closing her eyes, she tried to think of nothing. But her mind refused. Unburdening a year's worth of stories and grime should have left her feeling relieved and refreshed. Instead, she felt empty and irritated. It was Teddy's fault—an idealist who mistook himself for a pragmatist. Unburdened by realistic expectations and with an energy and vision uncannily matched to a new century ripe for their use, he succeeded routinely at what others knew to be impossible. But improbable success in worthy public causes was not the likely result in an unworthy private one. Adolescent lovers reunited in middle age could not live happily ever after in Panama or Montana. Not even Teddy could make that work, and it was not a worthy goal for either of them. He knew that. Or he would have torn up her letter and followed. Easing her body lower into the tub and allowing the tepid water to lap at her ears and chin, she mused over Mr. Wilde's claim that virtue was its own, and only, reward. She did not believe it. But for Teddy to be president again and do what only he could do, dreams of adolescent lovers reunited must remain just that—dreams. If the price of world peace was a pair of saddened hearts, so be it. It was as simple and as sad as that.

Gazing at her half-submerged limbs and the almost forgotten image of bath-wrinkled skin, she fantasized about remaining immersed in rediscovered luxury until inauguration day. But with her name append-ed to a Hearst international exposé of the Belgian king's atrocities in the Congo and without the protection of Teddy's safari, she would have to regain the security of civilization before King Leopold's Force Publique came looking for her. Pere de Clercq had once urged her to make "God's speed." The advice seemed timely.

But the temptation to linger remained, running circles in her mind with thoughts of its consequence, until an apologetic knock at the door interrupted. "Beggin' your pardon, ma'am," Corporal Flannigan called through the door. "There's a pair of Americans downstairs looking for your Colonel Roosevelt. I told them someone was here that just come from his safari."

Dear God. She stepped quickly from the tub and wrapped herself in a clean white towel, grimacing at the sight of her filthy clothes and the prospect of stepping back into them.

"Did you mention the telegraph?"

"No, ma'am. I turned off the dynamo as it was starting to spark some. These fellows say they're with some museum."

"All right, Corporal. I'll be down shortly."

Gritting her teeth, she stepped into her unlaundered garments and then hurried downstairs and across the courtyard to the reception room off the street. As she entered it, two men as unkempt as herself broke off their conversation and turned toward her.

The shorter and younger of the two extended his hand. "Elliot Cashman." He turned to his companion. "This is my colleague, Jack Ketchel."

"Maggie Ryan," said Maggie, omitting mention of her well-known journalist name.

"Corporal Flannigan says you just come from the Roosevelt safari. We've come from New York with correspondence for Colonel Roosevelt from the safari sponsors."

The slight, sandy-haired young man, already beginning to bald at the crown, didn't look like a rival reporter—too hesitant and perhaps too educated. But she had no intention of sharing the fruit of her hard labor. "What newspaper do you work for, Mr. Cashman?"

He should have looked surprised at the question. But he didn't. "I'm employed by the Smithsonian Museum."

"To deliver mail?"

His mouth turned. "Please, I have important information for Colonel Roosevelt. Do you know where we might find him?"

"We crossed paths about a month ago in the Congo. He was hunting some kind of rare rhinoceros."

"And what were you doing there?" Ketchel asked. He looked at least ten years older than Cashman and as hard as his companion was soft. His voice held no deference, and if he had claimed to be working for a museum, too, she would have laughed in his face. Instinct warned that the less these men knew about her or Teddy, the better.

"Missionary work.," she replied. Ketchel snorted.

Cashman interrupted. "Do you have any idea where Colonel Roosevelt intended to go after you last saw him?"

"I'm afraid not. I tried to interest him in our mission, but he was entirely occupied with killing animals for your museum. It was not a successful encounter from my point of view."

The two men exchanged glances, neither friendly nor scientific.

"You traveling alone?" asked Ketchel.

"I beg your pardon?"

Cashman glared at his companion.

"Will you excuse me, please?" She left the room before either man could reply. Corporal Flannigan, standing on just the other side of the visitors' room door, closed it behind her.

"Did you hear any of that, Corporal?"

"I did indeed, ma'am. Nasty bit of goods, that big one. If he's a museum poof, I'm a Hindu."

"Can you get me out of here without either of those men seeing me?"

"I can, ma'am, if you'll hurry." He led her across the courtyard to an enclosed kitchen at the back of the enclave. There he pulled hard on a small door next to a dry goods cupboard and dragged it partway open. "This here leads to an alley what comes out in the Souq. You can lose Mr. Sherlock Holmes in there. But it's no place for a lady to stay overly long."

"Neither is Africa, Corporal. But if you can keep those two men busy, I'll do the rest as you suggest."

"I'll do me best, ma'am. That big fellow looks like he might enjoy the yarn about the bishop and the belly dancer. Takes a bit of telling."

"Thank you, Corporal." She touched a hand to his arm and stepped out the door into the alley. After following it for what seemed a mile or more, the alley ended behind a stall in the Souq market as the corporal had promised. Wandering among carts and stalls piled high with brass and colored cloth, she waited until she was certain that no one had followed her before leaving the crowded market and making her way toward the river.

Despite the hundred-degree heat, she suddenly felt chilled. Who were those men, and what did they want with Teddy? If she could find a boat and buy passage down the Nile, it might be prudent to leave immediately. Those men weren't Belgian, but that didn't mean they weren't on the Belgian king's payroll. She had telegraphed her stories only an hour before. Surely the Force Publique was not that efficient. Still, her instincts warned that no good would come from lingering in Khartoum. Teddy was supposed to meet with the kaiser as soon as he left Africa and landed in Europe. If she got to Berlin first, and if Teddy made the same pitch to the kaiser that he'd practiced on Sergeant Fussner, she could break that story, too. Mr. Hearst wouldn't argue payment for that.

The river smell was strange and startling after being so long away from water. Walking along the riverfront quay—lined on one side with dhows filled with lumber, dates, and grain, and along the other with empty boats waiting for cargo or hire—she looked for something that might be fast, safe, and capable of leaving immediately. Clean and cheap would be welcome as well.

The river simmered under a cloudless sky, and rays of afternoon sunshine skimmed off the water, making it hard to see beyond the closest boats. Several of the boatmen called to her. One looked cleaner than the others, as did his dhow. She spoke to him from the dock, dispensing with preamble. "Can you leave for Cairo today?"

The boatman looked startled. "Cairo, *sabu*? Boat to Merowe. Fifty pound, Egypt money. Camel to Aswan, then boat to Cairo."

Maggie opened her satchel and removed the Maria Teresa silver she'd received in partial payment for Teddy's horse. "This is yours if we can leave now."

The boatman looked past her and opened his mouth. A voice from over her shoulder chuckled. "You're overpaying."

It was the American called Cashman who had accosted her at the consulate. Ketchel, his companion, jumped into the boat and stood in front of her. "Not nice leaving us scratching our asses back there."

She reached inside her satchel and placed her hand around the handle of the Colt pistol that she'd taken from Teddy's tent. She tried to keep her voice and hand from trembling. "I've told you where I last saw the man you're looking for. What further assistance do you require?"

"We require you to come to look for him with us," said Cashman.

"So we don't get lost," said Ketchel.

The boatman's face turned from one to the other as if watching the promised silver disappear in a contest he couldn't follow or understand. "Two silvers, Wadi Halfa, go now!"

Ketchel put a hand on the boatman's chest. "The lady's coming with us."

Grateful that her former husband had insisted she learn to use all manner of firearms, Maggie lifted Teddy's pistol from her bag and pointed it at Ketchel's chest. "I take it you're no friends of Colonel Roosevelt. As it happens, neither is my employer William Randolph Hearst, the newspaper publisher. He sent me here to find Colonel Roosevelt and to interview him for the Hearst newspapers. I found him, as I said, in the Congo Free State near a place called Bukavu. We had a nice chat about natural resource conservation and European politics, which you may read in the *International Herald* sometime soon. All I know of his future plans is that Colonel Roosevelt hoped next to hunt gorilla in the forest near a volcano called Nyiragongo."

"You said you was a missionary."

"And you said you worked for a museum. I'm not in the habit of telling my business to strangers. I won't ask yours. But I've told you all I know about Colonel Roosevelt's whereabouts, including where you might find him next." Keeping Teddy's pistol aimed at Ketchel's belly and her eyes on his companion on the dock, she spoke to the boatman. "Two silvers to Merowe. Let's go."

"*Sabu!*" The boatman jumped on the dock and untied the lines that held the dhow to the quay.

Maggie gestured for Ketchel to disembark. "Or stay, if you want to accompany me to Wadi Halfa. But you won't find Colonel Roosevelt there."

Cashman motioned to his companion. "Let's go. We're wasting time."

Ketchel growled, "She's lying."

"It's my skin, not yours."

"And I'll be carving strips of it, if you're wrong. You remember that."

Chapter Twenty-Eight

There is not one among us in whom a devil does not dwell; at some time, on some point, that devil masters each of us... It is not having been in the Dark House, but having left it, that counts.

- Theodore Roosevelt

Small dark specks dropped from a cloudless sky. More circled nearby. Kermit turned his mount and headed toward them. Something had attracted the buzzards. Something dead or close to it. A scrum of razor-beaked carrion eaters screeched and drummed their wings at his approach. A few flew away. The rest regarded him with wide red eyes while they continued to tear hunks of suppurating meat from their chance meal.

A shot from the Winchester scattered all but the boldest, though what remained of their meal provided few clues. A shod hoof suggested it had been a horse, but not a Fulani's. Pop's horse would have had shoes, and so would Mrs. Dunn's. Scavengers, human or otherwise, may have taken everything else, or the rider might have carried it away. There were no human remains.

Wispy clouds drifted across the pale blue sky and buzzards circled impossibly high above a lone acacia a hundred yards away. Something had the birds' attention there, too. Remounting his horse, Kermit galloped toward the circling birds. As he drew closer, he saw the muddy brown pool on the far side of the tree and a dark bulge not covered by bark where the pale trunk met the ground. Cocking his rifle, he slid from the saddle. "*Hodi!*"

The bulge separated from the trunk. A sunburnt face above a torn khaki tunic turned toward him, lips cracked and skin splotched with sweat and dust.

"Pop!"

The figure struggled to stand. "Your turn to rescue me."

The voice was hoarse, the grip weak. Kermit eased his father back to the ground and propped him against the tree. "Are you hurt?"

His father shook his head. "Could use a good meal."

Kermit took the canteen and jerky from his saddlebag and watched his father tear off a hunk of rhino meat with his teeth and then swill with difficulty from the canteen. He placed his hand on his father's forearm. "Glad to see you in one piece."

"Glad to be in one." His father coughed, trying to clear his throat of sand. "Do you know what day this is?"

"Monday, I think. February 28."

"Well, Mrs. Dunn should be in Khartoum by now, if those fellows who shot my horse didn't catch up with her." He coughed again, lifting the canteen to his lips as he pointed the barrel of his rifle toward the horizon. "I rode up on four of those Fulani following her trail. Thank Providence they only had those Berber muskets or I wouldn't be here talking to you."

Kermit looked toward the squawking buzzards that had resumed their squabbles over the dead horse. "I saw only one dead animal out there, Pop, and it's shod. If it's not yours…" He didn't want to say the obvious.

His father coughed and took another swallow from the canteen. "It's mine. I winged one of the Fulani just as he shot my horse out from under me. I guess his buddies decided to carry him off to wherever they could patch him up rather than hang around to match muskets against a Winchester. I don't think they could have caught up to Mrs. Dunn at that point."

His father's face, so rarely in repose, was commanding now in its stillness. It was the picture he'd imagined while he was being held by the Fulani. Not the hard-charging Rough Rider, but the thoughtful, resolute leader who willed himself into an unstoppable force once a plan was in place and it was time to act. He was a phenomenon of nature, not to be trifled with. "I wished I'd gotten here sooner, Pop. I had a lot of time to think while I was with those Fulani, and I'd hate for it to have been for nothing."

"Revisiting your Aristotle?"

"Not for myself."

A gap-toothed grin split Roosevelt's sunburned face. "Examining my life, too? Well, I suppose that's every parent's fate. Your sister Alice made a regular habit of it before she turned her attentions to Senator Longworth. What charitable insights did you come up with?"

The Kermit of a year ago might have hesitated to criticize his hero father or subject his own adolescent thinking to the lion's critical analysis. But that was an age ago. "You have to run for president, Pop."

"Well, well, you surprise me, son. Why do you think I *have* to run?"

Kermit took a deep breath. He knew he was right. But a weak, dehydrated, and understandably distracted parent might not be of a mind to appreciate a flawed son's wisdom.

"You told Sergeant Fussner that his country could either have the Congo without a fight or start a war it can't win and might not survive. You made a good case. Everything we've seen and heard in Africa says that war is coming in Europe. But President Taft will never make the offer or threat that you proposed to Sergeant Fussner. And President Taft wouldn't be taken seriously, even if he did."

His father's face remained impassive.

"But you don't need to be president to make the threat and to have the kaiser believe it. All you need to do is run. You can tell the kaiser when you see him in Berlin that you plan to run for president again in 1912. He'd be insane to start a war before he knows whether you've won or not. Even if you lose, it will be the summer of 1913 before Germany can mobilize."

"And then what?"

Kermit had asked himself the same question. The answer was hard. "War. But France and England will have two more years to come up with a better plan than yours—letting Germany take the Congo Free State from that monster Leopold in exchange for peace in Europe."

His father smiled. "I've been sitting here for two days thinking the same thing."

Dooley looked up from stitching a piece of rhino leather to the toe of his boot and saw a half-dead horse, carrying a pair of half-dead Roosevelts, walking slowly down the patch of trampled grass between two rows of tents. He wanted to be sick. *Couldn't the bugger just die?*

As word of Bwana M'Kubwa's return spread through the camp,

porters and *saises* came running, chanting their happy native gibberish while they rid the overloaded horse of its burden. Potter and the others came running, too, all grinning like idjits. "Well done. Well done," barked Cunninghame.

Potter passed his hand over his hair. "You had me worried, Colonel. I sent Thompson off with a pair of trackers this morning. We're down to four able riflemen."

The natives carried the two Roosevelts to the canvas chairs beneath the mess tarp, where the cook handed a cup of chai to the politician and a calabash of something else to his kid. Roosevelt looked at the crowd of black faces. "Where are the others?"

Potter lifted his fingers, counting as he talked. "I sent the two Boers off with the last wagonload of skins. The track should be safe as far as Kampala if the Fulani skedaddled back to where they came from. Thompson's got the bubble shits and I sent his man, who took a musket ball in the hand, back to Kampala with the Boers. That leaves four of us able-bodied and armed. Six, with you two back and healthy."

Dooley suppressed a smile. So Potter was counting him as one of the guns. Well, that was happy news. He and Thompson had asked a lot of hard questions about Dooley's capture by the Fulani. They hadn't disguised their disgust at his answers, and they hadn't given him his gun back.

Potter pulled one of the mess chairs next to Roosevelt and spoke in a low, earnest tone. It wasn't exactly a signal to scram, but Cunninghame went to the far end of the tent and the Roosevelt kid drifted outside to talk with the natives. Dooley wandered over to the mess table and fiddled with his boot. Potter's twang was clear enough over the short distance.

"I'd tell you to rest, Colonel, but I'll save my breath till you read the newspaper that came through in the pouch from Kampala after the Fulani beat it out of here."

"War?"

"You may want to start one. President Taft fired the head of the national parks and the papers say he's thinking of letting loggers into Yellowstone."

A cup of chai flew past Dooley's head and skidded across the packed earth. "He gave me his word!"

"Sounds like he broke it."

"Damnation!"

"Frees you up to run for president, though. Unless you think you have to keep silly promises to someone who hasn't kept his."

Roosevelt slammed a blistered fist on the wooden table with a force Dooley would not have thought possible from the sun-fried mummy who'd crawled into camp less than thirty minutes before.

Potter lowered his head and his voice. "Did you find any sign of Mrs. Dunn?"

Roosevelt stood and paced. "Her trail. With Fulani on it. I caught up and managed to keep them busy for a while. Long enough for her to get to Khartoum, if she didn't run into more."

Potter looked away. "Well, I hope she made it. You'll be running for president again, if she gets her story out—San Juan Hill in Africa. Newspapers will stampede you to run, whether you want to or not."

"Oh, I want it, Johnny. I do now."

"Well, then don't bust a gut over this Yellowstone business. The lumber boys will run for cover when they hear you're saddling up again. You can fix whatever else needs fixing when you get back to civilization."

"It's getting to be a long list."

Chapter Twenty-Nine

I heard a shout. Starting and looking half around, I saw the lion just in the act of springing upon me. I was on a little height; he caught my shoulder as he sprang and we both came to the ground below together. Growling horribly close to my ear, he shook me as a terrier does a rat. The shock produced a stupor similar to that which seems to be felt by a mouse after the first shake by a cat. It caused a sort of dreaminess in which there was no sense of pain or feeling of terror, though quite conscious of all that was happening. It was like what patients partially under the influence of chloroform describe who see all the operation but feel not the knife. This singular condition was not the result of any mental process. The shake annihilated fear, and allowed no sense of horror in looking around at the beast. The peculiar state is probably produced in all animals killed by carnivora; and if so, is a merciful provision by our benevolent Creator for lessening the pain of death.

- Dr. David Livingston, *Adventures and Discoveries in the Interior of Africa*, 1872

"Mr. Dooley!" The voice outside the tent was surprisingly high-pitched for someone so full of his own manhood, piss, and vinegar. Dooley eased himself off his cot and hobbled to the tent flap. His foot was healing slowly and the first step of the morning was a painful reminder that the missing toe had not just been severed by a savage beast, it had been torn out by the root.

Roosevelt stepped inside the tent and waved a thin brown envelope in Dooley's face, his name written in pencil across a sealed fold. "This was inside the newspaper that came in the pouch from Kampala."

Dooley felt his heart race, but he took the envelope with a steady hand and placed it facedown on the canvas cot. "Thanks." He didn't trust himself to say more.

Roosevelt looked him in the eye. "Meet me outside the mess tent in twenty minutes." When he'd left, Dooley hurriedly ripped open the envelope with his teeth. Out fell a Brownie photograph of Mickey, all puffy-faced, his shirt covered in dark splotches, eyes swollen shut, and front teeth missing. Across the bottom, someone had scribbled: *Time's Up.*

Jesus! Potter had told Cunninghame that the safari would end in three

237

weeks in a place called Khartoum. If Mickey's photograph was as old as it looked, he could be dead by then, or would be soon enough. If Roosevelt marched into Khartoum alive, Mickey was as good as dead. *Mother of God.*

Hobbling toward the mess tent in his hand-patched boots, Dooley stumbled into Potter coming the opposite way with a rifle. "The colonel wants you to go with him for a hike while we break camp." He shoved the rifle into Dooley's chest. "Hop on one foot if you have to. But I'll do you worse than the Fulani if the colonel gets so much as a scratch while you're *protecting* him."

Dooley dipped his chin, not trusting himself to speak. If he could get Roosevelt alone, he'd kill him any way he could and blame it on the Fulani bandits. There was no time to come up with a better plan.

Roosevelt had a thousand questions about Dooley's adventure with the bandits. Dooley gave the story he'd rehearsed—how he had been captured while out practicing his shooting. But Roosevelt seemed more interested in the details of the Fulani routine and camp. What did they eat? How did they care for their horses? What were their defensive arrangements at night?

When they stopped for a midday break, Roosevelt laid his rifle across his knees and unwrapped a lunch of cold impala and *mahalagi*. He held out a waxed cloth with Dooley's portion, and, before Dooley could react, Roosevelt lifted his rifle and pointed it at his chest. "We opened your mail."

Dooley dropped the pieces of meat and beans to the ground.

"Looks like somebody's got a squeeze on you, son."

Dooley started to bluster, but Roosevelt cut him short with a telling exhibition of a professional politician's uncanny memory for names and faces. "I remember a young policeman who Tammany served up as a sacrificial lamb when I went after them my first year as New York City Police Commissioner. His name was Dooley, too, as I recall. I only saw his picture in the newspapers, but that's him all beat up in that Brownie they sent you. Isn't it?"

Dooley clamped his mouth shut.

Roosevelt bared his outsized choppers. "You think I don't understand, but I do. I'd have gone to Tammany for a job, too, if I'd grown up in Five Points. They control the work. I'd have been grateful for whatever they gave me, as I'm sure your brother was. Even if it meant kicking back a piece of my pay and doing other *favors*."

"S'only right."

"Is it? Do you have to kick back a piece of your pay here? Does Mr. Thompson ever tell you to look the other way and not do the job I'm paying you for?" Dooley didn't trust himself to answer. "Of course not! You've got a square deal here. That's what I wanted to give the people of New York. Jobs and basic services without the Irish having to go to Tammany, the Italians to their Black Hand, and everyone else to their strong-armed protectors who only get what they deliver by corruption and violence."

"There's nothing wrong with taking care of your own."

"So long as you don't take it from others. Only strong, honest government can deliver a square deal to all people and not just some; or make laws so there's enough for everyone, and no group needs organized thieves and head-breakers to get its fair share."

Dooley stiffened. "Tammany's done all right by me and mine. It was you sent Mickey upriver."

"You're wrong about that. It was Boss Tweed I wanted, not some dewy-cheeked patrolman. There's a lesson there. Were you listening to Kermit when he translated my talk with that German sergeant?"

"I heard a lot of talk."

Roosevelt clicked his choppers and ploughed ahead. "Europe's been fighting over turf and spoils for a thousand years, just like your Five Points gangs. This time it's the Germans against England and France. A hundred years ago, it was France against everyone else. Before that, it was the Catholics against the Protestants.

"Now they're all in America. What keeps them from slitting each other's throats for a fair share of the pie here, just like they did in the old country? A strong, honest government that treats everyone fairly, that's what. If the people have that, they don't need a Tammany or a Black Hand. And no group of corrupt head-breakers can ever be strong enough to deal with aggressive foreign governments, backed up by powerful armies and navies. All they can do is undermine the honest government that can. That's why they have to go."

Dooley listened. He had no choice. But if Roosevelt wasn't dead soon, Mickey would be. That's all that mattered. He waited, listened, and bided his time.

As the politician warmed to his speech, cutting the air with both hands to emphasize some pompous point, Dooley lifted his gun and pulled the trigger.

The gap-toothed grin split the politician's face like a harmonica stuck in a melon. He even had the nerve to laugh. "That's a Springfield Mr. Potter gave you this morning. It's heavier than the Winchester you've been using, and it's been modified with a double safety. It won't fire unless you flip them both."

Dooley looked down at the useless weapon and glared.

"He was worried about a possible accident."

"Piss on you."

Roosevelt bared his teeth again, making a sound like a horse begging for an apple. "Ha! I like your spunk, Mr. Dooley. When I get back to New York, I'll talk to Governor Hughes about a pardon for your brother. The governor wants to be on the Supreme Court. The next president might be able to put him there."

Dooley looked away. *Maybe the gaseous politician was a better man than he'd thought. Maybe he could cut a deal with the governor, and maybe he'd actually do it. But none of that mattered now. He hadn't killed Roosevelt, and now they were going to kill Mickey.*

The low, meditative growl started just after sunset. At first, the sound came from a distance, then from somewhere close in the tall grass beside the trail. "Keep still," Roosevelt whispered. "Lions don't growl when they're hunting. This one probably made a kill already and is just making noise to warn off the hyenas."

But the guttural sounds were close and moving closer. Sweat poured from Dooley's scalp, turning his shirt into a wet sponge. His gut knotted and his bowels loosened. When the growls become a roar, he leapt to his feet and ran. Thorns ripped his legs. A brace of birds burst from their hiding place as he stumbled past. Lungs gasped, but he couldn't breathe. Then his body suddenly lifted off from the ground and pitched forward through the cool evening air. Hot fetid breath wafted over his neck. He heard and felt the crunch of bone. His.

Epilogue

Two Years Later

Roosevelt was putting the finishing touches on his campaign speech when his son knocked on the door of the hotel room and pushed past the clutter of Bull Moose Party literature. The presidential election of 1912 was three weeks away.

"The car's waiting outside," said Kermit. "Surrounded by about twenty thousand well-wishers. We may have to run over a few to get you to the auditorium on time."

Roosevelt folded the fifty-page speech and put it in his breast pocket. "Mr. Potter will find a way to get us there without maiming any votes we may still need."

"He and your one-armed bodyguard have their hands full keeping Mrs. Dunn from tackling you on the street. She says you promised her an interview on how you bluffed the kaiser out of going to war with France and England. There's talk of you getting another Nobel Peace Prize."

"Balderdash! I promised nothing. The kaiser is just waiting to see who wins this election to know whether he'll have a free hand in Europe, just as you predicted. He may put off war for another four years if it means not taking on the United States as well as France and England. But Germany is going to war sooner or later, make no mistake. I didn't talk the kaiser out of it. I just helped him see the wisdom of delay." He smiled at his son. The African adventure and presidential campaign had matured him. He still drank too much and too often, but he was no longer a boy. There was much to hope for.

"You should give Mrs. Dunn the interview anyway, Pop. She's been hounding Mr. Potter since before Kansas City and he's starting to get that vigilante look. I know you were mad at her for running off to send that story from Khartoum. But look what that did for you. She also sent those bogus Smithsonian toughs off on a wild goose chase to the Congo, and who knows what they were up to? Her story on your charge up Fulani Hill made you a public hero again. If Morgan hadn't bought the bosses and the convention for Taft—"

"Enough. There's no such thing as a fair fight in politics."

"All I'm saying, Pop, is that you owe her. She's a sweet old lady who maybe is just a little sweet on you. You should give her the story."

The words "old lady" made him wince, but in the end he agreed. "All right. You tell Mag…Mrs. Dunn, that I would be pleased if she would join me for dinner after the speech. But let Mr. Potter know first, so he doesn't have the Dooley brothers lock her in a freight car."

Mounting the steps of the outdoor stage, Roosevelt waved to the crowd, feeling the roar of their collective voices wash over him. It was the moment of unconditional adulation that every professional politician lived for. He did not hear the gunshot. Striding toward the podium, he felt only a sudden blow to the chest and the sensation of falling backward. Light and pain filled his head as it bounced off the rough wooden planks. Blood spread across the front of his starched white shirt.

The Pinkertons swarmed a bowler-hatted man and wrested a short-barreled pistol from his grip. Someone opened his jacket—a doctor? Blood-soaked papers with a hole blasted through fell from his breast pocket. Behind them, the glasses case and locket that was always inside were punctured and bent in half. "This is a bit of luck," said the disembodied voice. Then Roosevelt's head began to clear. He tried to stand. The man who had opened his shirt told him to lie still. Kermit and Potter stood over him and repeated the instructions.

Balderdash!

He struggled to his feet, waved them away, and staggered to the podium. Blood covered his shirtfront from chest to trousers. The roar of the crowd rose in waves and fell in a deafening crescendo like the thunder of Victoria Falls. It restored him. Waving the bloodstained speech above his head, he waited for the crowd to grow still. "I don't know if you fully understand that I've just been shot." Then to them, and to the tearful reporter forcing her way toward the podium, he opened his throat and roared, "But it takes more than that to kill a Bull Moose!"